The Dragon and the Butterfly

by Abby Simpson

Lost Boys Press

ISBN: 979-8-9898476-3-1
First Print Edition – 2024
Cover Design by:
Dewi Hargreaves
Printed By:
Lost Boys Press
www.lostboyspress.com

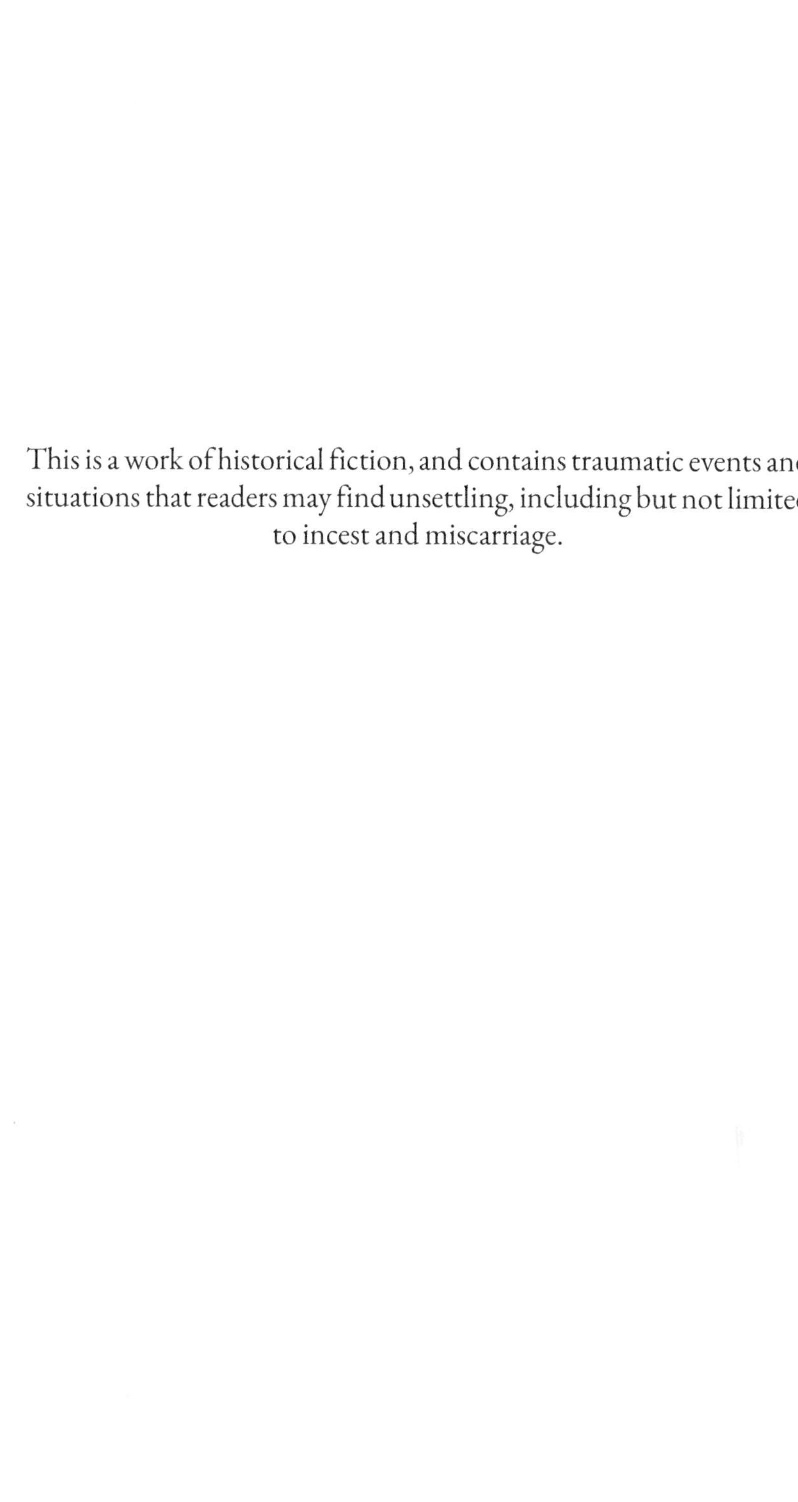

This is a work of historical fiction, and contains traumatic events and situations that readers may find unsettling, including but not limited to incest and miscarriage.

Dedicated to Dad, who loved all my stories.

Kingdom of Scotland
Northumbria
Durham
Yorkshire
York
Selby
Welsh Kingdoms
Walsingham
Kingdom of England
Norfolk
London
Old Wessex
Kent
Winchester
Canterbury
Hastings
Hampshire
Borne
Bruges
Zeebrugge
Boulogne
Lille
Flanders
Ponthieu
Beaurain
Hainault
Abbeville
Eu
Aumale
Vermandois
Barfleur
Lillebonne
Bayeux
Beaumont
Caen
Rouen
Lorraine
Coutances
Normandy
Mortain
Paris
Kingdom of Francia
Brittany
Maine
Blois
Anjou

DRAMATIS PERSONAE

(Geneological resources can be found at the back of the book.)

The House of Flanders

- ***Lady Matilda (Maud) of Flanders*** – a lady of Flanders who rose to become a duchess and a queen.
- ***Count Baudouin V of Flanders*** – Maud's father.
- ***Countess Adela*** – Maud's mother, born a Frankish princess.
- ***Lady Eleanor*** – the second wife of Count Baudouin IV, she's the same age as her stepson, Baudouin V. She's also Duke William II of Normandy's paternal aunt as a younger sister of his father, Duke Robert I.
- ***Lady Judith of Flanders*** – Lady Eleanor's daughter, Count Baudouin V's half-sister.
- ***Baudouin (Bodhi) of Flanders*** – Maud's elder brother.
- ***Robert (Robby) of Flanders*** – Maud's younger brother.

The House of Normandy (before 1050)

- ***Duke William II of Normandy*** – the man known to history as William the Conqueror, he became Duke of Normandy at eight years old.
- ***Adelaide (Addie) of Normandy*** – William's sister. They're both illegitimate children of Duke Robert I of Normandy, who died when they were children.
- ***Viscountess Herleva*** – William's mother, a low-born woman later wed to *Viscount Herluin de Conteville.*
- ***Bishop Odo of Bayeux and Count Robert of Mortain*** – William's younger half-brothers.
- ***Emme*** and ***Murielle de Conteville*** – William's younger half-sisters.
- ***Walter of Falaise*** – Duke William's uncle and Herleva's brother, skilled in embalming.
- ***Archbishop Mauger of Rouen and Guillaume Talou*** – Duke

William's uncles as younger half-brothers of Duke Robert I and Lady Eleanor; passed over for the Ducal Crown in favor of their illegitimate nephew upon Robert's death.

The House of Wessex

- ***Lady Emma*** – Queen of England twice as consort to King Aethelred the Anglo-Saxon and King Cnut the Dane. After Cnut's death in 1035, Lady Emma's eldest son with Aethelred, named Alfred, was murdered by her stepson, King Harold Harefoot, in a plot executed with Earl Godwin. Born into the House of Normandy, she's Duke William II's great-aunt as sister to Duke Richard II, who ruled Normandy from 996-1026. Duke Richard II fathered Lady Eleanor, Archbishop Mauger, Guillaume Talou, and two Norman dukes: Richard III and Robert I (William's father).
- ***King Edward*** – Emma's son with King Aethelred, he spent his youth in exile in Normandy.
- ***Queen Edith*** – King Edward's wife, born into England's Anglo-Saxon and Danish aristocracy.
- ***Edward Aetheling*** – a paternal nephew of King Edward, he spent most of his life in exile in Hungary but later became his childless uncle's Wessex heir.
- ***Agatha Wessex*** – Edward's wife, an orphan from Kyiv who married her husband for love.
- ***Margaret Wessex*** – Edward and Agatha's eldest daughter.
- ***Edgar Wessex*** – Edward and Agatha's son.
- ***Cristina Wessex*** – Edward and Agatha's youngest daughter.

The House of Godwin

- ***Earl Godwin of Wessex*** – the most powerful Anglo-Saxon thegn in England, Queen Edith's father.
- ***Gytha Thorkelsdottir*** – Earl Godwin's Danish wife.
- ***Sweyn, Leof,*** *and* ***Wulf Godwinson*** – Godwin and Gytha's eldest, third, and youngest sons.
- ***Harold Godwinson*** – Godwin and Gytha's second son.
- ***Tostig Godwinson*** – Godwin and Gytha's fourth son and Judith of Flanders' husband.
- ***Hakon Sweynson*** – Sweyn Godwinson's son.
- ***Edie Swanneck, Lady Walsingham*** – Harold Godwinson's first

wife.

- ***Ulf Haroldson*** – Harold and Edie's son.
- ***Gunhilda*** and ***Gytha Haroldsdottir*** – Harold and Edie's daughters.

House of Normandy (after 1050)

- ***Robert 'Curthose' of Normandy*** – William and Maud's firstborn son and heir.
- ***Richard of Normandy*** – William and Maud's second son.
- ***Emma of Normandy*** – William and Maud's eldest daughter.
- ***Cecilia of Normandy*** – William and Maud's second daughter.
- ***Agatha*** and ***Constance of Normandy*** – William and Maud's twin daughters.
- ***William (Rufus) of Normandy*** – William and Maud's third son.
- ***Matilda of Normandy*** – William and Maud's fifth daughter.
- ***Adela of Normandy*** – William and Maud's youngest daughter.
- ***Henry of England*** – William and Maud's youngest son.
- ***Gundred van Oosterzele*** – Duchess Maud's young lady-in-waiting.
- ***Lanfranc*** – a religious scholar from Pavia who becomes tutor to William and Maud's sons.
- ***Bertrand*** – Duchess Maud's loyal steward.
- ***Celeste*** – Duchess Maud's trusted midwife.

In addition to:

- ***William (Fitz)Osbern***, ***Roger (Monty) de Montgomery***, and ***Roger (Beau) de Beaumont*** – Duke William's loyal stewards and closest friends.
- ***Brictric***, son of ***Algar*** – Maud of Flanders' first love. Born the son of a carpenter before his rise to ambassador of Flanders in King Edward's court. Married a woman named Goda.
- ***Cecilia Drengot*** – an old woman in Rouen descended from Norman mercenaries.
- ***Countess Richilde of Hainault*** and her children, ***Roger*** and ***Gertrude*** – Richilde was betrothed to Bodhi of Flanders after the death of her first husband, Count Herman of Mons.
- ***Pope Leo IX*** – the Great Schism separating Eastern Orthodox Christianity from Western Roman Catholicism occurred in the aftermath

of his death in 1054.

- ***Lady Berthe*** and her children, ***Marguerite*** and ***Count Herbert of Maine*** – allies and residents of the Norman court in exile. Lady Berthe was born into the House of Blois and twice widowed. She had Marguerite and Herbert with her second husband, Count Hugh of Maine. Until his assassination in 1040, her first husband, Duke Alain III of Brittany, managed the regency of young Duke William II.
- ***Duke Conan of Brittany*** – Lady Berthe's son with her first husband, Duke Alain.
- ***Count Enguerrand of Ponthieu*** – Adelaide of Normandy's first husband. He gave her the County of Aumale in tribute when they married.
- ***Count Guy of Ponthieu*** – Count Enguerrand's younger brother.
- ***Count Eustace II of Boulogne*** – an ally of the House of Wessex in England, his first wife, Godeva, was Lady Emma's daughter with King Aethelred, and his second wife, Ida, the nine-year-old daughter of Duke Godfrey of Lorraine.
- ***Count Lambert of Lens*** – Count Eustace's younger brother, Adelaide of Normandy's second husband.
- ***Count Edo of Champagne*** – Adelaide's third husband.
- ***Adelaide of Ponthieu*** and ***Judith of Lens*** – Adelaide's daughters.
- ***King Philippe of Francia*** – Countess Adela's nephew as the eldest son of her brother, King Henri, who died when Philippe was a child. Until his own death, Adela's husband, Count Baudouin V, served as regent to the boy king.
- ***King Malcolm of Alba (Scotland)*** – an ally of the Wessex kings and several Northumbrian lords, he killed King Macbeth in 1057 to take back the throne Macbeth had usurped from his father.
- ***Mistress Dzintra*** (**pronounced** ***Sin-tra)*** – A fortune teller in Caen.
- ***Archbishop Stigand*** – England's Archbishop of Canterbury at the time of the conquest in 1066.
- ***Earl Morcar*** and ***Aldgyth of Mercia*** – a powerful Anglo-Saxon earl before the conquest, Morcar's sister, Aldgyth, married Gruffydd ap Llewellyn, King of Gwynedd, and after his death married Harold Godwinson.
- ***Earl Gospatric*** – a distant relative of Wessex kings in England, he was Earl of Northumbria before the conquest.
- ***William of Jumieges*** – a monk and retired tutor compiling a chronicle of the Norman dukes.

PROLOGUE
The Butterfly

May 1068 – The Palace of Westminster in London, England

England's new queen stood at the window of the castle tower, high above the old Roman walls encircling the city of London. Maids fussed over her robes as she let the sun's rays warm her cheeks. She couldn't delay this day any longer than she had already.

"It's a beautiful day for your coronation, my queen."

She smiled at her ladies-in-waiting while they decorated her gold-embellished white robes. The weather was spectacular, just as they'd hoped, but this did little to calm Queen Maud's inner storm. For years this had been her dream. Now, she was a carriage ride away from her crowning moment.

Her heart bled turmoil she dared express to no one but herself. She'd been treated as England's queen since her husband's victory two years earlier, but her planned coronation by the Bishop of York was important to him. Further legitimizing their claim to the throne, their lords prayed it might help subdue the rebellions on their new lands.

Her maids straightened yards of embroidered blue butterflies, whirling across waves of woven gold over the heavy, white satin of her skirt. Above her auburn locks, they attempted to place her veil.

"Not today." Brushing them off, Maud eyed the golden coronet on her wooden vanity. Jewel-encrusted gold bangles chimed against her small wrists. "The crown will stand out much better without a veil."

Judith would have judged her for choosing not to wear a veil in a house of the Lord. Awash with sadness at the thought, she composed herself, fighting to enjoy the occasion.

She knew loss, and she'd felt unimaginable pain. Sacrifice had been expected on the way to her crown, but today of all days, she felt Judith's absence most.

Applying rouge made from crushed berries and beeswax to her cheeks and lips, the smell of sweet grease permeated her nostrils. Pulling her hair into two long braids, her maids placed the golden crown atop her head. Maud took a long, careful breath, feeling the molded spires between her fingertips.

This refined appearance hid sacrifices weighing on her heart like a shroud. Her reflection smiled back at her from a polished obsidian mirror—and though the pursuit of power could be a poison, her children were healthy. Her husband had more power than most men on the continent. She feared she was undeserving, but in her heart, she still wanted this moment. No queen before her ever had a coronation in England. Not even her beloved Lady Emma, who would have been prouder than anyone to see her now.

Maud couldn't muster the same level of satisfaction as her husband, but she performed it well after a lifetime of training.

"A crown adds more than a few inches of gold," said young Gundred, her loyal lady-in-waiting. She pinned a silk scarf across Maud's midsection with an opulent gold brooch, the metal pulled to resemble wings around a blue sapphire in the center. "You define elegance, my queen."

Carrying her train along the stone corridors, her ladies-in-waiting followed her to the Great Hall. King William, the great conqueror of England, shared a beaming glance with his wife as she came into view. "You look stunning, my love." His brown eyes twinkled with delight.

"And you're the most handsome king I've ever seen."

Over his gold tunic he wore a long blue-and-gold cloak lined with white rabbit fur, clasped together over his shoulders by a gold chain festooned with rubies. Fur-lined stockings hugged his powerful calves with gold linen wrapping, and the crown atop his closely cropped dark hair was taller and heavier than Maud's, befitting his fearsome Norseman's gait.

"The carriages are ready for the procession to the cathedral, Your Majesties."

They gave appreciative nods to their steward as her ladies-in-waiting tied a gold cloak adorned with white fur over her shoulders. "This will be warm in the sun today." Tension in her cheeks pasted over her placid expression.

"Anything less would be undignified for the occasion." William escorted his wife to the courtyard of their new castle with a gallant smile, helping her step into an open-topped black-and-gold carriage with the dragon of Wessex and leopard of Normandy carved into the doors. A line of similarly decorated wooden boxes, hitched to four strong black horses, snaked behind like a thread. Their world on a string. William glanced upon the elaborate procession as he took pride of place next to his wife on the carriage bench. "I promised you England, my queen."

Taking his face in her hands, she kissed him tenderly. "I've never known a man more deserving of calling himself a king."

God still favored them—even in her darkest moments, Maud knew this to be true. This grand coronation was proof enough.

Catching her children's faces in the carriage directly behind, she wiped a discreet tear from her cheek and smiled. Maud's eldest sons cast assured glances in her direction. They'd become young men before her eyes. "It doesn't feel that long ago Robert and Richard were running around the nursery."

"A lifetime can pass before you know it." William spoke over the din of revelers with his familiar, crooked grin. Indeed it had, but she could remember the day she and her husband met as children as though it were yesterday.

William gave her arm a gentle squeeze as they stepped toward the cathedral where cheering crowds waited for a glimpse of their glamorous new monarchs from south of the narrow sea. The waves of people mixed the faces of their loyal lords, finely dressed in expensive, colorful robes, with some of their new English subjects—citizens of London in embroidered fabrics, all awed by the procession.

Again, her mind drifted to those absent from this momentous day as Maud's gaze returned to William's sympathizing visage. He knew her glances so well. He'd always known her better than anyone.

As she waved instinctively to the onlookers lining the roadside, a blue butterfly passed over their heads. Watching it sail on the wind, she felt the golden diadem atop her head lean slightly toward her husband.

With a loving chuckle, the new King William straightened her crown. "You've always been the sun, my queen. Even the butterflies come to dance in your light."

She doubted his opinion, but on this auspicious day she smiled anyway.

PART ONE

Childhood

Chapter One

May 1039 – Lille, southwest Flanders near the border with Francia

A blue-winged butterfly fluttered in the breeze, dancing between wisps of white clouds marking the sky above. Maud of Flanders played with her auburn braids as she watched the bug float through the air, reaching out in hope it might mistake her for a flower and land.

Following the butterfly's zagging path above the city, free to go wherever it might please, Maud escaped into a memory of a dream. In that dream *she* was the butterfly, but she had nowhere to take flight.

"Get out of the carriage, Maud," came her mother's voice, cutting through the murmuring chaos of the marketplace. She turned to meet Countess Adela's steely-eyed stare.

"There was a butterfly, Mama." She pointed toward the sky. "It was blue, but its wings looked dipped in white rabbit fur."

"I've seen butterflies like that in England," Lady Emma of Normandy said as a carter in a blue tunic, his legs wrapped in golden herringbone wool, held out a hand to escort her from the carriage. "They love the sea breezes in the south."

Lady Eleanor, the youthful dowager countess who had been married to Maud's grandfather, raised an eyebrow. "You love any chance to talk about England, Auntie. One might think you still see yourself as its queen." She smiled wryly, her tongue sharp as her features.

"It was my home for thirty-five years." Lady Emma's blue eyes burned with conviction. "Exile won't keep us away forever. My sons will reclaim their land from my wicked stepson, King Harefoot, *and* Earl Godwin of Wessex." The old woman's lip curled in disgust at the mention of their names. "When that day comes, I'll finally return to England, but my days as queen are over."

Maud stared thoughtfully at Lady Emma, hanging on her every

word. "Maybe I could be like a blue butterfly who goes to England." Climbing down the carriage steps, her sewn linen slippers crunched pebbles beneath her small feet.

At her side, her father's half-sister, Judith, fiddled distractedly as her mother, Eleanor, pulled her hood over her blonde braids. "It is your favorite color." Judith grinned, adjusting the wool fabric of her cloak. "Half your robes are blue already!"

The air smelled faintly of vinegar from the monks' infirmary nearby, and one of their horses relieved himself as Maud plugged her nose. Lille was more modest than Bruges, Flanders' capital, but the market still bustled, with ales and fresh fruits emanating a crisp, sweet scent from tented stalls. Six Flemish soldiers escorted them, sword hilts resting against their waists. The sheaths bobbed against their legs as they dismounted.

When Maud and Judith accompanied the women of their house to make offerings to the local church, the girls, eight and six years old, could see part of the world beyond their castles' stone walls. People with dirt on their faces, including barefoot children younger than Maud, carried heavy sacks of grain along cobblestones. They all stopped to stare at the finely dressed women in the horse-drawn carriage.

At one end of the open-air market stood a cathedral with a wooden spire so tall it looked like it could touch God in the clouds above, but a puppet show in the square tugged at Maud and Judith's attention. With an impatient sigh, Countess Adela tapped her foot but let them stay.

Puppeteers balanced on wooden stools over a stage draped in alternating red and orange wool, painted to resemble a tower overlooking a field of wild grain. Marionettes dressed like princes, knights, and even a black-painted dragon, fought a battle for the tower in the meadow. In the end, princesses came out to congratulate the winning men, dancing and kissing and drinking until the puppets fell over sideways. One princess in blue took the dragon and saved her prince before killing the others to take the tower for themselves.

Judith gaped at Maud. "Won't they be lonely now they've killed all their friends?" The puppets flew away on the dragon, and Maud nodded. As the audience applauded, the marionettes rose from the dead to take wooden bows from the stage.

"Come, we're here to greet the bishop." Countess Adela gestured to the church. Her veil, covering her long, dark hair, danced a little in the wind. Maud and Judith followed the women toward the cathedral, their cloaks dragging across the stones.

"Get out of the way!"

The shout rang across the yard, followed by the din of screams. Maud turned to see a man wrestling with a black horse. The creature bucked its head with a ferocious grunt as people rushed forward to help. Tossing its rider with a mighty jolt the horse took off, thundering in Maud's direction. She felt frozen in place as the wild steed careened past market stalls, toppling vendors jumping desperately from the horse's path.

Seconds passed in a blur. Judith grasped the fabric of Maud's cloak when the horse drew near. Staring down the beast as the screams of their mothers grew louder, Maud stepped in front of her. Hooves clattered across the stones. Her hands shook. Squeezing her eyes shut, she hoped it was nothing but a nightmare.

Strong arms took Maud and Judith by the shoulders. A Flemish soldier tossed them to the side just in time to meet the horse's bony breast with his bearded face. The women screamed and the earth turned red beneath him.

Maud craned her neck as the remaining soldiers formed a tight circle around their fallen man, conscious of a gathering crowd building in their midst. "Stay back. Don't look," ordered her mother, her voice grave. "Get the girls to the carriage. The Boy Duke and his family arrive soon, and we must take care of him now."

Blood pooled under the soldiers' leather turnshoes as Eleanor and Emma ushered the girls into the carriage, pulling the tapestry across the window. Undeterred, Maud peeked through a hole in the fabric before Emma's thin fingers emerged from her embroidered sleeves to brush against the linen. "You don't need to watch." She took Maud's face in her soft hands, her stern gaze shrouded by her gentle voice. "You were both very fortunate!"

"He's dead, isn't he?"

The woman pushed stray blonde hairs from Judith's small, curious face. "As a soldier for the Count of Flanders, his sworn duty was to risk his life for your safety. He died with great honor," she insisted. The girls knew better than to press, and Maud listened silently to the commotion outside the carriage.

A quiet ride followed the soldier's death as the women returned to the family's chateau in Lille. Spots of blood dotted Countess Adela's leather slippers, and when she noticed Maud staring at the red stains they left on the carriage bed, she hid them discreetly beneath her gray linen skirt.

"What was the soldier's name, Mama?"

"His name was Draco, and he was every bit as strong and fierce as his name implied."

"We should send his sword to his family, and I'll pray for his soul tonight."

Crossing the bridge to the island they called their second home, Lady Emma placed a comforting hand on Maud's shoulder. "You're a very thoughtful girl," she said. Maud's heart fluttered with pride.

"En garde, swine!"

In the tree-covered courtyard, Maud's ten-year-old brother, Bodhi, taunted their six-year-old brother, Robby, knocking a wooden sword from his hands with a swipe of his own. Wailing playfully, Robby pretended to be killed.

"Boys are dumb," said Maud loudly, hoping her brothers would hear. "They think blood and death are so exciting."

As the carriage pulled to a stop in the courtyard of their estate in Lille, Bodhi stopped mimicking chopping his brother to bits. "We're not as dumb as girls. Girls can't even make decisions without a man to tell her they're good ones."

Maud ignored him, but her mother snapped, "Stop it, Baudouin!"

"All girls are foolish, Mama." He creased his brow. "They don't even have tutors. Robby's younger than Maud, but he has a tutor."

Countess Adela shook her head while Lady Eleanor snickered quietly.

"We are not fools!" Maud poked her head from the carriage as their soldiers unloaded the body from the back. At the sight of the corpse her brothers' jaws dropped, tongues silenced. The countess jumped from the bench in a futile attempt to shield her sons from the blood-caked soldier.

"Get away."

"What is the commotion out here? Are we trying to awaken every nymph in the forest?" Maud's father, Count Baudouin the Fifth of Flanders, emerged from the wood-and-stone manse where they spent most summers. His voice was strong but welcoming as he held out his hand to help the women step down, but when he noticed the body of one of his loyal men, his face fell.

"We weren't able to visit the church." Countess Adela spoke with gravity in her voice. "He saved the girls from the path of a runaway horse."

The count forced back his shoulders, turning to the men standing over Draco's body. "Take him to his sons for an honorable burial *before* the arrival of the duke." They obliged their lord and Count Baudouin returned his attention to his wife. "I hope that's not why the children are fighting."

Adela shook her head. "Bodhi says all girls are fools because they don't have tutors." Her husband sighed, then cast a discerning glance at his eldest son.

"Bodhi, you don't even know all girls. And with that attitude, you never will." Countess Adela turned her cheek, hiding a smug grin while Bodhi sulked. He stared at his feet as Count Baudouin continued. "You wouldn't dare say all women are fools in front of your mother and Lady Eleanor. Lady Emma, who was Queen of England twice and escaped civil war with her life, doesn't deserve such abasement. Women are the reason boys like you are allowed, by the grace of God, to grow up thinking themselves so superior to other girls."

Bodhi's dark locks hung low over his eyes, and he had no reply. Robby stood, launching onto his toes to appear taller under his father's towering presence, settling for puffingout his tiny chest. Both boys wore brown wool cut from the same threads that made Count Baudouin's fur-trimmed cloak.

Each year, Maud's father wore more dark-red hair on his face than his head, but his charming smile was as sprightly as ever. To greet the Boy Duke of Normandy, he topped the thinning hair on his head with a wool cap pinned with a raven's feather. Maud had only seen him dress finer in the presence of Countess Adela's brother, King Henri of Francia.

"There's nothing special about girls. They can't become dukes or kings or anything that matters. And they smell funny."

"Robby, I've told you before, that's just rosewater oil. It's perfume." Adela smiled softly when her youngest son scrunched his nose.

"Is this the kind of education my endowment is sponsoring?" Lady Emma moved slowly to a stone bench by a healthy bush of pink roses gifted by a Flemish noble returning from a pilgrimage to the Holy Land. In exchange for Count Baudouin's shelter during her exile from England, Lady Emma made generous contributions to church poets, educators, and artists throughout Flanders, but she couldn't read herself and had no say in what tutors might impart on their male students. Slipping out of her linen shoes, she sat with her shoulders slumped in exhaustion.

"Come inside, Judith," said Lady Eleanor. "We must be ready for your cousin's arrival."

"I *am* ready!" she protested, but Eleanor shook her veiled head. Flicking her wrist toward the house without a word, she turned with such speed her burgundy robes rippled, creating a short breeze in the grass. Judith followed quietly.

Countess Adela clicked her tongue when Eleanor and her daughter had gone inside. "I know it's strange to be a dowager three years younger than your countess, but I don't think she'll ever forgive us for your father dying."

"Not in this lifetime." Count Baudouin smirked, offering his wife a slight shrug. "Boys, come with me. Let's see that the stablehands made enough room for the duke's men to keep their horses while they're here."

Her brothers followed eagerly, but Maud was happiest with Lady Emma. Sitting next to her on the bench, she placed a protective hand on her arm as the old woman rubbed her toes.

"Do your feet hurt, Lady Emma?" She lifted her long, embroidered robes, the style in her beloved England, to glance sadly at her soles. The sight made Maud's stomach churn, but this couldn't cure her spirit of inquiry. The skin was so thin on the old woman's feet that her bones gleamed white through red, blue, and black shades of flesh. Downy was added to her shoes for extra comfort, but Lady Emma never liked to stand for very long.

"I'll be all right," she said. "I always am. I just need to rest for a few minutes."

"You said when I was older you would tell me how you hurt your feet."

Glancing between the young girl and Countess Adela, Lady Emma met Maud's hopeful gaze again. "Your mother doesn't want me to tell you that story."

"But I'm older!" Maud's braids bounced as she threw up her arms in exasperation.

"Not that much older."

"Oh, go on. Tell her." Sitting next to Maud on the bench, Countess Adela studied the old queen and her daughter with a sigh. "You're too inquisitive for your own good, Maudie."

Practically feverish with curiosity, she waited impatiently as Lady Emma massaged her mangled soles. "I was very young," the old woman began. "Older than you are now, but barely what I thought of as grown up. Without a choice, I was given in marriage to Aethelred, and I became his queen in England. He was much older, but Wessex men are prone to war, and he needed more sons. I gave him Alfred and Edward, but Aethelred never loved me. Not like your mother loves your father." Maud smiled. "Aethelred believed a rumor I broke my vows to him and God, so he ordered the Bishop of Winchester to walk me blindfolded across a line of red-hot ploughshares as punishment."

In her lifetime, Maud had only seen a ploughshare brand the livestock in her father's barns. Imagining the same hot iron singe itself against the soles of her feet, she cringed, frowning earnestly at the old queen. "Did you break your vows?"

"You must understand, Maud. What's true, or not true, is known only by God. What's true to man is whatever he believes, and I knew they'd believe my innocence if I survived the ordeal. Many men in my husband's court broke their own vows to God, and their wives, but they weren't ordered to walk across hot irons in shame. I walked over fire in that church because death was my only alternative, and as much as it hurt, I was determined to make it all the way across. I found a place inside my mind where the heat couldn't touch me, and I imagined myself walking barefoot across cold marble. When it was over, I collapsed from the pain, but I refused to shed a tear even though I could smell my own flesh burn."

"It's not fair!"

"Life is scarcely fair." Countess Adela ran a comforting hand down one of her daughter's long braids. "And queens have it better than most women."

Lady Emma nodded. "In some ways, life is easier without a crown. Being queen often felt as though I was judged against God. Queens must represent the very best of their people, their soldiers, and themselves, but I'll tell you a secret." Maud leaned forward, enraptured. "A queen can do many things other women can't, but she pays for that power with sacrifice."

Chapter Two

May 1039 – Count Baudouin V's chateau in Lille, Flanders

As Maud digested Emma's words, Countess Adela groaned. "There's no version of that story safe for a child."

"And yet today she's already seen a man trampled by a horse." As Emma spoke with an apologetic shrug, Maud tried to push the image of Draco's bloodied skull from her mind.

"I won't have nightmares," she insisted.

Eyeing her daughter with concern the countess stood, extending a hand to assist Lady Emma. "It's time to gather the household for the arrival of Duke William and his entourage." White locks peeked through the old woman's veil as she stepped into her linen shoes.

Maud followed the women through the manor to collect their attendants, past the stone kitchen where the cooks were hard at work. Smoke wafted from the large, open windows of the building separate from the main house, decreasing the likelihood of a kitchen fire setting the wooden beams and painted tapestries ablaze. Rich smells of garlic, sage, and goose emanated from boiling iron pots and large stone ovens.

As they passed through tall doors, held to stone-carved arches on steel hinges, servants dusted for the Boy Duke's arrival. Timber beams and cut stone formed the foundations of the peaceful two-story home, situated on the largest island in the River Deule. A bridge connected their island to the leafy sea of charcoal forests and rolling green countryside beyond the river. The thin waterway, a shade of dark blue like a raven in moonlight, kept marauding boats at bay. Most of their home's windows faced southeast, letting in more light than the family's larger, fortress-style chateau near Bruges—about a day's ride north by carriage. Maud was often happiest with her family together in Lille, which felt brighter and more inviting.

The women's long robes brushed pebbled stones at their feet as the household converged in the gravel courtyard, where their bannermen hung flags from the second-story balcony, each blue and yellow with a red shield in the center. Birdsong floated on the warm spring breeze.

"Nice hair, Judie!" Robby laughed, running ahead of his father and brother on their way back from the stables. "You look like you're wearing a basket."

Her braids had been tied into one elaborate bun atop her head. Maud hid a smile, but Judith pouted. "I hate when Robby's right." Maud let go of a chuckle at her expense.

The household staff stood straighter when Count Baudouin returned from the stables. His cavalry arranged themselves in a line, their horses brushed, and hooves polished. The blue tunic of all who served the county of Flanders danced in the breeze, hanging across the wide shoulders of her father's Flemish men. Yellow wool wrapped their legs, and many hid their faces behind bushy beards just like Draco, their fallen man.

"Lady Emma, when the Boy Duke gets here, we're going to take him fishing."

The old woman smiled warmly at Bodhi's excitement. "I know you three better than I know my own great-nephew, but I think the Boy Duke would like that very much."

"You know us better because they exiled you from England after both your kings died."

"Robby, don't be rude," Maud said gently, but Emma laughed.

"No, he's right. My son would be on the throne if not for my stepson's alliance with that traitor, Earl Godwin. I long to return to England, among the people I cherish, but my remaining sons *will* avenge Alfred's murder and take back our home."

Nearby, Maud and Judith's ladies-in-waiting giggled amongst themselves. They cared nothing for England as Lady Emma did, and Maud overheard them refer to the Boy Duke as William, the Bastard Duke of Normandy, but this garnered a deathly glare from Countess Adela. The ladies cowered and apologized, their shoulders folding inward behind the more senior ladies-in-waiting.

"What does 'bastard' mean, Mummy?"

At her daughter's query, Lady Eleanor smirked. "It means someone whose parents weren't married when they were born. But of my nephew, they say it's his awful temperament too."

Interjecting quickly, Adela shot a disappointed glare in Eleanor's direction. "We will not be calling the duke by that name while he's here," she announced, loud enough for all to hear.

"Illegitimate sons don't inherit titles," Maud protested. "And if he wants Papa's support, why isn't he entertaining us at his own castle, like when King Henri invited all of us to Paris to ask Papa to fight at his side against the Count of Blois?"

Count Baudouin smiled at his daughter with a gleam in his eye. "Duke Robert never married and had no legitimate heirs, so he left Normandy to his only son before he died," he explained. "As for us, an alliance with Normandy would strengthen Flanders, too, and the young duke insisted on a meeting between our families here in Lille."

"Ruling a duchy at twelve is no easy task," said Lady Emma. "My great-nephew has the support of most nobles, but he's weathered countless betrayals since his father died—mostly from relatives who disagreed with Robert's choice to make him his heir. They all want more power for themselves."

Judith looked up at her much older brother, fiddling with the sash on her dress. "If my mother and Lady Emma are Normans, the Duke of Normandy should already be our ally."

"We're Normans in our memories, Judie," said her mother. "When we married, we gave that part of ourselves away."

"That isn't true," said Adela. Eleanor glared stiffly in her direction. "The duke is their nephew, and this is the key to our families' alliance."

"The real secret to the alliance of our families is how quickly you remarried the future Count of Flanders after my brother's death. You don't forget your first husband, do you Countess?"

Countess Adela rolled her eyes in frustration. "You'll never let me, Dowager Countess." Knowing Lady Eleanor despised the title, Adela enunciated with a satisfied smirk. At nineteen, Eleanor became the second wife of Baudouin's father, when the last count was an old man. A widow at twenty-three, younger than the new countess, Eleanor responded to her new title with resentment. Countess Adela celebrated the end of her third decade soon before the family left for Lille, at a grand fête hosted by Count Baudouin at their castle in Bruges. Lady Eleanor, who was still just twenty-seven, celebrated by complaining the whole day.

Keeping a measured calm in her voice, Adela turned to Maud and

Judith. "It's no secret our husbands were chosen for alliances, but we're fortunate to be in Flanders."

"Can I choose my own husband?"

The countess frowned, sharing a glance with her husband. "We'll see, Maudie."

Interrupting their chatter, a servant rushed back to the house from beyond the wooden bridge. "The Duke of Normandy is arriving!"

At his pronouncement, the household hurriedly arranged themselves outside the front door to greet the Norman entourage. Maud's brothers stood with their hands behind their backs, playfully slapping one another. Catching their parents' attention, Count Baudouin turned to stare them down. As they pulled apart, still giggling, Judith found them irresistible and fought to stifle her laughter. Ignoring them all, Maud craned her neck to spot the Norman party in the leafy green woods beyond the river.

It was customary for the whole household—including the family's advisors, ladies-in-waiting, and servants—to greet the arrival of an allied duke or king. The House of Flanders was well-practiced in this regard, and the number who stood ready to greet the Boy Duke was higher than Maud knew how to count.

"Stand up straighter, Maudie," Adela said sharply when the first cavalry appeared among the trees. A long procession of ornately carved red-and-gold carriages emerged from the forest, passing over the bridge before stopping in a row on the gravel path to the front of the house. Maud made out an intricately carved wooden leopard with a knotted tail on the door of the largest carriage and looked to her parents with excitement.

"I think the Boy Duke and his family will like it here, Mama."

Chapter Three

May 1039 – Count Baudouin V's chateau in Lille, Flanders

Stars twinkled through the window, bathing Maud in silver light. The scent of roasted goose wafted through the walls as she tossed and turned in Lady Eleanor's sparse bedchamber. Whenever they made space for visiting nobles, the girls squeezed together on the dowager countess' eiderdown mattress with goose-feather pillows.

Too young to be invited to the raucous feast welcoming the young duke, the clang of chalices and plucky lute music kept her from slumber. Sitting up, she disturbed the covers, waking Judith next to her. "How can you sleep?" Judith shrugged as Adelaide, William's half-sister, lay wide awake at their side.

"Could we go see Lady Emma?" She sat up when they stirred. "I've heard so much about my great-aunt. And with the party going on, I'll never sleep anyway."

"Me neither."

"Me neither," mimicked Judith, even though she'd just been sound asleep. She often played the part of Maud's shadow, which Maud didn't mind much. As her father's half-sister, Judith was Maud's aunt by blood, but the two of them were as sisters.

"Lady Emma may not have left the feast yet," said Maud.

"Can we see?" Adelaide was tall, older by almost two years, with a pretty heart-shaped face, and Maud felt slightly intimidated. Still, she loved any excuse to see Emma, growing excited at the thought by virtue of Adelaide's suggestion.

With Eleanor downstairs at the feast, and their ladies-in-waiting retired for the night, the girls freely exited the chamber to head down the hall where Emma slept. They found the door to her room unlocked, illuminated by a torch on the wall, but unattended. Disappointed, Maud turned to leave, stopping when Adelaide walked inside.

"We shouldn't," Maud warned. Adelaide continued as if Maud hadn't spoken, and the younger girls followed slowly. They'd never been in Lady Emma's room without her there before.

Adelaide fell backward into her linen bedsheets. "There's no bed this comfortable in all of Normandy!" Adorned with a canopy of white silk and fur-lined blankets, the wooden bed took up much of the space. Hung from the bedposts, silk curtains cast angled shadows against the wall from the torch, but even in the firelight, the room seemed dark and cavernous without Emma.

Maud was drawn to a large, glass window, with views of the meadows across the river where she loved to play. In the moonlight, the grass glistened in shades of blue and gray.

Under the window stood Lady Emma's polished oak desk, ornately carved with Celtic infinity knots down each leg. She'd brought the desk, among her most beloved possessions, to Flanders upon her exile from England. A short stack of papers sat on the smooth surface under a heavy red stone of smooth marble.

"Encomium Emmae Reginae," Adelaide read aloud from over her shoulder. "She's writing a book about herself? Praise for Queen Emma—that's what it says."

"Lady Emma doesn't read. Maybe someone wrote it for her," Maud offered.

"It's not even bound," she pointed out, and Maud eyed the pages with interest.

"Are you sure you can read it?"

"The nuns teach me Latin in Coutances." She nodded proudly. "Mother said being a poor man's daughter was hard for her to overcome at court, but she wondered if things might have been different if she could read. Since William and I are both bastards and I have no title, she wants me to have the best opportunities one can get."

Maud listened with yearning.

"What are you three doing out of bed?" Whipping around with guilty faces, Adelaide secreted the stack of papers behind her back as Judith grabbed Maud's hand in the torchlight. They stammered nervously, barefoot in their cotton nightgowns, as Lady Emma glared at them inquisitively. "What's behind you?"

Maud passed Adelaide an anxious nod, and she nervously revealed the papers they had taken from her desk. "I'm sorry. We didn't read it.

Only the title!" Adelaide said.

"You can read?" Emma gasped, but then she grinned. "Nobles rarely send daughters to learn."

"My mother insists on it." She handed over the papers, and Emma palmed them carefully.

"I received this draft before we came to Lille for the summer, but I haven't asked anyone to read it to me yet. They're my stories, but I'm afraid someone might have got them wrong."

"But it's called Praise for Queen Emma. It can't be bad," said Maud. Emma gave a rueful laugh.

"I'll read it to you. Maud and Judith too." Adelaide bounced as Emma smiled.

"I can't ask you to do that," she said gently. "If your mothers found out, we'd all be in trouble."

"I can read fast!"

Giving in with a cheeky grin, Emma headed slowly down the corridor to the girls' room to tuck them in. Adelaide splayed the pages of Emma's book across her lap as the old queen sat in a leather-backed chair.

"May our Lord Jesus Christ preserve you, O Queen, who excel all those of your sex in the amiability of your way of life," began Adelaide, reading the dedication on the hand-scribed parchment. "That your excellence transcends the skill of anyone speaking about you is apparent to all to whom you are known, more clearly than the very radiance of the sun."

"That's really nice." Judith smiled, yawning softly, but they were all too enthralled for sleep.

Emma's eyes were smiling, too, even as she quietly rubbed her soles, hiding her grimace in the torchlit shadows as Adelaide read aloud. The story spoke of King Cnut, her second husband, but made no mention of Aethelred—the husband who burned her feet. Maud listened as Adelaide recounted how, when Cnut decided to marry Emma, he was unwed in the eyes of God. Cnut's first marriage was in the handfast tradition of the Danes, unrecognized by the Catholic Church, so he was free to marry Emma and secure new alliances in England.

"What's handfasting?" Maud wondered aloud.

"It's a very ancient pagan ritual. The Danes consider it just as binding as a wedding in the Church, and where I grew up in Normandy too," Emma said. "During the ceremony, the couple's hands are bound together with rope or long fabric to symbolize the coming together of two lives. Although we were married at the cathedral in Winchester, it was important to Cnut that we bound our hands during the vows."

"It sounds romantic." Adelaide grinned dreamily.

Untying a blue scarf from her wrist hidden under the long sleeves of her robes, Lady Emma ran her fingers along the softly frayed edges with a wistful sigh. "I remember both my weddings like they were yesterday. King Cnut was a great man, and wearing the scarf still ties me to him, even though he's gone."

Lapping at the edges of the River Deule, the meadows danced in shades of vibrant green and gold under a cloudless, pale-blue sky. The whole house slept late following the feast the night before. Maud, Adelaide, and Judith sunned themselves by the riverbank shortly after lunch, when the boys, led by the young duke, appeared with fishing nets.

Dressed down in bloomers and a cotton shirt, Duke William removed his shoes. Jumping into the shallow bank of the river, he stood in water up to his waist. Bodhi followed, while William's younger half-brothers, Odo and Robert, waded out slowly with Robby.

Nearby stood William's stewards: William FitzOsbern, Roger de Beaumont, and Roger de Montgomery. William addressed them casually as Fitz, Beau, and Monty, but only the duke could be so informal with these tall, sharply dressed young men, each descended from Norman nobility. Swift glances passed between the trio and the girls' pretty ladies-in-waiting, who also stood watch over their charges, though far less attentively.

"Why don't you girls join us?" invited William, practically submerging himself with the net each time he dove for a fish.

"No, thank you." Adelaide sniffed. "It looks wet. Can't you fish further away?"

"Water is wet, Addie." William ignored her request and she groaned.

Maud usually enjoyed fishing with her brothers, but today she was distracted. Staring beyond the bridge at branches of tall oaks swinging in the gentle breeze, she pictured the beautifully formed but foreign letters in the pages of Emma's book. She longed to know them as Adelaide did, to have the opportunities afforded women with an education.

Her brother laughed, followed by unintelligible whispers from the boys in the river, before Maud was showered by a short burst of heavy droplets. Once, then twice, before Adelaide was screaming and the water hit them like a wave.

"William, you fool!"

"Is water wet, Addie?" William laughed hysterically with the other boys as the girls stood to let their soaked dresses drip to the earth below. Addie screeched at her brother, but all were struck silent by a splash. Robby gasped, poking his head above water.

His thin arms flailed before he fell under again, pulled by the waves. "He doesn't swim!" Bodhi cried. Maud's thoughts drowned in a cacophony of shouting. She raced forward, but her ladies-in-waiting held her back. She didn't swim either. Fitz leapt past the riverbank.

Pulling Robby's head above water, Fitz scooped him up and hurried him to the shore. Maud watched, unblinking, as Fitz pressed slowly on his chest. A silence fell, lingering heavily in the air until Maud's brother expelled the last of the river from his lungs. She raced to his side.

"You almost killed him!" Adelaide shrieked, the boys denying any intent as Monty, Beau, and the ladies-in-waiting tried to calm them down. Too far from the house to be heard by the women, and with the men out hunting, Beau still reminded them voices carried along the water.

Stunned silent when she feared her brother's drowning, Maud felt emboldened by relief at Robby's recovery and rubbed his back while he coughed. Yanking at her wet dress, she eyed the boys. "Fools," she said. Breaking her gaze, they looked down at their empty nets, soaked and standing in the river.

"You bastard."

Everyone but Robby held their breath as the words left Judith's lips. William's knuckles went white as his grip tightened on the net. His lips wavered. Words he dared not say, and fists he dared not throw, waited behind them. Even his stewards looked afraid.

"She doesn't know what the word means," Maud lied, stepping between her and the angry Boy Duke. "Judith, say sorry."

"I'm sorry, Your Grace," complied Judith. William's features softened and his shoulders dropped. Shaking her head, her wet robes pasted to her skin, Maud turned toward the house. Adelaide, Judith, and their ladies-in-waiting followed, and William leapt from the river.

He caught up breathlessly. "I'm sorry," he said. "It was all just a joke."

"I wasn't going to tell. We'll get sick if we don't change our robes," said Maud stiffly, cracking a broad smile as a small red butterfly sailed on the wind. Dipping low, it preened on the young duke's shoulders, which were broad for a boy of just twelve. His face fell as she laughed, but she pointed to the insect. He flinched. The butterfly dodged his waving fingers, catching its wings on the breeze and flying free. "It's only a butterfly, Your Grace. You should be glad it trusts you enough to land."

Cracking a crooked grin, he bowed his head, stepping aside to let her pass.

River water dripped onto the stones as the girls marched back to the house. From the back garden where she sat with Emma, Eleanor, and William's mother, Herleva, Maud's mother heard them and stepped inside.

"How did you get so wet?" Countess Adela looked aghast at her soaked offspring, and Maud padded toward her mother while the others headed off to change.

"We were just playing by the river, Mama. I came in to get dry."

"Get upstairs then." With a disapproving nod, she turned to head back to the garden.

"Mama..." Maud steeled her nerves, and Adela turned again. "May I learn Latin?"

"Why do you want to learn Latin?"

She sighed heavily. "It's not fair! Boys get tutors, but I have to ask people to read me things."

"Monks aren't permitted to teach women in Flanders, Maud."

"Or the nuns? I could be as smart as any boy." She drew her arms to her hips in frustration.

"You won't need an education to run a household. I'll teach you everything you need to know about that." Equally exasperated, Adela studied her daughter's face. "Where is this coming from? Why should you have something thousands of other women can't get, including women from more powerful families than you?"

"It's stupid that we can't." Maud's protest caused the women in the garden to glance curiously from beyond the open door.

"One day, you'll lead a powerful family and set many rules of your own, but we can't bend *every* rule to our whims just because we don't like them." Countess Adela knelt to meet her daughter's precocious face. "It's too dangerous. Women are meant to be pillars for their family, devoted to God and their husbands, but they don't need to learn to read." Maud sulked, but her mother raised a stern finger to silence her. "I love you," she said. "But learning Latin for fun isn't worth the risk."

Temporarily defeated, Maud retreated upstairs to dry her hair and change.

Chapter Four

June 1039 – Lille, Flanders

For days Maud, Judith, and Adelaide slipped their ladies-in-waiting, all of them distracted by the visiting Norman men. Finding quiet, clandestine spots to huddle over Emma's pages, the girls went undetected until Lady Eleanor caught them one evening in the tower, guided by the candlelight they huddled around as night fell.

"Your mother wouldn't approve," she told Maud sternly, but rather than scold them, she smiled. She allowed Adelaide to teach Maud and Judith late into the nights in her chambers, long after the household had gone to bed. "The torchlight is brighter there," she reasoned, but Lady Eleanor, who couldn't read, liked sitting up listening to Adelaide's stories too.

One morning, the girls were found by Bodhi and Duke William on the other side of the river, leaning against the trunk of a large oak. "You're reading. Mama won't be happy."

"Don't tell her," she pleaded. But Maud could see in Bodhi's eyes that he wanted to.

"They're just reading," said William. "What else should girls do all day?"

"Someone should sew the tapestries. Besides, Mama says an education can be dangerous for girls." Bodhi shrugged. "And Papa says girls are clever enough already."

The Boy Duke wore a smug grin. "Must be how they learn to read even when they're not allowed to."

"What if a girl became so smart, she raised an army against you?" asked Bodhi.

"I *have* an army, and I don't read or write well at all. Whether she can read or not makes no difference. My men would cut her down like they will anyone who'll rise against me. The rebels may have forced us into safe harbor in Flanders for now, but my cousin, Duke Alain, is strong. Soon I will be too."

Adelaide smiled, holding tight to a copy of Herleva's Bible. Painted gold on the outer edges, it was a treasured gift from Adelaide's father, Duke Robert, given on the day she married their stepfather. Because she couldn't read herself, Herleva had passed it to Adelaide, who treasured the heirloom from her deceased father with pride.

Viscount Herluin de Conteville called to the boys from across the bridge. William and Adelaide's stepfather was spending the day training them with swords in the yard, and the blades were sharpened and ready.

"Don't stab anyone, Brother." Adelaide shot William a snide grin as the boys raced each other toward the viscount.

"Some people say mean things about Duke William." Maud picked at a blade of grass beneath her yellow robes. "Sometimes, I think he's the rudest boy I've ever met, but I've never met a boy who was also a duke before, so it's hard to tell his true nature. Sometimes he's nicer than any boy I've ever met too."

"My brother is incorrigible." Adelaide shook her head. "Except for rare moments when he's not. His guardian, Duke Alain of Brittany, put in his head you'd make a suitable wife one day. When Robby almost drowned and you stood up to him, he respected it. He hates anyone else telling him off."

Maud scrunched up her nose. "I'm only eight. I don't want to get married yet."

"Neither does he, silly. But years from now, I think he'll probably ask your father."

"I want to choose my own husband."

"Mother says no one gets to choose their husband themselves," said Judith quietly, and Adelaide nodded.

"I'm going to."

"Would you not choose my brother?" Adelaide countered. "We could be sisters!"

Exasperated, Maud's cheeks flushed. "Can we please go back to reading?"

Adelaide obliged with a soft grin, returning to the Bible in her hands. At her side, Maud and Judith listened as she read each passage, showing them how to sound out the inky words across the pages.

The morning of departure back to Normandy, Adelaide hugged Maud and Judith tightly. Behind them, her family's stewards hitched stocky black mares to their elaborate carriages loaded with crates—each filled with sets of clothing, bows, arrows, and tributes from the Count and Countess of Flanders, including gold and polished marble from the southern quarries.

"I hope we'll see each other again soon," said Adelaide. "It's only been a few weeks, but I feel I've known you all my life. Come visit us in Normandy when the rebels aren't so dangerous." Regretfully, Maud said goodbye to her new friend.

The first family of Flanders stood to see off the Duke of Normandy and his entourage, dressed in the stately robes they'd worn on arrival. With his family by his side, he bowed gratefully to Count Baudouin and his wife, a radiant peacock feather in the duke's cap dancing in the breeze. "Everything Alain told me is true, Count Baudouin. You are a man of great honor, skilled with a sword, and God has blessed you with a beautiful family."

Count Baudouin grinned proudly as Maud and her siblings smiled graciously, presenting the polite hospitality they were trained for.

"You honor me, Your Grace." Maud's father bowed regally to the young duke. "Alain said you were much like your father, and his magnificent spirit is indeed alive in you."

William showed a hint of a smile before pulling it from his lips, bowing his head regretfully. Next, he kissed Emma and Eleanor's outstretched hands, their fingers heavily adorned with gold rings newly gifted by their Norman kin. "Dearest Aunties, it's been an honor to finally get to know you. Lady Emma, your sons were great influences on me during their exile in Normandy, and I've always wished to tell you how sorry I was to hear of Alfred's murder. He deserved an end more dignified."

Curtsying low, Emma's face contorted into a grimace she tried to hide. Pushing through the pain in her feet, she looked determined to show the utmost respect to her great-nephew for speaking so graciously of her sons.

"You'll always be proud Normans to me," said William. "We're grateful to solidify the alliance between the Duchy of Normandy and the great County of Flanders. I hope we'll be aligned for decades to come." He glanced quickly at Maud, catching her gaze before he looked away. "I look forward to the day I can repay the hospitality shown to me and my family."

Maud waved as the Normans climbed into their carriages and mounted their horses, watching until their convoy crested the bridge and disappeared.

One overcast morning, while Count Baudouin and his cavalry taught Bodhi and Robby to ride horses outside the stables, Maud and Judith accompanied their mothers and Lady Emma into town. Returning to the scene of Draco's death weeks earlier, the marketplace bustled as Maud eyed their entourage of soldiers on horseback. A new soldier had taken his place among the retinue, dark-haired and bearded and almost indistinguishable from the man he replaced.

As they approached the church with sky-high spires, the bishop smiled. The women knelt before him, each kissing the top of his hand in turn. From under the hoods of their cloaks, the girls curtsied to the sunken-eyed bishop when he spotted them behind their mothers.

"Hello, young Lady Matilda and Lady Judith. You look more like your mothers each time I see you. But the magnanimous women of the House of Flanders bless our humble chapel so scarcely of late."

"We've had guests, but we haven't forgotten our God, nor his disciples." Countess Adela looked down at the balding, droopy-faced man, smiling as she spoke. She curtsied again, handing the bishop three gold coins stamped with the face of her husband.

"Your generosity is truly a sign of your goodness, Countess. We are but humble servants of God, and He smiles upon your patronage."

"I've brought Lady Emma of Normandy, who wishes to discuss a patronage of her own."

The bishop's sunken eyes lit up. "We would be most gracious, my lady."

Maud and Judith followed the adults inside. Painted brass statues of Jesus and the Virgin Mary adorned stone walls, and a winding wood staircase ascended the steeple housing their brass bell. Bowing to the altar, the women crossed their chests; watching closely, the girls tried to emulate their movements.

Lady Emma turned to speak with the bishop in the nave while Judith knelt at the foot of the gold-painted altar, raising her hands to her face in prayer. She eyed the statue of Jesus and whispered, "Pray with me that my horse has a healthy foal while we're away from Bruges."

Maud turned up her nose. "I don't know what you like so much about horses."

"They're beautiful. Most aren't mean and wild like the one in the market," she protested. Standing at the end of the aisle with Countess Adela, Lady Eleanor shushed her daughter, and Judith struggled to keep her exasperated voice at a whisper. "You don't have to like horses to want them to deliver healthy babies."

To Maud, horses were heavy, dangerous beasts with black eyes and steel hooves. But she knelt all the same, raising her hands to join Judith in silence. Her mother and Lady Eleanor spoke in hushed tones behind rows of wooden benches, their voices echoing off the rafters.

"One of my ladies-in-waiting found papers in your room about Lady Emma. She said the girls were reading with Adelaide, with your blessing."

"The ladies are always making up stories."

"I'd have thought that, but Maud asked for Latin lessons while the Normans were here." Lady Eleanor's spine straightened.

"The girls found those pages in Emma's room the night of the duke's welcome feast," Eleanor said. "Adelaide knew how to read it, and I think the girls envy her."

Countess Adela looked with frustration toward her daughter. Trying to avert her gaze, Maud nervously studied the statue of Mary.

"I wanted to read it too," admitted Emma, returning from the nave. "Come, my business with the good bishop is done. Perhaps we can find some honey cakes in the market before we head back to the estate."

Maud and Judith forgot their praying and stood, giggling excitedly at the thought of gooey, sweet white cakes drizzled in fresh honey. Before stepping into the overcast air, Countess Adela dropped three more coins into the bishop's grateful hand.

Their cavalry stood guard in front of the cathedral doors, making a path to the carriage at the end of the cobbled walkway and helping the women climb the benches with gloved hands. Each remounted before the driver prodded the horses forward along the uneven stones.

"I think I'll let the nuns teach Judith." Eleanor challenged her countess with a stare as they passed thatch-roofed timber buildings fortified by stone foundations, and three gray-clad nuns walking in the sunlight. "Maybe it will give her an advantage. Perhaps if I had been educated, I might have foreseen your failed rebellion against your own father-in-law, rather than his son betraying the old count in his last, most vulnerable, years."

"I doubt he foresaw the loss of his mind," Adela snapped with a scowl, bumping shoulders with Lady Eleanor as the carriage plodded through the busy streets. "Eventually, he didn't know his own name. He could hardly feed himself and couldn't remember Judith was his daughter. How can you forget how our hearts ached? Baudouin was already running everything and the true nature of his relationship with his father was never your concern. We thought it was for the good of the county if his father stepped aside."

"It wasn't your right!" Eleanor's brow creased with bitter resentment. "You always think you know what's right. When you came to Normandy, I lived as a lady-in-waiting in my own family. You were the daughter of the King of Francia—the angel sent to enrich the Normans—and I was always tucked behind your wings." Adela crossed her arms dismissively, pushing Eleanor to continue in anger. "Even now, I bow to you, but you couldn't steal the throne from Judith's father before his death, and you won't stop me giving my daughter an education. I know how you feel about it, but I don't care."

Maud examined the faces of the people in the street, frowning as they rode past the bustling market. Countess Adela and Lady Eleanor were in no mood to present themselves among chaotic food stalls, jewel peddlers, and craftsmen today. The smell of hot, fresh honey cakes lingered in the air and Emma gave the girls an apologetic shrug.

"I was a child! I was being groomed by the ladies at court to marry your brother and become the next Duchess of Normandy." Eleanor rolled her eyes as Adela spoke, both glaring at one another like a cat about to scratch. "But Richard died, Elle. Things changed. God had a different plan for both of us. Turns out He's got a wicked sense of humor, sending you and I to follow one another around the low counties, from one house to the next, so I could be saddled with your nagging the rest of our God-forsaken lives." Eleanor had no immediate rebuttal, and Adela pounced. "I'm not having this argument again," she said. "Thanks to him calling in the support of your brother's Norman army, the old Count Baudouin thwarted us anyway. But to use your bitterness to undermine us with our own daughter is low, Elle. Even for you."

"Maybe it's God's plan for Maud and Judith to learn to read." Eleanor shot the countess a sly grin, throwing her own words back in her face. Maud shared a knowing glance with Judith as Lady Emma raised her hands in frustration.

"Please," she interjected. "Let your past go. You're family."

"Let your past go? Are you sure you can say that with a straight face?" Adela howled. "I may not be able to read your book myself, but I know what it's about. Who wrote it for you?"

"No one," said Emma. Adela threw her brow skyward in disbelief. "No one...but a monk inside Bertin's Abbey in Saint-Omer, who said he wished to write it in honor of me."

"How much did you pay him?" wondered Eleanor.

Emma frowned, silently defiant, even as Adela and Eleanor found common ground.

"Earlier this spring, you said your days as queen were over," recalled Adela. "My husband thinks you'll use this book to undermine the Godwins and Harold Harefoot to put your own sons on the English throne."

"Earl Godwin turned on my family." Emma's cheeks burned red with anger. "I know how badly he wants it, but as long as I live, the earl will never have the throne of England. My sons are raising a fine battalion, and when they're ready, the rightful heirs *will* rule again."

"Lady Emma, I beg you. Do not print this book. Not yet, not this way." As the carriage returned to the dirt roads beyond Lille's central marketplace, the ride smoothed out considerably and Countess Adela leaned forward. "You declare your own stepson, Harold Harefoot—

the sitting King of England—a murderer and Godwin his accomplice, but the Godwins are both Saxon and Dane. They have too many allies in England and you're in exile. If you release this now, it's treason. They'll raise the barricades before you get close."

"My God-awful stepson hasn't long left," said Emma assuredly. "Harefoot has no heir, but Earl Godwin will never take what belongs to my sons."

Adela sighed. "My husband and I aren't hosting you here to make war in England. If you insist on releasing the manuscript while in exile in Flanders, we'll have no choice. St. Bertin's will have to take you until you're ready to sail back to England with your sons' army."

"No!" Forgetting she was supposed to be invisible, quietly watching the people in the street, Maud threw her arms around the old woman at her side. "Please don't make Lady Emma leave. I won't ask to read Latin. I don't need to, I swear."

"Don't worry." Emma smiled her soft, soothing grin. "Convents are cold and drafty, and they won't let me bring you. I'll ask the monk for rewrites and save it for another day."

Relief cascading through her, Maud hugged Emma firmly as the tears quickly faded.

Chapter Five

March 1040 – Zeebrugge, north of Bruges, Flanders' capital city

Buoyed by expectation, Lady Emma floated gleefully through court from the moment her sons arrived in Flanders in late autumn. Her old bones and mangled feet all but danced through the halls of the castle just beyond the city walls of Bruges. Once her son, Edward, fashioned a knotted cane from the branch of a cherry tree, not even her burns could slow her down.

For an entire winter, the castle courtyard was full of soldiers and mercenaries practicing with swords—some Danes, some Normans, and some Flemish, convinced to join the fight for England with a piece of Emma's vast fortune in their satchels. The grounds brimmed with men unbothered to sleep amidst hay and horse dung. When Maud saw how they gobbled the food prepared for them in the kitchens, eating scraps the cooks wouldn't serve the count or his royal guests, she better understood why none complained about sleeping in the stables.

Now spring, the time had come for Emma to return to England. Her stepson, the English King Harold Harefoot, was dead. Earl Godwin wrote to declare his support for Harthacnut's claim to the throne, and Emma's sons prepared their fleet to sail.

With two carriages and a few cavalries, Maud and her family escorted Lady Emma to the harbor north of Bruges, in Zeebrugge, a seaside fishing village with small wooden houses that gave Flanders' capital a crucial artery to the sea. There, Emma's sons, Harthacnut and Edward, waited with thirty ships and almost one thousand men.

First, they stopped by a lake her father said was formed when the canal from Zeebrugge was built. "They tried to dig here but the ground was too soft, and water rose like a flood. The canal needed to be able to support buildings along the shoreline for trading, so they built it further east and left this a place for nature." The water was reedy and overgrown with tall grasses, but the horses drank ravenously from the freshwater shore.

Maud loved this unkempt lake as much as the butterflies, but her heart sank when she spotted none fluttering through the verdant weeds. Instead, she stood with Lady Emma, who leaned on her gold-rimmed cane with a warm smile.

"I know how happy you are to return to your home in England, but I wish you didn't have to leave," she said, trying to hide her sadness. The old woman grinned. She placed a comforting arm around Maud's small shoulders while Count Baudouin and his men gathered the grazing horses. It was time to go.

"England is so dear because I lived there from the age of thirteen. It's where I raised my children and lived as a queen," said Emma proudly. "It's a wonderful place, my child, but you're wonderful too. The very best part of staying in Flanders has been getting to know you."

"After everything he did to your family, you're a gambler at heart if you trust Earl Godwin." Countess Adela spoke freely when they reached the harbor, helping the old woman down the carriage steps.

"I don't trust him," Emma replied. "Harthacnut was finally ready to take the throne by force if it came to it. Earl Godwin might think he has us fooled because he sent an envoy to welcome us triumphantly into London, but we have legitimacy, and he doesn't."

"That doesn't mean he wants you there."

Lady Emma grinned at the headstrong countess, cavalier and unwavering as she leaned on her cane. "Godwin needs us as much as we need him, for now. Besides, we're taking our own ships into the city, and we'd never go down without a fight."

"Those are the biggest ships I've ever seen." Stepping to the ground, Robby stared in awe toward the sea. Blue water met pale-blue sky, dotted with puffs of white clouds. Inside a stone-packed breakwater, tall ships with billowing red sails bobbed near the shore.

Salty sea air filled Maud's nostrils, and the cool north winds played with her braided hair. Seagulls dove into the water surrounding the boats, emerging with silvery fish flashing in the sunlight before gliding into shore to devour them. "How long will it take to sail?"

Emma smiled at an awestruck Bodhi. "Not more than a few days, if the weather holds."

"You must be excited!" Robby gaped, his eyes fixed on the ships.

"I'm just as excited to go as I am sad to leave all of you. Most of my life's memories are tied to England, but I'll forever cherish the past three wonderful years of your hospitality in Flanders." She bowed graciously to each family member in turn.

Afraid to look away from the boats in the harbor, Maud feared she might burst into tears if she met the old woman's wistful gaze. She hated the thought of waking each day without Lady Emma to turn to for guidance.

Her sons strode up to them with broad smiles. Harthacnut, a tall blond with piercing green eyes, walked ahead of Edward, a shorter, more rugged man with dark hair and a thick beard. Following a few steps behind was a third man Maud didn't recognize, with sandy-blond hair and the early wisps of a beard on his chin.

"Mother, we've been waiting for you." Harthacnut kissed her cheek.

"We stopped by a lake," she explained. "You wouldn't leave without me." The old woman next greeted Edward, who planted a kiss to her other cheek.

Harthacnut, the son of King Cnut, was already King of Denmark—younger than Edward, who was vile King Aethelred's last male heir. Harthacnut was the better speaker, and by far the better swordsman. His charisma could command a room of drunken lords distracted by beautiful women and rich wine, but Edward's greatest skill was diffusing his younger brother's temper when the feisty Dane couldn't get his way.

"My brother and I are grateful for your hospitality." Harthacnut bowed respectfully to Count Baudouin and his family. Dressed regally, in fine threads that glistened in the sunlight, Harthacnut looked every inch a man who would wear a second crown in a matter of days. Maud and her family returned the bow reverently.

"The men have the sails ready," Edward told Emma, his robes just as fine, poised as he was to serve at his brother's side. With two kingdoms soon to manage, Harthacnut would need the help. "The winds are favorable, so they'll set sail as soon as you've settled on board the ship.

They'll have your desk set by the window, just as you like it."

"I wish you'd change your mind and sail with us into London, Edward."

He chuckled softly. "I've got to tie up a few things, but I'll sail from Normandy when my brother's been crowned. The last time I landed in England, Alfred was left to bleed out in a riverbed by Earl Godwin's men and I barely escaped with my life. I have good reason to wait until England's ruled by a king I can trust." Emma pouted, but Edward nodded to the young man standing behind him. "I'm told this is Maester Brictric, son of Algar. He's just fifteen, but Earl Godwin personally entrusted him with your care for the voyage to England. He'll protect you as a son would protect his mother, and he's vowed on his own life he's here on peaceful orders."

"What does Earl Godwin want of one so young?" She looked upon him with keen interest and a warm smile, as she did most new people she met. Removing his hat, Brictric bowed respectfully to the old queen.

"My father is a builder. He owed the earl a debt for some materials, and Earl Godwin thought I could be the one to pay it."

She met mention of the earl with disgust. "It can't be easy being away from your family."

"No," he agreed. "But he does favor me. The earl let me take to the sea for the first time to escort you home." Brictric exuded just enough charisma to sound humble as he spoke. "I thought the sea would be rough on me, my lady, but I might be a natural."

"Perhaps you'll be an ambassador one day, young Brictric, and get to spend a lot more time on the open water." She placed a soft hand on his shoulder. "Your father, the builder, could never have imagined such a life for one of his sons."

Brictric grinned wide. Harthacnut corralled his men to prepare to pull up anchor, while Edward ordered more to cart Emma's belongings to her room below deck.

In preparation for sailing across the narrow sea, Emma had donated most of her possessions in Flanders. Acquiring the heirlooms throughout her years in England, only the most treasured of her worldly goods—including a few dozen vases and her wooden desk with Celtic carvings—would return with her.

Leading Maud and Judith, Emma took a few steps toward the boat, pulling them in for a long hug goodbye. When they parted, she lifted a cloth bag from her shoulder to reveal a copy of her book, bound in vellum and embossed with gold. Maud's eyes brightened.

"I had the monks at St. Bertin's make a copy so you girls can practice." Maud took the tome in her hands. Clutching it to her chest, she hugged Emma tightly. She'd stopped asking her parents for lessons, but still hoped to one day read Emma's ornate *Encomium* on her own.

Countess Adela eyed the gift with a mix of frustration and suspicion weighing down her features. Raising her brow to her husband, Count Baudouin turned to watch the army load the boats with feigned interest. Clearing her throat, she glared at Lady Emma. "Restraint," she said quietly.

"Once my son becomes king and secures his court, if it keeps Earl Godwin from the throne, nothing will stop me from releasing it." Emma met Countess Adela's gaze without fear. She no longer needed to oblige the terms of Count Baudouin and Adela's hospitality in Flanders; any heed she paid them now was a courtesy.

"Will we see each other again?" Seven-year-old Judith clutched the pink fabric of Emma's dress, and the old woman's heavy gold bracelets dotted with colored glass jingled as she embraced them. The old queen had no intention of arriving in England looking anything less than regal.

"I hope so. Maybe you'll find paths that will lead you to England. But whatever fate waits for me, the minute I set foot on English soil, no one will ever force me to leave again."

Hugging one last time, the book nestled between them, Maud dabbed her eyes through another short burst of fresh tears. "I'll miss you," she managed between sobs. Her brothers laughed at her emotion, but their father silenced them with a steely glare. She stood straighter, mustering conviction as she composed herself. "I hope you grow old and happy surrounded by your sons. Someday, I *know* I'll see you in England."

Flitting nearby was a blue butterfly, with wings that looked dipped in rabbit fur. Maud smiled despite her tears, wiping her cheek with her sleeve as azure wings sailed on the wind.

PART TWO
The Student

Chapter Six

January 1048 – on the road from Bruges, Flanders to Rouen, Normandy

"It's the middle of the night, Papa. Where are we going?"

Wrapped in yards of wool to guard against the frosty winter chill, Maud hurried toward the stables, Judith following close behind. Rushing through the open courtyard with their family, under the raised steel gate and across the lowered drawbridge, they crossed the murky moat encircling their home beyond Bruges' fortified walls.

"Emperor Heinrich sends his men to Flanders. We'll be ready, but you and Judith will be safer in Normandy now the anarchies against the duke have subsided. His mother agreed to shelter you until we've pushed back the Empire's latest threat."

"Can't we stay and fight?" asked Judith.

"We can't even wield a falchion," Maud cut in, carrying her robes over the dirt path.

"Your brothers will help us defend Flanders." The glint of torch-lights cast a dim yellow glow upon her mother's face, but even in the shadows Maud could see her steady gaze. "We sent your ladies-in-waiting to safe harbor in town, and we'll rest easier knowing you're both in Normandy with the duke and his family."

Maud was quiet. Bodhi and Robby were there to see them off, but the shadow of darkness blended them into the night, almost obscuring their newly grown facial hair.

"Will we go to the convent for lessons with Adelaide?" Judith wondered aloud, and Maud caught a knowing glance from Eleanor to her daughter. Tutored in Latin by the nuns in Bruges for years, every night Judith reported to Maud what she learned when they were supposed to be asleep, while Maud spent her days meandering with her embroidery. Each time they were caught they were confined to their rooms for a day, except to follow their mothers when they donated to the churches.

"We always knew you weren't given a copy of Emma's book for it to sit useless on a shelf, but we've only ever thought about your safety." The countess' rueful voice cut through the dark, and Maud halted in shock as they ran. Her brothers pushed her forward.

"Who will take us?" Judith noticed no one else was quite as bundled against the chill.

A sandy-blond figure emerged from the stables, a leather harness circling his left shoulder. Standing straighter, Maud eyed him sheepishly.

"Ser Brictric has agreed to take you before he returns to England," said Count Baudouin. "You'll have better cover if you leave in darkness under the English banner. Emperor Heinrich has eyes from Lorraine to the North Sea, but he has no quarrel with England."

"How long?" pressed Judith. Count Baudouin pushed away a nervous glance with a plastered smile for his sister. This midnight evacuation was more serious than he wanted to let on.

"It might be half a year or more." He failed to hide the shudder in his voice. "The emperor is angry I aligned with Godfrey of Lorraine against him, after the Empire took Valenciennes from me. But all the soldiers in Rome couldn't take Flanders from our family."

"I still don't understand why we have to leave." Judith tugged at the hood of her fur cape. "You've been at war with the Holy Roman Emperor for years."

"Because Emperor Heinrich says he'll have you both kidnapped and wed to any man he wants, to annex Flanders acre by acre and take control of it for himself."

"Quiet, Robby!" Count Baudouin hissed as his shoulders dropped.

It was unlike Maud to let Judith be more outspoken, but she'd been woken in the middle of the night and forced to flee. Her thoughts were clouded with fatigue and worry, but while Judith begged to stay, and Maud feared for her family, another part of her couldn't wait to get to Normandy—or her Latin lessons—fast enough. "Be careful."

"I'm meant to say that to you." Count Baudouin turned to the English seaman, his voice strong. "You're a trusted envoy, Ser Brictric, with my family's most precious cargo."

"I'll get the ladies to Normandy safe and sound, Your Grace." He nodded assuredly. The girls hugged their parents, the chill forming clouds from their lips as they spoke. Helping them into the carriage, Brictric gave each a gallant smile. Only fourteen, Judith was tall and lithe like her mother, and she climbed the ladder with grace despite her long gown.

He turned to Maud, gingerly taking her hand as she stepped forward. "Lady Matilda." He gave a respectful nod and her heart fluttered. Smiling back nervously, she averted her gaze as she sat next to Judith on the bench inside the simple wooden carriage. No longer a scrawny young serf but a handsome, strapping young man of twenty-two, Brictric flashed his wide and welcoming grin as he covered them in a hide blanket to guard against the cold.

"Sit up straight, Maudie." Her mother approached. "We'll come collect you both when things have settled down. Be good for the de Contevilles, and for the nuns. Show everyone in Normandy how smart you are."

"I love you." Maud's voice broke as tears swelled.

Brictric lashed the horses, hooves plodding heavily in the night. Maud's heart beat in time with each click-step echoing inside the wooden box.

The carriage rolled past the city to start their journey. Once the firelight illuminating their home faded slowly in the distance, only the wolves slowed them down, but Brictric was skilled with a bow and sword. Squaring his agile frame against the gray beasts, he waited until they lunged forward. The wolves always met a bloody end by the point of his blade, and each became offerings to the nobles who took them in on the way to Rouen.

The first night, they stayed at Saint-Omer with the van Oosterzeles, hereditary advocates of the Abbey of St. Bertin and long-time allies of their family. Their hosts thanked Brictric graciously for the food, blessing it at the altar of their chapel before serving it that evening.

"Is the monk who authored *Encomium Emmae Reginae* still in residence here?" Maud picked at the gamey wolf, and Gerbod, the head of the family, gave a nod while he chewed.

"But our monks aren't permitted to speak with unmarried

women—only wives and widows. Your parents made it law in this region, and it's good for the monks to remain focused."

She sighed, taking a small bite of meat. "Please tell him how much I enjoy his work."

Chewing carefully, Maud was conscious of Brictric at the end of the long table, afraid to appear unladylike with her food. She always wore her nicest robes in his presence. But rushing out in the middle of the night, for a long stretch on the road, prevented her from looking anything like the Lady Matilda worthy of his usual greeting. She felt exposed and nervous.

For three years she'd been caught in the crush of her emotional attachment to the charming, long-haired English thegn—one of King Edward's closest advisors and able-bodied men. When Harthacnut dropped dead two years after sailing with Emma from Zeebrugge, Edward took over the crown of England on his own. Within months, Brictric was promoted to the position of English ambassador to Flanders.

Maud loved his visits, with his stories of the sea and his elegance as he moved about her family's castle. He always danced beside her at her father's feasts, and when her parents began to talk about her marriage prospects, young Maud found herself dreaming of Brictric. Now, as if drawn by fate, they were closer than ever.

The second night, they pulled up to the coastal home of Count Eustace of Boulogne, a distant relative on her father's side. Lady Emma's daughter, Godeva, was married to the count's eldest son and heir, but the Counts of Boulogne and Counts of Flanders had a violent history.

Maud watched Brictric cast his blond locks from his face before he unloaded two wolves from the roof of the carriage. He tossed both over his shoulder as if they weighed no more than a feather-stuffed pillow. "Why would Count Eustace let us stay with his family if he dislikes my father? He might tell Emperor Heinrich we're here."

"Probably because the Duke of Normandy asked him." He brushed a loose strand of hair from her cheek with his free hand. "Don't worry too much, Lady Matilda. Your father asked me to keep you safe, and I gain nothing from disappointing him. Besides, I'm fond of you. I'd like to see you and Lady Judith safe in Normandy too." Her anxiety dissipated with his assurance.

Leaving his second son, Lambert, to host the daughter and sister of the Count of Flanders, Maud and Judith had neither seen nor spoken to the Count of Boulogne by the end of their short stay. This was no accident of timing, but Maud tried to capitalize on Lambert's amiable nature.

"If we let Emperor Heinrich take cities by force, it won't always be someone else's cities. Eventually, he'll come for Boulogne-Sur-Mer," she said, as Lambert escorted her through his family's dormant gardens the morning of their departure. Though the winter winds were fast and cool, it felt good to stretch her legs knowing she'd spend another full day bundled inside a wooden carriage. She inhaled the salty sea air as seagulls cawed by the shore.

"I admit I'm fonder of building works than swordplay and diplomacy, but I'll bring up an alliance with my father," promised Lambert, returning her to the carriage where Brictric and Judith waited patiently in the cold morning air. The success or failure of this maneuver wouldn't be apparent for weeks, but Maud felt she owed her parents because of what they'd done for her education. Gratitude compelled her to fight for them.

Their third night on the road to Rouen, they stayed with Count Hugh of Ponthieu and his wife, Bertha, the hereditary Countess of Aumale. Their second son, Guy, took a particular interest in Judith, and she spent the night at their grand limestone chateau trying to avoid him. "Don't get too close," she warned Maud in disgust before for dinner. "His breath smells like blood."

Maud thought Guy and his older brother, handsome, raven-eyed Enguerrand, spoke like frivolous cads, but she knew the importance of the alliance with Ponthieu in both Flanders and Normandy, so she held her tongue while they ate. Enguerrand, on the other hand, didn't bother.

"Ser Brictric, is it true you yanked an old Roman spatha from a stone to try to pay off your father's debt, but Earl Godwin took you to pay it off instead?" Enguerrand smiled, his voice dripping with disdain. "Praise be to anyone indebted to that bastard."

Brictric shifted with discomfort but spoke assertively. "My father was indebted to Earl Godwin, but I serve King Edward. When my brother died I inherited my father's land, not his debts. Any lands I've gained since have been with the tip of my sword. On the king's honor." Maud swooned.

By the fourth night, they reached Rouen. Maud and Judith shared a glance as they passed a wooden bridge lined with heads on spikes, marking the path to the chateau. Maud cringed at the sight of white maggots gleaming in the moonlight, chewing at rotted flesh. In the dark, she couldn't tell whether their eyes had been removed before they were mounted or pecked away by birds.

Despite the late hour, two trumpeters blared a harmonious fanfare from the ramparts to announce the arrival of the esteemed Count Baudouin's daughter and half-sister to the Norman court. William and Adelaide's half-brothers, Odo and Robert, were young men now, almost as tall as the duke. Their baby sisters, Emme and Murielle, who spent most of the time in Lille in the nursery, were young ladies with long braids and pink dresses. All nearly a decade older than when they'd seen each other last, they recognized one another as if no time had passed.

Adelaide, now a statuesque, stunning, and self-assured young woman, rushed to embrace the girls. "Maud, Judie, I've missed you both so much!"

"We're very happy to have you here in Normandy," said William's mother. "But God willing, the time will be brief, and the war will come to a peaceful end."

With reverence, they said in near unison, "Thank you, Viscountess Herleva."

"You'll both be staying in the large room next to mine!" Adelaide jounced with excitement. "The views of the city are wonderful from our side of the chateau. It's dark yet, but the torchlights look like fireflies this far up the hill. The view is just as beautiful in the daytime."

"It sounds wonderful." Maud glanced in awe at the large hall, with high wood ceilings as tall as any steeple in Flanders. She caught the duke looking at her and offered a low curtsy. "Your Grace, thank you for agreeing to shelter us. We're truly grateful for your hospitality."

"Welcome to Normandy. But please, while you're here, my home is your home. Your parents have always supported me, and we're proud to have you." Smiling warmly, he stood tall and broad-shouldered with a gleam in his brown eyes. With a respectful bow to his guests, his clean-shaven face and crooked grin sparked with confidence.

"We look forward to spending time in your great duchy, Your Grace. My parents speak so often of your successes, I think it makes my brothers jealous."

"And I look forward to sharing all my successes with you." He proudly puffed out his chest before turning to the Anglo-Saxon. "You must stay the night, Ser Brictric." Maud beamed, and William cocked a crooked grin. "Did you know my father once tried to conquer England? He said crossing the sea was a battle unto itself and turned his ships around, but we'll send you off with a strong morning meal to aid your travels, in gratitude for delivering the Count of Flanders' daughter and sister in such good health."

Brictric bowed to the duke with respect and a charming smile as a servant handed each of the guests a golden chalice of wine to greet their arrival. "I'm sure you'd strike fear in the hearts of men if you followed in your father's footsteps. The Wessexians may call themselves dragons, Your Grace, but I know Normans are Norsemen at heart, like the Danes who conquered English lands for centuries." He raised his cup. "I'm grateful instead to break bread at your table."

At daybreak, Maud was anxious to say goodbye. Brictric kept her safe, as promised, and she felt fortunate to spend so much time with him.

Hugging him in the courtyard before she could think too much about it, she felt his warm hands on her back, fanning the flames of her desire. Falling into the softness of the fur he wore to guard against the winter wind, she felt safe in his arms, but pulled away dutifully.

"Thank you, Ser Brictric, for your service to our family, and to me and Judith. We are, and certainly I am, in your debt."

"It's my honor, Lady Matilda."

He smiled at her one last time before turning toward his horses, leaving her standing on the castle bridge, bundled against the cold. As he disappeared over the gray horizon, she felt a chill from the air, stronger than she had in three days.

The high-arched stone-and-wood ceilings of the Abbey of Saint-Armand made Maud, already short in stature, feel small as a mouse. Looking up, she stood in awe under a wax statue of the Virgin Mary over the altar. Adelaide spent three days a week here, sleeping in the dorms while learning Latin from the nuns. Now, Maud and Judith would join her.

Taken to the rectory, Abbess d'Ivry waited to greet them. "Welcome, Lady Maud and Lady Judith. It's a pleasure to have you." Big eyes looked down her long nose while she spoke, her hair hidden under a pristine white veil and gray robes. "Please, tell me what you'd like to learn while you're here."

"Adelaide and Judith are miles ahead of me already." Maud stared hungrily at the books laid out before them. "I don't know if I'll catch up, but I want to see shapes turn into letters."

"The beginning is the hardest, but most rewarding, place to start," said the abbess. "Or, as they say in Latin, *Initium semper gravem esse et maxime praemiando locum incipere*."

She smiled. Adelaide and Judith said they wanted to work on their penmanship, but this meant so much more to Maud, who sought to understand the world through her own eyes.

With the abbey more than an hour away by carriage, the girls commuted between it and the Norman chateau in Moulineaux south of Rouen. Both ways, they'd pass the bridge with heads on spikes. Occasionally, Maud noticed a new head, less rotted than the rest, eyes still embedded in the skull—the price paid for challenging the authority of a man descended from Norsemen. She still felt compelled to pray for their headless souls, fearing one day her father and brothers could face a similar fate at war with the Holy Roman Empire.

Abbess d'Ivry said she'd never had another pupil work as hard as Maud. Month in, month out, she immersed herself in her lessons. She was at a disadvantage with Addie and Judith so far ahead, and only the abbess to teach them, but she didn't mind. She was happy to be there at all.

On her own, she practiced by writing letters to Brictric she dared not send, professing her desire to become his beloved wife. Keeping them under her pillow until Addie and Judith found them, they teased her saccharine-swept prose until she burned the letters in the convent's stone hearth, ridding herself of the embarrassment.

A letter from home arrived a few months into their stay in Normandy. Using what she'd learned, Maud tried to read aloud amid the fresh blossoms in the castle garden, but stumbled over the penmanship and offered the letter to Judith. In it, her father wrote, "*Our fight against Emperor Heinrich is strengthened by Count Eustace of Boulogne's decision to join the cause. He told Duke Godfrey of Lorraine his sons insisted after Maud spoke to young Lambert en route to Normandy. You make us proud, dear daughter, and you have a gift for diplomacy.*"

Maud took the letter from Judith's hands and studied the words for "you make us proud." Beaming, she kept the letter inside her Bible at the convent.

Each morning in the abbey she prayed for her family's safety. Every night before bed, she prayed again. Though grateful to God for all she had, every day she missed her family terribly.

Chapter Seven

June 1048 – Rouen, the largest city in the Duchy of Normandy

By summer, eighteen-year-old Adelaide was ready to wed. She had the interest of a few suitors, but "the one" was handsome Enguerrand of Ponthieu, whom Maud and Judith met on the road from Flanders with Brictric. When Enguerrand preened in front of any surface that shined inside the magnificent stone castle at Rouen, Duke William could scarcely mask the annoyance on his face.

"I'd like to visit your market today," announced Enguerrand over lunch, picking his teeth in the reflection of his knife. "Unless it's unsafe. It's quite a collection, all those heads on the bridge."

"We could all go," said Addie. "Uncle Walter moved the family's embalming workshop further beyond the square and the market aromas are bearable now. Besides, he's still got allies in town who'll shelter us if anything seems out of order, like before the rebels were defeated."

"I have no time to wander today," Duke William groused, piling his trencher with cuts of meat next to his own gravy bowl for dipping. Enguerrand's beard caught small drips of sauce, but William's bare face—rare among the nobility—kept him from such indignity. "Archbishop Mauger is bringing a man who used his bishopric to steal from me."

"Between the heads on spikes and rebellions, Normandy's reputation for danger goes well beyond Ponthieu." Enguerrand sneered. "It's not safe for a beautiful lady like your sister."

Duke William glared at his guest. "My sister has never been unsafe in my court. She's very precious to me. Even more so than the small gold trinkets you brought in tribute."

"The roads are wild with bandits, Your Grace." Enguerrand laughed off his insult. "Should marriage be agreeable, my mother's title in Aumale should more than impress."

Adelaide's eyes gleamed at the thought, as Mauger, the Archbishop of Rouen and William's uncle, entered the room with a smile. "Still eating, I see. Even with a Norseman's appetite, you needed the help of King Henri of Francia to stop the rebel march at Val-ès-Dunes."

He wore fine robes lined with gold-embroidered silk, which couldn't mask the brown stains on his crooked teeth. Though he wasn't that much older than his nephew, he spoiled his youth enjoying the excesses of wine and bread heaped upon his diocese. William greeted his uncle with a frown, refusing to stand despite Mauger's position as a powerful representative of the Catholic Church in Normandy. "I didn't appoint you to the position of Archbishop so you could monitor my eating habits, Uncle. I appointed you to manage the bishops, but under your stewardship they rob Normandy blind."

Mauger's belly danced when he laughed. Maud thought it rich he would insult his athletic nephew with his own constitution so indolent, but she held her tongue as she chewed the last of her bread. "About that, Your Grace. You needn't worry about the Bishop of Lisieux. I came to tell you everything he stole has been returned to the treasury, and he's agreed to exile to spare his life from the end of your sword. I'll manage his diocese until you agree to his replacement."

The duke searched Archbishop Mauger's face, his distrust more than evident. Slowly placing his knife across his empty trencher, he stood. "Thank you for the report." He refused to make small talk, waving his uncle toward the door. "I don't wish to keep you from your duties at the cathedral."

Mauger looked just as pleased to take his leave. As one of the relatives who disagreed with Duke Robert's choice to make an unlawful son his heir, Mauger loathed making time for his brother's only son, and preferred exercising his authority elsewhere.

Shaking off his uncle's visit, Duke William turned to the table. Glancing quickly at Maud then his sister, he smiled. "There's time for a trip to the market after all."

As the late afternoon sun set long shadows over the market in Rouen, Adelaide prattled on. "You know the Brionne brothers? They spent some years in Flanders, after their father was assassinated by rebels trying to kill my brother." Maud and Judith nodded, recalling the rambunctious duo with polite smiles. Maud was often distracted from her own longings—for her family in Flanders, or for Brictric, wherever he was across the sea—by Adelaide's love of animatedly sharing family secrets, and Enguerrand seemed equally taken by the legendary lives of others. "They're two of my brother's best young swordsmen, but already they're barred from half the taverns in Normandy because the barmaids can't work when they're around."

Enguerrand listened insatiably as they were escorted by Walter, William's maternal uncle, with Fitz, Monty, and Beau not far behind. Older now, with even more refined threads in their tunics, the stewards carried steel swords in leather sheaths around their waists. With their right hands resting on embossed golden hilts, they watched people scurry about the stalls.

"Rouen has been much more peaceful since William and the King of Francia splintered his rebel lords last year. According to Mama, it's the least hectic life at court has been since my father died, and the longest we've been able to stay in one place."

Walking through the bustling market, they drew stares from commoners as they went. But Addie only had eyes for Enguerrand and his glossy, raven-black stare, holding his attention with the story of her dubious lineage.

"Everyone knows she's my stepmother. Lady Herleva had a son with my father, but I'm her daughter. Although my existence meant he was unfaithful, she loved me as her own even before my father died. Mama said she felt a duty to him, and to me, but my father spent every night with a woman in his bed; it was never a secret. He loved Herleva more than anyone, but they couldn't wed, and he couldn't be denied his appetite."

"What of the stories she seduced the old Duke Robert while working in the palace courtyard?" Enguerrand walked with a dreamy look in his dark eyes. Behind them, hovering by the apple carts, Judith, Maud, and William watched in bemusement.

"Some stories are just stories," said William stiffly. Adelaide nodded vigorously.

"Herleva's father was the best embalmer in Falaise, and skilled in tanning," she said. "He provided hides for the duke's chief clothes-maker, and they met one day while she was making a delivery. Everyone says my father fell in love with her instantly and wanted to marry, but the Church forbade it because her father had no land. So he arranged for her to wed our stepfather, Herluin, his favorite noble. He even hosted the wedding at his own castle in Falaise because he wanted our mother to have the best life he could give her."

"Enough family gossip in public, Addie." William was firm, but unimposing, and Adelaide leaned toward Enguerrand with a flirtatious laugh.

In the years since they first met as children, Maud heard brutal stories of William, the Bastard Duke of Normandy, who beat back anarchists to his authority with both ends of his sword. He could—and had—taken just about any lands he wanted. Maud had seen the heads on spikes and had even watched a thief or two lose their necks, but the dynamic between William and his sister had grown in respect since their childhood, revealing another side to him entirely.

Purchasing an apple with a small silver denier, Maud turned to the young duke. "If your father could have married Viscountess Herleva, would he have strayed from her as he did?"

He shook his head with a disapproving shrug. "I looked up to my father, but he thought loyalty was only of value when it was useful—he told me so before he left for his pilgrimage."

"The one he never returned from?" pried Judith. "My mother was told her brother got sick from some lamb coming back from the Holy Land, then was buried right where he died to lessen the load for his fellow pilgrims."

"One day I'd like to have him returned from Nicaea for a proper burial, with full rites. Maybe I'll even go myself," he said. "For now, there are still those who distrust the sanctity of my rule because I was born illegitimate, but we've shown great strength and even greater generosity many times, just as my father did." He looked both proud and mournful as sunlight reflected sharply off his sword's hilt.

"My parents worried for your family's safety for years, but after a while they never doubted you'd be victorious against the rebels," said Maud. "They were pleased to let Lady Herleva and Lord Herluin stay in Lille with your younger siblings when you went into hiding."

He scowled playfully at the memory. "When I was stuck on Jersey. Nothing but beaches and monasteries. I remember Adelaide stayed in Rouen with the nuns and became such a voracious reader even I grew jealous of her mind."

"I just hope she's learned to use it for more than sharing secrets." William let out a rare laugh, and Maud smiled proudly to herself. "When you're not trying to be such a serious duke all the time, you have a warm smile, Your Grace."

"Look out!"

Beau shouted as an arrow pierced a wooden post above their heads. The peaceful courtyard marketplace turned to chaos, as a second arrow came so close it set a quick wind through Maud's braid. She fell against the apple carts as produce tumbled into the square. Under a mess of tents and broken wood, panicked screams rose from overturned market stalls. "Oy!" shouted Fitz. He raised his sword toward the assailant.

With only an archer's bow, a hooded figure jumped an overturned cart to scale the stone wall. Fitz and Beau gave chase as William rushed to Maud's side. "Are you all right?"

"This way!" shouted Walter.

Rubbing a sore spot on her elbow, Maud nodded. Walter's voice sharpened, and William helped her from the ground. As the duke pushed her from the square, she grabbed Judith's hand. Walter led their run from the open yard, with Monty pulling up the rear.

On either side of a thin alley, three-story timber buildings gave them shelter. Stopping at a red door hinged into the beams, Walter knocked heavily. A few silent seconds passed and Maud could hear her heartbeat in her chest. He knocked again—this rap quicker, more expectant. His shoulders dropped in relief when an old woman let them in. Standing by her stone hearth, she studied them each in turn.

"I thought you said you never left home." Stalking inside, Walter shut the door behind them, checking over his shoulder with a nervous glance.

The old woman shrugged, her thin shoulders heaving under her billowing robes. "Lot more of them than last time."

"I know you," said William. "Years ago, you led us to the men who escorted us to Le Havre."

"Aye." Her brittle bones moved slowly, her face worn as an old leather hide.

"I never had the chance to thank you," he said eagerly. "What is your name?"

"I am Cecilia Drengot," she said, bowing respectfully. "I'm but a humble servant of the Norman throne. My ancestors were mercenaries for the Norman dukes. Our will is to serve you."

"Madame Drengot, you're a hero to the Norman throne," William said graciously. "We escaped that night certain my death was barreling down on us. I owe my life to you."

The old woman flipped her toothless scowl to a grin. "Hydromel? It's been brewing since sunrise." She took a ladle from an iron cauldron bubbling over a fire warming the stone hearth.

"We'll share," said William. The woman filled three glazed clay cups with fermented honey water, which stung Maud's nostrils with its sweetness. Taking the first sip, Walter nodded his approval to the duke. William and Walter took small sips before passing the homemade beverage, but Enguerrand held his cup longer, taking a larger drink, before finally passing it to Adelaide. This bothered Maud, but she could see the doe-eyed look on Addie's face.

Only Maud looked concerned with Enguerrand's selfishness as they drank. William eyed Walter pacing in front of the window, looking outside cautiously to see if he might spot their attackers skulking in the alleyway.

"I thought the rebels were all defeated." Adelaide looked concerned, but not afraid. She'd grown used to avoiding danger lurking at the Norman court. A year after William and his family came to Lille, the Count of Flanders was shocked by a letter announcing William's guardian, Alain, the Duke of Brittany, had been poisoned. This betrayal of Duke Alain encouraged others to attack the Boy Duke and his guardians, with each successive protector killed within months of taking charge of him, including old Gilbert of Brionne and Fitz's own father, Osbern.

"Resistance to power has been around a lot longer than the Duchy of Normandy," said Walter, wiping sweat from his brow with a linen cloth pulled from a leather belt around his waist. "The attack in the market shows the threat of anarchy in Normandy isn't over. The rebels' defeat at Val-ès-Dunes forced them to regroup. But they can, and they will."

"I've never lost a battle," William reminded them. "And rebels smart enough not to fight have become some of my closest allies. Isn't that right, Monty?"

Sipping hydromel, the loyal steward cleared his throat with a lighthearted smirk. In his youth, under sway from power-hungry men, he'd cursed the infant duke in his crib. "You're not a man to war with, Your Grace."

"All of life is war," said Madame Drengot. "I lost my sons when they marched with you near Caen years ago, and my life has been scarce ever since."

William frowned, sipping from his cup before handing it back to Maud. "I owe your sons a great deal, and I honor you for your sacrifice."

"Stay vigilant. One day, your assailant might have better aim with an arrow than that fool I sent to the market square." The old woman drew close, pulling her hand from a fold in her robes. Between her skeletal fingers, the dull sheen of a knife reflected in the flames over the hearth as her eyes flashed wild with vengeance. Still hot to the touch, Maud reflexively tossed the remaining contents of the cup of hydromel. The old woman shrieked as alcoholic liquid burned her vision.

Unsheathing his sword, William sliced downward in such a quick, unexpected motion that the old woman's hand, still clutching the knife, hit the floor before anyone registered the attempted assassination. Madame Drengot screamed, the kind of pain-induced, curdled growl that Maud heard men describe after returning from the battlefield. She'd never heard one like it herself, and her ears rang as the old woman fell to the floor. Blood pooled around her, turning Madame Drengot's blue robes a shade of deep purple on her right side.

"Go!" yelled Walter. "Back to the castle before more traitors come. I'll handle this hag."

Monty picked up the hand and confiscated the knife, tossing the useless appendage into the bubbling cauldron of hydromel.

Madame Drengot would see her next sunrise from a spike on the bridge to Moulineaux.

Avoiding the market, they raced in the direction of the castle keep. Monty and William kept their swords unsheathed, ready to swing, but people passed by in a blur as Maud followed. Still, she tried to read their faces. Looking for what? She wasn't sure. But she hoped if this were the end, she'd see it coming. Fear coursed through her, willing her forward.

Sweaty and exhausted by the time they made their way back to the castle through a servant's entrance, Maud's cheeks turned red as heat burned off them. She'd never run for her life before. Her lungs pounded inside her chest as her breath rang hollow.

"I was right," Enguerrand announced to Adelaide. "You're not safe here. I must marry you and take you to Beaurain. I'll protect you myself."

"I will marry you," she squealed, the ends of her smile locked into the upper edges of her cheekbones. Despite her reservations, Maud beamed with happiness for Adelaide's infectious joy. At her side, William looked equally conflicted.

"You make my sister happy, Lord Enguerrand, and her happiness is our happiness. If you vow to keep her safe, I won't protest. Come discuss the dowry before we inform the nobles."

Adelaide had nowhere to channel her excited energy, so she draped her arms around Maud and smiled. "You and Judith must be there as my attendants!"

Judith beamed, and though Maud kept her reservations to herself, she smiled. "We wouldn't miss it, Addie."

Chapter Eight

August 1049 – Count Baudouin V's castle near Bruges, Flanders

Dearest Maud,

Your last letter fully warmed my heart, to hear you wrote to Rome on my behalf to protest their intent to annul my wedding. I've come to think of you as my sister through all our years of friendship—especially that most marvelous year when you and Judith came to stay with us. You inspire me with what you learned from the nuns in such a short time.

Married life is truly wonderful; I should wish it for you soon. Enguerrand is a good husband and a fair man. He says he loves me, but if we are too closely related as the Church claims, Enguerrand says we'll be forced apart. This looming decision could only be made worse if I am with child—and my dear Maud, I fear things are the worst.

Please pray for me and keep yourselves well and safe while Emperor Heinrich's war rages. I think warmly of you, always.

Your dear friend,
Addie

Nearly two years earlier, after the feast of Michaelmas, Maud and Judith traveled to Beaurain in the County of Ponthieu. Returning to the chateau that gave them shelter for the wedding of Addie to Enguerrand, they were once again reunited with Adela and Eleanor. Count Baudouin sent word he'd won back Valenciennes and the worst tensions with Emperor Heinrich had passed, paving the way for Maud and Judith's safe return to Flanders after the traditional Catholic ceremony.

Carrying Addie's heavy lavender-and-white cape, Maud marched past limestone that stretched higher than the tower at William's castle in Rouen. Walking as tall as the pillars, Addie wore a smile bright enough to overpower the sun. The great celebration, with fire dancers and musicians, was a joyous and exuberant occasion befitting the bride and groom.

At the feast, Enguerrand's younger brother, Guy, asked for Judith's hand. Maud would never forget the look of terror in her eyes as she considered devoting her life to a man whose breath smelled like blood. Before leaving again for Flanders, Eleanor and Adela declined his proposal on Judith's behalf, saying Maud, the elder among them, was to be wed first. A total lie, but Maud played along for Judith.

"I don't think I'd like her hand in marriage." Lanky Guy looked down at Maud with a cynical glare. "Not even a dance, to be honest with you."

Rolling her eyes, Addie whispered, "I'd love you as a sister-in-law, but I'd rather you marry my brother." Maud smiled politely, but whenever marriage was discussed, she thought only of Brictric.

She danced twice next to William in the standard circle around the musicians, though he wasn't very graceful on his feet. She even danced once next to Enguerrand at Addie's insistence. They talked of nothing, listening only to the lute players while Maud imagined she clasped hands with Brictric instcad.

Now eighteen, Maud sat by a large window in her father's library as she reminisced in a daydream until birds cawed vigorously outside the window to disrupt her thoughts. As they flew southward in a V-shape, Maud smiled. This time of year, the birds had their compass pointed south, but Maud's had been pointed northwest since Emma sailed for England nine years earlier.

"Your father and brothers return from Hainault this afternoon with their soldiers. Put your books and letters away." Adela's voice was more exuberant than usual, but still stern, as she entered the library with a frown. "Emperor Heinrich may wish to turn the whole of the known world back into the Holy Roman Empire, but your father and brothers secured Hainault for Flanders and we'll greet them proudly when they come through the castle gates."

Clutching Addie's letter, written in Latin, Maud set it in her lap to retwist a loose braid, turning her head away when one of her ladies-in-waiting approached.

Maud didn't mind their help to dress in all those yards of fabric, but she'd grown up more independent than many women in her position. Part of that was because she'd learned to read, though she couldn't read or write as well as Addie. Even Judith, now sixteen, was better than Maud. Still, she was good enough, and for that she was grateful. With a large, south-facing window to let light in, and a wooden chair lined with fabric and stuffed with wool on the seat and back, she found her father's library a perfect sanctuary. He had fewer books than Abbess d'Ivry at the convent, but she didn't mind. She'd already pored through Emma's book at least a dozen times, cherishing the words as if they were pure gold.

"Mama, will the Catholic Church really excommunicate Addie and Enguerrand?" Maud stood to put her books on a stone shelf. "I feel for her, especially if she's with child."

"The Church has more power over them if she is, because it proves they committed sin."

"But the Church hasn't even proven they're third cousins by blood!"

"It was their mistake not to get the consent of the Pope before their wedding." Adela shook her head with curt disapproval. "Pope Leo does whatever Emperor Heinrich wants, even though being under the emperor's thumb makes him feel small. A tiny county like Ponthieu is a perfect target for someone like Pope Leo to pay forward his emasculation at the whims of the Holy Roman Emperor."

"God wouldn't want the Pope to lie."

Adela shrugged. "I doubt He would, but this is one of those rules you won't change simply because you don't like it, Maudie."

The Church claimed when Enguerrand's sister married Adelaide's uncle, Guillaume Talou, it made Enguerrand and Adelaide blood relatives, but Maud knew better. Before he left for Hainault, Count Baudouin assured his daughter blood relatives had to descend from one ancestor—but he also made sure she knew this didn't matter.

"One can hardly rule a county, duchy, or kingdom while excommunicated. Power descends from God to the divine, but without the Catholic Church a man is not a king."

Maud's letter to Pope Leo, written with her father's help, attempted to promote the godly union shared between Addie and Enguerrand. They were married by a Catholic priest on Catholic ground, she said, and their love was a blessing from God Himself. Maud thought it probably true Enguerrand loved her, but Addie's latest letter confirmed what Maud had long feared: If the Church ruled against them, Enguerrand would choose ruling the County of Ponthieu over his marriage to Adelaide. Maud would do almost anything to help her, and sending a letter to the Pope in their defense was the least she felt she could do.

Maud and her mother met Judith and Lady Eleanor in the castle courtyard. The household stood behind, and soon they heard horses' hooves in the distance. As they slowed, their gait grew louder. The bridge lowered and the steel gates raised, and her father rode in on his favorite black steed, flanked by Bodhi and Robby to his left and right. Two carriages pulled into the walled enclosure surrounded by a dozen more soldiers on horseback.

The wooden boxes were painted with the striped black and yellow colors of Lord Herman of Mons, the deceased Count of Hainault. Count Baudouin and his sons dismounted, and Maud ran to embrace them. Relieved to see them returned in good health, she smiled earnestly.

"My dear Maudie," said Count Baudouin. "How many books have you read since we left?"

"Not that many, Papa."

From behind her father, Maud watched the door to the first carriage swing open. A woman's leg popped out, draped in a long silk skirt and embroidered black shoes. She stepped down carefully, her hair pulled back under a black veil.

She was followed by a young girl, who looked about five years old. When her feet touched the hard-caked dirt of the courtyard, the woman turned back to help a young boy. He looked older than the girl by a few years, but his right leg curled outward, bending in again sharply at the knee. His ankle bent downward, and his right foot curved in toward the left one. He could scarcely walk, and the woman supported his weight as Bodhi stepped forward to introduce them.

"I present Lady Richilde of Mons, the Countess of Hainault and my future wife. These are her children, Roger and Gertrude."

Lady Richilde didn't smile. Only her children graciously accepted the women's respectful bows.

"When will the wedding be?" asked Judith excitedly, seemingly oblivious to Richilde's clear unhappiness.

"Autumn will be a perfect time to hold the wedding, though it doesn't leave much time to inform our allies," Adela gushed proudly. "We'll host a celebration for the ages."

By the size of her children and the lines in her cheeks, Richilde looked years older than Bodhi, who was a young nineteen. Feeling for her lack of choice in the matter, Maud spoke up for her. "It's been a long journey for you, Countess. Can we offer anything? This is your home now too."

Softening slightly at Maud's overture, Richilde shook her head. "No, thank you." She looked to the ground with a distant glance, her children's hands hanging limply from her grasp.

"Who will be invited?" wondered Judith.

"Everyone," Lady Eleanor replied. "The wedding of the heir is an event second only to a coronation. Everyone who wishes prosperity to the County of Flanders will be invited."

"Including the peasants?" asked Maud rhetorically.

Bodhi scoffed. "The unbathed are sad and can't pay their taxes."

Robby chortled. "You had no problem cavorting with the unbathed at the whorehouse." Countess Adela's grin fell from her face, her cheeks reddening with rage.

"He's joking," insisted their father with a nervous laugh, but Adela wouldn't placate him with a smile.

"Will anyone from England be invited?" asked Maud.

"We'll certainly invite Lady Emma, though we're told she doesn't travel much these days," said Count Baudouin. "I'm sure we'll receive representatives of King Edward."

"Why do you ask, Maud? Hoping a certain ambassador will be there?"

Maud's cheeks flushed at Bodhi's snide observation, but she had no time to react. With the gate still open, two men in red tunics embellished with gold rode through on magnificent brunette horses. As they pulled to a halt, Maud recognized them when they dismounted.

"William FitzOsbern? Roger Montgomery? To what do we owe this honor?"

"We've come to see you, Lady Maud. And your family, of course," said Fitz.

"And where is Roger de Beaumont?" she asked, surprised not to see them in trio.

"His wife just had a son. The duke didn't want to pull him from his family," said Monty.

"We were just welcoming my son's betrothed and her children from Hainault," Adela interjected.

"Pardon our interruption, Countess." Fitz bowed apologetically. "His Grace, the duke, wished to be here himself, but he's entertaining the Norman bishops in hope they'll convince the Pope not to annul his sister's marriage."

Maud spotted gold glistening from a satchel around Monty's shoulder. Tributes for her mother and father; she suddenly knew why they were here. She froze but didn't stop them.

"Lady Maud of Flanders, the Duke of Normandy wishes to ask for your hand in holy matrimony." Monty spoke with a hint of ceremony in his voice. "He says you would be a divine duchess, and he wishes for no other lady on the continent but you to fill this role."

Maud deflated. It was so precise and unromantic—exactly the sort of man she thought William to be. He couldn't bring a smile to her lips in the same way she beamed at the sight of Brictric. Though she trusted William, he could be a petulant snob with a distinct temper, quick to act or speak without thinking—the bastard son of a man left to rot in the place where he died. But most of all, William sat on a throne across the sea from the shores of England.

Her parents smiled expectantly. By their wanton looks, they believed she would agree to become Duchess of Normandy, providing Flanders with a powerful alliance. Speaking slowly, and carefully, because she could feel her mother's eyes on her neck burning holes into her skin, she said, "Please tell His Grace I'm grateful for his proposal, but I can't accept."

"And why not?" Lady Eleanor's sharpness surprised Maud until she remembered the dowager countess was a born-and-bred Norman.

Countess Adela stepped forward anxiously, grasping the sleeve of her daughter's gown with a surprisingly solid grip. "Allow us to apologize, gentlemen. Perhaps our daughter needs time to consider the duke's proposal more thoroughly."

"I mean no disrespect to Normandy. My heart isn't with the duke," she said honestly. "It's in another place altogether."

Robby scoffed, laughing ruefully. "She won't marry a bastard, but her torch burns for a sailor."

"He's an ambassador!" protested Judith on Maud's behalf. "And his landholdings are significant."

Usually grateful for Judith's penchant to act like her shadow, as she met Richilde's spiteful stare and the embarrassed glances of Monty and Fitz, ignominy got the better of her.

"Thank you for your visit," she said stiffly. Bowing her head to Duke William's stewards before turning on her heels, she straightened her shoulders as she marched inside the castle. Climbing the dark, spiral staircase to her room, she locked herself inside so they wouldn't see her cry.

Chapter Nine

September 1049 – Flanders Castle near Bruges

By early autumn in the County of Flanders, plans for the wedding had taken over the Flemish court. Leaves had turned from green to orange and red, but there was still a warmth in the air. Adela believed the weather sent by God, to bless her eldest son for his impending nuptials.

With a knock at the door, Maud bid her father inside, her shoulders tense. He felt compelled to knock before entering his own library because she spent more time alone with her Latin books than ever, hiding from her parents' disappointment after turning Duke William down.

"Your mother asked me not to tell you that Brictric arrived with Tostig Godwinson, but I'm far less concerned about you and Brictric than I am about the drunk Dane he came with. Tostig wrote ahead to say his brother, Sweyn, advises: 'the Flemish court is rich with potential brides.'"

"When you let Sweyn Godwinson stay here in exile a few years ago, before Judith and I went to Normandy, you told us never to stay in a room with him without our mothers present," she recalled, closing the embossed Bible in her lap.

He nodded. "I did say that."

"Wouldn't a marriage alliance with the Godwins be a good thing for Flanders?"

"Only if Earl Godwin stays in King Edward's good graces," he said. "And I'm not sure he wants to, in all honesty. He's a snake if I've ever seen one walk on two legs, and I think his sons learned from the best."

She frowned. "Why did you let Sweyn stay here if the Godwins are so dangerous?"

"Because, Maudie, I could keep you protected while he was here, and one day Earl Godwin might win." He sighed. "Even if their relationship is dysfunctional bordering on murderous, the Godwins are

King Edward's in-laws and the most powerful family in England."

Maud considered this, forming a slow smile. "Makes sense. Keep friends close, but your enemies closer."

"And friends' enemies even closer than that." Her father grinned, nodding his head slightly as he placed a hand on her shoulder. "I don't like the Godwins much, but I need to pretend I do. The earl has friends all over Europe."

"You've never said what Sweyn did to earn his exile from England."

Count Baudouin scowled but gave a reluctant sigh. "King Edward refused to give him an earldom, so he kidnapped the abbess of Leominster and tried to steal her land. Even when she refused to marry him, he raped her to try to prove they were husband and wife. The abbess recovered, but Sweyn's exile lasted less than two years."

Curling her lip in revulsion, Maud thought carefully. "Lack of justice for the abbess aside, is Tostig duty-bound to be like his brother?"

"No," Count Baudouin said. "But what if he's worse? He smelled of wine when we greeted him. When my father was alive, he loved his wine. When he loved his wine, he hated everything else, like my mother before she died. The dowager countess wants to see an engagement for her daughter, but my father had already started to fade from illness by the time she arrived to marry him. She doesn't remember how violent he could be. Judith trusts you. If Tostig is the wrong man for her, she might listen to you."

With a nod, Maud stood from her favorite spot near the window. "Papa, if I wanted to marry Ser Brictric, would you allow it?"

Count Baudouin looked into his daughter's eyes with some sympathy. "Get him to propose first, Maudie. Then ask me again."

"And Mama?" She pouted as she returned her books to the shelves.

"Maudie, if you haven't noticed for the last eighteen years, your mother is always the one who capitulates to you first."

"I had to ask for Latin lessons for eight years." She crossed her arms defensively.

"And when we had to send you to safety, we could have sent you to the abbey in Saint-Omer with the van Oosterzeles and you'd have been no less safe, but you could get a better education in Normandy."

"She wanted to send us to Normandy so I might get better acquainted with Duke William and decide to marry him."

Count Baudouin laughed, pulling his daughter in for a friendly squeeze. "She had multiple motivations, Maudie."

Finding Judith with Tostig and Brictric by the stables, which reeked of horse dung, Maud placed a hand in front of her nose to block the stench.

"Lady Matilda." Brictric greeted her with his wide smile, his blond hair bouncing over his shoulders as she marched up the stone path.

"Ser Brictric." She braved the stench to smile. "It's always a pleasure to see you."

She held out her hand, but Tostig Godwinson reached out to kiss it instead.

"We've not been introduced, lovely lady." A long, faded scar shined across his left cheek.

"Lady Matilda, this is Tostig Godwinson, son of the great Earl Godwin of Wessex," said Brictric. "Tostig, this is Lady Judith's niece, Lady Matilda of Flanders."

Tostig smelled of red wine and, probably, beer from one of the abbeys in Flanders, brewed by the monks. The region was growing famous for open-air yeast fermentation, a brewing style unlike any in the known world. Maud loved it; of course, a reputed drunk would love it too. "Is that lambic beer? How do you like it? It's new. I love the taste, but not half as much as my brothers do." She kept a genial wit so as not to offend him.

"It would have been insulting not to try the beer Flanders is famous for all the way to the north of England." Tostig's scar stretched across his cheek as he laughed. "It's just as good—maybe even better—than I've heard."

"Maud, we were just talking about taking the horses for a ride!" said Judith excitedly. "Or for you, a stroll, maybe."

"Yes, it's true, I still don't like horses. They make me think of the man we watched get trampled." Judith halted laughing at her expense. Brictric didn't laugh with her, which was all that mattered to Maud.

"Horses are nothing to fear, Lady Matilda. Not like us." He held the leather reins of a saddled, raven-haired stud with a chestnut coat.

"Look into the horse's eyes. They're proud creatures, but soft-hearted. Sound familiar?"

Maud's heart skipped as her breath caught. Brictric looked back at her with his enchanting smile and a gleam in his golden-brown eyes, with lips that spoke such affirming words of her. Stepping tenderly toward the horse at his urging, she looked cautiously into its large, glassy black orb. Her memory of the day in Lille rushed back. The charging horse. The pool of blood on the cobbles and the crippling fear. She straightened her shoulders, steeling her nerves.

The horse stared back calmly, and Maud's breathing evened. Brictric was right. There was a peacefulness in the reflective eye of the horse that humans rarely managed. Gazing back at Brictric, she realized she felt that same peacefulness in the eyes of the Saxon thegn—warrior, advisor, and ambassador, with the landholdings to match his station. Rising from servitude as the son of a builder, paying his father's debts to one of the king's most powerful men had benefited him well.

The horse leaned into Maud as she slid her hand down his coat. "He likes you, Lady Matilda. You can ride with me. We'll keep a slow pace."

Using Brictric to support herself as she climbed, Maud placed her left foot in the stirrup to hoist herself up. She sat sideways, both legs hanging over the horse's left shoulder.

Holding tightly to the reins as he pulled himself up behind her, Brictric's leg locked in underneath her thighs. His leather-gloved hand brushed softly against her bare fingers as he reached around her to take the reins. Smiling, she felt his breath on her cheek as he urged the horse forward.

"You look good on a horse, Maudie!" said Judith. She'd mounted the flaxen-haired mare they prayed for in the cathedral all those years ago in Lille. Maud knew Judith patronized her, but she sat so close to Brictric she was paralyzed. She smiled awkwardly as a mixture of fluttering butterflies and white-hot fire rose in the pit of her stomach. Soon, Tostig and Judith were several paces ahead of them.

Over a jug of strong Frankish wine, Lady Eleanor and Countess Adela had once reminisced about a courtier so excited by the women of Normandy they called him "The Bulge." Sitting practically in his lap Maud knew, from that old memory, Brictric was excited by her too. His arms tightened around her sides as a new and dizzying sensation rose inside her.

"Let's go back," she said, and Brictric slowed the horse.

"Are you not enjoying the ride?" His breath warmed the blushing skin of her cheek.

"No, I'm enjoying it very much." She looked up to meet his gaze. He swallowed hard, and the hairs on her neck tingled as he ran a gloved hand through her auburn locks.

"Tonight, Lady Matilda. After the welcome feast." Desire dripped from his voice as he clasped around her hands to grip the reins. "Let's not leave Tostig alone with Judith."

"Is he not good for her?"

"He's the smallest of his brothers," said Brictric. "Even smaller than the younger one. He drinks to feel less like the runt of his family, but thinks the drink adds ten feet of charm. He's easily the least liked Godwinson in all of England—among his own family too. The only sibling who shows him favor is Edith, and if she wasn't the king's wife, Tostig would never be invited to court."

Brictric kept one hand on her waist, caressing the fabric of her robes with his thumb while Maud forced her mind to return to protecting Judith from Tostig's advances. On their leisurely ride through the charcoal forests outside Bruges, they listened as Tostig regaled Judith with tales of life in England.

"I'm in line for an earldom like my brothers, but I've told the king I'm happy to wait for one in the south if it means keeping my future wife away from the savages in the north." Judith laughed like a lark, her blonde tresses bouncing in the wind as they rode. She was falling for him.

By the time they returned to the stables, Judith was thoroughly smitten, and Tostig was on his best, most charming behavior, according to Brictric. Maud wasn't thrilled, but she was distracted. How wonderful it would be if she ended up in England, as Brictric's wife, with Judith not far away as the wife of one of the powerful Godwinsons.

Tostig playfully smacked Judith's backside as he helped her down from her horse. It would never be tolerated if their parents were around, but she tried to make light of it when Judith giggled from his touch.

"Ser Godwinson, if my father catches you doing that, he'll have you hunted down and marched through Bruges without your clothes."

She painted a sly smile across her lips.

"He'd enjoy that," quipped Brictric with a snort. Tostig joined them at his own expense, but Brictric's laugh played in Maud's head like a song as he dismounted.

"I never thought I'd say this about an afternoon on horseback, but that was fun!" Brictric held out his hand to help her down, and Maud lingered in the stable while he handed the reins to the stablehand. The boy's father, Rene, had worked for Maud's family all her life, but she spent so little time near the horses she could only smile politely. She didn't know his name.

"Thank you, Jean," said Brictric casually, his hair sailing with his striding gait. "Come, Lady Matilda. A feast awaits!"

"You're the only person who calls me that," she said. "Why are you so formal?"

"Because you're of noble birth, and I'm not. You should be addressed with due respect."

As they entered the castle courtyard, Maud's buoyant heart sank. Familiar red flags adorned with the golden leopards of Normandy hung from carriages just pulling in.

Addie leapt out first, embracing Judith and Maud. From the bump visible under her robes, she was, indeed, expecting a baby. "You look wonderful, Addie!" said Judith, gleefully placing her hands on her bulging stomach. Enguerrand wasn't with her, which Maud noted silently, as Duke William dismounted a speckled grey horse in front of the carriages.

Maud looked at him with a quick, cumbrous smile, conscious that Brictric's hand rested inconspicuously on her lower back. William didn't return it, giving her a short, polite nod before turning his attention to Count Baudouin.

"Take Adelaide up to your room," the countess said to her daughter, keeping a stern eye on their Anglo-Saxon guests. "Help her settle in before supper this evening."

With a grateful nod, Maud escaped the uncomfortable moment in the courtyard.

Chapter Ten

September 1049 – Flanders Castle in Bruges

At the welcome feast, Maud avoided William's gaze from her seat at the head banquet table, impatiently counting the seconds between every slurred, celebratory speech welcoming Richilde to the family. The bride wouldn't even fake a smile. She sat stone-faced for the duration of the evening, but Maud was too distracted to concern herself with much besides her own plans.

Sashaying in her pale-blue dress through the crowds, she was charismatic and engaging with the guests. If she looked too happy, her mother would suspect something, but the same would be true if she didn't look happy enough. She drank one beer too quickly, playing a drinking game with empty chalices and a set of gold rings with Robby, Tostig, and Judith before pretending to fall ill. Excusing herself, she glanced discreetly toward Brictric as she left the stone-walled hall, turning slowly up the stairs.

When he reached her, they took a quick look around to ensure they were out of sight before he wrapped his arms around her from behind, leaning in close to kiss her neck. Tasting his lips on hers, Maud's nerve endings shot off like stars in the night sky.

"I shouldn't get caught in the family quarters. We should go to my room."

Maud felt dizzy, as though she floated on her feet. Falling into him as they moved through the stone halls, their footsteps echoed on the stairs.

It seemed to take forever to reach Brictric's room in the east wing, and Maud considered what she was about to do. To the Church it was forbidden. Her parents would be horrified if they found out, but Brictric had been the one Maud set her heart on from the time she'd begun to feel anything for the male sex at all.

She wanted this. She wanted all of him, forever. She was sure God would forgive her for lying with Brictric before their wedding day.

They reached his room and he shut the door behind them. Lifting her blue kirtle above her shoulders, he pressed against her skin. Under her billowing white underdress, her stomach twisted. He pulled at the knots holding the linen in place, pushing it to the floor at Maud's feet as he left kisses on her neck. Torches lit the walls, casting shadows across the blond hairs in his beard as he studied her wantonly, caressing her breasts. She eyed him self-consciously. No man had ever seen her like this, and she worried she might disappoint him.

Brictric leaned forward to kiss her again, letting his lips linger against her cheek. Leading her to the mattress, he knelt over her on the bed, tearing off his tunic. His solid biceps tightened around her naked body while his lips traveled the length of her bare skin. Smiling down at her as he slid inside, she shuddered from his touch.

Grimacing, because it pinched, she pleaded for him to be gentle as he pushed himself further inside her. Brictric's feather-and-wool mattress pricked her skin, but though her stuffed eiderdown would have been more comfortable, she didn't care.

"Is this all right?" he asked, and she nodded until it started to feel less painful. "Look at me," he pleaded, and she stared deep into his golden-brown eyes, writhing underneath him in a sweaty, uncoordinated rhythm. When it was over, he fell onto the mattress, his arm splayed over her naked chest. "Wonderful, Lady Matilda." He nuzzled breathlessly against her neck, kissing her forehead.

"I love you."

The satisfied smile fell from his lips. Nonplussed, he spoke gently, squirming as he met her doe-eyed stare. "Lady Matilda, I should tell you, I'm engaged to be married."

"You're *what*?" Her whole body tensed under his heavy, hairy forearm. "If you're engaged to be married, what are you doing in bed with me?"

"Goda and I talked about a seaman's life. She understands."

Maud wished she could scream at him, but she knew it wouldn't make her feel any better. "I'm a port whore to you? You're just like my brothers, using women like playthings."

"Lady Matilda, please. That's not what I think." He objected calmly, but she was already mentally atoning to her parents and her God. They would have had to forgive her indiscretions the day she walked down the aisle to become Brictric's wife—but now? All she had was disappointment.

She pushed herself out from under his arm, refusing his offer of help as she reached for her robes. "Why didn't you mention the engagement?"

Fur blankets fell to the floor as he sat up in bed, exposing him, naked and aghast. "I was going to tell your father after your brother's wedding."

She tied herself in her clothes haphazardly, just enough to get her through the dark halls. "No. Why didn't you mention the engagement to me?"

He sighed. "Lady Matilda, you're bound to lead a house far greater than any I could ever give you."

"You coward. You're a liar and a cheat," she spat. "I broke my vows to God! I dishonored my parents! Until the day I die, I may never understand how I ever loved you so much."

"I never asked you to love me, Lady Matilda."

Her heart sank. Tossing her kirtle on backward, she decided against fixing it because it meant spending more time alone with Brictric. Stalking angrily from the room, she glanced around nervously, wiping her tears before racing to the curled stairwell in shame.

The upstairs halls were quiet, but Maud could hear the feast echo from the Great Hall. She pinned herself against the wall as her numbing rage melted away in the darkness. Bitter tears stung her cheeks. The weight of her sins hit her stomach and she fought the urge to be sick, loath to return to her chambers. Judith would likely come to bed soon, but Maud felt too much indignity to face her.

A creak from the floor above punctured the din. Looking up the stairs as a shadow slipped out to the castle bridge, red robes trailing behind them, she followed instinctively. "Countess Richilde."

Moving quietly, she reached the door left open and looked to the night with a gasp. Her brother's betrothed removed her jewel-encrusted shoes, climbing atop the castle rampart.

"Stay back!" she hissed, teetering on the stone. "Come closer and

I swear I'll jump."

"Please," Maud begged. "What about your children?"

"What about them? No one thought to mention Roger or Gertrude in any of the speeches tonight, because they'll be disinherited after the wedding whether I live or die. Now all my Herman had to his name belongs to Flanders, including me and my family."

"Why would you rather die?"

Richilde laughed—a pitiful, scornful gesture. "Don't you have any idea what your father and brothers did? Less than a month after the death of my husband, Count Baudouin and those two snobbish pricks you call brothers brought their army to my door. Every one of them drew swords, and your father and brothers each killed one of my husband's men. Just to show they were serious. The only reason I'm marrying a man young enough to be my own son, who only wants me for my titles, is because I'm as good as dead otherwise."

"Before they left, they said you favored an alliance with Roman Emperor Heinrich. They said if they didn't take back Hainault, you'd send your men to march on more than Valenciennes. They said your husband never would have supported it."

"My husband left Hainault to me, to pass on to our children."

"Please, come down," Maud said. "Would you really leave them?"

"Didn't you hear what I said? They're being disinherited. As soon as they're both old enough, they'll be forced to take vows and enter the Church. Their father's birthright disintegrated in a bloodthirsty political coup."

"That doesn't sound like my father."

"You think because you can read the gospels that you know so much?"

"I don't know half the things I wish I knew." Maud fought to hold her composure. "I know I've been sheltered, bred to carry myself like a lady who's only meant to know enough to run her own household and support her husband's goals. I've thought about it for as long as I can remember."

"You are sheltered." Richilde's face softened. "There's so much violence in the world, and you and Judith know next to none of it."

"Please come down." Maud stepped closer gingerly, and Richilde did not object. When she was close enough, she held out her hand, and Richilde reached for it slowly. Eyeing the ground below one last time, she turned back toward the rampart with a dejected groan.

Collapsing against the half-wall, she sobbed quietly. Sat next to her in silence, Maud began to recognize her own anger. With Richilde's tears providing a contagion, she felt her face warm again with embarrassment, as though Brictric had only just said, *"I never asked you to love me."*

Surprised by her tears, Richilde wiped her eyes long enough to notice Maud's fussed clothing with a raised eyebrow. "What happened to you?"

"I thought I met the man I was going to marry. Turns out he was just a reason to feel sorry for myself and seek forgiveness from God."

"Was it the Saxon thegn?" Richilde leaned forward with interest. "The handsome blond with the big smile? I saw you looking at each other over dinner."

With a short nod she looked away nervously, afraid she'd revealed too much to a woman who had good reason to want revenge on her family.

"Your mother talks of nothing but an eventual marriage with the Duke of Normandy."

Maud sighed. "I trust the duke with my life, but I insulted him when I turned down his proposal. My mother seems to think he'll ask me again if I decide to change my mind."

A grin spread across Richilde's tear-stained cheeks. "I'm surprised she's pushing so hard for a Norman alliance. Have you never heard the rumor that your mother wanted out of her marriage to Richard of Normandy before he died? They say he fell asleep with a belly full of wine and wolfsbane so the poison would take effect peacefully, but my husband said when Duke Robert took the throne, he let Adela marry Baudouin in exchange for the support of her family in Francia, even though Baudouin and Adela fell in love while she was married. People wondered if Richard was poisoned by his brother, who was desperate for the ducal throne, but men kill with swords. Women kill with poison." Maud wondered if the distressed bride was being antagonistic to have her revenge. "Your secret's safe with me, if my secret's safe with you," said Richilde.

"What secret?" Deciding to trust her new sister-in-law, Maud gestured to the door as they walked back inside. "I came out to get some air and I found you looking at the stars."

Following Richilde down the stairwell, Maud kept a smile on her face. Inside, her mind raged, thinking of all tonight had revealed about the world she thought she knew.

PART THREE

Marriage

Chapter Eleven

September 1049 – Flanders Castle in Bruges

For days, celebrations for the wedding roused the chateau, and Maud played doting sister to the dashing groom. Brictric, in his capacity as England's ambassador, couldn't make himself as scarce as they both wished he would. Her pride was deeply wounded, but she allowed herself only fleeting thoughts of vengeance, more frustrated with herself than anything. She was happiest to lie on her pillow at the end of each day, exhausted while she healed from her first heartbreak.

When the morning of the wedding finally arrived, Maud gazed out the window to the castle courtyard. Stablehands prepared the horses for the carriage procession to the church, dressing them in cloth of blue and gold to note the importance of the occasion. She itched under the wool robes she would wear to carry the bride's elaborate red train, her fingers nicking a gold-and-sapphire pin in the shape of a butterfly as it shimmered against her chest.

Richilde wouldn't smile as she was dressed by her ladies-in-waiting. Days earlier, she was ready to kill herself rather than spend one more minute at the mercy of power-hungry nobles, and Maud couldn't get this out of her mind. She felt lied to by the people in her life she'd placed the most trust in. Now that she'd begun to accept her mistake with Brictric, Richilde's inference Adela was responsible for her first husband's death weighed heavily on her mind.

Her head pounding, Maud watched Countess Adela, who watched the ladies-in-waiting dress Richilde. Maud sidled up quietly. "I need to talk to you."

Adela looked at Richilde talking cordially to Eleanor and Judith. "I expect this conversation to be more interesting," she said brusquely, her daughter anxiously trailing her from the room. Once alone, Maud turned with her hands on her hips.

"Did Papa, Bodhi, and Robby force Richilde's men to surrender

Hainault under threat of death? And now we're forcing a thirty-two-year-old woman to marry Bodhi, the youngest nineteen year old I've ever met."

Taken aback, Adela quickly regained her composure. "She'll be a countess in two counties one day. It's not a fate worse than death." She scoffed. "Matters of state are complex, Maud. If Richilde had aligned with the Holy Roman Emperor, none of us would have been safe."

Frowning, Maud lowered her voice to a whisper. "Richilde told me a rumor about the death of Duke Richard of Normandy. She said William and Addie's father let you wed Papa after Richard's death, and that poison is a woman's weapon of choice."

Adela's face turned ashen, but she recovered and straightened her neck. "That clever, devious woman," she mused. "What reason could I have to poison my own husband?"

"You were having an affair. You were in love with Papa, not Duke Richard. Maybe you figured it was poison or hot ploughshares." She offered a tone both charitable and sarcastic.

"Duke Richard's death was a tragedy, but make no mistake, his brother wanted control over the Duchy of Normandy." Countess Adela pressed her hands together in front of her green skirt. Maud refused to cower as her mother pursed her lips into a scowl, leaning close to talk low. "Richard and I were just a month married before Robert's failed coup. So much time we could have spent together was wasted on his brother's pointless insurrection, but I had nothing to do with Richard's death."

For the first time in her life, Maud did not believe her mother. "You speak poorly of Duke Robert, insinuate he's capable of murdering his own brother, but you look down on me for declining a proposal of marriage from his own bastard son."

"It's true I didn't love Duke Richard," Adela said forcefully, keeping her voice quiet. "I was performing a duty to our families as his wife. Marrying your father was no less a duty to our alliances, but I was fortunate the second time to fall in love."

"And I want love and desire to guide my choices, not duty."

"You're frivolous and unrealistic! Powerful men don't marry women like this."

"Frivolous and unrealistic," she countered. "You mean moderately educated and romantic. Are people really so worried about a woman who thinks for herself?"

"You're worldly enough now; don't act so surprised. Not like me when one of the servants reported whose room you were seen leaving a few nights ago." Her father always said her mother could see and hear better than any hawk, or any spy, in the known world, but Maud still flinched in surprise. Countess Adela leaned closer, her voice quiet, as her daughter stood agape. "Let's hope there will be no child to sully your prospects. A servant had to burn the soiled mattress."

Countess Adela turned on her heels, and Maud followed angrily back to Richilde's dressing room. "I want to marry someone who sees me as more than a good investment."

Turning around, her face annoyed, Adela threw up her hands in frustration. "You turned down the one man who loves you as you are, Matilda. Ever since you were children, he's seen you in a way no one else has. We've all seen it, but you blind yourself with your affections. Yes, marrying the Duke of Normandy would be a good alliance for Flanders, but Duke William is more than meets the eye. He's certainly deeper than that Brictric fool."

"I've had second thoughts about Brictric," she admitted bitterly. Adela gave no obvious expression, but Judith stood stunned. Maud's performance had kept her from revealing her embarrassment even to her.

"Girls, we're almost ready to head downstairs," said Lady Eleanor. "Tell the men to have the carriages ready, and we'll meet you in the courtyard."

Judith practically pushed Maud out the door away from the others. "Did something happen after you went to bed with a headache the other night?"

"I didn't have a headache." Judith flashed a knowing grin. "But I don't have Brictric either. He's engaged," Maud said.

Judith stopped in her tracks at the top of the stairwell. "He's engaged?" Her words echoed off the stone, ringing in Maud's ears.

"Yes, Judie, and he didn't tell me he was engaged until after I lay with him."

"You *what*?" Judith chased her down the stairs, lowering her voice to a whisper. "You *lay* with him? What was it like? Was it painful? Why did he lie to you?"

Judith's invigorated curiosity overwhelmed Maud's sense of

melancholy. She felt sore—a dragging reminder of her sins weighing the fine-threaded wool against her skin.

"He's a rogue, Judith. He's not who I thought I loved." Fighting her bubbling anger, Maud stopped them both in the quiet stairwell. "He warned me not to let Tostig alone with you, and I can only wonder how he must be if someone like Brictric thinks low enough to say so."

Her smile faded. "I don't get it. Do we trust Brictric's word, or don't we?" She sniffed, continuing down the stairwell in silence.

When they reached the courtyard, Maud spoke to the lead footman, who greeted her with a reverent bow. "We're just about ready for the procession to the church, Lady Maud."

She turned to Judith with quiet sincerity. "I'm not saying you shouldn't marry him, but there's no rush. Take time. Learn more about him. But in my honest opinion you can do better."

"This doesn't have anything to do with the fact that without Brictric, you don't have your own reason to sail to your beloved England, does it?" Judith asked angrily.

"No, it's because Tostig's a drunk," Maud balked. "What if he can't keep you safe?"

Lady Eleanor emerged from the castle, announcing the arrival of the bride. When Richilde, draped in miles of red fabric, stepped into the courtyard, trumpeters blared joyfully in her honor. But she wouldn't smile as she strode toward the carriages. Her own death march.

Attendants assisted Roger and Gertrude into the carriage with their mother. Richilde was right: they'd be disinherited when she gave birth to Bodhi's heir, but Maud was heartened to see her family wasn't erasing them entirely. At this point, she felt sure they could if they wanted.

She sat next to Judith and across from Eleanor and her mother in a chariot-style carriage. All four sat tense on the way to the cathedral, spines straight, waving to curious people pulling carts of hay along dirt roads snaking from the castle to central Bruges. Some beamed at the sight of the glamorous bride, but Richilde did not return their expressions of joy. Outside the church, onlookers stood and cheered as Maud and Judith straightened Richilde's gown, grasping the red fabric as chanting monks welcomed their presence from inside the cathedral choir. Baritone voices echoed from the stone arches, pulsing through Maud as they approached the altar.

Bodhi stood, head down, looking up when Richilde was only a few steps away. Maud saw regret in his eyes, but it was too late. This was the plan, and the bishop stood before them.

She scanned the crowd of well-wishers sharing in celebration of this farce. Addie and William, dressed regally in purple, watched from across the nave. Not far from them stood Brictric, side-by-side with Tostig. She scowled.

The chanting of the monks grew louder. The reciting of false vows before God, and the presence of those who masked their own sins—herself included—made Maud's head swim. Her stomach lurched. Her body warmed rapidly beneath the wool and her heart ached as her skin itched. She raced for the exit.

Ignoring the din of guests who spotted her interruption, the bishop continued. She took a deep breath when she reached the cathedral's steps, grateful to fill her lungs with fresh air. Among a line of horses hitched to wooden posts outside the church, her gaze fell on the chestnut steed she and Brictric rode days earlier, munching hungrily on a pile of hay. Marching forward, she steeled herself as she looked into his black eyes.

"Remember me?" She ran her hand down the horse's raven mane as her heartbeat slowed.

A man called her name from the cathedral steps, but she ignored him. Lifting her foot into the stirrup, she hoisted herself upward, hands clasping the cantle of the saddle. Unsuccessful, she cried out in frustration. Her robes weighed down her legs like an insect in a spider's web.

"Lady Maud, what are you doing? You don't like horses."

She looked down to see William at her side, staring at her with sincere concern in his brown eyes. His purple cap tipped slightly, revealing small wisps of his closely cropped dark hair. With her foot in the stirrup, she met the tall duke at eye level. "I need to get out of here," she hissed. "They're all liars. I can't breathe around them."

"Please, Lady Maud, will you get down? You need to calm yourself."

"No." She again tried in vain to lift her leg over the horse, batting away his outstretched hand. "I won't stay and watch this mockery on parade."

They'd begun to draw a crowd, and William and Maud both

noticed. A few of her ladies-in-waiting had made it to the steps outside the cathedral with Fitz, Beau, and Monty at their side, watching her anxious conversation with the duke.

He wouldn't budge. "If you don't get down, I'll throw you down in front of all these people."

"No, William. You can't order me around in my own county. I'm not one of your lords, and I didn't agree to be your wife." He stepped forward with a stony glare, but she wouldn't cower. "Are you going to put my head on a spike?"

His nostrils flared and the blacks of his eyes swallowed the brown rings around them. He reached for her skirt in one hand, silk veil in the other.

"Get off!" she shouted, fighting him as the horse jostled beneath her. With a yank, he threw her from the stirrup, her skirt torn to the thigh and her clothes dappled with mud. Staring at him, unintimidated, her lip bled from hitting the cobblestones.

"You insult me by denying one proposal of marriage twice over." His voice shook with anger, but he softened at the sight of her. "If you need to escape your brother's wedding, I'd be happy to take you anywhere you want to go. But you can't steal Ser Brictric's horse."

Maud winced at his name. "I'd sooner escape to Lille and never come back, but there's a lake north of here, and I like to watch the water there. No splashing this time."

He raised his crooked smile, and she accepted his hand as he helped her from the ground and into the stirrups of his own speckled mare. "No splashing, I promise." She grinned despite her anger, her golden butterfly pin bouncing as she settled into the long saddle. "That's a pretty brooch," he said coyly. "Where did you get it?"

"My mother gave it to me a few days ago. She could tell I was upset and hoped it would cheer me up enough to be a charming and dutiful lady during the festivities, but she didn't say where it came from. Just that she couldn't keep something that so clearly belonged to me."

"She knows you love butterflies. So do I." He chuckled softly as he mounted with Maud in front, sitting more timidly with her on his horse than Brictric.

"The brooch is from you." She felt foolish not to realize it before.

"It was among the tributes I sent with Fitz and Monty, and the only one I refused to take back when you turned me down. It wasn't

Norman wealth. I had it made for you."

"And my mother waited to give it to me until you'd see me wearing it, knowing it would draw us together even though I'd insulted you." She eyed the bauble incredulously.

"Now I know where you get your genius."

Though reticent at the thought of being compared to her mother, she forced a smile as they left the city.

Chapter Twelve

September 1049 – the outskirts of Bruges, Flanders

"Why did you propose to me?" Maud probed his stoic gaze as they rode toward the reedy lake on the way to Zeebrugge. Moving quickly to the countryside to avoid chase by Flemish guards, William slowed his speckled horse when they reached the woods. Fitz, Beau, and Monty, his faithful stewards, rode a safe distance behind their duke.

"I didn't know it when we were children, but I couldn't forget you after we met." His eyes didn't have Brictric's sparkle, but Maud thought them more earnest. "Over time, you became the sun. Every day, the sun would rise and set, and I'd think of you."

Her heart ached, struck by guilt for failing to notice him before she'd ruined herself. "I need to tell you something. And then I have another question, if what I say doesn't offend."

"That's unlikely," he said. His arms rested at her sides.

She looked him dead in the eyes, challenging him to change his mind about her. "I'm not a virgin. I've lain with another man."

"I lay with a prostitute Monty hired for my seventeenth birthday, and I'm the bastard son of a duke and an undertaker's daughter." He shrugged. "I know it's all supposed to matter, but it doesn't. Not to me. All I care about is whether it's still true that your heart is with another."

"It's not true anymore. I'm still processing the whole turn of events, to be completely honest with you, but he hurt me. I was so wrong about him." Desperate not to think about Brictric too long, she returned her attention to the road. "Turn left at the next fork in the path."

William took her direction, holding the reins with his arms tighter around her waist than before she confessed. "You said you wanted to ask me something?"

"When you proposed, why didn't you say anything as romantic as 'you became the sun?'"

She looked back and caught him blushing. "I should have waited to speak to you and your parents myself," he rued. "I'm not great with words. And I couldn't bear to have Fitz and Monty be the ones to tell you I felt that way."

"So it's 'he thinks you would be a divine duchess, and wishes for no one else to fill this role?' You might as well have reminded me my mother descends from Charlemagne and Alfred the Great, and your murdered cousin, Duke Alain, told you years ago I'd make a suitable wife."

Maud rolled her eyes and William's face fell. "Duke Alain was right about you, Lady Maud, but he couldn't have known how I'd love you."

"We're here," she said, blushing as they came upon the lake. Jumping from the horse, William tied the leather reins to a tree before helping her step down. Her torn skirt billowed in the wind as she surveyed the familiar, lily pad-dotted lake surrounded by tall reeds along the shoreline.

"I'm sorry I threw you from the horse and ripped your dress." He looked away as she pinned the wool together with her hands. "And about your lip." Reaching for a silk napkin attached to his leather belt, he wet it at the lake's edge before handing it to her.

The sharp taste of blood pierced her tongue as she dabbed her lip with the cloth. "I'm sorry I insulted you, but don't worry about the robes. My legs felt trapped in the fabric."

He nodded coyly. "Next time I'll ask permission first—not to rip your..." His cheeks flushed with embarrassment, but Maud found herself smiling. They sat together in the grass as she spotted Fitz, Beau, and Monty in the brush, far enough away to be out of earshot. "They'd rather be back at the wedding where there's plenty of wine, believe me. They just go where I go." He raised his shoulders in a hopeful shrug. "Ideally, they'd go where *we* go."

"And where would we go?" Chuckling, she flashed an inquisitive eye.

"Anywhere! Where do you want to go?"

Taking a deep breath, she looked into his eyes. "The man I fell for was an Anglo-Saxon."

"I know it's Brictric," he said. "I saw your interest when he brought you and Judith to Normandy, and Addie confirmed it."

She frowned. "I've been in love with the thought of England since Lady Emma stayed with us years ago. I've had a few days to think about what I saw in him, and I think I connected him with a place I've always dreamed about. But I was a fool to think my future was with him."

"If it's England you want, we'll get it." William's lips coiled into a smile with his vow. "King Edward is old and childless. He shares my Norman blood through your beloved Lady Emma, and we grew close when he and his brother spent their exile at my court, but he'll be more inclined to make me his heir if I have a wife who shares his Wessex blood. Earl Godwin is a snide man with more power than he deserves, and most of his sons are a disappointment. I might have to battle for it, but I could get used to the idea of finishing what my father started. The English people deserve a better fate than if the Godwins take the throne."

"If we use force, I'll be just like my father."

"I heard your father forced Hainaut's surrender by spilling the blood of three, not three hundred. If that's the standard, I should tell you I'm already like your father. Probably worse. If given the chance, do you think Countess Richilde wouldn't have used force against Flanders?"

She paused, remembering the heads on spikes on the bridge to William's castle in Rouen, and her father's warnings Richilde was aligning with the Empire against them. "I'm sure she would have. I know power is precarious, and a lot more violent than I've borne witness."

"It's better not to fight," he agreed. "War is unpredictable, but you've got to be ready to spill blood or you'll die. It's a weakness sniffed out by all enemies."

Considering this, Maud took deep breaths, her heart beating heavily in her chest. "I have more to confess. It's part of the reason I wasn't myself at the cathedral," she said carefully. "I think my mother killed your uncle to help your father become Duke of Normandy."

"I've heard that rumor," he said with a shake of his head. "I don't give credence to it. We know your parents, Maud. They're not evil people, and you're not evil by association."

Tears burst onto her cheeks. She wiped them away with her wool sleeve as William put his arm around her in comfort. Pressing his cheek softly against her forehead, he pulled back to pick at a few long pieces of grass as she leaned into his shoulder. "When we were children at the river in Lille, disappointing you that day was the first time I'd ever felt remorse for something I'd done. I felt remorse because you have a good heart, and sometimes I wonder about mine."

She lifted her head to look into his earnest eyes, with Brictric's cavalier disloyalty weighing on her mind. "Promise you'll never betray me, William."

"I'll never betray my love for you," he insisted. "Before my father became duke, no noblewomen would marry a seducer without a crown. Once he had one, he could have forced any count to volunteer a daughter to be his wife, but his heart was with my mother, and he chose to marry none. Sounds romantic, but leaving a bastard to tend his throne hasn't made it any easier on me, and I'd never do that to my—our—children. I'd never do that to you."

She leaned in, pressing her lips to his. Conscious of her split lip, he kissed back gently. A few sparks ignited, and she didn't pull away as his tongue slid slowly over hers. His hand caressed her cheek, and the same lightning bolt of feeling that coursed through her with Brictric returned. She smiled. The old Duke William was no more.

"I don't deserve a better proposal after turning you down, but if you were to ask me again, what would you say?"

He gave it a moment's thought with a crooked grin. "I would say, 'Lady Maud of Flanders, you are the sun, and you glow like the stars. I was a fool to wait so long to tell you I love you, but I love your strength, your capacity for love, and your intelligence. Being your husband would be a great honor, and that you have the perfect bloodline is only ninth or tenth on the list of reasons why.'"

She laughed. At that moment, a vibrant blue butterfly fluttered from a nearby bush to pass through the air in front of them. She hadn't seen one in years, and after a picturesque flight through the reeds it was gone, headed northwest.

"It's going the wrong way. The butterflies should be headed south for winter." William pointed at the winged creature as it floated by.

"Maybe it knows exactly where it's going." With a smile, she considered his proposal thoughtfully. "Could you win England with diplomacy, William?"

"As diplomatically as possible," he countered. "You could help me with that. But in the name of my father, who always wanted Norman lands across the narrow sea, I'll get it for us and our children, and our children's children. Will you be my duchess, and my future queen?"

Lady Emma's words a decade earlier flashed in her mind, etched into her subconscious. *"A queen can do many things other women can't, but she pays for that power with sacrifice."*

She'd never imagined herself as a queen. The role seemed too magnanimous in her childhood worship of Lady Emma. Not even her parents spoke of marrying her to a king. She thought about what it meant, but her heart leapt to accept William's proposal this time. "I will marry you," she said, confident she could meet the demands of sacrifice. Grinning, she leaned in to kiss him as his stewards hooted and hollered by a grove of trees in the distance. "Your future duchess requests the three of you turn around immediately!" she shouted with a laugh, and they cheered her announcement before obliging her. Kissing William again, she tasted his lips with her tongue as they fell backward into the grass.

Maud had no interest in returning during the wedding feast or running into people she wasn't ready to see, so William and his stewards made a fire and camped with her by the lake's edge. Passing around Beau's canteen of wine, they talked and laughed amid the din of crickets in the still autumn night.

"Won't your father's men come looking?" wondered Monty, tossing brush on the pyre.

"They're busy patrolling the wedding." She sipped from the canteen of bitter wine before passing it to Fitz. "But my parents have wanted a marriage alliance with Normandy for years. When they realize we're gone, Addie and Judith will convince them to give us one night."

By daybreak, with fog rolling in to chill the air, dew-frosted grass had stained Maud's wool gown. "I should face my parents," she said. "Maybe my reputation."

"No one will question my betrothed's reputation without wishing they were dead." Pride pushed through William's fatigue as he rose. "As for your parents, at least we come bearing good news." She smiled, but neither his assurances, nor the touch of his forearms against her skin, could make the ride back to her parents' castle any less nerve-wracking.

The wooden drawbridge lowered on an iron chain, pulleys spinning on either side as it dropped. Simultaneously, iron bars raised with a heavy *clink* as they rode into the courtyard wearing yesterday's finery, covered in stains. Judith and Addie stood waiting as the rest of her family joined them—even Richilde, all in black for her first day as a newlywed, stood among them with curiosity.

Her father leapt into the courtyard, angrily brandishing his sword toward Duke William. "Where the hell have you been? Get down and answer for yourselves."

William leapt from his horse, placing a protective hand on his sword hilt though he refused to draw. "Lady Maud was kept safe by me and my men."

"Liar!" hissed the count, and William gripped his hilt tighter. "Maud's ladies-in-waiting said they saw you pull her from a horse by her hair, before dragging her off in the middle of her brother's wedding. You dishonor not just her, but the whole County of Flanders!"

Maud looked down at her torn robes. "That's not what happened!" she insisted. "I was upset. I was running away and about to steal a horse, so the duke stopped me. He didn't drag me anywhere. I needed a friend and I wanted to go."

"And quite a scene you made," her mother snipped.

"Please help me down." William held out his hand to help Maud place her feet into the stirrups. Gasping when they saw her torn dress, she raised a hand to quiet her family once she was back on solid ground. "I was suffocating in these robes."

"The dress is filthy, but your face is worse." Adela's disapproving glare enveloped her. "Graciously, the guests have all gone and can't see you."

"Duke William didn't do this. Not with malice," she said, turning to her brother and sister-in-law as she touched the sensitive flesh on her lip. "Richilde, Bodhi, I'm sorry I made a scene on your wedding day. It was rude and I can't excuse it. I know I missed the toasts last night, but I'd like to say I wish you both happiness for the rest of your lives. As your sister, I'll do all in my power to support you." Bodhi smiled. So did Richilde, if only slightly, before Maud turned to face her parents' demanding glances. "I'm sorry I ran off, but William did nothing wrong. We had an opportunity to talk, and I've decided to accept his proposal of marriage."

Her family suppressed looks of surprise. "You're certain of this," her father pressed.

"It would please me well. There's no one else I wish to marry, Papa."

Countess Adela grabbed her husband's arm and grinned. "Maud's mother and I have long hoped for this union." Count Baudouin's face softened. Sheathing his sword, he shook Duke William's hand.

The duke's other hand found Maud's, and he wrapped his fingers around hers as their relatives happily congratulated them. Addie took them both in a gleeful hug and Judith beamed. She wished Maud and William true happiness and "more babies than you can count!"

Amid their joyful celebration, Lady Eleanor spoke. "We must send our request for a papal dispensation right away." Addie moaned scornfully, rolling her eyes.

"Pope Leo has no reason to step in," Count Baudouin said. "He granted dispensation to Bodhi and Richilde, and the Normans aren't even at war with the emperor."

With a wink, William squeezed Maud's hand. "It's just a formality," he assured her.

Chapter Thirteen

October 1049 – Flanders Castle in Bruges

After William rescued Maud from the wedding and proposed again, she felt lighter, returning somewhat to herself. William returned to Normandy with Adelaide to inform the nobles of their wedding plans while she stayed behind preparing to move.

Wooden boxes stood stacked in the castle courtyard, nailed shut with the dresses and possessions she saw fit to bring with her to Normandy. Emma's book took pride of place in a polished mahogany chest, along with gold jewelry from her mother and a battle-worn shield from her father, with blue, red, and gold paint chipped and fading against the wood. Pierced by arrows and slashed by swords, the shield maintained its structure, the colors still visible. It was hardy and strong, he told her, just like their family.

A request for papal dispensation for the wedding was sent to His Holiness, the Ninth Pope Leo. Set to announce whether it was granted at a continental gathering of bishops, the wait for word made Maud uneasy.

"I think the Pope will deny our engagement." Setting out for a walk in the woods beyond the castle walls, tailed by three cavalry soldiers, Maud walked in step with her mother. "Despite everyone who spoke in their favor, Addie and Enguerrand think the Pope will annul their marriage at the bishops' council in Reims, and Flanders is still at war with Rome."

"The Pope gave dispensation for Bodhi and Richilde's marriage, and it meant the Empire ceding control of Hainault to your father. You're overreacting," said Adela.

"Maybe Uncle Henri's in on it too. What if he called a feudal levy on behalf of the Kingdom of Francia so our bishops couldn't be in Reims to support our engagement with the council? The longer Flanders fights the Holy Roman Empire, the more we need Francia's military support and Uncle Henri keeps us under his thumb. But if ceding Hainault motivated the Empire to try to impact our alliance with Normandy, we've antagonized the Church right before the annual council where they decide the fates of all in their dominions."

Adela eyed her daughter impressively. "The Pope still needs to find a lawful reason to deny the marriage, and we had no choice. I know most of my relatives are entitled prats, but our alliances with Francia have kept Normandy and Flanders autonomous from the Empire for decades. When my brother the king levies our service it's no worse than an act of war to turn him down. We can't insult your uncle by sending bishops to the council instead, especially if there's no legal reason for Pope Leo to deny the alliance."

Maud and her mother spotted a messenger with a large leather satchel riding a gray horse toward the castle. Pope Leo's decision regarding her future was inside and Maud's stomach twisted.

"Let's get back," said her mother. Maud followed nervously, her legs caught between a desire to finally learn her fate and run from it, prolonging her potential disappointment. Clinging to the promise of a simple formality carried her forward.

When they returned, the messenger had already left. Count Baudouin stood in the castle courtyard with the letter, Judith and Eleanor at his side as his young sister tried to read over his shoulder. Bodhi and Robby were fencing in the yard nearby and couldn't be moved to care about the contents.

But Maud cared very much, trying to read Judith as she approached beside her mother. She knew Judith's face best, all its quirks and expressions. Instantly, she knew it wasn't good.

"What does the letter say?" Her voice cracked nervously.

Her father cleared his throat with a stern look in his eyes. "The council annulled the wedding of Adelaide and Enguerrand, and they've been excommunicated. They've also excommunicated the new Count Eustace of Boulogne for marrying Ida of Lorraine."

Maud rolled her eyes. "The new Count of Boulogne left his wife—Lady Emma's daughter—on her deathbed to marry Duke Godfrey of Lorraine's nine-year-old child," Maud reminded everyone, but their faces were crestfallen already. "We're in this war because of Godfrey of Lorraine. Let them excommunicate the Count of Boulogne for his dishonor all they like. His child bride hasn't even had her first communion! But Addie doesn't deserve it."

"And the Pope has refused to give dispensation for your wedding to William." Her father spoke gently, though this had already become clear to her. "They cited the same reason for denying the weddings in all three cases—consanguinity. But neither of you have been excommunicated because you have yet to wed in sin."

"So which abbey should I retire to? I won't marry anyone else."

The last thing Maud wanted was to live her life as a nun, but if she refused to submit to marriage to anyone the Pope might approve of, she knew the convent was among her few choices.

"We'll appeal this decision with Rome," Count Baudouin said. "We have the right."

"But both Del and I descend from Rollo, the first Duke of Normandy, which means both William and Maud do too," said Lady Eleanor.

"A whole lot of married nobles are a lot more closely related than that. Your mother and I both descend from the kings of Francia." Count Baudouin scoffed. "If the Church can turn a blind eye when it wants, we'll appeal until this Pope dies and another takes his place. As long as it takes."

"Or until we're all swallowed up by the Holy Roman Empire," said Maud, bereft again.

"Maud, Tostig Godwinson will be here soon." Judith stepped quietly into Count Baudouin's candlelit library. "I know how you feel, but I'm going to marry him when he asks." Looking up from her books, Maud forced a smile as Judith stood over her pleadingly. "You've spent all winter moping by yourself, but when I go to England with Tostig, I don't know when I'll see you again." Judith spoke cautiously, careful with Maud's frustration over love, politics, and religion since the Church ruled against her marriage to William. Nearly a year after his proposal, Maud still languished in Bruges with her family.

In her hand, she carried the latest letter from Addie, signed "the Countess of Aumale." Other than their daughter, little Adelaide, whom Enguerrand effectively disowned, Addie refused to relinquish the hereditary title from his mother after the annulment. Now she used the title with fervor, writing it on both sides of the parchment of all her letters.

Addie often wrote of William's increasing frustration, as each letter of appeal to the Pope on their behalf came back with the same denial. All her life Maud had been warned the duke was capable of frightening rage, but even she was shocked to read how he spent increasing weeks on the road, plundering churches and villages in his wake.

William was so sure the Church would approve your engagement. I worry my brother finds solace fleecing the churches he can control in a way that is becoming self-destructive, even with his power in Normandy as solid as ever, Addie confided in her latest letter. Maud prayed for a solution, as her heart grew more and more determined to commit to no one else but William.

"Are you coming?" Judith turned when Maud didn't immediately follow, caught up in thought and less than anxious to greet Tostig Godwinson. "Addie will probably never tire of calling herself Countess of Aumale," she said, peering at the letter in Maud's hand.

"Do you blame her? She left Ponthieu with child, without the man who promised to love her. Even if she never sets foot in Aumale a day in her life, Enguerrand's family tossed her aside."

"That title will give her the respect Enguerrand wasn't capable of showing her," said Judith in agreement. "She deserves to use it."

Maud stood from her favorite chair by the window in the library, anxiously picking at her nails. "Judith, I want to tell you something, but I've been afraid because I know I won't convince you not to marry Tostig. I'm worried about you and your future. If the Godwins rebel against King Edward, or if the king dies without sons and the Godwins make a play for the throne, William's loyalty to the king means we might not be on the same side."

Maud was careful not to mention their designs on the same throne. Judith wouldn't keep it from Tostig once they wed, and Maud didn't trust what the Godwins might do with the information. Besides, without a wedding or a son and heir of their own, there was no point broaching the subject with anyone.

"Tostig says in some parts of England the Godwins could muster a larger army than King Edward, but Tostig wants an earldom in the south, not a crown," Judith said. "My mother says I'll marry well if he proposes, and I'll be just across the sea from you."

"Wherever that will be." Maud frowned as she entered the Great Hall where Tostig and his men stood to greet Judith's family. Long, tousled hair couldn't hide the redness of Tostig's eyes from too much drink, nor could it mask the faded scar under his left eye. Standing beside him was a middle-aged man with a yellow beard, and when Maud and Judith approached them with a polite curtsy, Tostig introduced him.

"This is my older brother, Harold Godwinson. After our eldest brother, Sweyn, the warrior, Harold's got our father's brilliant mind."

Tostig leaned into their greeting and Maud smelled wine. She wondered when he was ever sober before she turned to greet Harold with a polite smile. "It's a pleasure to meet you, Lord Godwinson."

"What did you inherit from Earl Godwin, Lord Tostig?" wondered Countess Adela.

"His appetite," Harold interjected. Maud thought it didn't sound like a joke, but when Adela broke into a beguiling laugh, Tostig joined in and cut through the tension.

"We'll feed you both well while you're here," Lady Eleanor promised with enthusiasm.

"Yes, once you and your men get settled—" began Count Baudouin, but Tostig cut him off.

"Forgive me," he said, "but my men and I can't get settled in until I do what I've come here to do, which is ask lovely Lady Judith to be my wife. My future countess."

Maud caught Tostig looking at Harold as he said this; he was here less as a brother than a guardian to the Godwin family runt. Tostig and Judith would have the protection of his family in England, but this didn't soothe Maud's unease.

Judith didn't notice any of this, and as Tostig approached she wore a grin as wide as the castle bridge. "My dear, beautiful Judith, hold me in your hands and watch me fall to my knees." Clasping her hands in his, he dropped dramatically to the ground at her feet. No one proposed like this, and Maud thought the show absurd, but said nothing as Tostig continued. "I would be honored if you would say yes to being my wife."

"Yes, of course I will!" Judith practically screeched. Tostig stood, his smile so wide even Maud believed his love was true. Lifting her off the ground in a short spin, laughing gleefully, they stole a kiss in their embrace, which shocked Count Baudouin.

"Manners." He cleared his throat. Tostig and Judith pulled apart sheepishly, and Maud covered her mouth to hide her amusement. She met Judith's gaze and smiled warmly. Despite her misgivings, which she had voiced, Judith would always be family.

"What kind of ceremony will you have?" Robby wondered aloud. "Catholic, Saxon, Dane?"

Maud could tell he was being snide, but she thought of Emma's book, which she'd been too sad to read since the bishops' council in Reims. She remembered how Lady Emma married Cnut, the conquering Danish king, after his first marriage had been in the handfast tradition of his native kingdom. It gave her an idea, and she grabbed Judith's hand excitedly.

"I don't wish to be rude and leave our guests, but something's just come over me and I hope you won't mind if I excuse myself."

"What is it?" Judith eyed her with eager curiosity.

"I must write to Normandy. I think I've come up with a way for William and me to marry without facing excommunication by the Pope."

"How?" Her interest piqued, Countess Adela stepped forward.

"Handfasting. It's legally recognized in most courts, but if the ceremony isn't performed with Catholic rites, then the Church can't say we broke their rules."

"They could say your marriage is illegitimate and declare your future children bastards," pointed out Richilde.

"You might be onto something," Harold said to Maud, thoughtfully scratching his beard. "Forgive me. I heard of your predicament from my brother on the ship over, and this could at least buy you time to work to convince the Church to give assent to your marriage. I'm told Pope Leo is easily swayed by tributes."

"Aren't we all?" said Tostig with a chuckle, but only Judith seemed to know he was expecting the room to laugh. They grinned together, eyes gleaming. Maybe Judith and Tostig were right for one another after all.

Chapter Fourteen

August 1050 – a hilltop near Eu, Normandy on the border with Aumale

"I can see the Normans! There are so many torches it looks like an army of fire standing on guard for you." Judith craned her neck out the window of the carriage, pulled by horses toward Duke William and his men. Her parents, each on their own horse, led the procession up to the highest point on the border between Normandy and Aumale, the county Adelaide refused to return to her ex-husband. Her mother wouldn't normally ride, but on this occasion of marrying her only daughter to a duke, she rode tall and proud, sitting side-saddle while her ladies-in-waiting marched in step alongside her.

Maud caught a peek out the carriage window. Afraid to rush a single moment, she didn't want to see too much too soon and looked to the sky. Several stars had begun to shine their light in the darkening air, and she found the brightest one. "Mama says that's the same star that led the Wise Men to Jesus," she mused. "I'm not sure she knows as much about Jesus as she thinks."

Judith gave her a piteous grin as Lady Eleanor scoffed. "Adela told me what you said to her on Bodhi's wedding day, and it isn't right to be so cold to her. She's your mother."

"Her life with my father is built on a terrible lie." Maud glowered, enveloping her hands in the heavy burgundy fabric of her dress. A gold sash across her midsection, pinned with her gold-and-sapphire butterfly brooch, let the robes hang somewhat at her shoulders. "I understand why you fight with her all the time."

Eleanor sighed, glancing toward the torchlit hilltop before dropping her voice low and leaning forward in her seat. "I've known your mother for most of my life. Despite what you may think, you have her all wrong."

Maud raised an eyebrow. "I'm surprised at you, Lady Eleanor."

"Your mother and I have a relationship like you and Judith—we're not sisters, but we've lived that way for years. I may not always like the countess, but no matter what, we're family."

Maud stared at her mother's wedding robes, like a heavy blanket holding her against the wooden bench inside the carriage. She wore them because Eleanor and Judith said she looked wonderful. Wearing them also made her parents happy, so she dressed for them too, despite her complex feelings of anger at them both.

"The countess used to frighten me," said Judith. "She watches more than she ever speaks."

"I'll tell you a story your mother would be too proud to tell you herself." Eleanor glanced cautiously outside the carriage. "Consider it a wedding present."

"She'll be angry with you for talking about her," said Maud, raising her brow with an impish smile, and Eleanor suppressed a fitful laugh.

"We haven't bickered since Bodhi's wedding. We're due."

"Of course you wait until Maud's leaving to fight with Countess Adela again." Judith let out a playful moan. "Who will I gossip with about whose mother's argument is more entertaining?"

"What's the point in gossiping when the clear choice is always me?" With Judith now betrothed to a lord with a powerful family, Lady Eleanor was more lighthearted with her daughter. Spending time with them had been Maud's greatest joy in the anxious months leading up to her wedding.

"I'd like to hear that story," Maud said. "There's time to the top yet."

"Constance of Arles was your mother's mother, but her spirit lives on in you, Maud," she began. "She was raised in a free-thinking Christian court in Provence before she was forced to wed your grandfather, King Robert of Francia, as his third wife. But Constance wasn't the marrying kind. She didn't believe marriage was a duty, and as soon as she arrived in Paris, she rebelled."

"Sounds like you, Maud." Judith spoke with a roguish laugh, but Maud hardly reacted as the carriage plodded forward. Her grandmothers died before she was born, and though Lady Emma filled the role for a time, she felt an instant connection to this woman Lady Eleanor described as having a mind of her own.

"Constance dressed provocatively at the Frankish court, had almost as many lovers as her husband did, and responded to each punishment imposed on her with further rebellion. She gave Francia four sons and two daughters, each one ripped away to be raised by others almost as soon as they were born."

"That's terrible!" said Judith fretfully, and Eleanor met Maud's captivated gaze.

"Adela was sent to Flanders and raised at the court of Judith's father. He intended to marry her to your father once they were old enough, but when she was twelve, something happened. She told her maids one of the monks at St. Peter's in Ghent attacked her. Within days, she was put on a horse with a hooded man and delivered to Normandy."

Eleanor's retelling of the dark secrets Adela was too proud to share made Maud rethink her new perception of her mother. "Why was she at St. Peter's without guardians?"

"The monks were her guardians. She was learning Latin."

Maud's jaw dropped. "She says she can't read."

"She never asked to keep up her lessons when she got to Normandy, and let the ladies throw her into preparations to become duchess to my brother," explained Eleanor. "What little she can read, she finds it expedient pandering to the more paternalistic nobles in Flanders."

Maud considered this new information. "I think I understand why she pushed so hard to enforce clerical celibacy laws. And why monks are barred from teaching girls in Flanders."

"She wanted to protect you," Eleanor said with an emphatic nod. Her veil brushed against her neck. "Your mother was sent to Normandy under the condition I'd replace her in Flanders, but Adela threw a mighty fit, refusing to marry Richard if I was sent away. She said she wanted a friend, but your mother had no friends before me and treated me more like a pet. I was always angry with her, but mostly jealous of the attention she received from my father's courtiers."

There was a heaviness to Lady Eleanor's voice, but Maud pressed for more. "What does this have to do with the death of your brother, Duke Richard?"

"Richard had no interest in your mother. He had no interest in any woman. When his engagement to your mother was announced, he accepted it as part of his duty to the Norman alliance with Francia but carried on as though he was still unwed. Your mother reconnected with your father once he started joining his father on campaign, and they fell in love naturally because God knew Baudouin was her intended all along. After they were married, when Countess Ogive passed away, Adela recommended me to her father-in-law as a second wife." Lady Eleanor smiled as the carriage rolled forward. "When she says God saddled us with one another, she knows she chose me, and she knows I could have married again but chose to stay in Flanders so you girls would have each other. But anytime I get her angry enough, she'll say it anyway."

"You love to get her angry enough." Judith grinned cheekily.

Looking out the window at the approaching torchlights, Maud couldn't laugh with them. "How did Duke Richard die?"

"I'm certain it was poison, but not sure it had anything to do with your mother. Yes, Robert and your mother benefited from his death, but Duke Richard's personality made him enemies. Anyone could have poisoned him as they did."

"She looked guilty when I mentioned it to her."

Eleanor shrugged, looking dubiously at Maud. "You didn't just infer she murdered her husband. You also told her—quite correctly—that she'd been having an affair."

"Thank you, Lady Eleanor." She sighed. "I needed to hear this. It comforts me somehow, to know you two will gleefully antagonize each other long after I've crossed into Normandy and Judith's sailed to England."

"We certainly will." Eleanor chuckled. "But it's not without love that we mourn our fate to grow old together. I hope you and Judith will always be able to say the same."

"We'll always support one another, no matter how far apart we live." Judith grasped Maud's shoulders as the carriage leveled out near the crest of the hilltop. The bride wrapped her arms around her, smiling at her closest friend.

Drawing a long breath in when the carriage came to a stop, butterflies fluttered in her stomach. Outside, Robby jumped down from his horse to open the door. "Ready, Duchess?"

Stepping out last from the carriage procession, Maud took Robby's hand to walk down the wooden step, careful not to catch the fabric of her dress beneath her slippers. She heard a collective, quiet gasp among those waiting on the hill, as though she were the most beautiful bride the world had ever seen. Beaming, she took her father's arm to begin the slow, symbolic march under the torchlit walk.

Flames cast shadows across the face of the duke, who stood waiting for his bride on a patch of earth surrounded by a circle of stones. His men had corralled their horses, tearing away the grass to mark exactly this spot—the highest point on the border, closest to God. Maud reached the outside of the stones, and her father let go of her arm with a kiss on her cheek. One of Count Baudouin's tears landed on the fabric of her gown. Sniffling with an embarrassed laugh, he brushed another away with his thumb.

"Blessed days, my daughter," he said. "You make your mother and I so very proud."

"I love you." She kissed his cheek, catching sight of her mother's tear-stained eyes behind him. With a nod, Maud tried to convey solemn respect for her mother on this, one of the biggest days of her life.

Stepping over stones dragging slightly under her skirt, she reached for William's hands. Moonlight cast shadows upon his loving gaze as he caressed the soft skin of her palms.

Adelaide, with her baby girl sleeping peacefully in a sling around her shoulder, stepped forward to hand the vicar a blue silk scarf. "It's from Lady Emma," said William. "Adelaide wrote to tell her of our wedding plans, and though she said her bones are too old to cross the sea, she sent the cloth that tied her to Cnut on their own wedding day. She said you would like it."

Maud wiped a tear from her eye as she felt the weathered fabric between her fingers. Though no replacement for her beloved Lady Emma, she beamed at the thought of her playing some small role in her ceremony. "It's perfect."

The vicar cleared his throat. He had agreed to perform this unconventional ceremony for his duke, but it was against the orders of the Catholic Church and without rites, and he appeared the least happy to be there. Even Richilde, standing next to Bodhi and her two children, had a smile for Maud on her perfect night.

The bride felt herself vibrate with excitement while the vicar spoke in the warm evening air, as stars danced in the sky above their heads. Maud was aware they were surrounded by their immediate families and close friends, and a retinue of tunic-clad soldiers from both sides of the border. But as she pledged herself to him, the scarf bound around their hands and wrists, everything melted away but her new husband.

When the vicar presented the newly wed Duke and Duchess of Normandy, a swell of cheers rolled down the sloping mound. Maud beamed as their loved ones joined them in the circle with hugs and congratulations, before the party moved down to a small valley inside the Norman border. They feasted into the night on braised oxen in saffron sauce, served on trenchers stale enough they could be held like a plate. The Normans and Flemish drank merrily, singing songs to the fireflies as they dined by campfire.

Of the row of lavish tents set up at the base of the hillside, none were more luxurious than the one for William and Maud. The grassy floor was covered in wool fleece, dressed in dozens of feather-stuffed pillows over bear-hide blankets. From the ceiling hung a shimmering gold ornament that picked up the fire from the torches, casting a glow across the canvas walls. Tomorrow they would ride into Rouen to greet the nobles and Norman subjects, but tonight they had each other.

Finishing their chalices of wine, they retired to their tent at the urging of their families. William's mother, Herleva, declared she wanted a grandchild, and Countess Adela jovially agreed. This led the rest of the party to gleefully lead them to their tent. Tying it closed with thick rope from the outside, they laughed and raised their chalices.

Maud fell into Duke William's secure arms. Taking her face in his hand, he smiled. "Hello, my wife," he said, pulling her lips to his for a kiss.

She could taste wine on his tongue, and she smiled up at him hungrily. "Hello, husband."

His hands traveled to her back, and he untied the rope belt from her burgundy robes while she removed the leather vest he'd worn all night. Gently tugging at his cotton shirt, she kissed his strong, scarred biceps, weathered and worn from countless battles—even more than was common for a man of twenty-three. When her robes hit the floor and she was exposed, William licked his bottom lip and picked her up with one arm. She wrapped her legs around him as he carried her to the bed, gently laying her onto the pillows and lowering himself over her.

Arching her back, pleasure swathed her skin from her swooning head to tingling toes. She wouldn't bleed as she had with Brictric—he took that from her. But now, as their bodies writhed in time in the muggy autumn air, she knew Brictric gave her a gift. She could enjoy her wedding night with a man who knew exactly what to do with his hands.

Their first night as husband and wife, she slept soundly in William's arms.

Following a breakfast of pancakes chased by what ale was left from the night before, the parties prepared to separate. Hugging each of her family members one last time, Maud's eyes welled with tears as she took William's hand. Unable to leave without one last embrace, she let go to hold tight to Countess Adela, who held her back just as hard. "I love you. I'm sorry. Thank you for everything," said Maud.

"No need," she insisted, standing back tearfully. Wiping her eyes with her fingertip, Adela smiled. "Stand up straighter, Maudie. You're a duchess now."

Chapter Fifteen

May 1051 – Château de Moulineaux outside Rouen, Normandy

With Adelaide's help, Maud rose to her gold-painted throne inside the imposing stone fortress on the edge of Rouen. Built by William's father, Duke Robert, before his fatal pilgrimage to Jerusalem, it was decorated inside with beautiful tapestries and hand-carved furnishings to showcase her husband's wealth. William, in fine black threads, entered from the door to the castle's great room, leaping forward to assist his wife.

Maud was nearly to the end of her first child-bearing, and the entire court doted on her. For months she'd been treated like an egg, confined mostly to the chateau grounds. A midwife followed everywhere she went. Today, excitement added to the anticipation of the impending birth as the court buzzed with preparations for a supreme arrival to their gates.

"If the Pope is late, he may get to see the birth of the Bastard of Normandy's heir." Laughing to himself, Mauger, the Archbishop of Rouen and Duke William's conniving uncle, bared his brown, old teeth. Maud shot him a scowl beyond her black veil.

"Your mother was a Duke of Normandy's mistress too, Uncle." William scoffed.

"And yet, the Church approved my parents' marriage." Shrouded in the protection of the Order, Mauger feared no retribution for his disrespect. Maud turned up her nose at him. He was so much worse than she remembered.

"We know how you and Uncle Guillaume feel about my father naming me his heir before either of you, but that is the choice he made," said William forcefully. "We *will* show a strong, united front to the Pope if we want the Church to legitimize our marriage."

"We don't feel unmarried. It's a shame the Church has so much power over whether we can say we are," Maud lamented bitterly, cradling her large stomach. "Our marriage was legal."

Mauger forced a smile. "The bishops in Normandy just want the matter settled, Your Grace. Our congregations' perception of a duke wed outside the Catholic Church can have repercussions." Waiting in a silent line, those bishops gathered in the courtyard beyond the castle walls, waiting to pay respects to their esteemed Holy Father.

Climbing down the platform, Adelaide looked ready to boil. "He's only coming here to make more deals in his favor. We should be focused on the baby's arrival."

"The midwife says it'll be another week or two." Maud patted her bump.

Since learning she was expecting six weeks after the wedding, she prayed daily for the safety of her unborn child. While the newlyweds toured Norman villages in the east of the duchy, Maud could eat nothing but apples, sick morning to night in the earliest months. Gratefully, Normandy cultivated some of the finest orchards on the continent, so in every town they stopped, William bought her all the apples he could find.

When her body started to expand and she could feel her child moving, her appetite returned. She grew to appreciate her changing shape for the life it grew inside her, though she was glad to be seated on her padded throne, with eiderdown-stuffed velvet to support the weight on her spine.

"Pope Leo is never late," said William nervously, and sure enough, the Pope and his entourage arrived as if summoned by his words. His Eminence stepped onto the stone platform raising the duke and duchesses' thrones above the marble floors beneath. William stood reverently to kiss his ring. "Holy Father, welcome."

Maud kissed his ring respectfully but didn't stand. "Forgive me, Holy Father. I'm unable stand and sit as easily as I could just a few months ago."

His Eminence grinned. "Children are known for their unreasonable demands. Especially those born to parents whose union is yet unsanctioned by the Church."

William cleared his throat. "We trust your journey from Rome was comfortable."

"It was lovely, Your Grace. So many grand churches in the smaller parishes these days. I had plenty to see on the way north."

Maud smiled proudly. "We visited some of them ourselves after the wedding."

"Ceremony."

Biting her lip as the Pope corrected her, she continued. "While we toured the countryside, I witnessed how the people cherish my husband as their duke. Their protector."

Leo laughed. "I'm sure they do, Duchess. Still, God insists on marriage by His own laws. But the Normans, and their duke and duchess, are deprived of His divine proclamation."

"We can't wed in the Church, or we'll be excommunicated." Maud fought to sound polite. "That was made clear to the Countess of Aumale, and we do listen well, Holy Father."

From across the marble tile, Adelaide eyed the Pope carefully. His Eminence caught her stare and threw back a smile. "The Countess of Aumale's marriage was annulled. I could cancel the excommunication, but the Count of Ponthieu wants the return of his mother's hereditary county. He says it was part of a dowry for a marriage that legally never occurred. I have to say, on paper, I agree with him."

"So, it's my sister's title or her good name?" William asked angrily. As her husband's ears turned red Maud grabbed his hand, looking up at him pleadingly.

Mauger turned to the Pope with a sneer. "There's the Bastard Duke of Normandy."

"You mentioned the beautiful new churches you visited on your way to Rouen." Maud spoke over the archbishop, shooting a wretched glare in his direction. "I imagine they must have been stunning. Every building in Normandy is among the most beautiful on the continent. But tell me, Holy Father, have these new churches been built by dukes and duchesses?"

"No, my lady."

"Then imagine how beautiful a gift to God *two* grand cathedrals would be."

"It would be magnificent, my lady."

William looked at Maud, wide-eyed. They hadn't discussed this, but Maud continued. "They'll be the grandest pillars of worship in all of Normandy. They would house monks, in the duke's church, and nuns in the duchess' church, who would teach both boys and girls. In Normandy, children of God will have equal opportunities for education."

"I'm sure it will be a struggle to fill the girl's school, but I absolutely love the idea," said Leo. Maud squeezed William's hand.

"Then it's settled," said William as he stepped forward, ready to dismiss the pompous Pope. "Two cathedrals, both centers of education, in exchange for recognition of our marriage."

His Eminence bristled. "Once the bishop's council rules on a decision it becomes law. I know common perception is I make these decisions myself, but I can't simply reverse laws." He leaned forward, a mischievous glint in his eye. "I'll be frank—some think excommunication is the best thing for Normandy, because of all the bastards. The question of your marriage will have to go back to the council, but two cathedrals should help reverse the original decision." He grinned, stepping back onto the platform. Again, William and Maud kissed his ring.

"I wish you a safe delivery, my lady. I'd like to see this matter resolved quickly for the sake of your child."

Though she suspected he was disingenuous, she smiled. Finally, they'd found a way to legitimize their union with the Church, and the child growing inside her too.

Maud forced herself to be polite as she bade the Pope farewell, grateful when Archbishop Mauger took his leave soon after. She waddled in her long, cinched robes to see them off in the courtyard, but when she could see their carriages turn a corner and out of sight, she unapologetically cursed both their names. Her child kicked her, and she flinched. William placed a protective hand on her stomach. "I'm all right," she said, catching her breath. "The baby's happy to see them go too."

William patted her stomach proudly, taking her for a walk through the courtyard as dusk brought out the fireflies. They were interrupted when his younger brother sped up on horseback. His face white as a sheet, he stumbled slightly as he leapt from his black steed. "Odo, you should be at Bec Abbey for your studies. I can't have my Bishop of Bayeux shirking his duty." The duke approached his younger brother with concern. "You look like you've seen a ghost."

"It's Mother. She was at the abbey in Grestain while father had his leprosy treatment and came back coughing. Robert rode to me when she coughed through the night and into yesterday. The monks fear she can't seem to get her breath and suggest you come. Now. It's dire, Brother."

Maud held her arm behind her husband as he stumbled back, processing the news of his mother's sudden illness. "We should go," said Maud, and William nodded.

The midwife, silent through the Pope's visit, said sharply, "The duchess will not go."

"This is an important family matter," Maud protested.

"My lady, the road isn't safe should your child come early."

Maud wanted to object further, but William shook his head. "Celeste is right. Besides, if my mother caught anything to make the baby sick, I don't want either of you anywhere near it."

With a frustrated sigh, she gave in. "Please let Lady Herleva know how grateful I am for everything she's done for us over the years." William leaned in to kiss her. She held him in her embrace for a moment, feeling his strong arms fall limp on her sides. "I love you," she said, and he stayed in her arms a few moments more, prolonging the inevitable, heartbreaking goodbye with his beloved mother.

He finally sped out on his horse with Adelaide riding sideways and Odo on his own steed at their side. A dozen soldiers followed because William never left home without bodyguards, and Maud ached with guilt as they disappeared over the horizon.

PART FOUR

Life and Death

Chapter Sixteen

August 1051 – Château de Moulineaux outside Rouen, Normandy

"You don't have to carry him so much," said the wetnurse. "That's why I'm here."

With her son against her chest, Maud forced a smile as she left the room with Addie. The wetnurse always returned her son when he was done feeding; these were Maud's orders. She was anxious for him to become attached and to know her, which he couldn't do in another woman's arms. "Tell me again why there are no other wetnurses available?"

Adelaide laughed. "There are plenty, but they won't be different from any other. They all judge us for not feeding our children from our own breast, as if we weren't working harder than anyone else in the room when our children took their first breaths."

"She seems too attached to Robert. I'll be glad when he's eventually walking and can be weaned." Although the duke and duchess knew and loved so many Roberts in their lives, their son, who would one day become Duke of Normandy, was named to honor his grandfather. William and Adelaide's father, Robert, loved Herleva, the undertaker's daughter, who had joined the old duke in eternal life on the same day their first grandson was born.

"Once they're walking, then they start to talk," said Addie. "Right now, Little Adelaide says no to everything. It doesn't matter what it is. 'Do you want to feed the ducks, Adelaide?' 'Do you want supper?' 'Are you happy?' 'Are you sad?' 'No, no, no!' I love my daughter, but this stage is insufferable."

As they walked the dark stone halls of the chateau, they stopped to pick up Addie's daughter from her nursery before making the long walk to Duke William's chamber, where he and his advisors often discussed matters of state. Normally, the women wouldn't join him here, but he called them to his side this time, and asked to see the children.

Entering with her son fighting sleep against her chest, Maud barely bent to kiss her handsome husband in his gilded, leather chair. "How are the two stars in my life?" He leaned forward to inhale the milky scent of his young son. "He's bigger every day I see him."

"We're blessed he eats well," Maud told him proudly. "He'll be strong like you."

In the duke's muscled arms, their son appeared even smaller. Her warrior husband placed his finger inside the grasp of his son's tiny hand and laughed as Robert tried to suckle from it fruitlessly. "He looks like a great eater to me. A Norseman's appetite will serve him well."

Adelaide put down her daughter, who toddled to a guard in full steel armor clutching a spear. "You asked us here, Brother?"

William nodded, glancing at Maud. "We received a dispatch from England. Lady Emma isn't well. Her physicians think she'll be fortunate to make it to spring."

Maud felt a short rush of blood to her head and sat down. "Do they know what it is?"

"A stomach issue. Not contagious."

She was quiet. Death was always so heartbreaking for her to think about. She hadn't lost her parents, like William and Adelaide, or grown up without her father like Judith. Until this moment she had been spared, but tears welled in her eyes as a wave of grief settled over her.

William shifted Robert in his arms as he stirred. "I was thinking you, me, and Addie should go. To England."

Maud looked at her husband as though he suggested they fly to the heavens. "The monks haven't cleared me to venture further than the castle garden, let alone Robert."

"The monks say you can go where you please, but you don't want to leave Robert's side," William chided her, staring down at his smiling, blue-eyed baby boy. She wavered. "Eventually you'll have to, my love. It won't be for long—a month at most, depending how long you wish to stay with Lady Emma. Our son is magnificent, but he won't be walking or talking before we return."

"You've recovered better from Robert's birth than any mother I've ever seen," Adelaide added excitedly. "You told Judith and Tostig you'd miss the wedding so soon after giving birth, but I know you, Maud.

You'll regret missing her wedding day."

"I'm still trying to process her going through with the wedding, and across the sea! My father would have thrown her a beautiful wedding closer to us in Bruges."

"Don't you like to skip those?" Maud blushed playfully as her husband teased. "I'm guessing Judith couldn't turn it down—the wedding will be hosted by the groom's sister, Queen Edith, and King Edward at the Palace of Westminster. We'll bring Monty with us and leave Fitz and Beau here in Normandy with their families. They'll keep Robert safe," William said.

"Say yes, Maud," Adelaide begged as her daughter waddled back to sit in her lap. "The wedding sounds like such a magnificent spectacle, and we've never been to sea."

"After the wedding festivities, which I understand will take place over several days, we'll visit Emma on the way home," said William. "The new Count of Boulogne and his brother, Lambert, have been invited. They'll share the cost to run the ship."

Maud hadn't seen Lambert since she fled for Normandy with Judith years earlier, convincing his family to join her father's war with the Holy Roman Empire. She'd never met his older brother, Eustace, but knew of him, though she didn't like what she knew. "And what of Count Eustace's child-wife, Ida of Lorraine?"

"Godeva was already dying when Eustace made his alliance with the Duke of Lorraine," William reminded her gently. "I know you feel protective because his first wife was Lady Emma's daughter, but Eustace was acting in the best interests of the sovereignty of Boulogne."

Maud frowned. "It's not just that he dropped his first wife so unceremoniously on her deathbed. Pope Leo banned their union at the same council in Reims that annulled Addie's marriage to Enguerrand and forced us to wed outside the Church. Leo already reversed his decision on Eustace and Ida's marriage, but we still wait for word from the bishop's council."

"Emperor Heinrich had Eustace and the Duke of Lorraine over a barrel, quite literally, submitting to his authority to save their heads," said William with a smug laugh. "Pope Leo's puppet strings haven't been pulled in our favor because your father valiantly refuses to fold."

She sighed, her resistance fading. "Judith knows I'm not Tostig's biggest fan, but I owe her better than failing to support her on her wedding day, even if I watch with a guilty conscience." Looking at their sleepy son in her husband's arms, she smiled, caressing his soft cheek with her finger. "A month away from you will feel like an eternity," she said as he snoozed. "But it'll be over soon enough."

While Adelaide excitedly prepared for the trip, Maud allowed her ladies-in-waiting to arrange her dresses for their journey, squeezing in as much time as possible with her son. A week later, they kissed their babies goodbye, accompanied by a small retinue of attendants and soldiers as they boarded at Le Havre. The smell of salted fish hung in the air.

"We should make landfall in a few days," said William, escorting his wife and sister onto the wooden deck of the single-mast boat that would carry them to England. Half a dozen men pulled thick ropes to hoist the red-and-white striped sail, while others wound rope around a wooden crank to bring up the anchor. Steering the ship from the harbor with oak posts half as tall as the mast, they guided the boat into the bay until the posts no longer reached the seabed.

A soft breeze caught the sails to drive them northward, each man pushing the great oars forward in lockstep, back and forth. The ship's mahogany planks glided across the water as the northern beaches of Normandy disappeared in their wake.

After a night at sea, Maud woke after her husband. He always rose before she did, like a rooster with the dawn. She dressed, stepping from the bunks below deck to join Adelaide, staring out at the endless water reflecting the bright sky. Soft waves lapped against the sides of the boat as it carved through the narrow sea.

Addie's voice cut through the wind ripping through their long veils. "It's amazing that a bunch of wood can hold so much weight and move so quickly."

Maud nodded with a yearning glance toward the horizon. "The waters have been calm, and the sea air is so invigorating. I almost miss the days when I didn't have to wear a veil. I'd like to feel the wind in my hair this far out to sea."

Walking alongside the men, William approached his wife and sister on the deck and smiled. “It’s an unfair advantage for the mighty sea, if I’m to share your hair with the waves.”

“But my brother has never lost a battle,” Adelaide reminded him with a grin.

“Only God can beat the sea, Countess,” said Count Eustace, his tone more pedantic than philosophical. “Everyone else gets blessed with good weather.”

Flecks of gray shone in his beard as he smiled in the sunlight. Maud couldn’t raise a grin, stifling the urge to remind Eustace his sense of reverence might have extended to his first wife, rather than discarding her when she was dying for a new political alliance. “It’s a shame your wife couldn’t join us. How old is Ida now? Eleven?”

Eustace nodded, oblivious to her dismissive tone. “She’s in Boulogne-Sur-Mer with her guardians, awaiting the birth of our first child. I’m quite sure it will be a boy.”

Maud looked to the sea to avoid speaking her mind to Count Eustace, thinking back to the night her adult-sized womb felt ripped apart when her son was born. William took her delicate hand in his strong, rough fingers. “You’re quiet today, love.”

“I was thinking of Robert.”

He smiled as gulls cawed on the horizon to the north. The shore wasn’t far away now. “I’ve told you, he won’t be walking and talking by the time we get back.”

Letting go of his hands, Maud paced the deck, holding her blue robes to keep water on the ship’s wood from soiling the linen. “I was thinking back to when Lady Emma left for England, and how much I hoped I would join her there one day. We’re close to reaching shore in Emma’s England, the mythical garden of my childhood.”

“When I was a little girl and King Edward was exiled in Normandy, he told me London had a smell. Like a pig who ate a garlic plant then rolled in its own shit. And ale on Sundays.”

Maud looked at Adelaide’s earnest, smiling face, laughing to imagine the specificity of the pungent odor. Addie would never tire of court gossip—Maud was sure of this. Lambert, now grown enough to sport a bushy beard, smiled behind his whiskers. He was over a decade younger than Eustace, but before the death of their father, he’d been given his own county in Lens. Though he carried himself quietly, as he did years earlier when he hosted Maud and Judith in

Boulogne-Sur-Mer, the spark between him and Addie was plain to see. Stolen glances across the ship seemed only the beginning.

"I was also thinking of the wedding, and I was thinking about Robert because I feel guilty," Maud said. "I feel guilty because I want to be here. I want to go to the wedding, and I want to be with Lady Emma before it's too late. I want all of it more than I want to be in Normandy right now."

William pulled her close. "He will be fine, love. Odo, Fitz, and Beau are watching over the duchy while we're gone. My younger sisters will watch over his nursemaids, and we have no reason to fear for Robert's safety while we're away."

"I don't fear for his safety half as much as I fear he won't recognize me when we return."

"Of course he'll recognize you, Maud," Addie cut in. "Your son is from you and will always know you as his mother."

Watching the horizon, Maud fell into the comforting embrace of her husband and sister-in-law like a warm blanket. A soft spray of salted sea brushed their cheeks and her heart brimmed with anticipation. Beyond the vast expanse of water was the shore of the land she'd longed to visit above all others, and excited butterflies rose in her stomach as the wooden boat drove them forward.

Chapter Seventeen

September 1051 – Borne, England (modern-day Eastbourne)

"Land ho!" shouted one of Duke William's men, and Maud looked eagerly across the bow of the ship. Chalky white cliffs fell into the sea from a piece of land south of the settlement of Borne, growing taller the closer the boat sailed to shore. Lifting their wooden posts, the retinue of men steered them toward a landing stage jutting out from the sand, fastening the boat with knotted ropes. Here, they'd unload for their planned journey north to London.

Maud could smell fish curing in the air. The few residents milling about the quiet village took notice of the regal visitors when the captain blew his horn, signaling they weren't raiders from across the sea. Accustomed to invasion, the English made note of them warily until the finely dressed ladies stepped onto the floating dock—the surest sign of their party's peaceful intentions.

The sun hid behind a pocket of clouds as the anchor dropped. Taking Maud's hand to escort her down the shallow gangplank, William flashed his crooked smile. "Welcome to England, love."

Taking it in, she breathed deeply. The rotting scent of fish guts reminded her of Zeebrugge, but this part of England outshone her homeland with its verdant wonder. "It's so green!" she exclaimed, smiling toward the sloping hills beyond huts of mud and straw dotting the village. The church's wooden steeple, standing high above every other fortification in Borne, paled in comparison to the vast acres of green that stretched behind it.

"I've heard it rains here more than anywhere else on the continent," Addie said matter-of-factly. "And the peasants live in mud houses even in the cities! I can't imagine it."

Lambert pointed inland from the pier as they walked the wooden pathway carved into the beach. "The straw roof keeps the water off the walls, Countess. And it looks like they've built a trench through the lowest part of town, to drain water away from their foundations."

Eustace laughed. "My brother, the engineer who never was."

"With knowledge like his, he'll oversee projects in Lens to rival any buildings in Boulogne. A great legacy in two counties for your noble family." Grinning, Maud turned on her heels without waiting to read Eustace's reaction. Would he know she was insulting him? She didn't care. Not today, with the soil of England at her feet. Letting go of William's hand, she stepped onto the shingled beach, dotted with rocks flattened by the tides.

The hem of her blue linen robes danced atop the powdery crystals. William joined her away from their entourage, and she leaned into him as she listened to the whistling breeze.

"And what of Emma's England so far?" he asked her.

She smiled. "Dried fish isn't my favorite smell, but it's beautiful."

"One day, this will be ours." The duke pulled her in for a warm embrace. "I plan to bring up the issue of English succession with the king while we're here."

Her heart skipped a beat. "In front of the Godwins?"

"If King Edward agrees to make me his heir, they'll need to be present. They need to hear Edward's intent from his own lips, or they'll never support us when the time comes."

The sound of thunder rose from the distance, but the clouds were too small for a rainstorm. The noise grew slowly louder the closer and faster it came, and William instinctively put his arm around the small of his wife's back. The people of Borne hurried into their mud huts as a wall of dust rose over the hill behind the church. Dozens of horses crested the ridge. Monty drew his sword, calling back his duke and duchess with urgency in his voice.

Maud and William hurried across the stony beach, rejoining their party as the charging beasts raced in their direction. With the horses closing in, a white dragon became visible on red flags carried by the bannermen at the front of the stampede.

"They must be the king's men," said William. "That's the flag of the House of Wessex."

Maud froze in terror as they drove closer—a mess of men and beasts racing through a cloud of spoiled earth. Slowly, she recognized the face of the man leading the charge. With no helmet, his dark beard couldn't disguise the rabid look in his eyes, nor the zest for danger her father warned her against years earlier.

"It's Sweyn Godwinson," she said, frowning as the horde came to a stop at the end of the beach. Earl Godwin's eldest son laughed with manic timbre as fear turned to annoyance on their faces. Instinctively, William had unsheathed his sword, though he'd have been no match for this horde. Sliding it back into his slim sheath with a sharp clink, he glared uneasily.

"My lords, welcome to England. We come in peace," Sweyn said, chuckling to himself for a successful prank. Harold Godwinson, whose beard was much lighter than Sweyn's, was on horseback at his side, wearing a look of embarrassment for his elder brother.

"The king sent us to escort you safely to London," Harold said.

Sweyn grinned. "And no one told Lady Judith you've come to attend the wedding. Now we won't need to get the lovebirds a wedding gift."

Maud resisted the urge to roll her eyes in plain view of him. Sweyn made her loathe Judith's chosen future even more than she thought possible, but she silently reminded herself this trip was far more important than her annoyance with his family. As William said, they needed the support of the Godwins, just as Lady Emma and her sons relied on their support when they returned to England a decade earlier.

"We've brought a carriage for the ladies. Wouldn't want them falling from their horses on the ride north."

"A great relief indeed," replied Maud with a grin, assuming Sweyn thought his condescending tone was simply hospitable. As she walked toward the carriage with Adelaide and her ladies-in-waiting, her butterfly pin gleamed in the sun. Her short stature meant the English soldiers towered over her on their stealth-backed steeds, but some of them might be under her husband's command one day, so she walked tall and stoic to mask her insecurity.

Her mother's words echoed in her mind: *"Stand up straighter, Maudie."*

The ride to London was split over two days, with an overnight camp in the hills. Maud and William hadn't slept in a tent since their wedding night, but once their stewards set up their temporary domain, they christened it just as they had their first time.

She cherished the warmth of his breath against her neck while he slept. Whether at war, pillaging towns of those who stood against him, or collecting tributes from loyal subjects, William was often away from home. Some campaigns were short, others long, but there would always be campaigns for a duke. She rested better when he was near.

Snuggling against him, she drifted peacefully to sleep.

They reached the Thames by late afternoon. At Southwark Cathedral, imposing over the southern banks, they stopped before the wooden bridge into the city. The sun cast long shadows against the water, glistening in the angled light. Spotting a band of soldiers to the east, Maud beamed. This time, she knew the flags when they were small drops of yellow and blue under a blood-orange sky.

As the retinue from Flanders approached, her father waved when he spotted her by the riverbank. Men on horseback, including her father and brother, Robby, escorted the family's most elaborate carriage—the same one of black and gold that carried Maud to her wedding near Eu. When they emerged from the wooden box, Maud raced to greet them warmly.

Life in Normandy had been so busy since her arrival the previous year, Maud didn't realize how much she missed her family until she looked upon their faces again. Tears stained her cheeks as she fell into the waiting arms of her father, enveloping him in a hug that caused him to step back against his horse. "Maudie, my dear, it's wonderful to see you."

They dressed even finer than they had on either Bodhi or Maud's wedding day. Lady Eleanor, as the mother of the bride, wore gold-embroidered robes of white satin and a veil to match. Golden ropes cinched her waist, highlighting her thin frame.

"We were so glad to hear you'd changed your mind and would come to the wedding," said Eleanor. "Though your mother and I were sad to hear you wouldn't be bringing the baby."

"Still a bit young for a sea crossing," William said, bowing respectfully to his in-laws.

"My grandson is part Norseman." Count Baudouin chuckled. "It won't be long until he's got his sea legs, I assume."

"Let's get him walking on dry land first."

"We may need to come and visit just so I can hold a babe in my arms again." Adela gave her daughter a wistful sigh. "At this rate, Bodhi and Richilde may never give us an heir."

Maud had a letter from Richilde detailing why, but she knew it wouldn't help to explain Bodhi was often too drunk to perform his role in making heirs. *Your brother and I have one thing in common,* Richilde said in her letter, *and that's how much we dislike each other. He drinks to forget, and I try never to look at him.*

"I'm sure a child will come," Maud said comfortingly. "Though I doubt either is enjoying themselves, watching over Flanders while you're all here for the wedding. Besides, if Flanders is desperate, they'll always have Robby."

He frowned in mock protest. "They should be so fortunate," he said. Maud smiled, her heart full.

At sunset, they prepared to ride into London across the long bridge into the city. Some of Sweyn's men lit torches to accompany their grand arrival under growing moonlight, but the march was so slow, so regal, none of the men appeared threatening. Crowds stopped to watch as they passed. They seemed to know the procession was part of a royal wedding celebration, tossing flowers at the cortège. Others poured drunkenly out of taverns, copper mugs aloft in their waving arms as they cheered.

A small pink bloom with a short stem landed on Addie's lap inside their carriage. Laughing, she picked it up and sniffed. "I'd say it smells faintly of my family's old embalming workshop here in London, but this is magical. Judith must feel like a princess with all this excitement."

The procession pulled through a wide gate lined with English soldiers. As they entered the royal enclosure beyond the Roman walls at the Palace of Westminster, copper bulbs atop five stone towers glowed by torchlight in the dusk. Approaching the home of England's King Edward, they rode through an iron gate under the rampart wall, coming to a stop in the courtyard.

Gold-painted tapestries hung on the walls, lit up by a thousand torches. Exiting the carriage, Maud turned back to help Addie, whose skin burned orange in the firelight, but she bowled over as Judith's long, golden hair sailed across her face.

"You're here!" she cried as they enveloped one another in a hug.

"What about Robert?"

Maud righted herself, laughing. "Addie and William convinced me I couldn't miss this."

Greeting her family, Judith beamed excitedly next to Tostig, as healthy and polished as Maud had ever seen him. Today, he smelled of rich wine instead of beer, and the scar on his left cheek seemed to dignify his presence in the glow of the occasion like a badge of honor. "Come," said Judith. "There are so many people I want you to meet."

Maud allowed Judith to drag her toward their hosts, William striding behind to keep up. At the top of the yard, closest to the central keep, King Edward and Queen Edith sat in gold-dusted chairs on a wooden stage. Since Maud last saw him in Zeebrugge when she was a little girl, a few gray hairs now refined the king's dark locks. They bowed reverently as he stood.

"Dear cousin, how long has it been?"

"Long enough I didn't need to shave when you last left Normandy." Looking around the gorgeously decorated courtyard William laughed, nodding at the golden crown perched atop King Edward's head. "The years have treated you well since then."

"What I have, this week I share with all of you." He gestured to his wife, who smiled warmly. "Queen Edith's family has planned quite the celebration for her younger brother's wedding, and we pray you all enjoy the festivities."

In smaller chairs on a second stage sat Earl Godwin and his Danish wife, Gytha, Tostig's mother and father. The earl was the largest man Maud had ever seen—even larger than her husband. But Gytha, whose nephew was a king in Denmark, was petite, with delicate lips that smiled warmly, like her daughter, Queen Edith.

Crowds cheered to welcome the arrival of a troupe of jugglers, rolling around on wooden wheels fixed with seats. One tossed a ring into the air, catching it with his teeth as partygoers in the courtyard urged him on. Maud watched for a moment, but soon Judith pulled her away.

"Maud, meet Princes Malcolm and Donald of Alba," she said as two young redheads in green tunics smiled at her side. They met Maud's height at eye level, as they were not yet men, but they were surrounded by a crowd taking note of their status. "They've been in England since they were small children, when King Macbeth killed their father and usurped Malcolm's throne. King Edward and Earl Godwin say they're going to help them take it back someday."

Maud smiled as each kissed her hand politely. "It's a pleasure to meet you both."

"Getting to know Lady Judith has been a pleasure since her arrival at Edward's court, and she speaks of you often," said Malcolm, the older of the two.

"How is your new son, by the way?" wondered Donald.

She grinned. "He's perfect. Every mother says it, but in Robert's case, it's true."

Behind them, through a crowd of faces unfamiliar, Maud spotted one she hoped she'd never see again. He stood, laughing jovially with a pretty, long-faced woman. It had to be Goda. Her heart sank like a stone into her stomach, and she excused herself with an apologetic smile.

Following her gaze, Judith let the young princes turn to speak with another guest as Maud dragged her from the courtyard. "I'm sorry. I can't give Tostig a reason to uninvite him without giving you away. Brictric is too close to the court."

Maud took a deep breath, steeling her nerves. "Deep down, I'm sure I knew he'd be here. I wouldn't let myself think about it."

Judith lowered her voice and smiled. "His wife is such a bore. Apparently, they have no children because she's barren."

Maud raised an eyebrow. "He left me no child either. Maybe it's not Goda's fault."

As they laughed to themselves, William appeared in the dark hallway. "There you are. What are you two snickering about?"

They froze. "I saw Brictric," Maud said slowly.

William's nostrils flared, but he composed himself. "And it made you happy?"

"No, it upset me." She shook her head. "Judith was making me feel better. After all, I found a much better husband than poor Goda."

William grew quiet, his brown eyes darkening with rage as Judith excused herself to the courtyard with an anxious smile. "It frustrates me that he still upsets you this way. Have I not given you everything I could and more, just as I promised?" Careful not to raise his voice, his angered tone sounded eerie. "Will I not give you the world at the first opportunity?"

"You have, William. I'm sorry, but I haven't forgiven him for what happened, and I can't look upon him with indifference," she said. "It doesn't mean you're not the man I love. My devotion is to you. Only you."

He fell against her as she spoke, checking to ensure they were alone in the hallway. Leaning in, he stole a kiss, letting it linger as his hands explored her skin.

"I love you," she said. "Nothing is truer than my love for you."

Chapter Eighteen

September 1051 – the Palace of Westminster in London, England

Exchanging vows in the chapel of Westminster Palace, the Archbishop of Canterbury bound Tostig and Judith's hands with a blue scarf, just as Lady Emma and Maud had done. A raucous feast carried well into the night, and the next morning Maud awoke with a headache. Accepting the help of her ladies-in-waiting to dress, she splashed her face with water before fastening her veil.

Taking William by the arm, they walked downstairs to find a long table in the dining room set for another drunken breakfast. Piled high with hearty breads and meat, cooked grouse and boar sent heady smells to Maud's nostrils before she dug in.

Looking down the table, she couldn't see Brictric or his wife. Having spent much of the week skillfully avoiding them both, and after several days trying to appear to William as though they didn't bother her, she was exhausted.

"I think this one is the grouse I killed myself." William laughed, taking a swig of ale as though last night's celebrations barely affected him. Maud sipped gently from her own cup.

"What makes you so sure? All the men went out hunting, and I saw how many the cooks brought in the night before the wedding."

William grinned. "Mine was the biggest."

"He's right," Tostig said from across the table while Judith gazed at her beloved with a foppish smile. "Everyone tried to shoot one as big, but it's not just on the battlefield where the Duke of Normandy always wins."

Maud looked proudly at her smiling husband, slicing herself a piece of his grouse. Fatty juices filled her throat, relieving her aching head, and she helped herself to seconds.

"Your lady eats well." Tostig's scar over his cheek stretched with his grin.

William winked at her, turning back to Tostig to raise his mug. "My lady does everything well, but I'm told all the ladies of Flanders have this in common."

During breakfast, while servants packed their masters' accommodations at the palace, a plan to carry celebrations to Dover where Maud and Judith's relatives would sail home began to circulate. Most of the Godwins were going, except for Harold and another brother, Leof, who had business in the Welsh Marches. Even King Edward and Queen Edith joined, but Maud wouldn't think of delaying her visit to Lady Emma, nor her return to her infant son.

"May I join them?" Adelaide spent much of the wedding week at Count Lambert's side, and this morning was no different.

"I'll return her to Winchester myself, once most of the boats have sailed for the continent," Lambert promised. Maud knew William didn't want to agree, as much as she could see in Addie's eyes that his approval was the only response she expected. She pulled her husband aside quietly.

"Lambert is nothing like Enguerrand. I trust his character, and your sister will be safe with him," she said assuredly.

He nodded gruffly, a hint of reluctance still etched on his face as he grudgingly allowed her to go. When Addie hugged him, his rough exterior slowly evaporated.

Maud and William thanked their hosts before bidding a warm goodbye to her family. "You must visit soon and meet young Robert," she said.

"Perhaps soon there could be more," her mother prodded hopefully.

Maud smiled. "God willing."

She saved her tears for Judith because this was her celebration, but also because, despite how she glowed with happiness, Maud worried for her. The Godwins wore warm smiles, but Maud couldn't trust them. Earl Godwin betrayed Lady Emma's family when Alfred was murdered; he could do it again and Judith, Lady Emma's great-niece, might find herself in his crosshairs.

"Congratulations, Judith." Her voice wavered as she pulled her in for a hug. "You were the most stunning bride anyone will ever see. I didn't think anything could outshine the décor or the entertainment, but of course you did. You always have." Tears wet Judith's cheeks and Maud laughed, wiping her own face with her sleeve. "We're not sisters by blood, but I've known you better than anyone else for all my life. No one deserves the happiness you wear on your face more than you do."

"It's not just my face," said Judith assuredly. "Everything about this week was so perfect, I can feel happiness in my bones. I feel like I'm vibrating."

Maud smiled. "I hope you feel this way forever."

That night, as Maud and William camped on the road to Winchester, they lay together in the candlelight of their tent. Enveloping her, the hairs on his muscled arms tickled her soft skin.

"On the hunting trip, King Edward agreed to make me his heir." She was so lost in his touch it took a moment to register what he said.

When she did, she shot up in bed. "That was days ago!"

"I had to be careful inside the king's palace. I had no idea who had eyes anywhere, or what their motivations would be if they overheard."

She beamed as William sat up next to her. "How did it happen?"

"We were with Monty and Harold Godwinson in the woods, and you came up. Harold mentioned you were descended from the great King Alfred of Wessex, and Edward joked, 'Then your son is an Englishman!' I couldn't resist. I knew that was my moment. I said he would be proud to be an Englishman someday, if the king is looking for an heir."

Impressed by her husband's campaign, she laughed. "What did Harold Godwinson say?"

"He said, 'An heir who's only three months old won't do the English people any good.' So I said, 'His mother and I are more than capable of running a state.'"

"And King Edward agreed?"

"He said, 'You would rule England well.' He knows the English kings of Wessex have been murdering their brothers for so long they've all but killed themselves off, but Harold mentioned rumors of a son of Edmund Ironside in the east."

"A son of King Edward's half-brother would have a strong claim."

"The king thinks if Edmund's son was alive, he'd have come for the throne already. He'd be almost forty now." With a shrug, he pulled her body close, breathing in her scent. "I promised you England, love, and one day we'll have it. The ground on which we sleep will be ours."

She sank into his chest as the heat from the candles warmed their bare skin. Looking into his chestnut eyes, she purred, "King William of the English. I like it."

He gazed back dreamily. "And his Queen Maud."

Two days into their journey to Winchester, Maud called for a rest. Riding her own horse, she hated every second of it. Despite their slow pace to the cathedral town Emma called home, she was plagued by the discomfort of the horse's gait and longed to stretch her legs.

Under mild skies a shade of bluish gray, their horses stopped to drink from a roadside stream. Sliding down the horse's back, Maud bent down to wash her face in the gently trickling brook, letting cool waters wash the stench of gelding from her hands.

Standing again, she spotted a small band of horses on the horizon, brandishing the Anglo-Saxon flag. They came much less threatening than Sweyn and his men, but Maud felt the same rush of dread when she realized the sandy-haired blond leading the charge was Brictric.

"What now?" William's voice clipped as he registered Brictric's chiseled jawline and hair waving in the wind.

He stood with Monty, but Maud stayed back. She stared into the eye of the horse drinking closest to her spot by the stream, attempting to mirror its calm demeanor as she listened.

"King Edward says you must come, Your Grace. There's been a riot in Dover and your sister is barricaded in the fortress with the counts from Boulogne."

"Is this another prank? Where's Sweyn Godwinson?"

"King Edward was drinking with Count Eustace, and he attempted to make him castellan of the Dover fort, but Earl Godwin was opposed and rallied the locals to riots. The king ordered Godwin to make them stand down, but he just put down riots in Worcester and said he wasn't about to do it again over some foreigners. He told the locals to fight harder. Count Eustace's allies were barricaded inside the castle tower, and two dozen of his men were killed."

Maud stood, unable to feign disinterest in what Brictric came to say. "And my parents?"

"The boat for Flanders had already sailed, Lady Matilda."

She held in a gasping breath. Her heart used to skip when he said her name, but this time she hated the sound of it, dripping like poison from his lips.

"Duchess." William glared disdainfully as he corrected him. "And Lady Judith?"

"She's with the Godwins outside the walls, but she's been unsuccessful convincing her husband's family to let the nobles go," said Brictric. "The king and the earl are in a standoff, and no one thinks this latest disagreement will end in peace. King Edward believes if you come to retrieve your sister, you might help him gain the upper hand against the earl."

Even before she read his frantic stride, Maud knew William would ride to Dover to save his sister, and he'd ride at least twice as fast as Sweyn stampeded down the hill at Borne.

"Monty, carry on to Winchester with Maud." His loyal steward tried to object, but William ended the debate with a charming smile. "I'll send word if anything goes wrong, but protecting our duchess is the most important job I'll ever ask of you. Should anything happen to me, she'll be regent for our son."

"What of your safety, my lord?"

"I'll bring half a dozen soldiers with me, and I trust Ser Brictric and his men know the quickest, safest route to Dover from here."

He glanced at Brictric, as if challenging him to lead him into a trap, but protecting his sister was too important. Despite the danger, he wouldn't waste another minute.

After pulling his wife close for a long, lingering kiss goodbye in clear view of her first love, he remounted, speeding over the crest of the hill with his men.

Chapter Nineteen

September 1051 – Royal Lodge at Kings Worthy near Winchester, England

At midday, Maud arrived with Monty in Winchester, which boasted two glorious monastic cathedrals built in polished limestone: Old Minster, where Lady Emma walked across burning ploughshares for King Aethelred, and New Minster, where she joined in marriage to King Cnut. Maud marveled as monks inside each building competed with the other, sending a melodic, chaotic chant over log houses spread out in every direction. The expansive lodge at Kings Worthy, built by Wessex kings two centuries earlier, sat two miles north of the cathedral town, and Maud's robes felt hot as her horse marched along the pebbled road. She smiled with relief as the royal residence, a timber hall with glass windows, pulled into view.

Lady Emma stepped outside gingerly, dressed down in plain gray robes and leaning on her knotted wood cane. Maud barely gave her horse time to stop before she slid off its back, practically running to Emma's waiting arms. "I've missed you so much," she cried, emotion welling in her throat. The old woman smiled weakly. Emma felt different than when Maud would hug her as a girl. These days, she was thin as a flagpole. Even under yards of fabric, Maud's fingers could fit in the ridges between each rib. "You didn't have to come out to greet me. You need your rest."

"I didn't expect to see you come in on a horse," said the old woman with a laugh. Her voice was softer now, and her cane wobbled in her grasp. "I had to see for myself, and who knows how many sunny days I have left."

"Horses and I tolerate each other a little better these days," Maud explained. "Not much, but there were so many wedding guests, the king was out of carriages."

Emma smiled at Monty as he dismounted his own horse, and Maud helped Emma adjust her weight against her cane. "Where are William and Adelaide?"

"Long story. Let's sit and rest, and I'll tell you all about it."

Servants led them inside, where they sat at an oaken table in a plaster-walled room. "What trouble has my grand-nephew gotten in now?"

"Not William. Adelaide. She's fallen for Count Lambert of Lens and went with the royal party to Dover the same morning William and I left to come here. We were almost to Winchester and stopped on the road for a rest when Ser Brictric rode up in a panic. King Edward and Earl Godwin are in a standoff over Edward's desire to appoint Count Eustace of Boulogne as his castellan at Dover."

Emma shook her head. "I don't know what my son sees in Eustace of Boulogne, but Earl Godwin can't stand interference from anyone loyal to the king before him. He's been trying to have the Archbishop of Canterbury returned to Normandy ever since my son appointed him."

"I think the earl finally snapped. Brictric said he encouraged the locals to riot and refused the king's orders to make them stand down. My family sailed for home already, but Adelaide was barricaded inside with the other nobles. William left to rescue her because Brictric said he doesn't think this standoff will end in peace."

"What irony!" The old woman wore a gleeful smile, willing herself to endure the pains in her stomach. "I'm glad I lived to see the earl finally overplay his hand, but I would have drawn the line at my useless former son-in-law too. Earl Godwin can't hold England without us. We have too many allies in the south who will never bow to the Godwins, and the north doesn't even want to be English."

"I wish I could laugh about it." Maud picked at a loose thread on her dress. "I worry for all of them, but most of all Judith. Once the standoff ends Addie will likely be safe with her brother, but Judith will be stuck with the Godwins."

Emma frowned. "You should worry for her. I'm disappointed your father let the marriage go through."

"Did you tell him so?"

"Of course not." She shook her head regretfully. "Edward's kept me isolated out here because he said it was impossible to have a working relationship with the Godwins while I was at court. Interfering in the wedding of Earl Godwin's drunkard son would just isolate me further."

"When was the last time King Edward came to visit you?"

"Two years ago, at least." A sadness buried behind her blue eyes rushed forward. "I don't think he's ever forgiven me for backing Harthacnut once I knew he was the one Earl Godwin supported. Edward was older, but he's never had his brother's strength. Once Harthacnut died and the throne was his, Edward's been having his revenge with me a little at a time."

An attendant entered the room with a plate of bread, which he placed on the table in front of the women. Lady Emma's face turned green at the sight of it.

"Do you remember when I told you that a queen paid for power with sacrifice?" Maud nodded, looking piteously upon the frail old woman. Emma's sullen eyes looked out a long window, but colored glass made it impossible to see outside. "Outliving four of five children and becoming a stranger to the last has been harder to bear than I imagined."

While they waited more than a week for word from Dover, Maud delighted in entertaining her with stories, or losing to her repeatedly at various dice games. Each time Monty returned from a day hunting in the fields, Maud and her ladies-in-waiting would eat guiltily while Emma pushed food around on her trencher, tasting morsels but always leaving the rest behind. Even when her stomach had no food, Emma spent her days nauseated and retching up blood.

Some days, Lady Emma stayed in her room, and Maud would visit her bedside to read to her. She read sermons and the epic poetry of the Greeks, because Emma said the words painted beautiful scenery. Her beloved desk took pride of place under the window.

"Why do you love a desk so much if you don't read or write?"

Emma grinned wistfully. "It was a gift from a friend a long time ago. One of the first friends I made when I got to England. They're long gone now, but the desk reminds me of a time of peace. Hope for an unwritten future."

Running her hands along the smooth wooden finish, Maud smiled. Outside the window, a monarch butterfly caught her attention, flapping its orange-and-black wings on the wind.

One morning, the air was warm and the sky was blue, so Maud and Emma sat outside on a wooden bench. "I don't think I'm ready for you to die, Lady Emma."

The old woman laughed. "I'm ready. When you get to be my age, you realize death is just a part of living, and most days your old body hurts so much you think death would be a comfortable alternative."

"Are you afraid?"

Emma stared out toward the sea and smiled. "I used to be."

They watched the sky on the horizon, and the old woman wrapped her crooked fingers around Maud's hand. "I feel for you, Lady Emma. You've seen so much loss in your life, and I've seen so little. You even lost your father as a child like William and Judith."

"You're young. You shouldn't know loss like I do. My father was an old man when I was born, like your grandfather when Eleanor had Judith. I didn't know I was meant to be sad my father was gone. I hardly remember him being there."

Maud understood what she meant. "I don't remember my grandfather well. I do remember he liked to bounce me on one knee, and Judith on the other, and he would laugh when we laughed. Then he died, and I was four. I remember the funeral. We walked through the streets of Bruges, from the castle to the cathedral inside the city walls. Lady Eleanor and my mother were sobbing. People in the streets were in tears. Even Papa cried, but not loudly. At some point, he picked me up and carried me the rest of the way, but I remember wondering why I wasn't sad like everyone else. And you're right, I barely knew him. But I know *you*, Lady Emma."

She accepted Maud's head against her shoulder. "When my old, broken body dies, I'll still live on through you, my dear."

Tears dripped down her cheeks, but Maud smiled at the thought. "And through your book."

"It may not have done enough to win me favor over Earl Godwin, or convince the English of his true character, but it did inspire you to follow your dreams."

"My father said you secured England for Edward after Harthacnut's death because your *Encomium* kept allies from trusting Earl Godwin."

Emma smiled, exhaustion worn on her face. "And yet, my last son has no children, so in the end, the book hasn't been the legacy I'd hoped for."

Maud raised her head from Lady Emma's bony shoulder. "King Edward and Queen Edith may have no son, but he does have an heir." Lady Emma looked at her quizzically, and Maud continued with excited eyes. "My husband. He may not be your son, but he is your Norman kin."

"When was this agreed?" Surprise crossed her cheeks as a breeze brushed their veils.

"The men went hunting before the wedding. William was with the king, Roger Montgomery, and Harold Godwinson when he raised the possibility. He knows his Norman heritage won't interest the Anglo-Saxons, but I'm a great-granddaughter of King Alfred, and we have a son already."

Lady Emma seemed unconvinced. "If Harold was there for this conversation, I wouldn't doubt that's why Earl Godwin chose Dover as his moment to rebel. He's so close to the throne now. His daughter is the queen, but you have an heir."

"You think he'll build resistance against us?"

The old woman nodded plainly. "I know he will."

Maud missed the soft cries of her son, but it was another week before William finally returned to Winchester with Adelaide. He rode alongside a horse-drawn cart carrying two blond-haired boys, their hands tied together with ropes. Eustace and Lambert were nowhere to be found, and William scowled at the mention of their names.

"They can rot in Dover. The king and Earl Godwin refuse to stand down. Even after the king's men kidnapped Wulf and Hakon, Earl Godwin refused to let the nobles out of the fort."

"And I told you, I wouldn't have escaped the walls without Count Lambert's help! He wants to marry me, William, and I want to accept."

"Addie, enough! You could have been killed. I have no interest in setting up a marriage alliance with anyone loyal to Eustace of

Boulogne." William stalked away from his sister as he forced the boys to stand with a menacing glare. "Lady Emma, will your staff prepare them a meal?"

She nodded to her steward, who shuffled inside to find the cooks. Maud helped the old woman find her balance. "Who are Wulf and Hakon?"

Frowning, Emma shot a rueful glance at the boys. "Wulf is Earl Godwin's youngest son, and Hakon is Sweyn Godwinson's only acknowledged child."

"The king asked me to take them to Normandy as hostages." Her broad-shouldered husband sneered toward the lads. "They're still standing at the gates of Dover hoping the other blinks first. Edward said to take them back to Normandy; he'll send word when they can return."

"Should we get involved in their dispute like this?" A regretful look filled Maud's eyes.

"Edward said if I want the throne of England, I have to involve myself in her affairs."

"We may be making enemies of the Godwins unnecessarily."

"If you want England's throne, the Godwins *are* your enemies," said Emma assuredly. "The only ascendancy left for the earl is the Crown. If he can't take it himself, he'll find someone he can control to take it instead."

William turned to his great-aunt with an inquisitive glance. "Lady Emma, Edmund Ironside was your stepson. What do you know of rumors a son of his lives in the east?"

"I know when Ironside died and Cnut took control of England, he had the Aetheling sent to King Olof's court in Sweden with orders he was to be murdered." She sighed at the vicious memory. "Olof ignored every request to produce a body. To the end of his life Cnut doubted the boy was dead but wouldn't go to war with his brother over a child. If he's out there now, with a family of his own, he may be no threat, but that could change with Earl Godwin in his corner."

Maud's final goodbye with Lady Emma was prolonged and tearful.

Among her possessions in Kings Worthy, the old woman gifted Maud and Adelaide ceramic vases. Adelaide's was red and gray, like fire and ice dancing together on the earth. Maud's was gray, adorned with blue butterflies. Emma said she'd chosen them with each in mind, and the women cherished them all the way to Normandy—first by cart back to Borne, and then by sea.

Winter passed before they received word of Emma's death. She died with her son at her side, and Maud was grateful the king forgave his mother in time to say goodbye. Observing a period of mourning at the Norman court, Maud and William made donations to several churches in her honor. Determined to keep her spirit alive though her body was gone, Maud's maids potted fresh wildflowers in the butterfly vase every morning, and she read pages from her gilded copy of *Encomium Emmae Reginae* each afternoon.

Chapter Twenty

November 1053 – Rouen, Normandy

Chanting monks lulled Duchess Maud while she prayed at the chapel of Nôtre Dame du Pré in Rouen. Kneeling at the altar with hands clasped to her chest against the butterfly brooch he gifted her, she asked God to bless her husband. When the duke was on campaign she attended chapel daily, hoping to aid him with the love and support of God to hold his duchy.

She also prayed for Judith, clutching her latest letter against her chest. Maud studied the words once more, willing the Lord to bless Judith as He had her.

My dearest sister,

The last few years have been filled with strife, and still I watch the sunset each night and know I've been blessed to see another day. As you know, Tostig gave in to the drink during our year in exile in Flanders. Every alehouse in Bruges revered his patronage as though he were a duke. He's only gotten worse since our return, and after Earl Godwin's death at Easter with the king, he was gone for six days. I thought he'd gone mad, but he returned in time for the burial.

I know Tostig loves me. He tells me every day he doesn't mean to make our life so volatile, but drinking consumes him. He doesn't realize how he hurts me. I've asked God if I could be a better wife and make him happier, but what Tostig wants most—what we both want—will not come. God takes every child before they're ready to live outside my body. I know it's selfish, but I can't comfort myself knowing God makes angels of His chosen children when I long for one to look upon me as his mother. He's given you and William three healthy babies in three years, and I yearn to know the love you must have in your heart.

The letter also revealed potential new plans for the succession of the English Crown, and Maud prayed God would bless the promise King Edward made to William two years earlier.

Harold says the Aetheling has been found in the Kingdom of Hungary. The king refuses to believe it until someone has looked upon his face, so talks have begun to send an emissary to meet him in Germany. I know King Edward said he would pass the crown to Duke William, but the Aetheling is the son of an Anglo-Saxon king. The king's council will ultimately decide succession, and since the Archbishop of Canterbury was unseated and returned to Normandy, the council are all Anglo-Saxons themselves.

All of this has prevented the king from fulfilling a promise to give Tostig an earldom in the south. We languish at court without a household of our own, and he grows ever more impatient.

The ink was smeared by a dried drop of water where she signed her name, and Maud had no doubt Judith composed her latest letter with sadness on her face.

Alone inside the chapel, as always when she said her prayers, Maud studied the crucifixion of Jesus on a tapestry over the altar. "Why forsake her when it was me who sinned, God?" Maud hadn't forgotten her night with Brictric, so she knew the Lord remembered too. "Judith is a good and devout woman. She deserves Your blessings more than me."

After kneeling a few more moments in silent prayer, she closed Judith's letter and straightened her blue robes. Two attendants opened the tall wooden doors of the chapel, escorting her back to the carriage where a small crowd of Rouennais were gathered.

Women often reached out to touch her, sending prayers to God that Maud's fertile womb might be contagious. "Oh, gracious, beautiful Duchess!" they cried. Maud smiled, enamored of their adoration. She didn't know any of them by name, but their faith in her strengthened her heart, and she loved them all for loving her.

"God's blessings to you." Smiling warmly, Maud clasped their hands in hers while attendants cleared them from the cobblestones. The driver hitched the horses, crossing the familiar bridge with traitors' heads on spikes rotting in the sun.

The carriage rolled to a stop in the courtyard. William's brother, Odo, named Bishop of Bayeux by his brother to aid his dealings with the Church, offered target practice to Wulf and Hakon nearby. They all stopped to bow as she approached.

"That's enough archery for today," announced Odo. "Gather your arrows."

"How are lessons coming along?"

"Fine, Duchess," said Wulf, returning her welcoming smile. He was fifteen now, and his nephew, Hakon, was ten. "Has there been a dispatch from King Edward about our return home?"

She frowned, staring upon their dejected faces. "Not yet."

"I'm sorry, Duchess. You've treated us well here. It's just...now that the king and our family have reconciled, we wonder why we've been unable to return."

Maud had no answers for them. After the standoff at Dover, Earl Godwin and most of his family spent a year-long exile with her relatives in Flanders but made no effort to cross the border to visit them at William and Maud's court. According to her relatives, the Godwins were fixated on returning to England above all else. In exile, Harold and Leof escaped from the Welsh border to Ireland, gathering support from the powerful King of Leinster to return with numbers. Unable to mount an army strong enough to take on allies of the vengeful Godwins and paid Irish mercenaries, King Edward had no choice. He reinstated the earl and his sons to their lands and titles to avoid war.

Only Sweyn was barred from returning with the rest of his family. His previous insults to the Crown had been too grave, and the king kept Sweyn in exile in exchange for removing his closest advisor and most loyal appointment, the Norman-born Archbishop of Canterbury.

Less than a year after his return to England, Earl Godwin died suddenly at Easter, but no word came from England to return the boys. A letter from the king said to leave them in Normandy "until advised."

"When it's safe, the king and Earl Harold will send word for you." She tried to sound reassuring.

"What if I'm not wanted because my father is dead?" Hakon's lower lip wavered.

Maud put her hands on his small shoulders, forcing herself to empathize with Hakon's heartbreak. From Flanders, Sweyn Godwinson's permanent exile began with a barefoot pilgrimage to Jerusalem, wearing nothing but pauper's cloth tied with rope. Judith wrote that he vowed to cleanse himself of his sins and drink the water of the apostles, to heal himself of the devil in his soul. He never made it home, murdered on the road out of Antioch, but only rumors existed as to how he was killed. In one, he raped a woman in a village and her father beat him and sawed off his genitals, drowning him in the Mediterranean, alive and screaming, inside a leather sack. If true, Sweyn finally met justice for his crimes against women, including the abbess of Leominster, but Maud was careful not to share her opinion.

"The Godwins are your family, Hakon Sweynson." She placed a gentle hand on his shoulder. "You are wanted, but your stay here in Normandy is...political. Nonetheless, I hope we've made clear we are happy to have you." They bowed graciously as Maud turned toward the stone keep. Odo followed. "Do you bring a report from this year's bishops' council?" He nodded, and she halted with interest. "And? Has Pope Leo finally decided to address the question of our marriage?"

Odo nervously shook his head. "No. He didn't bring it up to the council."

Exasperated, she kept walking. "I doubt he'll do anything about the marriage while my father still feuds with Emperor Heinrich."

"He's also preoccupied with divisions between the Catholic Church in Byzantium and Rome. There's talk a *split* could be imminent."

She took a deep breath. "Forget him. We'll forge ahead with plans to build both churches anyway. William and I toured Caen while I was expecting Richard. It's a gorgeous town not far from the sea, and its place in the center of Normandy is a perfect location for our two grandest cathedrals." Odo followed as she entered the tower, soldiers standing at attention. "And we'll build new hospitals in every city in Normandy, to show we don't need the approval of the Church to do God's work."

"You'll show the Church you don't need it, in order to gain their approval," said Odo, and Maud grinned. "Building hospitals is an inspired idea, but you'll need an advocate from the Church to defend your marriage to the bishops." She raised an eyebrow in his direction. "It can't be me. I'm a relative. You need someone with a good reputation in Rome who has no claim to any feudal seat in all of Europe."

"Well, Bishop, you know most clergymen in Normandy. Please, find this advocate for your brother and me."

He bowed. "Yes, Duchess."

As he headed back down the stairwell, Maud continued to the nursery. Robert was now a dark-haired, blue-eyed toddler, and had since been joined by Richard.

Born just over a year after Robert, he entered the world unlike his brother, who wailed as though his lungs were larger than his body. Richard let out a single cry before settling peacefully in his mother's arms. His brother's heir, he was named for several previous Norman dukes, including William's uncle and grandfather. In her second son's thoughtful gaze Maud believed Normandy in good hands, with two perfect sons to nurture its future.

Their daughter, Emma, suckled hungrily from her wetnurse. Born so recently, William had yet to look upon her rosy cheeks while he battled his rebellious uncles, Archbishop Mauger and Guillaume Talou, at Arques. Smiling down at her, Maud hoped Emma would one day embody the spirit of the great queen she was named for.

That night, removing her veil, Maud brushed out her long, auburn hair. Retiring alone, she went to bed with thoughts of her husband's touch to lull her to sleep.

Days later, as Maud finished a late-morning breakfast of sweetbread, a short, balding, cleanly dressed man appeared in the dining hall with a reverent bow. "What news today, Bertrand?"

"There's good news, Duchess." Hearing the excitement in her steward's voice, she sat forward in her chair. "The duke secured Arques. His uncles had the support of Count Enguerrand of Ponthieu and your uncle, King Henri of Francia, but the king's men retreated, and Odo detained Archbishop Mauger on the road south of Rouen. The duke's army should return this afternoon."

Maud suppressed a grin. Bertrand, meanwhile, didn't take his leave, pausing nervously. "Is there more news from Arques?"

He shook his head. "Not Arques. Flanders. Your father writes to say the Holy Roman Emperor is planning a siege on Lille in early spring. He's hoping to reinforce his borders with the support of neighboring soldiers, and he asks for Normandy's help."

She thanked her steward, excusing herself to prepare for William's arrival. Setting the servants to work, they scrubbed and dusted the halls while she helped dress the children.

Outside the castle walls, horses marched over cobblestones toward the gates. Maud watched in anticipation, but the approaching cortège belonged to Adelaide and her new husband, Count Lambert of Lens. She raced down the winding staircase to greet them in the yard, and Addie jumped into her arms excitedly.

"What are you doing here?" Maud smiled in surprise.

"William sent word from his victory feast in Arques to meet him in Rouen. He says he has good news for me." Adelaide grinned. She always loved intrigue. "Do you know what it is?" When Maud shrugged with a clueless laugh, Addie cheerfully wrapped her arms around her besotted husband. "Just as well. I have good news for him too."

She smiled proudly at Count Lambert, who stood next to her with raven-haired Little Adelaide, Addie's now four-year-old daughter, in his arms. Addie looked down at her stomach with a grin and Maud squealed with excitement. "Are you with child?"

Nodding happily as she placed her hands against her purple robes, Addie grinned again. "The midwives say she'll arrive in late spring."

"She?"

"I feel the same as I did with Adelaide," she said. "But a son will come. We plan to have as many as God will grant us."

Addie's eyes gleamed, looking upon her beloved Lambert before she stepped away to walk with Maud through the courtyard. "I'm so glad we finally convinced William to allow you two to wed," said Maud gleefully. "I've never seen you so happy, Addie."

"Lambert is everything I dreamed a husband could be," she said. "I'm relieved. I was worried real love only happened to other people." Little Adelaide raced in circles around her stepfather, giggling madly. "He's the father my daughter deserved all along."

"My heart bursts for you, Addie."

They pulled their furs tighter around their shoulders as Maud glanced over the hill, trying to spot her husband's cavalry. Returning to Count Lambert's side, Addie cozied up to him against the autumn chill, making faces at her daughter as she spoke. "How are your relatives?"

"My father wrote to ask for reinforcements in Flanders. Emperor Heinrich plans a siege on Lille in the spring, and he needs help defending his borders," Maud said.

Addie frowned. "What will you do? If my brother joins a war against the Holy Roman Emperor, the Church will never grant dispensation for your wedding. They might even have him excommunicated. Adversaries of an excommunicated, bastard duke would circle like vultures."

"We can't join officially, but I can send mercenaries under someone else's banner."

"I'll join him," said Lambert. "Boulogne joined the war against Emperor Heinrich once, and I can certainly do it again now that we're family."

"But the baby." Pulling his nervous wife close, he kissed Adelaide's forehead.

"I won't leave right away, and promise to return before our daughter's born," he said. "Don't worry. I might talk about irrigated ditches until you fall asleep, but I can use a sword."

"Count Lambert, I can't thank you enough," said Maud. "I'll send three dozen men to Lens in the new year, when you're prepared to march."

The sound of horses clattering on the stones again rose over the castle walls. From the top of the rampart wall, an iron-helmeted guard shouted down to the courtyard, "The duke returns!"

The guards straightened their backs as the gates drew open. William entered, leading a procession of two dozen men on horseback—among them, Fitz, Beau, Monty, and his brothers. The horses surrounded an ornate carriage shrouded with red-and-gold cloth, and as Beau stepped from his horse to open the door, he forced out Archbishop Mauger.

The shamed uncle, who could hide behind God no more, stumbled out with his wrists bound with rope. Maud ran to her husband, the linked chains of his armor clinking as he wrapped his arms around his wife. For a quick moment, it was just the two of them again inside the courtyard, and she sank into the comfort of his touch. "Welcome home, love."

He kissed her, his rough-skinned finger caressing her soft cheek, before he noticed Addie and Lambert waiting with broad smiles. He turned to bow theatrically to his sister. "Hello, Countess. At Arques, I ran Enguerrand through with my own sword. He fought well enough, but his brother, Guy, sold him out to take his title. Squirrelly little prick. Guy's nobles don't support him yet, so convincing him to give up his family's claim to the County of Aumale was the easiest negotiation I've ever had. The county is yours, Addie, to pass down to your children."

Addie was jubilant, hugging her brother gratefully for defending her honor. Little Adelaide's father was dead, but she joined the joyful celebration with her loved ones, the man she knew as "Papa" bouncing her in his arms.

Chapter Twenty-One

April 1054 – Château de Moulineaux outside Rouen, Normandy

The bells of every church in Normandy rang out, swinging slow and steady in mourning when word of Pope Leo's death reached the duchy. The bishops convened in Rome for his funeral, and all the ladies of the Norman court switched to robes of black for a week. Maud wasn't particularly troubled by the passing of Leo, but she knew the importance of respecting the tradition.

Walking through the gardens, Addie and Maud admired early spring blooms with Lady Berthe, a daughter of the Count of Blois. Twice their age and twice widowed, she neared fifty but had no gray hairs. Refusing to hide under a veil, she dressed her brown locks in a black lace hood.

Maud held baby Emma in her arms as they walked. Small and soft, the infant looked curiously at the world beyond her nursery walls. The women laughed as they watched Little Adelaide play with Robert and Richard, toddling in the grass with their nursemaids.

"I miss this stage," Lady Berthe mused dolefully. "When Geoffrey of Anjou killed my husband and exiled me from Maine with nothing but the clothes on my back, I never imagined I wouldn't see my own children for three years. They must be so big now."

"When did you last hear from them, Dowager Countess?" asked Adelaide.

"Marguerite wrote to say she won't leave without her brother, but the Count of Anjou refuses to ease the guard trapping Herbert in Maine. Our allies can't get him out yet."

"If Geoffrey of Anjou can't hold Maine without kidnapping its seven-year-old count, he must know the people will turn on him at the first opportunity." Maud scoffed, shifting Emma on her hip. "Lady Berthe, you've known my husband since he was a child. As the widow of his old guardian, Duke Alain, I know he'll do all he can to help your children escape."

Bowing gratefully, Lady Berthe smiled. "I'm proud of Marguerite's loyalty to her brother—she's much like her ancestors in the County of Blois and will make a fine wife to a great and powerful lord one day. Someone just like your sons. And Herbert will be a great leader to Maine when he's strong enough to win it back from Geoffrey of Anjou. Knowing this is the only way I sleep at night."

"When the bishops return from Rome, perhaps they could convince the Angevins to release your son on humanitarian grounds, as a gesture of goodwill in honor of the late Pope?"

Maud was hopeful, but Addie laughed, shaking her head. "I wonder who they'll elect to be the next Holy Father," she said, waddling in black robes that couldn't hide the size of her stomach. The midwives said Addie would deliver soon, and while her husband fought for Maud's father in Flanders, she waited at her brother's court in Normandy.

Lady Berthe walked regally. "With the power struggle over Church laws in Byzantium and Rome, who knows if they'll even agree on one Pope to rule between them," she said.

"Bishop Odo thinks the Church may split in two if they can't compromise," said Maud. "We may not hear word of a new Pope until they've figured out their differences."

"They will." Addie rolled her eyes before adding regretfully, "Though there's no telling how long it might take, which isn't great news for a decision on your marriage to my brother."

Maud forced a smile. "At least Pope Leo reversed your excommunication before he died, after Guy of Ponthieu dropped his family's claim to Aumale. That's something."

"I still can't believe Count Guy wrote King Henri after that and tried to get his help to take it back," mused Adelaide. "He really is a squirrelly little prick." Laughing as she stopped to smell a bush of pink peonies, she cupped her fingers around the stem to breathe it in before changing the subject. "Has Odo found an advocate for you yet?"

Maud shook her head. "So far not one is willing to challenge canon law amid the current schism. Not even for their duke."

"The duchy grows in power every day," said Berthe with hopefulness in her voice. "Even the King of Francia knows Normandy's a vassal state in name only."

"Maybe he should start bowing to my brother." Addie scoffed. "William's soldiers beat back the king's men at Arques, despite the Frankish army being three times their size!"

"We want no trouble with Francia," said Maud, subduing a prideful grin. "William hasn't needed to call in the support of King Henri since the battle at Val-ès-Dunes before we were married. Whether or not my uncle is maliciously trying to take down my husband, I hope his loss at Arques was enough to convince him to leave us to our own devices. If my father's long war with the Holy Roman Empire has taught me anything, it's how much it costs to defend your lands from an emperor, or a king."

"Have you heard from Count Lambert?" wondered Lady Berthe. Adelaide frowned.

"My husband said they surrounded Lille and were ready if the emperor's men got through the woods."

"We'll hear from Flanders," Maud insisted. "Count Lambert, my father, and brothers will be fine."

The women bowed their heads as they prayed for the fate of their men. Leaving the gardens, they stopped to watch William and Fitz practice swordplay in the courtyard. Baby Emma fixed her eyes on her father while Maud silently admired her agile husband, his steel blade crossing with Fitz' in the sunlight.

William spotted her and winked, pinning his long-time steward under his blade with a prideful roar, but the moment was interrupted as a guard raced into the yard.

"Your Grace, it's Mauger. He cracked the stone and escaped through the privy hole."

Furious, William threw his sword to the dirt before helping Fitz stand with one arm. "When?"

"Just now, Your Grace. He swam through the moat and ran toward the city. A few of the guards already made chase."

"Saddle the horses!" he shouted angrily. Fitz sheathed his sword as the crowd of men sprang for their steeds. "I want him brought in alive." His cheeks burned red with rage. "And anyone found helping him to be brought in on their knees to answer to their duke."

Mauger crouched before his nephew, his arms bound in iron chains. Oozing blood from his battered face, he smelled of waste from the walls of the broken privy he'd slipped through. Duke William stood over him, his hand on his sword hilt as he seethed. At his side, Beau stood tall and imposing with his grizzled beard. Maud lingered with Addie and Berthe near the doorway of her husband's chambers, trying not to stare at Mauger's unsightly wounds.

"You've betrayed me for the last time. Now we decide what's to be done with you. Throughout the winter I have kept you here—"

"As a prisoner," the disgraced archbishop spat.

William leapt forward, coming within inches of his face. "I should have locked you in the cells. Your deceitful brother found exile in Lombardy, and I guess you hoped you'd join him there after stopping in Rome to smear my name?"

Defeated with blackened eyes, Mauger shrugged. "Something like that."

William yanked his sword from its shaft. "I could cut you down where you kneel. I could have a band of mercenaries sent to Lombardy to find you both, returned to Normandy in disgrace to be drawn and quartered."

Mauger let out a nervous laugh but wouldn't yield. "I underestimated you. But I'm done being your prisoner. Kill me or let me go."

"My lord." Maud spoke gently to distract her husband, his eyes glimmering with darkened rage. "We've been generous to Mauger during his confinement because he's been a man of God. Perhaps exile, far away from Rome or Lombardy, is the better option. We don't want to appear heavy-handed with your relatives, to keep other nobles well at ease."

Beau nodded. "With the legitimacy of your marriage still outstanding with the Church, we shouldn't risk alienation by keeping one of their former bishops imprisoned for life without so much as a trial. Especially if he has connections in Rome, as he says."

"Fuck the goddamned Church!" William roared, sheathing his sword inches from Mauger's puffy, battered face. When the old archbishop flinched, he grinned in satisfaction.

"Your hold on Normandy is so strong, your vassal King of Francia dreads your expansion." Duke William grinned reluctantly while his wife lauded his accomplishments. "Even if you paid your uncles to stay away, they'd never field a stronger army than the one they lost at Arques."

William scoffed. "Why should I pay them to walk free for their treachery?"

Lady Berthe stepped forward. "Your Grace, I assure you there's no freedom in knowing you're not welcome in your own home, among your own flesh and blood."

"I could be motivated to stay away with enough to live comfortably," Mauger volunteered. "I could convince Guillaume to do the same."

"Shut up, rat." William seethed over his rancid prisoner, baring his teeth like a dragon about to strike. "The world will know there's a price for treachery against me."

Grabbing an iron poker from the fireplace, he heated the tip like a ploughshare before branding a cow. Satisfied when the poker burned orange and red, he swung hard across Mauger's battered face. The shamed bishop screamed in agony, his eyes bloodied as he fell to the tiles. William ignored his cries.

"I am the rightful Duke of Normandy. You may descend from proud, powerful Northmen, but you're nothing. No one. A blind fool who thought he could defeat me."

Maud cringed witnessing her husband's brutal retribution—the side he never displayed inside their home but saved for his true enemies. Shadowed figures appeared in the doorway behind them, as Fitz and Monty emerged into the torchlight of the room. Behind them, Wulf and Hakon frowned, looking down at their shoes.

"What's going on?" William glared, his hand resting on the hilt of his sword.

Fitz cleared his throat. "Your Grace, they've admitted to helping your uncle in his escape."

"Is this true?" The duke loomed over them and Hakon cowered. Maud's heart sank.

"He said he'd find us a boat home, if we helped him," said the boy quietly.

William chuckled. "What does my uncle know about boats? He's afraid of water." Suddenly struck by an idea, he turned back with a wicked grin. "That's where you'll go. On a boat to an island you'll be too afraid to leave. With lots of beaches. When your rebels sent me into hiding on Jersey, there was so much sand I wanted to shave every hair from my body." The duke smiled devilishly, kicking Mauger's battered ribs out of spite. Turning to Wulf and Hakon, William frowned. "I'll have to keep a tighter leash on you until King Edward takes you back. No more archery or sword training. And no more books."

"That just leaves caring for the horses!" Wulf's tone stopped short of complaining, but William shrugged at the disappointment on his face.

"If it was anyone else, I'd have their heads. Count your blessings. Get out of my sight."

A messenger soon arrived carrying a letter, which he handed directly to Duchess Maud in the throne room. Mauger's blood had been wiped from the stone floors, and the room again looked impeccable, dressed in fine tapestries and golden candlesticks. "Your father, Count Baudouin, sends word from Flanders."

Adelaide held her breath, placing one hand protectively over her bulging stomach. Slowly, Maud unfurled the parchment and read her father's note. His handwriting grew worse with the years, but Maud could recognize his scribbled formations more easily now.

"He says their forces were decimated at Lille. The town was sacked by Emperor Heinrich and his army, and they lost close to two hundred men." She paused, her heart heavy, preparing herself to relay the next part by stiffening her spine. "Count Lambert evacuated women and children...but didn't make it out in time to save himself."

A mournful shriek rose from Adelaide, devastating Maud more than the letter itself. Palpable grief echoed off the high-arched stone above their heads. Maud ached to soothe her.

"My Lambert, no!" she sobbed. "Our baby!" William rushed to hold his sister as she collapsed to her knees in sorrow, wailing as she came to terms with the news.

"Addie, I'm so sorry." Maud knelt to meet her tear-soaked face. Reaching out to place a comforting hand on her shoulder, Addie recoiled, glancing at the hand in disgust. She blinked, staring at Maud. Her blue eyes glimmered.

"This is your fault."

"Addie!" William arched his brow in protest, but she shrugged him off.

"I didn't want Lambert to go with our child on the way, but he wanted to prove himself and agreed to fight your father's pointless war with Emperor Heinrich. For a decade they've traded cities over nothing but pride. When it all ends, they'll sign a treaty saying neither is any more powerful than before and go about their lives, but my daughter will never know her father."

Maud was almost speechless. Nothing Addie dared say to her was wrong. "I'm sorry."

"You live the most charmed life of anyone I've ever met. You have everything, yet you want more, and you always get more while the rest of us pile up our losses and lose our way." Cradling her womb, she stood slowly and brushed her skirt. "I hate you. One day your fortune will run out, and it can't come soon enough."

"Addie, please." William stood with her, but she refused to heed him.

"I want to leave Rouen immediately. Before the baby comes." She wiped her tears. "Set me up with a household at the castle in Falaise, and when you visit, come alone."

Marching out of the room, Addie refused to look down as her large skirt brushed Maud's horrified, tear-streaked face.

PART FIVE

Prophecy

Chapter Twenty-Two

March 1057 – Château de Moulineaux outside Rouen, Normandy

Retching, Maud pressed herself against the door to her privy chamber with sweat on her brow, greeting the glint of morning sunlight through a small window carved into the stone. Knelt over a bucket, she tried not to throw up on her nightgown as a polite knock came from the other side of the door. "Is there anything I can do, my lady?"

Wiping her face with a linen cloth, Maud swallowed. "Lay out my gown and veil. I have a meeting scheduled in the Great Hall, and it won't do if the duchess regent is late because of a little morning sickness." She cut off her own words to retch again.

"Yes, my lady."

Maud stood, ensuring her stomach had settled before walking into her bedroom where her ladies-in-waiting watched her nervously. "I'm fine. Help me get ready."

Stepping into a long robe spun with fine threads of gold that made the dress shimmer, her ladies-in-waiting helped her with her veil. Crafted from the same fabric as her robes, it rose at the brim with carved animal bone sewn inside. She pinned her cherished butterfly brooch to her gown and smiled. The robes felt tight at the stomach; her body was already changing.

"It seems just yesterday you were waiting to give birth to baby Cecilia," said one lady with a smile, pulling tighter than usual on the threads that tied the gown down her front. "Soon to be five babies in six years and you still have a waist. You're the most fortunate woman alive."

Maud frowned. She'd spent three years replaying Addie's words over and over inside her head. Her good fortune made her feel guilty.

Smiling, Lady Berthe entered the room. "It's because she's still just twenty-six. During my first marriage, I had three children at her age. It wasn't until my second marriage, when I gave birth to Marguerite at forty, that I didn't recognize the body below my neck anymore. And then I did it one more time with Herbert, which just added insult to injury."

Maud's ladies-in-waiting were her age and younger, all at court looking for suitors among the nobility. Thinking of their possible future figures made them grimace with nervous laughter and Berthe grinned, taking small pleasure in their bemused horror.

The door opened and Maud found her genial, balding steward in the stone hallway. He bowed low. "Good morning, Duchess."

He looked unusually distracted. "What is it, Bertrand?" she asked.

"It's a matter of household finances, my lady. With money being directed to pay the stonemasons laying bricks for the cathedrals in Caen, and the fort being constructed by your husband there, we may need to raise taxes on the nobles."

"By how much?"

"Not much. Barely noticeable. An extra denier a year if we downsize somewhere."

As they walked toward the Great Hall, Maud thought furiously. "What if we move a smaller court to the fort William is building in Caen? It's central, and when the cathedrals open, we won't need to travel back and forth between there and Rouen. The duke returns today from Falaise, but I don't think he'll dislike the proposition."

"It's an inspired idea, my lady," Bertrand said as they kept walking. "There's also word from Flanders: the son of Edmund Ironside has left Hungary." Maud stopped in her tracks and her steward stopped with her. "Your parents are hosting Harold Godwinson with Edward Wessex—the Aetheling—and his family. They're staying at the castle in Bruges until the rainy season lets up and the sea is fit to cross with young children."

"How young are the Aetheling's children?"

"He and his Kyivan wife, Agatha, have three. Margaret is twelve, Edgar is six, and Cristina is two."

Maud and her steward reached the Great Hall, lined with hanging tapestries depicting victorious Norman battles going back to the time of Rollo—the great Norse warrior given Normandy by the King of Francia a century and a half earlier. Her guest, dressed in the simple gray robes of a monk, was already in the room, waiting with Fitz at his side. Bertrand bowed low again before leaving the hall. "Your Grace," said the monk, kneeling reverently. "It is my honor."

"And I'm always grateful to be in the presence of a man of God. What is your name?"

"I am William, from the abbey at Jumieges. I served as a tutor in the court of the duke's grandfather, Duke Richard the First, for his young sons, Mauger and Guillaume." Maud raised an eyebrow. "Of course I know they were disgraced and sent into exile. They were well-behaved young men when I knew them," he continued. "I left the court after the death of their elder brother, the second Duke Richard, to retire to the abbey, and I've spent years compiling a chronicle of the great Norman dukes, from Rollo to your husband."

Maud nodded thoughtfully. "I am a firm believer in the power of the written word to educate and inspire, Brother William. Have you come seeking sponsorship to continue in this endeavor?"

"I would be most grateful, Duchess, but would not think to impose. I've come seeking more information about your Flemish relatives, to add to Duke William's section. I lost track of your mother when she left court after Richard's death to marry your father."

She smiled. "Do you think the Norman audience who'll read your chronicle want to be reminded of our family connections to the very same King of Francia who now sacks their homes and their fields of grain, trying to intimidate their duke into war?"

The monk cocked his head sideways. "Do you mean I should lie?"

"Not a lie," she said firmly. "A simple omission for a benefactor as interested in the success of your chronicle as you. I'm still the daughter of a princess of Francia and niece of the current king, but my mother never had a true chance to be Duchess of Normandy before her first husband died. The Church branded my own marriage to William consanguineous, and it will do Normandy no favors to remind your readers of my mother's marriage to his uncle."

As the monk read her face, wise to many of the secrets of the Norman court already, he could see she was inventing an excuse to obfuscate the record of her mother's first marriage. He stood straighter with a dutiful nod, pulling his hood back over his head as he bowed. "Your reasoning is logical, my lady, and your loyalty to Normandy is truly commendable. Sometimes it is better to mask the whole truth." Turning to leave, he looked back with a polite smile. "For what it's worth, Duchess, I never thought your mother could have poisoned anyone."

She blinked, forcing back a tear forming in the corner of her eye as she thought not only of her mother's past but her own. The Church approved more of a tale where her husband ripped her from a horse and beat her in the street for turning down his proposal than the truth of Maud's own sins and indiscretions. How eager they all were to lie turned her stomach. "Please write with any questions about my family for your chronicle. I'm pleased to be of assistance to your work."

When Fitz escorted the monk from the room, Maud raised her hand to wipe the tear as Lady Berthe entered from an opposite doorway. "Duke William is back from visiting his sister in Falaise. He's with the children in the courtyard and asked to see you."

Standing from her ornate gold-painted throne, Maud headed eagerly to the gravel courtyard with the deposed Dowager Countess of Maine. "It may rain soon," she said with a glance to the warm, overcast skies, and William whipped around at the sound of her voice. One-year-old Cecilia bounced in his muscled arms, smiling up at him and showing off her tiny teeth. He grinned down at her, making a face that made her giggle more.

"My love." Leaning in to kiss his wife, he held Cecilia to the side with one arm.

"Welcome home." She pressed her stomach against him subconsciously.

"Marguerite, Herbert, don't let Emma eat the mud!" Berthe called across the yard as her daughter and son, twelve and ten, raced to brush dirt from the curious toddler's tiny hands.

"Sorry, Mama. We were distracted," said Marguerite, before settling back into a game of peekaboo with Maud and William's eldest daughter. Nearby, Beau stood over Robert and Richard as they spun around him in circles.

"I'm sorry. They've been overstimulated by the children since their return from Maine."

"It's just mud." With a laugh, Maud nodded toward Beau and her sons. "My boys have eaten plenty of mud in their young lives, and they're perfect."

"They're so grateful to have other young children around. Saving Marguerite and Herbert from captivity under the Count of Anjou meant as much to them as it did to me. We never would have been able to pull off their escape without the help of Normandy."

William shrugged his broad shoulders. "Duke Alain would expect me to care for those he loved. It's been sixteen years since he was murdered, but your first husband was one of the best men I ever knew, and he led me to my beautiful wife. I wouldn't dare disappoint him. You and your children can stay in Normandy as long as you need." Cecilia cooed, and William smiled down at her. "What's that, Ceci?"

"I've always wondered, where did Cecilia get her name? It doesn't run in either of your families," said Lady Berthe.

"I chose her name," said William proudly. "She was named for an old woman who conned me into trusting her before she tried to assassinate me."

"What a dubious namesake for such a sweet little girl." Cecilia giggled, reaching for Berthe's exposed dark hair.

"Ceci is nothing like Cecilia Drengot," said Maud assuredly, and William nodded.

"No, but just before she tried to strike me down, a few of the last words Madame Drengot ever said were 'stay vigilant.' Ceci is a reminder of everything I have to live for, and why I'll take Madame Drengot's advice until the end of my days."

His explanation was sound, almost poetic. It was the only reason Maud agreed to name Ceci for the woman who once made them fear for their lives, racing through the crowded streets of Rouen. "He's already promised me the next one won't be named Mauger." She laughed as another bout of nausea forced her to steady herself on her feet.

"The next one appears not to like the name Mauger very much," said Berthe with a sly grin, and William looked between the women expectantly.

"Are you?" he asked Maud, placing a hand on her stomach.

She nodded excitedly and he hollered with joy. Behind him, Monty offered his congratulations. William handed off Cecilia so he could envelop his wife with both arms, but Monty held out the infant like a shield. William laughed. "You have children, Monty. Did you never hold them as babies?"

Monty's brow glistened with nervous perspiration as he laughed off his duke's chiding tone. He shifted his weight to support Cecilia, letting them chuckle at his expense. "You sound like my wife."

William called his sons, who sprinted to him eagerly. Patting both on their heads, he knelt to greet them. "My sons. Have you behaved while I've been in Falaise?" They nodded. "Robert, why have you let Richard grow as tall as you in just the last few weeks?"

Six-year-old Robert looked down at his feet, then at his five-year-old brother. "I didn't mean to."

The duke laughed. "You'll probably take after your mother. Little Robert Curthose!"

"William, really? Little Robert *Shorty*-Pants?" Maud looked at her husband with disgust.

"It's said with love, my love." He disarmed her with a short kiss. "You know, I was thinking, on my way home from Falaise—"

"And how is the Countess of Aumale?"

William wavered. He hated to get between their feud but decided to speak his mind. "Don't do that. She's still your sister. You both know it, even if she refuses to admit it. Little Adelaide and Little Judith are happy and healthy. Addie's getting on well with the nobles in Falaise and helping raise an army if King Henri and Geoffrey of Anjou want to cross swords again." Maud smiled with an anxious sigh. "She will move on," William insisted. "This time, she even asked about you."

Shaking it off, she stood taller, straightening her robes as she changed the subject. "You said you were thinking about something? On your way back from Falaise."

He nodded with a knowing grin. "I think we should pay a visit to your family. Now that your brother and Richilde have two sons, the cousins should get to know each other."

"You've heard the Aetheling is at my parents' castle in Bruges."

He nodded and she threw up her hands, wrapping her arms around her husband. "As long as you don't mind a slow journey with the entourage we'll need for the children, I think it's a wonderful idea."

Chapter Twenty-Three

April 1057 – Flanders Castle in Bruges

The castle where Maud grew up was just as she remembered it: not one tapestry or chalice was out of place. As she wandered the same familiar hallways with Countess Adela, she smiled. "It's been seven years, but it still feels like home."

Her mother laughed. "It will always be your home. And my perfect grandchildren will always be welcome. How are you feeling?"

"I've been sicker before, but hopefully it will pass soon." Maud caught a glance from her mother in the torchlight, eyeing her carefully. "You look as though you judge me."

"Your father and I know your husband secured English succession on no more than a handshake from King Edward. The Aetheling has a lot more Wessex blood than you."

Maud crossed her arms defiantly. "We're here to visit family. Not push our claim."

Countess Adela nodded. "I must insist on it. Harold Godwinson knew how much his father wanted to find the Aetheling before he died, and his family are throwing their support behind him and his son, Edgar. Whatever happens in the future, this is the reality for now. For the next week, the presumed heir to the English throne, inside these walls, is Edward Aetheling."

Maud understood, and hoped she'd convince William to do the same. "What else do we presume inside these walls? Bodhi and Richilde are happily married?"

Adela balked, aghast, before remembering her daughter and daughter-in-law shared their own bond. "Now that she's had two sons, she's moved into her own bedchamber. She won't spend another night with him unless we tie her to the bed kicking and screaming. Her words. Bodhi's happier now, so your father and I washed our hands of it because of Arnulf and Baldy."

"The baby will grow hair." Maud chuckled. "You can't call him Baldy forever."

"There are so many Baudouins in the family already." The countess laughed. "It might stick."

"Richilde might have been different if her children with her first husband hadn't been sent to join the Church." Maud chose her words carefully as they came to a balcony overlooking the courtyard. Below, Flemish stewards unloaded their carriages, carrying their clothes into the castle for their stay.

Across the courtyard, from an opposite balcony, Maud spotted a woman in red, carrying a toddler and singing. The toddler was stark naked, wrapped only in the long fabric of the woman's black scarf. Her song, bright and cheerful, was in no language Maud could understand.

"Roger, the poor soul, with his leg was not built to lead, and Gertrude turned mute a year after she got here. The kindest thing to do was let them devote themselves to the Order."

Avoiding an argument with her mother, Maud changed the subject as they continued toward the Great Hall, where they'd left their families to get reacquainted. "Who was that woman?"

"That's Agatha, the Aetheling's wife," Adela said. "She's from Kyiv, and her children speak three languages. Well, not Cristina. That's the little one in her arms. She's an interesting woman. Very impractical. You'll probably like her."

She accepted her mother's playful ribbing as they continued down the circular stone stairwell. "And how's Robby? Is he any closer to getting married?"

Adela threw up her hands in exasperation. "I can't even talk about Robby. He's in Frisia chasing any daughter set to inherit her father's lands and title. Since Bodhi will become Count of Flanders, and you're already a duchess, he's more interested in the titles than the marriages. All the women can see through him."

Countess Richilde met them in the hall, handing her youngest son, Baldy, to a nursemaid as he fussed. When she saw Maud, she grinned warmly. "Ser Brictric was here with Harold," she announced with a smirk. "When he saw the Norman cortège, he made an excuse to escape to Zeebrugge to watch for calm seas."

"What could he possibly be afraid of? I haven't set eyes on him since Judith's wedding. I don't even know what I'd say." Silently, she was grateful not to have to try.

"Any man in their right mind would fear your husband, but I've rarely known a man to admit when he was wrong. They'd rather fear us than take responsibility for themselves," Countess Adela said.

"He's not special," added Richilde. "Each time he visits, he seduces a new maid. The girls trade stories."

Laughing as they approached the doors to the Great Hall, shouting rose from inside.

Two guards pulled the doors open. The air was thick with tension as men hitched with swords stood back, watching Harold and William square off in the center of the room. Duke William was taller, but the earl still imposed his muscular gait.

"I don't buy for a second the timing's a coincidence," Harold spat. "The least you could have done is bring my brother and nephew along so I could finally sail them home."

Fitz stepped forward, his hand protectively over his sword, but William shrugged him off. He enjoyed bringing men to red-faced rage. "Until I get word from King Edward, I can't surrender them to you. I can't break my cousin's trust."

Harold sneered as Count Baudouin inserted himself between them. His once bright-red hair had turned mostly gray and he seemed shorter, but his presence still commanded the respect of other men. Harold and William stepped back from one another cautiously.

"Wulf and Hakon are prisoners in Normandy because the king won't bring them home, and you act like keeping them is an act of nobility."

Maud shook her head, approaching in defense of her husband. "I can assure you Wulf and Hakon are well taken care of at our court."

"Whether they deserve it or not," William said in a huff.

"We don't blame them for Mauger's treachery," Maud said quickly, cutting him off. "The day King Edward requests it, you have our word we'll send Wulf and Hakon home."

Footsteps echoed off the marble from the opposite end of the hall as Edward Aetheling, his wife, and three children entered the room.

Agatha still held Cristina in her arms, though now the babe was fully dressed in crisp white robes. Their daughter, Margaret, was tall; already she looked down to meet Maud's gaze. Their son, Edgar, was Robert's age. Sandwiched between his mother and sisters, he looked to Robert and Richard with interest.

"Are you making yourselves comfortable here?" asked Count Baudouin.

Edward smiled. "The accommodations have been very grand, thank you. But we're looking forward to landing in England just to put an end to all this travel. It's been hard on children so young, coming all the way from Hungary with a soldiers' caravan."

"I have some idea what you mean. It was hard enough traveling from Rouen with four children, the fifth making my wife sick the whole way here," William said.

"That stage was always difficult for my wife." Agatha looked up at her husband with a devoted gaze, and he smiled down at her with equally steadfast affection. They only had eyes for one another, and their three children looked on contentedly. Politely, Edward returned his attention to William. "I must say I'm thrilled to meet the great Duke of Normandy. My uncle wrote of how he spent most of the war between our fathers, brothers, and cousins at your court. He said you treated him like a brother."

William nodded. "You and your lovely wife and children can expect much the same from me. I hold King Edward in the highest regard. His friends are my friends, his enemies my enemies." He shot a sly look at Harold Godwinson as he spoke, but if he noticed, the yellow-bearded earl had no reaction.

Emma toddled curiously up to the Aetheling, her auburn ringlets bouncing as she moved unevenly across the marble floor. "Up!" she pleaded, and the Aetheling laughed. He was tall but thin and didn't carry himself like most kings-in-waiting. He was friendlier, more personable.

"Come here, Emma," said Maud, but Edward knelt to pick up the little girl.

"No, I love children," he insisted, laughing as Emma ran her tiny fingers through his blond hair. As she stared into his chestnut eyes, her face pinched into a sneeze. Lurching forward instinctively, William reached for their daughter as Edward cleaned his face with the sleeve of his tunic.

"I'm so sorry!" Maud apologized profusely as William wiped Emma's nose with his gloved hands. The Aetheling shrugged it off.

"Believe it or not, it's happened before. But her nose is much smaller. I'm relieved!"

Agatha spotted Maud's mortified gaze and smiled warmly. "Really, he loves everything about children. Ed and I would have had more, but my fortune teller said there would only be three, so we count ourselves blessed to have Margaret, Edgar, and Cristina."

"Your fortune teller?" Maud looked curiously at the woman in red, her white veil lined in gold-painted rope.

Agatha nodded vigorously. "She is very wise. I've entrusted my life to her many times."

Countess Adela stepped forward with a wide smile. "Perhaps we can move to the dining room to continue over a hearty meal. Our cooks have been roasting a deer since this morning."

Maud's stomach growled at the mention of food—a good sign her body was finally adjusting to the new life growing inside of her.

While their ladies-in-waiting corralled the children, the adults followed Baudouin and Adela into the adjacent hall where an oak table stretched down the center of the room. Wood panels lined the walls surrounding a stone hearth. Above the mantel, the stuffed head of a black bear, felled by the first Count of Flanders, roared in silence.

Maud straightened her robes to sit between her husband and Lady Eleanor, who looked years older than she had on Judith's wedding day. "You look well, Lady Eleanor."

Her laugh trailed ruefully. "You don't lie very well, Duchess. My days are spent worrying for Judith, and the worry has swallowed my youth. I used to look younger than your mother, but becoming a grandmother seems to have frozen her looks in place, while I look like the dowager countess I've been for so long."

Understanding her worry, Maud tried to comfort her. "King Edward finally gave Tostig an earldom, and Judith runs her own household now." Lady Eleanor shook her head.

"The king gave them Northumbria. Tostig never wanted to be so far north, and Judith tells how he refuses to get along with the locals. She says they don't like her either, and call her 'the continental mistress.' She's miserable, and still, she longs for motherhood."

Maud knew Judith was lonely. Her increasingly infrequent letters always sounded sad, as though life was something she was learning to endure for the sake of it and nothing more. "I pray for her every day," said Maud, knowing how fruitless prayer had been thus far. "I won't give up." Lady Eleanor smiled politely, but exhaustion clouded her usually bright eyes.

"It's hard to be apart, but the north is no place for my old bones. Judith says the old women in England ache when it rains, so every night, we say the same prayer to Sainte Anne."

"You must share it with me. I'll join you both."

"Have you spoken lately to Adelaide?" Lady Eleanor asked. "We haven't heard from her since before she moved to Falaise."

"Neither have I. It's been three years, and I've never laid eyes on Little Judith. She shut me out after Count Lambert's death," Maud answered.

"She'll forgive you in time," Eleanor said thoughtfully. "Grief hits everyone differently."

Maud picked at a piece of venison on her trencher as the kitchen staff brought more food through the doors, placing large platters of boiled vegetables and sweetbreads on the table. "It feels like she's determined to hurt me. Even naming her daughter Judith felt like an attack."

"You know my Judith and Adelaide's daughter were named in memory of their Norman grandmother, who died when I was a little girl."

She nodded. "No, I know. But she could have chosen from any number of relatives, and she went with the one that implied Judith was a better sister. If she did it to hurt me, it worked."

Eleanor raised an eyebrow, bringing a bite of venison to her lips. "It's just a name, Maud."

To her left, William piled his trencher with fatty, flavorful cuts of venison, leaning in to chat with the Aetheling. "I take it the king's council is looking forward to your arrival."

The Aetheling nodded with an amiable smile. "Harold tells me they're keen to keep the Wessex line in England. I had no reason to want to be king while in exile. I had no allies, no army, but when Harold and his men arrived, I had to heed the call of duty. It's in my blood."

"Indeed," said Harold between bites. Fitz sat next to him, watching him carefully. "Alfred the Great brought much of England together, and with so much discord still in the north, King Edward and his council believe only a true Wessex king can keep England united."

William frowned, and Maud placed a pleading hand on his thigh. He squeezed her fingers gently but continued. "I can relate. My wife descends from Alfred herself, and she's perhaps the best regent Normandy has ever seen."

Harold gave a polite smile, filling his mouth with venison before he said another word.

"That's enough politics," pressed Countess Adela. "Why ruin a good meal with such chatter?"

Chapter Twenty-Four

April 1057 – Flanders Castle in Bruges

The gardens in Bruges lacked the colors that once brought her family's estate to life in Lille—before the raids that destroyed the manor and killed Count Lambert. Still, Maud enjoyed wandering among the leafy branches of the willows, as gargantuan to her now as when she was a child. She walked with Agatha and Margaret, whose golden braids seemed to sail amid the long, drooping leaves.

"I never thought I'd miss the sight of my own hair," Maud admitted with envy.

"Don't you get to see it at night before bed?" asked Margaret sweetly.

She chuckled. "I do, but it's not the same."

"Mama's fortune teller says veils prevent the Holy Spirit from escaping a woman's body. She says that's why she doesn't wear one."

Maud's jaw hung open. "Agatha, is your fortune teller a practitioner of dark arts?"

Wide-eyed, Agatha shook her head. "She's very devout, but says when the Holy Spirit has her body, she's unable to see the world beyond what is. Without, she can read the future."

"I'm not sure I believe anyone but God knows the future," said Maud, continuing down a gravel path toward the castle as Agatha and Margaret tailed behind.

"Women who have God's gifts can only enter a convent to become a nun," Agatha protested, hands on her hips defiantly. "They can't join the priesthood and share God's love with others the way any man is welcome to do. I've known others who were, but my fortune teller is no fraud."

Maud wasn't prepared to argue for or against the art of fortune telling but was nonetheless drawn to the curious woman from Kyiv. "You've intrigued me these last few days, Agatha. I feel we'll be great friends."

She smiled excitedly. "I wondered if we would have friends on this side of the continent. I've spent my life in courts full of nobles as good as strangers to me now."

"Please consider my husband and I among your friends. I know William quite enjoyed getting to know your husband before he fell ill. Robert and Richard have loved playing with Edgar in the yard, and I'm sure Emma and Cecilia have bonded well with young Cristina in the nursery. I'm sorry your husband feels under the weather. We've been unable to get to know one another as I'd like."

"He says it's only a cold," said Margaret gently. "I had them all the time at Reka Castle, because winters were so harsh."

"I'm sure all he needs are some herbs and good rest, and he'll be back to himself in no time," said Maud, catching the wings of a blue butterfly dancing between the willow branches. She reached out as it darted in the opposite direction as quickly as it floated into view. "Agatha, tell me: What future has your fortune teller seen? Did she prophesize you would become England's queen?"

"She said a foreigner will win England's throne when fire lights the sky."

Maud regained composure as she processed Agatha's phrasing. "What sort of fire?"

She shrugged. "The prophecy foretells nothing else. I find it ominous myself, as if Edward taking the throne would be a bad thing."

"And yet you left Hungary."

"My husband felt like an outsider at the court of the Hungarian king, and he doesn't like to believe everything my fortune teller says. He thinks her premonitions are vague, and when she's right they're just coincidences."

Anxious to avoid giving too much thought to such a sacrilegious riddle, Maud couldn't halt her curiosity. "The uncertainty doesn't frighten you? You've crossed the continent for your husband already."

"I'll follow Ed anywhere, and not just because of our children."

Margaret looked at Agatha with her wide, blue eyes. "Tell your story, Mama. Please! I love the story of you and Papa."

Maud smiled eagerly. "Who doesn't like to hear a great love story?"

Agatha straightened her robes as they climbed the short hill to the castle keep. "I've known Ed since we were children, and I've loved him since then too. When King Cnut conquered England and sent Ed to his brother's court in Sweden, Cnut expected Ed would be killed. But King Olof was an old friend of Ed's grandfather, Aethelred, and he feared killing a child would anger the gods."

Lady Emma's rumors of the Aetheling's fate had been true. Maud kept listening with interest as the bridge lowered, letting them pass the garrison walls.

"Olof entrusted care of the child to a wetnurse named Cristina, who immediately fell for Ed as a mother would fall for her own son. She knew if Ed stayed at the Swedish royal court, he would eventually be discovered and likely killed, so with King Olof's help she escaped to Denmark by skiff in the middle of the night, finding exile in the Kingdom of Hungary."

"Don't forget the boat almost capsized!" Margaret pipped, and Agatha laughed.

"Right! Yes, the boat almost capsized when it started to rain, but Cristina prayed with every stroke of the oars while a servant emptied the floor of the skiff with a bucket."

"And by God's grace, they made it," said Margaret. It was clear she knew this story by heart, like Maud knew Emma's *Encomium*. Agatha nodded.

"They made it all the way to Hungary on the back of a wagon. She raised Ed in drafty, isolated Reka Castle under the condition that whenever the King of Hungary wanted to impress a visitor, Ed would be paraded at court. One day, a man requested to buy the Aetheling for five hundred gold coins. Cristina begged the king not to sell Ed to this strange Rus man with a long, thin mustache hanging down to his collar, but the price was too good. To be rid of her, the king threw Cristina into the deal for free. She tried to fight the sale, but the man wanted to move to Reka Castle with them and brought his entourage. He was a Silk Road merchant seeking to retire like a nobleman. Two years earlier, he'd picked me up from an orphanage in Kyiv."

"If he wanted children, why didn't he just find a wife?" wondered Maud.

"He wanted children, not a wife, but he only spoke to us in the evenings. The rest of the time we spent with Cristina until she died of fever. Ed kept me safe after that, and I found my fortune teller one morning while out for a walk in the valley. She knew I was in love with

Ed, and she told me to propose because he'd say yes if I asked."

"So she asked and he said, 'Of course I will, I love you!'" said Margaret with excitement, the glassy-eyed look of a romantic in her gaze.

Agatha smiled at the memory. "He said he was afraid to ask me himself because all he had was Reka Castle, and even the castle went back to the Hungarian Crown once the old merchant died too. But I knew we'd never want for anything if we had each other."

"Your love seems even stronger now, if it's possible."

Agatha smiled as they entered the courtyard. "It's possible," she said.

A monk raced down the stairs to meet them in the yard, Countess Adela following hurriedly behind. "Mistress, it's your husband." Her voice shook with fear. "The Aetheling's fever spiked. He's still up and walking around, but Harold Godwinson wants to get him on a boat to England today, and in the care of King Edward's court physicians as quickly as possible." Maud gasped as Agatha and Margaret raced for the stairs with the monk. "Maudie, you and your family should leave," said Adela. "I hate for you to go so soon, but we must barricade the castle to ensure sickness doesn't spread."

"Is anyone else ill?"

Adela shook her head. "Not yet, God willing. Your father and I would hate to see you or any of our gorgeous grandchildren shake like the Aetheling. He says he's cold, but his skin is hot like fire."

"Are you sure you'll be all right here? Can we help?"

The countess shook her head. "No, you must go."

"I'll pray for him, and for all of you," Maud said, helpless. "Please stay safe."

Adela gave her daughter a comforting hug, and she fell into the scent of her mother's rosewater perfume. Just as she remembered. "Send word from the road. Let us know you're keeping well."

When Maud and William crossed into Normandy near Eu, Fitz pulled his horse to a stop to halt the caravan. Stepping down from his own speckled mare, William ensured the children and their attendants had no fever. For days on the road, this was their ritual at every rest.

Satisfied, he insisted Maud walk with him to the top of the same hill where they wed seven years earlier. The circle of earth trod away by horses was still mostly bare, though pockets of grass had begun to sprout at their feet. She fell against his muscled shoulders as they gazed toward Normandy, the rolling hills of their domain brushed gold and red by the sunset. "This is blissful," she said softly, glancing at the contented face of her beloved husband.

Driving the caravan into Eu, they sought beds for the night from the monks at the church of Notre Dame. In the morning, William asked a monk to bless their union.

"What for?" Maud watched him curiously.

"The Pope can prevent us from being wed inside the Catholic Church, but a blessing of our union is a gift from God that can't lead to our excommunication. What better place to bless our union than the church nearest to the spot we married?"

She smiled. "Sometimes you are hopelessly romantic, my love."

He laughed, placing a hand on his wife's stomach as he pulled her in for a kiss. "I've been waiting to return to Eu with you since the day we were married."

As they knelt before the altar, the monk said a prayer in Latin, pressing holy water to their temples. Warm and wet, it dripped down to their collars. Their children watched the ritual in silent awe, sitting with their maids in the pews, but Maud's attention was fixed on her husband.

As he finished the blessing, the monk motioned for them to stand. Maud let William's large hands envelop her in a gentle embrace. "I'm grateful every day to love and be loved by a man like you," she said, sealing their long union with a gentle kiss.

After a small breakfast, their caravan was back on the road to Rouen, but soon Monty, with William's youngest brother, Robert, the Count of Mortain, rode up to them on horseback.

Both parties were surprised to meet each other on the road. "We were on our way to Flanders because we didn't expect you back in Normandy so soon. It's Geoffrey of Anjou, Brother," said Robert hastily, sitting straighter on his horse. "He invaded Normandy at Domfront with the assistance of King Henri of Francia."

"We've sent an army from Falaise led by the Warennes and Brionne brothers," added Monty. "But the rest of your soldiers wait to march behind their duke."

Angrily, William jumped down from his steed. "King Henri can't miss an opportunity to support rebels moving against Normandy." In frustration, he threw back the curtain of the wooden box carrying his wife and their children. "I need to go."

Maud reached her hand through the window. "Please be safe."

He kissed her, lingering a moment on the soft skin of her lips. "No matter how many times the King of Francia wishes to come for me, no matter who he uses to try to take me down, I'll drive out the rebels like all rebellions before it." His nostrils flared, but his eyes looked upon his wife with affection. "Take care of Normandy while I'm gone, love."

"Always." She gave a stoic nod as he let go of the curtain and adjusted his tunic.

"Be safe, Papa," their son Robert called, mimicked by Richard as their father remounted. With a swift kick, the horse was off, sending William into the brush with Monty and his brother.

Maud was ready for a bath when the carriage finally pulled into the courtyard in Caen, which bustled with activity as though they'd never left. Her anxious children bounced on the benches, but when they pulled to a stop, Robert and Richard flew out the door to freedom from the wooden box. Her loyal steward stood waiting for them with an anxious smile.

"Welcome back," he said, but there was no excitement in his voice.

"Is there news from my husband's men, Bertrand?" On her nursemaid's lap, Emma laughed without a care as the maid created shadows with her hands in the late-afternoon sun angling against the carriage wall. Scrunching her face, the toddler let out a small, snotty sneeze. As she craned her neck to listen to her steward, Maud reached for a kerchief inside her sleeve to wipe her daughter's face.

"Not yet, Your Grace. A dispatch came this morning—the Aetheling died minutes after his ship landed in England. His wife and children went on to London and his wife laid the whole way with his body. We worried you'd all be sick too."

"We were forced to leave early, but the fever didn't follow us from Flanders. You're sure he's dead? Oh, poor Agatha!"

Forgetting her desire for a bath, Maud's head swam with fresh worry—both for her battle-scarred husband in Domfront and her grieving new friend in England. She climbed down from the carriage in shock as she thought of Edward Aetheling. He lived with such vitality just a week ago, but now the man who would be England's next king would be dressed for burial instead.

Chapter Twenty-Five

August 1057 – Château de Moulineaux outside Rouen, Normandy

Maud took up her throne in the Great Hall next to her husband's empty seat. While William battled against the forces of King Henri and Geoffrey of Anjou at Varaville, she waited for the arrival of their next child, tending to the administrative business of running the duchy until his return.

"Your Grace, the duke's brother is here with a man from Bec Abbey."

"Send them in, Bertrand." She smiled as her steward left and her brother-in-law, Bishop Odo, entered next to a man in gray robes with a bent nose and disarming smile. A red rosary hung around his neck.

"I bring news, Duchess. This is Lanfranc, Prior of Bec Abbey. He's from Pavia in Lombardy, a renowned scholar of biblical law who trained in Rome before he brought his talent to Normandy twenty years ago."

Maud nodded, pinching her lips together. "I know this man. He was sentenced to exile last year for opposing canonical recognition of our marriage within Normandy. Why is he still here?"

Odo stiffened. "He's a great scholar, Duchess. He trained nearly half of all bishops on this side of the Holy Roman Empire, including me, and was asked to finish with his current students before leaving."

Lanfranc approached, raising a careful smile. "I tried to tell the bishops my horse is too old and lame to delay my exit this long, but they insisted."

Maud kept her gaze focused on her brother-in-law. "Why do we want a man who opposes the duke and duchess to teach our future bishops?"

Lanfranc bowed his head reverently before Bishop Odo could speak. "I don't teach them this, Your Grace. I no longer oppose your marriage at all, to be honest."

Maud leaned forward slightly. "And what changed your mind, Lanfranc?"

"You and your husband. You're raising a robust and healthy family, and have shown that consanguinity is not God's law. The downfalls to the mixing of blood too closely are not absolute, and your family is proof God blesses your union."

Maud grinned at her large belly, placing her hand to rest on the curve of her black robes. "Odo, you're right—this is very good news indeed. Lanfranc, when do you think you'll be able to present this evidence to Rome?"

"Upheaval in the Church still makes it difficult to gather for a bishops' council."

"I suppose the fact Pope Leo's successor just died himself doesn't help matters."

"It's true, Duchess. The unsteadiness of the papacy makes it hard to push for any changes or exemptions to existing laws, but the newest Pope is a younger brother to Duke Godfrey of Lorraine, your father's old ally."

Maud scowled. "My father's allegiance to Godfrey of Lorraine ended when he submitted to Emperor Heinrich, leaving my father and his men to fight the Holy Roman Empire alone."

"Your father was right to defend Flanders from the expansion of the Empire," Lanfranc said. "Heinrich's war wasn't about God, and everyone who met him knew Pope Leo was as crooked as a weeping willow. When Heinrich died a year after Leo, their old grudges died with them, but right now the bishops aren't certain who or what to support after the schism between Rome and Constantinople. But I think they're close." Maud smiled again. She found everything to like about this pragmatic man of faith. "If you'll allow me to dispense advice, Your Grace?"

She nodded.

"Don't allow yourself to be held to the same opinion of the Lorraines as your father's court. Look what submitting to the Empire in the time of Pope Leo did for the Lorraine family fortunes. Now, their second son is Pope Stephen of the Holy See."

Maud leaned back against a velvet cushion to rest her spine. "I'm pleased to have made your acquaintance, Lanfranc. Your sentence of exile is waived pending Church recognition of our marriage, and I should hope your efforts will be solely focused on this goal. You'll move to your own accommodations at court, and we'll provide any resources you need."

Lanfranc bowed nervously. "I do love to teach, Duchess. Perhaps your young sons need a tutor? I would most certainly be able to focus myself on both tasks."

She nodded thoughtfully. "Might you also find time to arrange a tutor for my daughters when the time comes? I want Emma and Cecilia to be able to receive an education comparable to my sons, and who better to find the right tutor for my girls than a man who has taught so many brilliant minds across the continent?"

"It would be an honor for any one of them, Your Grace."

He bowed once more next to Odo before both men left the room. Betrand entered with Lady Berthe and she smiled gratefully. "No more audiences today?"

"That was the last," said Berthe, supporting her weight as Maud raised herself from her throne. "Let's walk the yard. Maybe you'll encourage your next child to hurry up and join us."

"At this point, I'm always ready to be done, but this one feels heavier than my other children," Maud said. Her black robes spread across the floor as she shuffled through the stone-arched walls to the courtyard. The summer sun beat down on their mourning robes, worn in honor of the recently departed Pope Victor. "It'll be a short walk today, Lady Berthe."

"I don't blame you," she said, raising her hand to block the glare from above. "I was just hoping to speak to you about one thing."

Maud raised her brow. "I thought I had my last audience of the day with Lanfranc."

"You and William are like family to me." She straightened her black lace veil, transparent enough to still show her hair. "And we could be a family by law, one day. We could marry Marguerite and Herbert to Robert and Emma."

Maud laughed, agape when she realized Lady Berthe was serious. "Robert is six and Emma is three. They're too young to be married."

"It's just a contract," she said with a fitful shrug. "They don't need to be married in body for many more years. Your children could still get their education before either would be expected to perform their marital duties."

"What about Marguerite? Wouldn't she spend her most fruitful years waiting for her husband to be ready to have children?"

"For the next Duke of Normandy, she'll wait." Seeming to sense Maud's unease, she added, "As a dowager countess, it's my duty to help secure Maine's future. I can't do it alone."

Maud studied Berthe carefully. "It's something to think about," she said, forcing a smile. "I'll discuss it with William when he returns from Varaville. I know how much he respects you." As Lady Berthe smiled warmly, Maud brushed her veil from her face in the heat. "That's enough sun for me. I should write to Agatha Wessex before dark."

Berthe followed her inside. "How is she coping in England with her children?"

"They're devastated. But King Edward plans to make Edgar, the new Aetheling, his heir to please the king's council. So, Agatha's grateful they're cared for."

"I know what she's going through. When my Alain was murdered, my world fell apart. My children and I were tossed to the mercy of relatives, and I felt I had no choices when allies arranged my marriage to Count Hugh of Maine. It was my lifeline; King Edward's court is hers."

Stopping at the entrance to her private chamber, Maud sighed. Bertrand stood outside the door, tucking his tunic over the bulge in his midsection. "I just pray they'll find their way. I feel such a strong connection with Agatha and want to help her and her children any way I can."

Maud retired to her chambers, her steward following close behind. Bertrand helped write her letters because he remembered how to spell more words than she did, but she never let him pen them for her. The feel of the ink gliding across the parchment was like lifeblood, dripping from the end of a trimmed peacock feather dancing across her desk.

He lit four tall white candles on the polished oak surface as night fell, and her thoughts drifted from the parchment to Lady Berthe's offer. Was she so desperate to save Maine for her son that she'd align herself with a duke through his toddler? Disturbed, her thoughts were interrupted by her amiable steward.

"It's very good of you to be a friend of Agatha Wessex in her time of grieving."

"She made an impression on me in Flanders, and I feel so deeply for her. But...I can't stop thinking about her vague prophecy. Do you think Agatha's fortune teller could have merit?"

Bertrand clucked his tongue disapprovingly. "Fortunes take advantage of people's faith and offer false prayers for events only God has a right to know... How did she word it again?"

"She said, 'A foreigner will win England's throne when fire lights the sky.'"

He considered this for a moment. Maud watched him furrow his brow in deep thought, but then he shrugged. "The prophecy could refer to the duke as much as Agatha's son and may not come to pass at all. It's too broad, just like fortune tellers are supposed to be."

She smiled. "Thank you," she said gratefully, but as she picked up her quill, a familiar rolling twinge in her abdomen suddenly seized her. Crying out, she composed herself as the cramps subsided.

Bertrand looked on helplessly. "Should I call the midwives, Duchess?"

Nodding, she took long, slow breaths as she stood. "My letters will have to wait. Delivering this baby has just become my only duty this evening."

She moved into her bedchamber as her midwives hurriedly encircled her, removing her undergarments and preparing buckets of water. She labored through her contractions as the women held her up, examining her closely to be sure of the right time for Maud to start to push.

Through the night they wet her sweat-soaked face with a damp cloth, helping deliver a healthy, ruddy-cheeked little girl just before dawn. Her cries echoed through the stone walls of the castle.

After the midwives cleaned her off and made sure her throat was clear, Maud reached out to hold her. But the pains returned, and the midwives yanked her away. "What's happening?" Maud cried, keeling over as the young midwife pulled back her robes.

"Another baby, Duchess!" said Celeste, an aging midwife with thin lines over her cheeks. They'd been together since Robert's birth six years earlier. "I wondered if you were larger or just carrying differently, but I think this one's been hiding for the last nine months."

"Twins?" In too much pain to be more than stunned, Maud worked with her contractions as the surprise in her womb made its agonizing entrance.

"It's another girl!" announced the younger midwife, but Maud's bones tensed as she noted the silence—this babe made no noise as her sister had done. Leaning exhausted against her arms, grasping towels mounted to the wooden pillars of her canopy bed, she watched the midwife stick two bony fingers into the baby's mouth. Positioning the head low, she scooped phlegmy, thick bile from her airway.

"Is she all right?" Maud was frantic, and the midwives tried to calm her with soft strokes through her matted hair.

Finally, the second girl let out a solid wail, and Maud collapsed with relief onto her soft eiderdown-stuffed mattress. Two midwives helped her pass the placenta while two more cleaned her daughters with warm cloth. Helping her into bed, the elder placed both girls in her arms. The larger one had dark hair, and the smaller one—who only made her presence known in time for delivery—was as bald as an egg. They both rested, serene and soft, and Maud leaned close to breathe them in.

After a short rest, she woke to find her babies lying in a wooden crèche at her side. Maud rarely caught the light through the windows this early, basking in the yellow glow of her daughters in dawn's light as her maids appeared with bowls of fresh water. Entering the room with an exuberant knock, loyal Bertrand smiled at the cradle. "Twins, how wonderful! They're beautiful, Duchess. And we've received a dispatch from the duke's men at Varaville to complement this most auspicious day."

"I pray there's only good news this morning." Maud sat up, spellbound by her sleeping girls.

He nodded. "Duke William's forces waited until King Henri and Geoffrey of Anjou's men were split trying to cross an estuary at low tide. The duke commanded his men to attack the half who hadn't crossed before the tide came in, sending the remaining forces into retreat. They're being driven out this morning and the duke should return to Caen in a matter of days."

As the sun rose through long windows carved in stone, Maud's eyes welled with tears at the thought of her continued good fortune. Despite Addie's prediction she would one day run out, her fifth and sixth children slept peacefully, and soon her cunning and powerful warrior husband would return.

Lady Berthe tiptoed inside the room as Bertrand left, gasping as she set eyes on the babes in Maud's arms. She buzzed with excitement. "It's two girls! They look like your husband. Have you thought about names?"

Her eyes heavy with exhaustion, Maud grinned. She had everything she ever wanted, and her mind drifted. "The little one, the surprise, made her entrance in her own way. With spirit like that, it reminds me of a story I was told of my grandmother, Constance. And for this dark-haired beauty, I like Agatha."

Berthe practically chortled. "No one in Normandy is named Agatha."

"If William can name our daughter after the woman who tried to kill him as a reminder of everything he has to live for, I can follow his sentiment. Agatha came from nothing and found the man who loved her as every woman deserves to be loved. She embodies a survivor's spirit I can only hope our daughter will be blessed with."

Berthe smiled, leaning in to stroke the baby's fine dark hair. "Agatha then. It's a beautiful name for a beautiful girl."

PART SIX

Heartbreak

Chapter Twenty-Six

February 1062 – Château de Caen in Caen, Normandy

Eyeing her reflection through a handheld obsidian mirror inside her bedchamber, Duchess Maud could spot the years in new lines on her face. She frowned, but her husband smiled down at her with pride.

"You look beautiful today, love." He leaned in to kiss her as she adjusted her veil over her auburn locks.

"I feel old," she protested, pulling at the lines above her cheeks as she accepted his affection. The new lines in his clean-shaven face gave him more dignity than ever.

"Many women fail to look as stunning as you do after they've had children, let alone eight." He offered his hand as she stood from the leather stool. Accepting her husband's compliment, she smiled, pulling her gold-and-sapphire butterfly pin from her jewel case—a striking reminder of the strength she found in those who loved her. Now a woman in her early thirties, she masked creeping insecurities of age with expensive robes, custom-made from the finest fabrics imported from Venice, embroidered with gold, and encrusted with gemstones. She awed everyone in every room she entered, imposing upon them the gravitas expected of a duchess.

The wetnurses still tried her patience. The last who voiced her opinion nursed Agatha and Constance, now precocious four-year-olds with their father's dark hair, though they shared little else in common. Brown-eyed Constance had caught up to blue-eyed Agatha in size, but her temperament was usually twice as explosive—another trait inherited from her father.

"The people need you, Duchess," the wetnurse had said. "You coddle your babes so much you might as well breastfeed them yourself." Handing newborn Agatha back to Maud after a feeding, she pulled a cotton bib over her shoulder to cover her engorged chest.

Maud seethed, her cheeks red with anger as she looked down at the bare-breasted woman in her rocking chair. "The people of Normandy aren't strangers to me any more than they are to you. You know next to nothing of what it takes to keep all the people of Normandy fed and safe in their beds at night. My husband and I need a strong, committed household to help us bring success to all of Normandy. But tell me, why are you so committed to harming the duchy with your divisive ideas?"

Her face falling ashen, the wetnurse shook her head vigorously, cowering beneath her small, but powerful, duchess. "I only believe in the benefits of a mother's milk for her own young, when she's capable, but I'm proud to help the children grow strong and healthy."

Maud spared her but never said a word to her again. When the twins were old enough to be weaned, the wetnurse was given a stipend and released from the Norman court without honor.

Walking into the brightly painted wood-paneled nursery, Maud and her husband found two-year-old William toddling across white marble floors.

The family left Rouen in the spring of 1060, packing up a caravan that stretched from one end of the city to the other. Duke William had built a new motte-and-bailey castle in Caen for his growing family, situated around a raised hill of earth between the foundations of their two cathedrals.

Expecting again at the time, Maud hated the journey. Following an elaborate welcome parade in the center of town with jugglers and dancers with painted faces, the duke and duchess ceremoniously broke ground to mark the foundations of their cathedrals. Crowds cheered as their carriage rode through Caen.

William was born in the throne room a month later, his labor too quick for Maud to reach her bedchamber. Her husband laughed recalling the story of his namesake's birth. "A third son, born in the throne room! Maybe he's destined for it."

Maud frowned at his joke. "What would become of Robert and Richard?"

"Maybe I'll have to add a third crown after we've won the throne of England."

She smiled with reluctance. "My correspondence with Agatha tells me King Edward has all but accepted Edgar as the true Wessex heir."

William shrugged.

"Nothing's final until King Edward's dead. Hey-o, Rufus." He ruffled toddler William's red mop. "He gets his ginger hair from your father." Tossing his son playfully in the air, he grinned with every satisfied giggle that left his son's lips.

She smiled as they kissed the boy they called Rufus, leaving him with his nursemaids. "May that not be all he inherits from my father."

Stopping outside the door to the nursery, William chuckled at his wife's playful indignation. "How is your father getting on as co-regent to your cousin, Philippe? I can't say I've had anything to complain about since King Henri died. Having my father-in-law act as co-regent to the new Boy King keeps the Frankish army out of Normandy."

"My mother says my father and King Philippe's advisors quarrel often over the growing power of Normandy. Without my father, I'm sure they'd have sent troops north to us already."

The wetnurse finished Matilda's feeding as Maud entered the room alone. With a polite smile she handed the babe to her duchess, but Maud paid her no attention. Beaming down at her sweet, sleepy little girl, Maud tucked Matilda against her chest, returning to her waiting husband in the stone hall. He cooed at their youngest daughter.

Countess Adela, while visiting the new castle in Caen when their eighth child was born just before winter, remarked how much she looked like Maud as a baby. Hearing this, William insisted she share her mother's name.

"I wonder why King Henri, who was so hellbent on providing assistance to anyone willing to cross me—including the Pope!—gave the regency of his son to a man whose own daughter is Duchess of Normandy."

"My father has housed his allies' enemies before," reminded Maud. "But when my mother visited for Matilda's birth, she said she thought, deep down, Uncle Henri hoped my father's loyalty to his Frankish wife would trump loyalty to his Norman daughter. After all, she still co-signs edicts issued by my father as: 'Countess Adela, sister to the King of Francia.'"

"But Henri's father sent Countess Adela away as a baby to punish your grandmother, Queen Constance." His lips curled into a smirk, and Maud gave a smug, affirming nod.

"My mother's affection for the Frankish royal court is more advantageous than familial."

"We can hope Henri's son doesn't carry any of his parents' anxiety over Normandy into adulthood. I'd be more than happy to leave our sons peaceful territories to care for when I'm gone, without the Franks breathing down their necks."

"King Philippe is still young. Have faith in him, or at least in my father for now," Maud said, and William leaned in for a kiss. Despite the years, he still set butterflies aloft in her heart with a simple gaze. "I hate to interrupt the children's lessons, but I want to say goodbye before I go."

They headed toward a room with a short wooden door. This time, her husband walked right in without knocking, making a jubilant entrance as their daughters, Emma and Cecilia, looked up from their Latin books. They cried in excitement, jumping from a wooden table in front of a black wall. Their tutor, a kind-faced monk from Cluny handpicked by Lanfranc, put down the chalk rock he used to write. As he clapped his hands, a puff of dust fell from his fingers.

"Have the girls been good students today?" asked William, scooping up a daughter in each arm.

"They're very bright young ladies," said the monk with a nod. "They're already looking forward to when Agatha and Constance will be old enough to join them, and all they'll be able to show them. You and the duchess must be very proud."

"Papa, I can write my age," Cecilia told him. "Six is v, i. And Emma's eight. That's v, i, i, i."

Maud considered their accomplishments. At their age, she didn't know what they knew, begging her parents for an education even half as comprehensive as the one she ensured for her daughters. "Very good, Ceci," she said proudly. "Soon you'll both have to help write my letters."

They beamed at the thought, nodding excitedly, and William placed them back on solid ground. "Your mother sails to England to see her Aunt Judith today. Kiss her goodbye and wish her a safe journey."

Maud handed Matilda to William so she could embrace her daughters with both arms. "Keep up your lessons while I'm gone. I can't wait to hear about all you've learned when I return."

"How long will you be in England?" asked Emma, playing with the collar of her cloak.

"Judith is about to deliver a baby, and I'll only be there long enough to help her get settled. Then I'll be back here, to all of you, in time for Easter." They smiled, returning dutifully to their chairs as their parents exited the room. Making their way to the stairs, Maud sighed. "Should I really go without the children?"

"You've been away from them this long before," William pointed out. "But you're going so far north. The journey up to Durham will be harder than the voyage by sea."

"I'm looking forward to seeing Agatha and her children when I stay with King Edward and Queen Edith in London. And I'll see Harold Godwinson's wife again when I reach Norfolk. We haven't spoken since Judith and Tostig's wedding."

"It was nice of him to offer to host you on your way, considering how he feels about me."

Maud laughed. "I'm sure Harold's doing it for his brother and sister-in-law, if not to gain favor with you in the matter of Wulf and Hakon's return to England."

"I've never wavered. I'll return them the moment King Edward orders me to."

"It's been eleven years, William. We moved them to Caen so you could keep an eye on them, but every day they just clean up after the horses. Earl Godwin died almost ten years ago. Spite is the only reason King Edward's kept them here."

"That's not our problem." He shrugged as they reached the top of the stairwell, walking out to the rampart overlooking the sloping hills south of town. They found Lanfranc staring out over their domain with Robert and Richard at his side. The monk smiled at their arrival, the boys straightening their posture in the presence of their father.

"We're just examining the beauty of God's creation, to better understand the point of everything we're learning," said Lanfranc, a hint of exasperation in his voice.

Richard was taller than Robert already, and Maud related to the way her eldest tried to stretch himself as long as he could, hoping to measure up somewhat to those around him.

William refused to make it easy on him. "Curthose, can you see over the castle walls?"

"I'm not that short, Papa." Robert frowned.

"You're shorter than Richard." William laughed. "In a few months, you'll probably be shorter than Rufus. That boy grows like a weed."

"Lots of men are taller than you!"

His father's expression turned to rage. "Don't talk to me like Richard isn't just taller, but faster, stronger, and better with a sword. You're my heir, but you've got a lot to prove if you think you're worthy of my throne."

"Enough," said Maud forcefully, eyeing her husband stiffly. "Lanfranc, have I detected by your tone that our sons aren't dutiful students like their sisters?"

He nodded, exhaustion on his face, and Maud shot a stern look at her sons. "What is it about an education that bores you? You're two of the most fortunate young men in all of Normandy, to be taught by one of the smartest men on the continent—the one man who finally convinced the Catholic Church to recognize our marriage."

William smirked. "For that, she'll build you a statue one day." Lanfranc returned a bashful grin.

Robert and Richard looked at their leather shoes, shuffling their feet nervously as Maud continued. "Your father and I push for you and your sisters to get an education. It's a privilege you should act like you deserve. What good are two legitimate sons of a duke who don't learn the beauty and mysteries of the world they'll inherit?"

A grin crept over William's clean-shaven face as an idea slid from his lips. "That's brilliant, love. Perhaps Robert and Richard need a change of scenery to enliven their pursuit of education. Lanfranc and the boys should go with you to England."

The boys' eyes widened in excitement. "The carriage is already packed and ready to leave for the harbor at Barfleur," said Maud.

"It can wait. Monks carry little and the boys need only bring some clothes. King Edward should look upon the sons who may one day challenge Edgar Aetheling for his throne."

"I'd prefer to think of Edgar as our sons' future ally."

"For now, he can enjoy the company of Robert and Richard as he did in Flanders five years ago. Harold has children their age, and the boys can help you with Judith in Durham."

"I'd like to visit some churches in England. I've long wondered how they feel knowing the head of their church, their Archbishop of Canterbury, has been excommunicated for so long. The whole continent thinks the kingdom savages because of it." Lanfranc meandered slightly, catching up to his thoughts and smiling. "I think it's an inspired idea for the boys' education."

"I suppose it won't be long before they spend most of their time on horseback at your side and I'll rarely see them." The boys celebrated her decision as she gave in with a sigh. "I agree, it's a great idea."

Chapter Twenty-Seven

February 1062 – Château de Caen in Caen, Normandy

The second carriage was loaded within the hour, and Maud stood with Lanfranc and her sons at the gates of the castle. William carried Matilda in his arms, rocking her gently as he stood with their youngest children to send them off.

"When Lady Berthe and her children return from Falaise with Addie and her new husband, promise you won't move forward with the marriage contracts. Berthe says she thinks Herbert will be ready to take back Maine soon and the contract will have to come with it, but you know I want Robert and Emma to finish their schooling first."

He laughed before straightening his stance and looking into her anxious gaze. "Maud, I would never sign a marriage contract for any of our children without you at my side."

She tried not to show her relief on her face. "I know you agreed to a marriage contract with Maine because Herbert is so popular with the people there, and I know you don't see why I mistrust the dowager countess. She's just so eager to marry her sixteen-year-old daughter and fifteen-year-old son to our eleven and eight-year-old children. She knows Herbert won't hold Maine against Geoffrey of Anjou without Normandy's backing."

"I've known Lady Berthe since I was a little boy. She's always supported Norman interests, and a marriage alliance with Maine only advances our position in the county."

Maud stood taller. "But not at the expense of our children."

"You fought hard for your education, and they'll all finish schooling before we sign any marriage alliances with their names." William looked down at their sons waiting by the carriages. "Robert and Richard may take their lessons for granted, but they know how important it is to you. I'm sure while they're away they'll do whatever is asked of them by you and Maester Lanfranc." The boys nodded dutifully.

Traveling with two of her maids and a small retinue of soldiers riding on horseback, the journey from Caen to Durham would be long and uncomfortable. Two carriages loaded with wooden crates of fresh robes would slow their journey, but she yearned to see Judith again, and looked forward to seeing more of the land over which she dreamed of being queen.

Beyond the iron-gated walls, Adelaide's caravan rolled toward the castle. Maud ordered her retinue to pull to the side to let them pass on the thin gravel road, watching out the window as soldiers on horseback and two wooden carriages moved past. From the first, Lady Berthe and her daughter waved through the window. In the next, Adelaide kept her face forward, without even stealing a glance at the woman she once called sister.

In two years, Adelaide had never visited the new castle in Caen, planning her first to coincide with the voyage Maud decided to make across the sea. A letter from Judith revealed she was expecting, and said she felt healthy. Still, she admitted she was terrified of further heartbreak, and wrote to ask Maud to be there when the midwives said she would deliver.

This time, Maud was easily convinced to go to England. After eight children, she was much more at ease knowing her absences from court weren't enough to make her children forget their own mother. She knew Judith wouldn't ask unless she was desperate for comfort, certain her drunk husband, Tostig, provided her none.

Bitterly, Maud ordered her driver to continue once they passed.

"Why does Aunt Addie dislike you, Mama?" asked Richard.

"Why do you think she doesn't like me?"

"Because she says she doesn't want to see you," explained Robert.

Maud was floored.

"She talks about me?"

"Papa always tells her to be quiet."

"So, we don't know why she doesn't like you. Papa says she *does* like you," said Richard. "But you weren't at her wedding to the Count of Champagne."

She masked a regretful frown behind her veil. "I was sorry to miss the wedding, but I was expecting your brother Rufus at the time. The midwives wouldn't let me travel."

They accepted her explanation and she smiled, though her eyes stung with tears. Lanfranc gave her a sympathetic glance, turning his attention to the passing scenery as she swallowed the lump in her throat.

"Mama, can we see King Edward's armory with Edgar?" Robert and Richard ran out to Maud, who sat in the garden at Westminster admiring the boats in the river under an overcast sky.

"Will any men be present? Where is Lanfranc?"

"He's gone with the king to view construction of the new abbey down the road. King Edward says Westminster Abbey will be the grandest church in all of England and will rival any cathedral in Normandy in size and status."

She smiled, but still didn't like the idea. "I won't have my sons around weapons they have no training to use. Not without someone present who knows what they're doing."

"I know how to use them, Duchess," said Edgar precociously, but Maud shrugged.

"Someone with decades of experience," she countered. "Someone years older than ten."

Her sons pouted, maligning the unfairness of their lives as Maud rolled her eyes gently. "If boys today can't have fun without cleavers and spears, we might be doomed." She slipped each of them a silver denier from a pouch on the belt of her blue robes. Holding out their hands, they hollered excitedly. "Take this to the market. I'll send a few men with you, and each of you can spend that coin on anything you can afford."

The value of the coin in their hands was enough to buy them practically anything for sale in a public marketplace, and she delighted in spoiling them.

"I can take them," offered a voice from over a small hill. She froze. He sounded older, but his voice rang in her head like a song. The notes had changed, but still held her. "I know the vendors well. No one will think to take advantage of the lads while I'm down there."

She forced a flustered smile toward Brictric. "I couldn't ask you to do that."

"I'd be happy to. I have no children of my own, and I'm always happy to spend time teaching Edgar to hunt at the king's court."

She shifted uncomfortably, but her sons looked to her with wide, hopeful eyes. She couldn't say no. "You've always been a careful protector of my family, Ser Brictric." She sighed. "I'm grateful for your continued service on behalf of my sons with Duke William."

The words of courtesy fell from her lips without meaning, but she trusted the safety of her sons in his care. He seemed genuinely mournful not to have been blessed with children of his own, and Maud wondered whether he ever thought about their night together. Did he lament how she was mother to so many—all of them a greater man's child?

As she looked upon him now, his chiseled jaw still strong, blond hair now flecked with silver, he was as attractive as ever. But his beauty held no sense of mystery anymore, and she could stand in his gaze without wondering if she looked her best.

The boys ran off as Maud spotted Agatha and her daughters cresting the hill to Westminster Palace. With a nod to Brictric, she thanked him again for escorting her sons.

"It's only right to honor you, Duchess Matilda." His eyes were sad, apologizing without words. She questioned his sincerity but said nothing as she placed the safety of her sons in his hands. Waving him off as he chased after the boys, she greeted her old friend from Kyiv with a smile.

"How did you and your sons sleep last night? I hope Edith put out the good pillows."

"Everything was comfortable, which is double the blessing after our rough voyage. I don't think Robert will have many fond memories of his first trip out to sea."

"It's early in the season to sail such rough waters, but everything I've heard from Durham the past few years says Judith needs you up there," Agatha said gently.

"I just hope I can do anything to help give her a different outcome. I've prayed for years, sometimes until my knees bled."

"She just needs you to hold her hand through the hard part," Agatha said. Maud knew that could mean holding Judith's hand through her grief but didn't want to give voice to it, turning her attention to Agatha's daughters. Statuesque Margaret, now strikingly beautiful at seventeen, reminded Maud of Addie at a young age. Next to her stood six-year-old Cristina, with small, angelic features and white-blonde hair like her father.

"Enough about Judith for a moment. Your children have grown so much since we saw each other last. I want to hear everything about the last five years at Edward and Edith's palace."

"I never imagined my girls could have such opportunities. Margaret spent time at Wilton Abbey, and Cristina will be sent to begin lessons with the nuns there soon. And King Edward is considering a marriage for Margaret with King Malcolm of Alba," Agatha replied proudly. "His first wife recently died, and his two sons have no mother now. We met him at court when we first arrived in London. Before he left to battle King Macbeth and win back his throne."

Maud noticed Margaret's stiff gaze. "How do you feel about that?" she asked.

"I-I don't," she stammered, looking down at her shoes.

"She doesn't love him," Cristina said matter-of-factly. "She loves Ser Brictric."

Mortified, Margaret shoved her sister into a healthy bush of pink hydrangeas, racing down a leafy path of young oaks. "Margaret!" Agatha called desperately. Maud stepped forward.

"If you'll allow me, Agatha, I'd be happy to talk to your daughter about the potential of a marriage alliance with the Scots, but I really would prefer to speak with her alone."

"I've run out of ways to reach out to her." She sighed with a helpless shrug as she pulled Cristina from the bushes. "Please."

With Agatha's blessing Maud marched by the oaks, finally catching up to Margaret when she found her sitting on a rock by the riverbank. Sliding over to make room, the young woman dabbed her tear-stained eyes with the cloth of her navy dress.

Maud took a deep breath as she sat. "Believe it or not, I know exactly what it's like to be head over heels in love with Brictric. I assure you there are better men."

Her lip wavered. "He says he can't leave Goda now, or she'd be an old maid without him."

Letting Margaret rest her head on her shoulder, Maud asked her next question carefully. "Has Brictric ever taken you to his bed?"

Margaret nodded, her tears staining Maud's robes. "He says once

I'm married, I'll realize I'm bound to lead a household far greater than any he could give me."

Maud simmered as an old, familiar loathing returned to the surface. Fifteen years later, Brictric's script remained unchanged. "Margaret, you're a good and beautiful young woman. You have wonderful parents who loved each other deeply, and it makes perfect sense you'd want to marry for love just like them."

"How can anyone marry for anything other than love? I'll never know how King Edward and Queen Edith can stand being miserable with each other every single day."

"Some marriages are better as business deals than love matches," Maud admitted. "I met Malcolm, back when he was younger than you, and he seemed polite, respectable, and charming. You don't have to give yourself in marriage to him, but you must end things with Brictric, and recommit yourself to God before the court learns of these indiscretions."

"I don't even know King Malcolm. We've only met once. We'd just arrived, and I was only twelve. He was seventeen and already engaged. Apart from his bright-red hair I barely remember him."

"Maybe before you dismiss him outright, you should meet again to see if there's still no spark," Maud suggested coolly. "King Malcolm is a good friend of my aunt, Judith, and I believe him to be a good man too. He's been an ally to King Edward and uniting with a wife of Wessex blood could be a sign of great peace between the north and south."

Margaret chuckled. "My mother doesn't think Edgar will have the throne, but she's not worried for him, because her fortune teller said all her children would live well into adulthood. She said there would be lots of grandchildren."

"Her prophecy told of a foreign king winning the crown when fire lights the sky. It could refer to anyone—why not your brother?"

"The prophecy speaks of winning the Crown. Edgar would succeed by law, and the king's council doesn't vote for a successor—they select him after discussion reaches consensus. My mother thinks he can't win a crown that's already been promised to him, but she's not thinking about someone stealing the Crown from him. He still might have to win it, in the end. If not from Harold Godwinson, perhaps your husband."

Maud masked a smile so she wouldn't give herself away, but she was impressed by Margaret's shrewd intelligence. "Do you believe your mother's fortune teller?"

"I believe some people have a closer connection to God than others. I know the Bible warns against those peddling lies to the vulnerable, but my mother would never lie. If she believes something she was told, her conviction is not misplaced."

With a sigh, Maud returned to the subject of the young girl's misplaced affections. "Brictric doesn't love as good men love, Margaret. His wife is his obligation, and you're not the first, or last woman, who'll help him betray her. You deserve a man who truly appreciates you." Margaret frowned, fiddling wordlessly with her yellow braid. "Trust me," said Maud. "Love can grow from unexpected places. I can't tell you to fall in love with King Malcolm, but any fortune teller in the world would agree Brictric's not the man for you."

Chapter Twenty-Eight

February 1062 – The Palace of Westminster in London, England

On Maud and her sons' last night in London, Harold Godwinson joined a farewell feast in their honor. The next day, he would escort them north to his home at Walsingham Manor in Norfolk, the traditional estate of the wealthy and powerful Earl of Wessex. But tonight, there was merriment to be had. Lanfranc also attended the celebrations, and Maud let the boys stay up late to sip their first mug of mead. She laughed as they grimaced, switching the mugs for cups of cider.

"You've been busy in London." She looked down at them proudly. "We'll have to spend twice as long with your Latin lessons to make up for all the time spent running around the market or hunting in the hills with Edgar and King Edward. For now, it's off to bed."

They groaned at the prospect of more schoolwork as Lanfranc laughed, soon excusing himself with ruddy cheeks from his own mug or two of strong mead. Across the grand hall decorated with long, floral tapestries, Maud watched Brictric eye Margaret with a wanton stare, but Margaret ignored him. His gaze rose to Maud, and he glared in her direction.

Sidling up to her, Agatha grinned wildly. "I don't know what you said to my daughter, but she's agreed to meet King Malcolm and discuss the possibility of a marriage alliance. Just like that, she said she'd give love a chance with him."

Maud turned her face to mask a prideful smile. "I just told her she has the chance to get to know someone who could give her the life she wants, even if he was never part of her original dream. In my own experience, it's a leap of faith worth taking."

"Your story with William is romantic in its way," Agatha said. "He pulled you from a horse when you tried to steal it, but he loves you as much today as he did the day you were married under the stars. Your beautiful children will be your legacy, and he lives and breathes for you."

She nodded gratefully. "I know how it sounds to say he showed me compassion in my lowest moment, considering I ended up in the dirt with a split lip. But I was goading him. I was so angry at things and people I couldn't control, and he was there, trying to get me to calm down."

"I don't blame you, yelling at him for that." Agatha chuckled softly, clinking her chalice against Maud's. "To friendship."

"To friendship. And to Margaret finding something to love in King Malcolm that makes her forget she ever loved a womanizing Saxon thegn."

"I'll drink to that," said Agatha, laughing as fermented honey mead flowed from their brass cups, stinging their throats as they celebrated.

The road to Norfolk was bumpy, with weeds growing along the side of the dirt road. Passing through green villages and sallow fields waiting for spring planting, Maud admired the landscape in the late-afternoon sun. Children younger than Robert and Richard joined their parents in the fields, and Lanfranc raised a long finger to point them out.

"Children with nothing left to learn from a book pivot to learning from the seeds," he said. Robert and Richard stared as boys their age gazed back at the passing caravan.

"It's not long now to Walsingham Manor," said Harold, riding alongside their wooden carriage on a tall brown steed. A dozen men flanked them on all sides, escorting them through rural England with the king's red-and-white banners waving through the air.

"I've heard the grounds are beautiful," said Maud, smiling in his direction.

He nodded proudly. "We have over ten thousand cows to keep the grounds manicured for most of the year, and an army of serfs to work the fields that pay for the livestock."

She pretended the number impressed her, but the Duchy of Normandy managed close to ten thousand cows just outside the city of Caen. "England is a remarkably beautiful country," she said. "It's clear her stewards care about her very much."

"England does have a way about her," he said, accepting her compliment with a smile. "During my year in exile in Ireland, I missed Norfolk terribly. I spent my entire childhood out here, before I was old enough to join my father on campaigns. My brothers and I would go up to the salt marshes and try to catch birds. Tostig always wanted to catch one with his bare hands."

Maud laughed. "And did he?"

Harold shook his head. "He almost nabbed a gull once, but the bird squawked and flapped her wings knowing her life depended on it. The bird flew away and Tostig fell to the mud wailing with his hand over his eye. The gull pecked his face to free herself and almost took his eye out. The scar on his cheek, under his left eye? The bird won."

Maud cackled at the expense of a man whose history suggested she was right to think him such a fool, but she quickly contained her laughter to avoid appearing too insulting.

"Can we go to the salt marshes while we're here?" asked Richard with a hopeful glance toward his mother.

"It's cold up there this time of year," said Harold. "Still plenty of birds, though."

"We won't be staying long," Maud reminded them. "We must get to Durham in time to be there for Aunt Judith. Besides, you'll have plenty of lessons with Lanfranc while we're in Walsingham, and we might not find the time."

"Please!" they begged, but she shook her head as they pushed her.

"We'll see," she said finally. "If you're good students and good guests to Harold and his wife, we may be able to find the time."

The boys grinned at one another, and Maud smiled as her gaze returned to the rolling countryside beyond the window. The sun was nearly set when they arrived at Walsingham Manor, an imposing wood-and-stone manse. Gasping, she took in the forested landscape, and the small village of wood-and-mud huts sitting off the main road into the yard.

"It reminds me of my father's estate in Lille," she mused. "We spent every summer there, but the home was sacked and burned near the end of my father's old war with the Holy Roman Empire."

"My father remembered it well. He said Count Baudouin and

Countess Adela took my parents and brothers there during our exile, and it was the most peaceful two months of his entire adult life. When King Edward welcomed us back, he set right to fortifying Walsingham and took several design ideas from Lille."

She smiled warmly. "It already feels as though I'll be quite comfortable here."

Harold's family exited the door at the front of the manor, framed by a stone architrave carved in the same Celtic pattern that adorned Lady Emma's old desk. "We're pleased to have you. You've kept my brother and nephew safe in Normandy even though the king has no reason to keep them away this long," he grumbled, smiling when his youngest children raced to wrap their arms around his legs. "You remember my wife, Edie Swanneck?"

She sidled up to her husband with a warm embrace. Edie had grown older in the years since Judith's wedding, but her lines and wrinkles added refinement to her sharp features. Around her neck she wore an elaborate golden necklace with interlocking rings that hung to her waist. As she walked, the rings jingled softly, like chimes in the wind. "Of course. It's lovely to see you again, Edie."

"Duchess Matilda, it's wonderful of you to join us." Lined up beside the lord and lady of the manor stood Gytha, Earl Godwin's widow and Harold's mother as the Dowager Countess of Wessex. She was small but commanding of presence, and Maud bowed her head respectfully.

"It's been too long since Tostig and Judith's wedding," Gytha said. "Hard to believe your dashing son, Robert, was barely a newborn the last time you were here."

She stepped forward, cupping Richard's chin in her hands because he was the taller of the two boys. Robert's face fell, and Maud rushed to spare him further embarrassment. "I should formally introduce them. This is Robert. He's eleven." She placed a protective arm around her eldest son, who stood as tall as he could to greet their hosts. "And this is Richard, who was born only a year after his brother. I had no time to rest between the two of them! And their tutor, Lanfranc, is with us. He's a great scholar from the abbey in Bec, and he's become somewhat indispensable to my husband and me."

Smiling apologetically, Gytha greeted Robert with the same warm touch she'd offered Richard. "We're pleased to have you all here."

"Ulf has been marking the days to your arrival on a rock in the gardens," said Edie as her ten-year-old son approached. "He's been so excited to have boys his own age around, with his older brothers usually off with their father throughout the kingdom."

All their sons looked like they were here today. Puffing out his chest, Harold introduced his five sons and two daughters. The first four boys were well into their teens, all strapping young men just like their father. Ulf was scrawny like his younger sisters, looking to his older brothers with childlike awe.

"The duchess' boys were just saying how much they'd like to head out to the salt marshes while they're here," Harold told Edie, a wide smile growing across the woman's face.

"I haven't been there in ages." She raised her brow and shared an insoluble laugh with her husband before returning her attention to their guests. "We could all make a day of it."

Her sons gleefully grabbed the sleeves of Maud's robes. "I've told Robert and Richard they must focus on their schooling while we travel, but if they do well, I've said we might be able to go. How would Ulf feel about the possibility of joining the boys for lessons with Lanfranc? He's a very inclusive tutor, and Ulf need not feel out of place."

Edie smiled down at her young son, who nodded excitedly. "I think Ulf would be quite happy to spend time with your sons and their eminent tutor."

Lanfranc bowed gratefully to their hosts, looking down the road to the small church at the edge of the circle of village huts. "I'd be grateful for an introduction to your priest," he said, and Harold nodded. "I must admit I've never been to England before, and as a lifelong scholar myself, I want to learn everything I can."

"Of course, Lanfranc. Our stewards will arrange an introduction for you tomorrow morning," said Harold, unleashing the harness from his horse. "Tonight, everyone can settle in, then we'll eat!"

No sooner had he spoken of food did their stomachs growl, but a soldier clad in a red-and-white tunic sped up on horseback.

"What does King Edward need now?"

Edie chuckled, gently pushing her husband. "He's old, Harold. He needs you."

The soldier jumped down from his horse. "The king is too ill to travel and asked you to attend the funeral pyre for Burgheard of Mercia in his place. The pyre is in two nights, in Repton."

Harold looked apologetically to his wife, who nodded dutifully before he turned to his guests. "Attending the funeral for the son and heir of the Earl of Mercia is vital to English unity," he said, bowing to Maud and her retinue. "My elder sons and I must leave at once, but you're welcome to stay until you're ready to continue north."

The Earl of Wessex and his four eldest sons hastened to prepare their horses. Edie and Gytha kissed the men goodbye before escorting the women and children inside. Lanfranc tailed behind as the forested hills turned black with the sunset.

Inside, their servants lit candles to brighten the long dining hall. Ulf stared longingly out the window as horses' hooves pounding in the dirt faded into the distance. Edie watched them leave with a winsome glance before steeling herself, sending word to the kitchens for a meal.

Robert, smaller than Ulf as well as Richard, looked solemnly to his mother. "Am I too short?"

Maud scoffed and shook her head vigorously. "No, Robert, you're exactly as tall as you're supposed to be until you grow again."

"What if I'm never tall enough to please Papa?"

She sighed, placing her hands on his small shoulders. "You'll please your father by showing him the duchy will be in your capable hands some day, no matter how tall you are."

He accepted this, and the smell of fish in garlic wafted into the hall. Servants carried brass plates with thick salmon drowning in butter sauce, placing them in the center of the long table. They sat, using knives to cut pieces of fish and place them on their trenchers before Edie clasped her hands. "Who should say grace this time? Gunhilda?"

The eldest of Harold and Edie's two daughters nodded, curls bouncing as she closed her eyes and raised her hands. She was unable to get out a word before they heard horses in the distance, pulling a carriage at a blistering speed. The sound grew louder, carrying up the dirt road to Walsingham.

"Is Da back already?" wondered Gunhilda with big, inquisitive eyes.

"Your father and brothers didn't leave with the carriage." Shaking her head, Edie stood to look out the window. At once they all heard a woman's agonizing scream—guttural and low.

"Help me!" cried the voice, which Maud recognized through the open windows. She stood, joining Edie as they stared into the night.

"I know that voice," she said urgently. "It's Judith."

Chapter Twenty-Nine

February 1062 – Walsingham Manor in Norfolk, England

Behind the reins, Tostig called frantically as Edie and Maud raced outside with their ladies-in-waiting. "Help us!" he shouted, taking directions from one of the midwives knelt over Judith in the back of the carriage. "We need blankets and warm water."

Edie sent her servants to fetch the items as Maud crawled up to the carriage bed. "You're here," said Judith through a fog of sweat and exhaustion, grimacing as her muscles contracted. "I was worried we wouldn't make it before the baby."

"What are you doing here at all? We were going to head north."

"I woke up a few days ago and I had the worst premonition you wouldn't make it there."

Tostig grumbled, the smell of ale wafting from his pores. "I tried to tell her we should stay put for the baby's sake, but she sat in the carriage and pouted until I harnessed the horses and drove. Had to bring the midwives, but everything was fine until about ten minutes back on the road. The midwives started screaming, 'The baby's coming now!'"

"Let's get Judith to a bed," suggested Edie, but the midwives shook their heads.

"We can't move her now, Lady Walsingham," said one. "The baby crowns."

Judith screamed again, the sharp, body-splitting pains of childbirth shooting through her as the midwives encouraged her to breathe. Passing a damp cloth to Maud, one said, "Keep her cool with this while she labors."

Maud obliged, dabbing at Judith's drenched forehead. Judith screamed as her body pushed out the child, her golden hair spilled between wood slats at the base of the carriage bed.

The midwives muttered quietly to each other, their faces grave, when Judith passed the head and shoulders. Leaning forward, Maud noticed the child, which should have been pink, was purplish-blue. The cord was tightly wrapped around the child's neck, and the eldest midwife begged Tostig for a knife.

Leaning into his boot, he removed a dagger, passing it gingerly to the midwife as he noticed the color of the child with fear in his eyes. With one final push, the child was born. A boy, with ten fingers and ten toes, a thick head of hair and blond eyelashes. He was beautiful, and Judith leaned back, exhausted. "Why isn't he crying?" The midwife cut the cord and released the boy from its grasp. Sticking two fingers in his mouth to clear his airway, she patted gently on his chest. Judith wailed, "He should be crying!"

Their efforts were met with no success, and the midwives' chests sunk heavily as they looked upon the sweet angel in their arms. "He's stillborn, my lady," said the eldest one.

The devastated howl elicited from Judith's weakened body reminded Maud of the day Addie lost Count Lambert. She wrapped her arms around her, holding tight while she grieved for the loss of yet another child. Maud ached to take her pain away, but she could only sit helpless in the boot of a stained wooden cart, caressing Judith's forehead while she sobbed.

Edie had her servants prepare a sedative drink of ale and valerian root, which allowed Judith to sleep for two nights straight following her traumatic and exhausting ordeal. Maud stayed in the bed by her side while she rested, keeping vigil while Lanfranc watched over her sons.

The first night, Judith lay like a log from the effects of the root, but Maud's mind raced and she couldn't sleep. Spotting a fiery light at the end of the dark hallway, she found Edie alone in her dining hall, drinking a goblet of ale with glassy eyes. She still wore all her jewels, including her gold ring necklace, which clinked against the wooden table when she moved.

"Can't sleep?" Her cheeks wet with tears, Edie turned with a start when she knew Maud was there. She motioned to a chair, and Maud sat down as Edie called for a servant to bring another drink. He went quickly, and Maud filled the heavy silence. "That's a beautiful necklace."

"It was a wedding present from Harold." Her eyes darkened. "It's too heavy. Feels like a noose."

"Where is Tostig?"

Edie shrugged. "Drunk. Out." Evidently, Edie was on her way to a similar state, swaying slightly when she put down her empty goblet. "Do you ever feel guilty for having so many healthy children?" She stammered only slightly over her words, sitting up as she fought to retain the presence of a lady. "I only lost one baby, very early on before it could have survived on its own, just between Gunhilda and Little Gytha. I feel guilty for my great fortune every time someone I care for is faced with great loss, but Judith is another beast entirely. The Devil entertains himself in her misery."

With a sigh, Maud nodded. "I try to trust in God and His decisions, but I've often wondered why He spares some of us from tragedy more than others."

Edie groaned as her servant brought two full goblets. "He can only protect us from so much. Man is led by two sides, and in this world, God is no more powerful than the Devil."

"But God is the Almighty because we *want* to follow him."

Edie frowned. "I'm a Christian woman," she said assuredly. "I wasn't raised that way, but after my marriage to Harold I was called by God. I converted my husband and his mother to His word, but in my journey through this faith I've seen the powers of God and the Devil work against one another. I've seen men kill for nothing but a sickly old goat, but the Virgin Mary has three times come to me to warn of heartbreak."

Maud sipped her goblet of ale. "How so, Lady Walsingham?"

"The first was before the miscarriage of my child. The second before my husband told me he'll take a second wife. We were married years ago, in the handfast tradition, but now he wants a second wife in the Catholic Church."

"A second wife? What for?"

"For legitimacy. He supports Edgar Aetheling as king, but only if King Edward lives long enough for Edgar to mature. If Edgar needs a regent, he wants to show the council he has the appropriate qualifications for selection." Edie stared at Maud. "I know you and your husband have made clear your desires for the English throne, but Harold thinks Edgar is the only heir with a shot at selection by the council. Anything else would likely mean war."

"The best transition for England after King Edward's death would be a peaceful one," she said. "My husband and I both agree with that."

Edie shrugged. "It shouldn't interest me at all who becomes the next king. Once Harold finds a connected Christian wife, I'll never be his Lady Regent. All I'll keep is Walsingham Manor."

Maud frowned. "Edie, I'm sorry." They clinked their goblets together in a pitiful mood. "You said the Virgin Mary visited you to warn of heartbreak three separate times. What was the third?"

Edie circled the rim of her goblet with her finger. "Just after Judith announced she was with child again. But the warning was vague, and I wasn't certain it was about her. She was doing so well when I saw her over Christmas."

Maud sipped. "I wonder why she comes to warn you of vague heartbreak. It seems so tragic. You can't do anything to stop anyone's pain."

"She's the mother of God's only son. I imagine she knows the greatest loss a woman could know and seeks to comfort them."

Finishing her goblet of ale, Maud considered this thoughtfully.

With sunlight peeking through the windows on the second morning, Robert and Richard entered Judith's room. Each planted a kiss on one cheek and Maud wrapped her arms around them warmly. "What does Maester Lanfranc have planned for you today?"

"He says he's going to take us to the church to meet the priest, and then he said he would continue with the New Testament," said Robert, trying to look enthusiastic for her sake.

"At least Ulf will be there," said Richard. "He's lots of fun, Mama!"

Behind them, Judith finally began to stir, and Maud sent her boys from the room with one last embrace. "Go. Give Aunt Judith her privacy."

Maud sat on the bed as Judith awakened. She blinked as her eyes adjusted to the sunlight, pulling the fur blankets around her head.

"Have you been here the whole time?" She smiled when Maud nodded. "Remember when we were children? Always up late reading... We never wanted to fall asleep." Judith groaned. "Now I loathe the days and hate the thought of being awake."

"You can come back to Normandy with us when your strength returns," she offered, but Judith shook her head. "I can't leave Tostig. He'll die without me."

"Your husband finally returned this morning and passed out in the barn," Maud reported brusquely. "He left after you were put to bed and stayed out drinking for a day and a half."

"He does try, Maud," Judith protested. "Last year, he tried to quit drinking after his pilgrimage to Rome, but it made him ill. He couldn't do his duty as earl, and we couldn't live that way either."

Maud forced a smile. "I'm sorry. The last thing I want is to upset you. When he's awake we'll get him cleaned up and he can visit you."

Gingerly, Judith sat up in bed. "I know you wanted better for me, Maud, but I need you to want more for me in the life I've chosen."

She forced back a tear as it fell from her eye. "I do, Judith."

"Do better."

When Judith was feeling well enough to leave her bed, Maud took her to the garden where her son's body had been buried under the branches of a mighty oak. She prayed, tears streaking down her cheeks, and she kissed the freshly disturbed soil that covered him.

"Both Lanfranc and the priest from Walsingham Priory blessed him before the burial," said Maud. Judith nodded graciously, but her eyes were sullen and lost, the words of little comfort.

When Lanfranc reported the boys were dutiful students in the wake of Judith's loss, Richard again mentioned the salt marshes. Maud tried to object, but Judith insisted they should go. "I'll have to leave the cocoon of Walsingham Manor sooner than later, and I'd hate to be the reason the children miss out on a chance to ruin their clothing with salt stains!"

Maud smiled to see Judith laugh again, if only for a moment. Tostig, as drunk and bitter as ever, grumbled into his canteens of ale. He stayed in the village tavern when the women and children left the manor in late morning. On the shore, Judith and Maud parked themselves on a spot of dry grass, watching Edie, Gytha, and the children race the tides rolling in and out from the northern sea. After a few minutes, their robes were already caked in wet mud. "I just remembered that day by the river in Lille."

Judith grinned. "When Robby almost drowned. Oh, Addie was so angry that day!"

"Who'd have thought she'd be even angrier at me eventually?" Maud let out a wistful sigh.

"She's angry at God. She can't forgive you until she forgives herself."

Maud ran her hand through a dry patch of sand. "Did she tell you that?"

She shook her head. "Addie's letters always read the same. She's lonely. Even though she's remarried, the Count of Champagne was a business deal. Lady Berthe was as anxious to wed her nephew to Addie as she is to wed your children to Herbert and Marguerite."

Maud frowned, choosing her words carefully. "I wish you'd reconsider coming to Normandy. Maybe Addie would come back to court for the sake of her own company, if you were there."

"No. The life I chose is my penance." Maud scoffed, but Judith continued insistently. "When we moved to Durham, I was told women weren't allowed in the Cathedral of St. Cuthbert, because Cuthbert himself declared no women should enter when it was consecrated. But Cuthbert's been dead four hundred years, and I was the new Countess of all Northumbria." Her voice dripped with self-loathing. "I thought the church should receive my gifts personally. Everyone said terrible things befell women who dared enter, so like a coward I sent my maid, Nora. I watched and waited. She walked out ten minutes later with a smile on her face, but the moment the door to the church shut behind her, she bent over with violent convulsions. I shouted for help, but it was too late. Nora was innocent and she died in my arms."

"It's not your fault," Maud insisted, but her words felt hollow. All she could offer that meant anything to Judith was her shoulder.

"I sent Nora to her family in a box, like our family sent the soldier who jumped in front of a horse for us when we were children. I was selfish and wicked, and my heartbreak is God's will."

Chapter Thirty

March 1062 – Walsingham Manor in Norfolk, England

The morning of their departure was sunny and warm. The entire manor lingered outside to see them off—even Tostig managed to rouse himself for their goodbye.

She felt uneasy leaving Judith behind to suffer in England's north, but she gave her no choice, and Maud grudgingly respected her wishes.

Bowing graciously to Edie and Gytha, Maud thanked them once again for their hospitality before her sons politely followed suit. Ulf pouted, anxiously grasping his mother's cloak as he waved goodbye to his new friends.

In a long embrace, Maud feared what might happen to Judith when she let go. "I hope we'll see each other again soon," she said, holding a tear back from falling when she pulled away.

Judith nodded, steadfast. "We will. Until then, I'll write to you from Lady Emma's desk. She asked King Edward to give it to me before she died, and he kept it while we were in exile."

"She'd be happy to know it's in such good hands."

"Queen Emma loved that desk," added Gytha. "I think it was a gift from a lover, but of course she never said."

Maud's jaw dropped, and she thought back to Emma's story of her walk across hot ploughshares. "She did say once it was a gift from her first friend in England," she explained, and the noblewomen snickered out of earshot of Lanfranc and the children.

An uneventful ride south preceded another rough voyage home. Robert again spent most of the trip hurling his breakfast over the sides of the boat. "I doubt you'll be a sailor, my boy!" chuckled Lanfranc, but Robert eyed him defiantly.

"I'm just not used to it," he protested as Richard stood by, watching his brother silently.

Maud ran a comforting hand over his sweat-soaked brow. "You

will get used to it, my son. It takes time for some to get their sea legs."

When the boat pulled into the harbor at Barfleur, Fitz stood waiting with a fleet of two dozen soldiers on horseback to escort them. The procession moved slowly through towns and villages. People emerged from their homes to wave at the decorative gold-painted carriage with a dragon-winged leopard carved on the door—a nod to her Wessex origins mixed with the traditional Norman crest. Robert and Richard waved excitedly, making faces at the laughing crowds. Though she scolded them, Maud couldn't help but smile.

They were all weary from travel by the time their escort pulled into the gated walls at Château de Caen. Maud was desperate for a lavender bath to remove the soil of the road, but none of their household met them outside when they arrived.

The yard was too quiet. A scant number of soldiers stood watch over the valleys from the ramparts, and the usual bustle of servants and cooks was nonexistent in the empty courtyard.

Taking her driver's hand to step down from the carriage, Bertrand raced out to her. Stopping breathlessly at her feet, he heaved himself upward with an ominous gaze. "It's very bad, Duchess." He looked nervously at the boys. "Your sons should stay outside."

Frowning, Maud turned to Lanfranc. "Will you stay with them?" He nodded, and she followed her steward cautiously. "Are the duke and our children well?" Her voice shook in fear of his answer.

"They are, Duchess." She exhaled heavily, but his face was pale and weary.

"How do you look less rested than I, Bertrand?" She climbed the stairs two at a time to keep up with her portly aide as the sound of mournful wails began to waft through the stone halls. "Who is that?"

He stumbled over his words as he missed a step, righting himself to look upon his mistress gravely. "It's Lady Berthe, Duchess."

Her eyes widened as she quickened her pace, entering the hall where Lady Berthe and her children had rooms inside the tower. No longer muffled by the heavy bricks of limestone fortifying the castle, Berthe's cries pierced the walls. "My babies! My beautiful babies!"

William spotted his wife and rushed to embrace her. "My love, you're home safe." Relief punctured exhaustion in his voice. "When we received your letter about Judith I—"

She didn't want to talk about Judith, forcing back a tear as she focused on Berthe's torrent of devastated wails. "Why is Lady Berthe screaming? Did something happen to her children?"

"You did this, William. You bastard!"

With Berthe's accusation Maud pushed past her husband, finding her sobbing on the floor. Lying naked on her daughter's bed, embracing intimately, Marguerite and Herbert lay still. Staring at the tragic tableau before her, Maud watched the monks examine their cinched corpses.

"How did they die?"

"Your husband did this," Berthe spat from the floor. "He grew tired of waiting for my son to be ready to take back Maine from Geoffrey of Anjou and wanted an excuse to go get it for himself."

William marched angrily into the room, followed closely by Fitz, Beau, and Monty. "You lie, Lady Berthe!" he shouted. "If that's what I wanted to do, I could have done this years ago. And I never would have added insult to injury by leaving your two children in bed like lovers."

Lady Berthe sobbed, and Maud pressed her hand against William's chest to calm him. Slowly, she knelt to embrace her. Lady Berthe cried into Maud's dirty robes before pushing away from her grasp in disgust.

"You never wanted an alliance. He just wants Maine and poisoned my children for it."

Offended, Maud stood with exasperation in her voice. "After all Normandy has done to support you and your children, Lady Berthe. We loved Marguerite and Herbert as extended family, and we've done what we could to give all of you a good life since you lost Maine to the Angevins."

"Your Grace," said one of the white-bearded monks. He looked pitifully to Lady Berthe as she clutched the stone tiles in agony. "They died of poison. My guess is wolfsbane."

He held up an empty vial, passing it to Duke William. The acrid stench of the liquid that once filled the small glass bottle floated on the air like an unpleasant wind.

"If they were murdered, who would leave the vial behind?" wondered Maud.

The monk gave a nervous shrug, conscious that Lady Berthe's eyes were staring daggers in his direction. "They may have obtained it themselves. Whoever did it seems to have known if they took a small amount and went to sleep, they'd avoid the more nauseating effects of the poison."

"How dare you!" Lady Berthe lunged angrily at the monk, leaping from the ground and running into William's powerful grasp. Fitz and Monty entered the fray, subduing her raving spirit as the duke wrested himself free.

Maud approached as Marguerite's vacant eyes stared back at her from the bed. A beautiful young woman, with her life snuffed out by poison. Her fifteen-year-old brother lay asleep with his arm around her and a peaceful grin on his face. "Lady Berthe, I know this is devastating."

"Don't touch me," she spat, collapsing against the soldiers who held her arms at her sides.

"Get everyone out of here and burn the sheets," ordered William. "Lady Berthe, despite your insolence you've been a close friend, so the bodies will be released to you to honor as you please. I'll arrange an escort to your son's court in Brittany immediately."

Maud wavered. "So soon? William, she just lost her children."

Steely-eyed, Berthe spoke. "I'll go, but my son, Conan, will avenge the deaths of Herbert and Marguerite. Take Maine from Geoffrey of Anjou. We'll have it back by fire and blood if need be."

William stifled a laugh. "Neither Duke Conan of Brittany nor Count Geoffrey of Anjou will be able to take me, Lady Berthe. I don't think you've ever seen them in battle."

"Stop it, William," Maud scolded as Lady Berthe seethed.

"Pack her things," William barked. "The dowager countess leaves tonight."

He stalked out of the room, and with one last, sad look at Lady Berthe, Maud followed her husband. His body vibrated with anger as he grunted with frustration.

"The nerve," he groused. "Her deviant leeches end their own lives and she's shouting murder."

"She's in shock," Maud said. "She'll go to Brittany, realize her son's army is no match for yours, and retire to a fortress by the sea."

Leaning in for a kiss, he wrapped his strong hands around her waist.

"I suppose the upside is Maine should be an easy county to win on my own. Herbert was no warrior."

Maud nodded. "His heart was soft."

"I wonder where they could have obtained the wolfsbane. It's illegal to sell at the apothecaries."

Maud thought back to two months earlier, when Marguerite confronted her, alone, about Lady Berthe's plans for her future.

"Your son is a nice boy, Duchess, but I don't love him," Marguerite said.

All too familiar with her feelings, Maud was sympathetic. "Do you know love, Marguerite?"

She nodded eagerly. "Herbert is the man I love. I know it's wrong, but he loves me so tenderly, Duchess. If I marry Robert I'll have to stay in Normandy, with Herbert in Maine. Mother is so eager for the alliance she won't listen, but we'd rather die than live apart. Please, Duchess."

"I'll speak with your mother," she offered, but Marguerite wailed with desperation.

"She won't understand! If we run away, she'll come after us. Please help us. I'd never be able to ask at the apothecaries, but no one would dare deny a discreet request from their duchess."

Maud looked at Marguerite now, her expression stiff as stewards carried her from the room wrapped in a blanket. Disgusted though she was, Maud trusted the depths of love the young girl had for her own brother if she would poison herself rather than live a life she had no interest in. A sense of relief, for the sake of her own children, washed over her.

Perhaps their years as prisoners to Geoffrey of Anjou, without their mother, doomed Herbert and Marguerite to an inevitable conclusion, or maybe they were broken some other way. Whatever it was, Maud abhorred the thought of their tormented hearts affecting her children.

Lady Berthe's wails cast a haunted echo off the stone walls, and Maud was reminded of Lady Emma's warnings of sacrifice years earlier. So consumed with protecting her family's claims over Maine, Lady Berthe pushed her children to ruin.

"With the right motivation, perhaps they figured out where to look," Maud said, comforting her husband with an embrace.

PART SEVEN

The Unknown

Chapter Thirty-One

December 1064 – Château de Caen in Caen, Normandy

Robert's aim was improving. Watching her sons practice archery in the yard with their father and Fitz, Maud cradled her petite bump, visible under her green-and-gold robes.

"Well done, Robert. You're almost as good as Richard." She sighed. Nothing prevented William from comparing his firstborn son and heir to his second. "Normandy's future counts on you becoming just as good, or better, than your brother, my boy."

"Duchess, there's a new dispatch from Ponthieu."

Moving away from the window, Maud smiled at her new lady-in-waiting. Gundred followed as she left her chambers, meeting her worried steward in the hall with an unrolled parchment in his hand. "Harold Godwinson and his men were shipwrecked off the coast of Ponthieu," said Bertrand. "Count Guy imprisoned the survivors at his castle in Beaurain—including Harold, who told the count they were headed to Normandy before the wreck."

She scanned the letter. "Does my husband know about this?"

Bertrand shook his head. "Apparently Count Guy has been holding Harold and his men for months, but the dispatch just came in and I didn't want to disturb his lesson with the boys."

Carrying the letter in one hand, she picked up the hem of her robes and strode down the spiral stairs of their chateau. As she entered the yard, William smiled. Ordering the boys to put down their bows, he greeted his wife with a soft kiss before she relayed the dispatch in her hands. "Fitz and I will leave at once for Ponthieu," he said angrily, nostrils flaring. "Where the hell are Wulf and Hakon? Fucking headaches."

Maud looked apologetically at her sons. "No more archery today, boys. Go find your uncle. Tell him your father and I are to go to Ponthieu, and he'll be in charge while we're gone."

"But the baby," said Gundred quietly from behind.

"It's many months until this one comes," she said. "You'll come with me, and I'll bring Celeste."

William shook his head. "You shouldn't come, love. Guy of Ponthieu is a bigger jackass than his brother was. He doesn't even have a wife to entertain you."

"Any change of scenery will entertain me. Besides, I haven't seen Guy of Ponthieu since you arrested him when he rebelled with King Henri. Perhaps if I'm with you, he'll behave."

William searched her gaze, pulling her away from the others. "I can handle Guy of Ponthieu and his tricks. Why do you really wish to come?"

She sighed, her voice shaking. "Our children are learning most days, and I'm left with no one to talk to when you're off battling Duke Conan in the west. Addie still won't speak to me, and Lady Berthe has decided we're her mortal enemies."

"You still have Judith," he suggested warmly, but she frowned. She'd kept her own poisonous secret so long, she felt as though no one knew her now—even Judith.

"She's so far away. Her letters take so long to arrive... Gundred is very sweet. I'm fond of her and she's a bright, gentle soul, but she's thirteen. Emma is nearly the same age." She tried not to sound unkind. "When the van Oosterzeles sent her here to increase her marriage prospects, I didn't feel as though I was getting a new lady-in-waiting, but another daughter. I was happy to do it for such faithful allies of my family in Flanders, but before my confinement with this next one starts, I need to get out of Caen."

He wouldn't change his wife's determined mind and gave in with a sigh, barking orders to his men. "Prepare the carriage. The Duchess will be joining us in Ponthieu."

As Count Guy's foreboding castle at Beaurain came into view, Maud placed her hand on her stomach. "Don't be so active today," she told her bump cheekily. "Your mama and papa have an important meeting with a man disturbing enough. We won't need you disturbing us too."

The younger brother of the late Count Enguerrand, Addie's first husband, lived in opulence, with immaculate gardens and limestone bricks to fortify the towering keep. The iron gates rose to welcome their entourage, and she spotted the wiry, balding nobleman standing to greet them in the courtyard. When he smiled, his crooked teeth glimmered.

William dismounted to greet the count as Fitz helped Maud and Gundred from the carriage. "You have Harold Godwinson in your dungeons," said William brusquely.

"It's nice to see you, Your Grace. And Duchess, what a pleasant surprise. You're looking well."

Smirking, he leaned in to kiss her on the cheek. As the coppery stench of blood from his breath settled into her throat, Maud recalled Judith's horror in his presence at Addie's first wedding. William sneered. He despised pleasantries.

"You confiscated the earl's cargo when his ship wrecked off the coast. We're told he was en route to Normandy, so we're here to retrieve him."

"I must admit, Duke, I'm not the warrior you are," said Count Guy, laughing to himself. "I don't command troops with faithful bravery as you do, and I can't expand my territory with military might the way you've done in Normandy and Maine. But the County of Ponthieu must maintain its great noble status somehow, and I'm very good at that."

William scowled as Guy escorted them inside his castle. "You're nothing but a feckless bandit. I should have run you through on the battlefield the same day I killed your brother!"

"And if you did, I never would have given you the intelligence you needed to defeat the Franks that summer. All I asked in return was Enguerrand's crown." He shrugged, seating himself proudly on his wooden throne padded with white satin.

Noting her husband's aggravated stance, Maud intervened. "Let's not let old wars distract from what we came to discuss."

"Right," said Guy, smiling at his guests. "Three hundred gold pieces should be enough to release the Anglo-Saxon and his men."

William's nostrils flared. "You'd like me to mortgage a town for English soldiers?"

"Depends how much you want them," Guy retorted.

"Bring out Harold Godwinson. We'd like to speak with him."

The count balked as William seethed. "Put down your swords and I will."

"Don't test me. I could take Ponthieu any time I want. I had you behind bars for years when you tried to take back Aumale after our deal, and the only reason you live is because it's not worth starting a war with Francia for your tiny county."

William stood, broad and imposing over lanky Guy, whose beady eyes darted away from him fearfully. He turned to his men. "Bring up the prisoner. Chains on."

As the sound of iron dragging over shaved limestone echoed through the long hallways, Maud's stomach lurched. Harold entered with his feet and hands locked, clothing ragged. His face bruised and sallow, his fingernails were torn and caked in blood.

"Still get a kick out of torturing your prisoners, I see. Savage pig."

With a boastful grin, Guy chuckled at the insult. "Such language in front of fine ladies."

Gundred blushed and Maud forced a smile. "My husband's love for colorful language doesn't mean he speaks out of turn, Your Grace."

Catching the insult Guy scowled, and William shot his wife a grin before turning his attention to Harold Godwinson. "What was the purpose of your voyage to Normandy unannounced?"

Harold sighed, looking forlornly at his torn fingers. "I carried a dispatch from King Edward, but it was destroyed in the wreck because God knew it was a forgery," he confessed, continuing under the inquisitive glare of Duke William. "The king spends most days in bed, rising only to hunt or sign laws he barely pretends to understand. When I talk of Wulf and Hakon's return, he no longer remembers who they are, or that he sent them to Normandy. I worried if I wrote ahead to tell you I was coming, the king's men would intercept the dispatch and stop me, but I brought three hundred gold pieces to pay for them."

William looked down his nose at Count Guy. "You unloaded the cargo. Where's the gold?"

Count Guy offered an unconvincing shrug. "It must have been lost in the storm."

"Yet you ask for exactly three hundred gold coins to release him."

The count shifted in his throne with a sinister smile when he knew the act was up. "Any self-respecting man of business would try to double his profits, Your Grace."

"You test my patience, Count, and I'm not known to have much to begin with."

"We've only come to discuss the release of the Earl of Wessex and his men," said Maud, dulling her husband's menacing glare. "And since you seem to have the gold Harold intended for us in exchange for his brother and nephew already, perhaps you should consider our price paid."

With one hand on his sword hilt, William kept his gaze tuned to the count, who stared back meekly. "Let the earl and his men go at once. Or face the consequences."

Count Guy didn't ask what the consequences might be, his eyes beady with fear as he unspooled a ring of iron keys. Tossing them at Harold's feet, he watched with satisfaction as he struggled in his chains, cycling through several that didn't fit the lock before freeing himself.

When the chains were off, Guy frowned, sending his men to the dungeons to retrieve the others. Standing, he cleared his throat. "I'd invite you to stay for supper, but once a week I bring the townspeople in for a large meal, and there just won't be any room at the table."

None were upset to leave the inhospitable count's castle at Beaurain, but Maud's stomach growled with hunger soon after. William placed a comforting hand on her back while she stretched out a short ache in her spine. "We'll find you and the baby something to eat before escorting Harold and his men to the docks at Le Havre."

The Englishman stepped forward cautiously. "I'd like to continue to discuss the release of Wulf and Hakon. I no longer have gold to exchange, but perhaps something else could be arranged?"

As the sun set, a chill in the air settled into their bones. They found an inn on the outskirts of Ponthieu, firelight warming the abode from within. An old woman in a long white apron walked outside. "I'm afraid we don't have enough to feed so many."

William smiled. "We're only here to feed my wife and this man here. She's with child and he's been through an ordeal. Both need a good meal before we continue."

"We also wish to feed the girl," said Maud, motioning toward Gundred.

Nodding, the old woman escorted them inside. A wooden table with five stools sat in the center of a room with walls that looked like the interior of a stable. Dark wood slats were lit with candles on an iron chandelier strung from the rafters by a steel chain.

Gundred followed Maud to the table behind Fitz, Harold, and Duke William. The old woman disappeared out a side door, returning with three bowls of chicken broth and ale for all.

"I should say thank you for pulling me and my men from the dungeons," said Harold gruffly. "But I know you didn't do it for charity."

"I trust Count Guy less than any noble on the continent," William said. "I was happy to be able to help you, especially with our history, but I can't give you Wulf and Hakon for nothing."

"I told you, King Edward doesn't even remember them," Harold replied.

"What happens if they reappear in England, years older, and suddenly the king remembers? He'll remember he left them in my care and wonder why he suffers my betrayal. It's not like you'll need them around. They never could get the hang of a sword. Right, Fitz?"

"Nothing matters like family," Harold said, ignoring the insult. "There's plenty I could offer." Sitting up in his chair, he slurped his broth hungrily. "I could wed one of your daughters. Emma or... Agatha?" He struggled to remember their names. "I'd make any one of them the most powerful woman in England, after my sister, the queen."

Supping more daintily at her broth, Maud gasped at Harold's suggestion, choking on a small piece of chicken. Drinking from a mug of ale to clear her throat, she forced a smile. "Our daughters are too young to be married," Maud said plainly. "And you already have a wife."

At the mention of marrying her children, the empty, pallid faces of Marguerite and Herbert tumbled from her memories. She blinked the recurring image from her mind.

"My wife means we're not negotiating our daughters into marriage alliances until they've finished with their tutors," William said, rebuffing his offer politely. "Let Edie remain Lady of Walsingham before our girls, who'll one day have the advantage of calling their father England's king."

Harold dropped his spoon in frustration, and it bounced off the wooden table onto the straw-caked floor. "You insist on your loose claim to the Crown! What about Edgar Aetheling?"

"What about him?" William shrugged. "You're not here because you want to shore up family alliances in preparation for a time when you're the dutiful second to a boy king."

Harold's brow creased with sweat at William's accusation and Maud glanced covertly at her husband, certain they were right about his designs on the throne all along.

Chapter Thirty-Two

December 1064 – on the road south of Beaurain, County of Ponthieu

Neither Maud nor William had time to react before the wooden door to the inn swung open and Beau and Monty marched inside. Again, the old woman fretted she didn't have enough food, but William's loyal stewards waved her off. "Duke Conan of Brittany launched a full-scale rebellion from Fougères, and the Breton rebels are raiding Norman villages along the western borders," announced Monty.

"He's baiting me." William scowled, tossing back his mug of ale.

"Would you possibly be in need of extra men to beat back the Breton raiders?"

With a long gulp, William stared down his copper mug at Harold Godwinson. "You'll need more horses before we ride. I can use strong men and I'll even pay for the boat to send you home when the battle's won, but it isn't worth betraying King Edward to release Wulf and Hakon in exchange."

Harold cursed him.

"William, if it's true King Edward is near death, it might be time to risk upsetting him and sending them home," Maud said slowly. "You know I've always felt they were in Normandy too long, and only out of King Edward's spite for the Godwins. Wulf and Hakon were just boys when they came to us, and now they're young men. We should take no joy in imprisoning them, neglected and forgotten by the king who used them as pawns."

Beau shuffled impatiently. "We shouldn't waste time," he pressed, and William thought carefully.

"Fair enough, Earl Godwinson. I'll allow Wulf and Hakon to leave for England with you, if you and your men succeed in helping draw back the Breton invaders." The Earl of Wessex started to smile. "And you'll have to swear your allegiance to my claim on the altar at Bayeux

Cathedral, in front of God, all your men, and mine."

With an outstretched hand, Harold nodded uncomfortably. "We may not be steadfast allies, Your Grace, but on this we have a deal."

Maud placed her spoon to her lips, but fumbled the broth as she felt a strong, sharp pain across her midsection, passing as quickly as it came on.

"Should I fetch the midwife, Duchess?"

Waving off nervous Gundred and her husband's immediate concern, Maud smiled sweetly. "It's really nothing. I must have eaten too quickly."

William paid for their meal as the pain returned—low, long, and dull, pecking at the base of Maud's spine. She was anxious to return to the road and cross the border into Normandy, back to the protection of their castles.

"Are you sure you're all right, love?" William packed his wife into her carriage, covering her with fur blankets to warm her against the late-autumn winds.

"I'll be fine," she insisted. "Be safe on the roads. I'll have Fitz with me, so you won't have his protection."

William laughed. "I know riding double until we get through Ponthieu leaves one open to getting stabbed in the back, but Harold wants Wulf and Hakon badly enough. He won't let anything happen to me until that's done, and you won't release them if I die out there."

"Don't speak like that," she scolded him.

"We'll be back to Caen in less than a week unless Conan of Brittany's become a battle-hardened mastermind since last spring. I'll return long before this one comes into the world." He gently patted her small bump, leaving her with a kiss before he jumped from the carriage step. "Travel safe, my love."

She waved goodbye as her driver hitched the horses and the carriage wheels rolled forward through the night. "He loves you so much!" remarked Gundred dreamily. "It's wonderful. My father never loved my mother that much."

"The duchess is very fortunate to have such great love," said the old midwife with a grin. "To be loved as one deserves is never a given."

As shadowy trees rushed by in the black of night outside the window, Maud thought of Addie and Judith and knew what Celeste said was true. The women rode in silence well into Normandy, until the sun began to rise in the east the next morning. Discomfort from her cramps kept Maud awake for most of the night, and she watched the world pass by them groggily.

Sharp pangs, like a lightning bolt cracking through her insides, suddenly brought her to her knees in pain. She felt cold, then suddenly warm, her blankets splayed on the carriage floor at her feet. Gundred and Celeste shouted at the driver to pull to a stop.

"You're bleeding, Duchess," Gundred said with a fearful lilt. Throwing open the door to the carriage, Fitz stood in stunned horror at the sight of his duchess on her knees.

"Put these blankets outside," the midwife ordered Gundred, crawling over Maud to exit the carriage. "Can you get down, Duchess?"

The pain in her womb emanated throughout her body, catching her lungs and stomach, then pushing against her ribcage. Fitz supported her weight as she climbed gingerly down the steps, crumbling as the pain snaked across her spine. "What's happening, Celeste?"

"I think you're in labor, Duchess," the midwife said.

"But it's too soon!" argued Gundred as she hurriedly laid the furs. Celeste nodded solemnly. Frosty air cooled the sweat as it fell from Maud's brow. She breathed, slow and measured against the pain, just as she'd done so many times before.

"I can't give birth in the woods of Normandy at dawn." Maud fought against the pain, arguing with a grimace, "It's not safe for the baby."

"You must not fight nature," pressed the midwife. "Your child is coming now, and we can hope and pray they'll be strong enough to survive. But your health is more important, Duchess, and you *must* push."

Maud studied the midwife's worn, wrinkled gaze and understood implicitly. Angrily, she remained defiant. "Celeste, it's too soon."

She doubled over in pain from the next contraction as Fitz led her to the blankets on the forest floor. Their soldiers formed a perimeter around them, and Celeste pushed her through another labor. Moaning, delirious from the pain, Maud followed her order for one more push.

There was no smile on Celeste's wrinkled face when this child was born. Over the years, Maud had grown accustomed to her comforting smile in the birthing bed, but this time she turned away to cut the cord with a knife. "What's wrong?" Maud's voice shook in the quiet night.

The midwife turned back with sadness in her eyes. "It's a girl, but she's too small."

"I want to hold her."

"Duchess, she's gone."

"Let me hold her." Maud wanted to scream, splayed helpless over blankets soiled with her blood. Celeste carefully passed the wool-swaddled infant to Maud as soldiers emerged from the trees to the sound of their duchess' sobs.

Tears staining her cheeks, Maud peeled back the cloth to look upon the child—too impatient to wait but too small to survive. Sobbing, she held her close, lying with her daughter in her arms amid the bushes.

The soldiers allowed her to stay for close to an hour, standing silently, respectfully, in honor of the lifeless child. Crystalline flakes drifted over Maud and her baby girl, and she imagined being buried alive, washed clean by the wet drops of falling snow.

"We should continue before the snow falls too heavy, Duchess," suggested Fitz. "Please, let me. I'll keep her warm. When we get back, we'll ask Lanfranc to bless her and return her to God."

She wanted to cry, but her ducts had run dry. "Her name is Adeliza," she said weakly.

"Adeliza's a beautiful name. She's an angel."

Using the wool blanket, he tied the ends in a knot around his left shoulder. Gently unlatching Maud's arms from the child, he placed her in the basket of his makeshift sling. Maud reached weakly for her lost daughter, her arms outstretched in desperate futility.

"We should lay blankets on the carriage floor so the duchess can rest," suggested Celeste, and Fitz helped Maud stand while Gundred busily prepared a bed of furs for Maud to sleep. "She's not bleeding now but must regain her strength quickly."

Helping her climb into the carriage, Fitz forced her to drink a spot of ale to help her sleep. As he covered her with a heavy bearskin, Gundred and Celeste crept around her, seating themselves on the benches before Fitz secured the door.

With her auburn locks splayed out around her heavy head, Maud quickly drifted into slumber despite the bumpy ride.

Her eyes opened slowly in the moonlight. The other women sat asleep as the carriage rumbled through the woods, batting low-hanging branches as they moved to the trotting of horse hooves. A third figure, in blue robes, looked silently out the window. "Who are you?"

"I'm the mother of the Holy Son," she answered. "I'm here because you need me."

"What do I need?" The woman wouldn't answer. "What do I need?" she asked again, more forcefully, as the carriage pulled to a stop.

"You're not safe for them now. You must take time."

Tears crept into Maud's eyes. "Time for what?"

"Are you talking to someone, Duchess?"

The door swung open, and Fitz eyed her with concern, but when she looked back the woman was gone. "I...I was having a nightmare," she stammered. Sitting up, she winced from the dull, throbbing pain in her bones as old Celeste stirred.

"Go back to sleep, Duchess. You need your rest," she said groggily.

Maud noted the sling around Fitz's shoulder with tears in her eyes. "I *am* having a nightmare."

Adeliza wasn't buried in the family crypt in Rouen. Dying before her baptism, her body couldn't be buried in consecrated ground, so Fitz dug a small grave under the apple trees in the garden when they returned to Caen. Maud slept, then sat in the bath while her ladies-in-waiting cleaned the soiled earth from her pores. If they raised her arm to scrub, she let them.

Still too weak to stand for long on her own, her eldest daughter, Emma, now eleven, brought out a wooden stool from the kitchen. Maud could scarcely believe she sat before the grave of one of her own children, listening in a fog as Lanfranc led them in Latin prayer, bowing his head as he spoke.

"Amen," said her children. Maud was despondent, the world a blur through her tears.

"It'll be all right, Mama." Eight-year-old Cecilia spoke gently, wiping her mother's face with her small hand. "When Papa returns, we'll bring him out to the orchard to tell Adeliza he loves her."

"What good will that do? She won't even hear it," argued seven-year-old Constance.

"Be quiet," said Agatha with a firm yet gentle glare, but feisty Constance stood up to her twin with her hands on her hips.

"You're not in charge of me."

"Don't be a brat, Constance," groused Emma.

Four-year-old Rufus watched his sisters and sneered. "Girls are annoying!" he shouted. Maud tried to tune them out, Mary's words ringing in her ears: *You're not safe for them now.*

"Children, be calm," said Fitz, bouncing toddler Matilda in his arms. "Robert, Richard, take your siblings to the nursery. Give your mother a moment alone."

He handed Matilda to thirteen-year-old Robert, and Maud felt Emma's arms wrap tightly around the cowl of her robes. "Leave her, Emma. She's too sad," said Cecilia gently.

The children returned to the castle keep while Maud sat, staring despondent at the freshly turned plot of earth where her baby girl lay in a wooden box. As the wintry winds began to howl, she turned to her maids. "I'd like to go to my chambers," she said quietly.

As her ladies-in-waiting tucked her into her bed, Gundred leaned over her protectively. "You'll feel less sickly tomorrow, Duchess."

She shook her head weakly, the world spinning in her unfocused gaze. "I don't deserve it."

"Of course you do." Gundred pulled wool blankets around her.

"No! I don't want to hurt them," she cried, kicking at her covers. "When you leave, lock the door from the outside. Don't let me leave to walk free. It's too dangerous. Promise me."

Her ladies-in-waiting tried to counter, but Maud refused to sleep until they agreed.

Chapter Thirty-Three

March 1065 – Château de Caen in Caen, Normandy

"Marguerite begged for my help, but I helped her end two lives. I understand God is angry with me, but I don't understand why he had to punish our little girl." Maud spoke desperately to the silent apparition, sitting peacefully in blue robes at the end of her bed. "Is that how it works, Mother Mary? Judith sends a maid into a forbidden church to die, and she can never have a healthy child? Am I condemned to feel this aching hole of loss because of my sins, while God hands out undue punishment to our innocent children?"

Mary smiled warmly. "God does not punish children."

"Who does? Me? Marguerite said there was no other way." Maud's auburn hair hung unwashed in front of her puffy, tired eyes. "Have you seen my dreams, Mother Mary? Have you seen what I could do?"

The apparition nodded with a fearful gaze. "Adeliza was meant to be my child," she said. "God commanded it."

From outside the room came a knock at the door and her husband's forceful voice peeled through the wood. "There's lunch laid out with the children downstairs. We hoped you might join us before we all leave for the church."

"It's Pentecostal Sunday." Maud suddenly remembered, and Mary nodded. Maud called toward the door, "I can't join you."

He softened. "The children need you, Maud. You can't lock yourself away from them forever."

"The monks say I'm possessed. You know I can't see them." She crossed her arms vehemently. "I can't feast for a God who would permit me to hurt the children."

William groaned in frustration. "No one would let you lay a finger on them, Maud. Will you open the door? I'm tired of talking to my wife through a wall. I haven't recognized you since Adeliza..."

"The door must stay locked, William," she insisted. "I don't trust myself."

Grumbling, William threw his weight against the wood, knocking the door from its hinges with a mighty kick. Cracked boards fell in a dusted heap against the wall and she eyed him with exhaustion.

"Why not just use the key?"

William's nostrils flared. "Gundred van Oosterzele threw the key into the river this morning when she heard us talk about forcing you from your chambers." She managed a smile, grateful for the young girl's loyalty. "It's been months, Maud. You talk to ghosts and fear you'll suffocate the children in their beds. You rarely eat, and when you do there's always enough left to feed Robert and Richard a second meal."

"They're growing boys." She shrugged. "I'm happy they have plenty."

"You're thin as a rail!" William shouted. "Are you happy to meet death from starvation while your children cry over their mother's absence and neglect?"

Her eyes narrowed defensively. "I've rarely been absent from our children's lives, William. You're always off on campaign, fighting one battle leading right into the next, collecting from your loyal subjects and constantly on the road."

"I haven't ridden off to fight Conan of Brittany since Harold Godwinson and I returned from Mont Saint-Michel," argued William. "I've had to send my men to fight for me like a coward, to be here to care for you and the children."

"I'm keeping myself away *because* I care for them." She sobbed into the eiderdown-stuffed linen of her mattress. William's furious face softened at the sight of his wife, a shadow of herself soiling the sheets with her tears.

"Come to dine," he said pleadingly, but she staunchly refused, shaking her head. "The lords have begun to wonder why their duchess isn't at court. I can't tell them it's because she thinks the Virgin Mary told her to stay away."

"You mock me so easily," she cried, desperation in her voice. "Leave me alone, William. Please."

He looked down with wounded eyes, but rage filled his throat. "If you insist on staying in your chambers, you'll have no door. And you'll eat the food brought before you. You will not starve yourself."

Maud scowled, but the apparition of Mary nodded once more. "Yes, Duke." She turned against the stone as she crawled into bed, pulling up the covers to build a new wall between them. "I love you too much to let you near the world in which I live in agony every day."

He stepped forward, placing a hand on her shoulder as a solemn silence passed. With fresh tears in her eyes, she reached up to squeeze his gruff fingers before letting go, forcing his hand away.

Waking in a cold sweat one muggy August morning, Maud's hands shook clutching the blankets. She replayed the latest nightmare to rouse her in fear.

Marguerite's cold, lifeless gaze. Broken glass and Maud's children screaming before a sea of blood. Her husband on a wild horse, larger than life, barreling over Draco. Red blood dripped from Maud's hands to the earth below as a hollow voice echoed, *"You killed them."* The words fell from a black dragon soaring low overhead. Red eyes glistened, reading her as prey.

The dreams. Vivid, dark, snapshots of horror pervaded her mind every night. As spring turned to summer, William brought discreet monks, physicians, priests, and one pagan sorceress to Maud's doorless chambers. Their remedies made the dreams worse, often leaving her sicker or more exhausted. She preferred sleep to waking hours at their disposal, working to fix a malady none could fully understand.

Guards stood constantly outside her room. They returned her to bed if she walked asleep at night and kept out all but a few. She forbade her children from her quarters until William sent them to Beau's chateau in Beaumont. She knew they were safer there, far from her.

In a leather-backed rocking chair across the room, the apparition of Mary waited for her to awaken. Behind her, the battered shield of Flanders, gifted by her father before her marriage to William, hung on the wall. Its scuffed edges hid in the shadows behind rays of sunlight peeking through the windows. Mary didn't speak, nodding toward the floorboards.

The effects of the monks' latest remedy still potent, Maud raised a finger to her lips. Rolling out of bed, she pressed her ear to the floor.

"If you're not here to talk about how we're going to muster the support of Norman nobles against Brittany, why are you here?" her husband bellowed in his throne room below.

"It's the duchess, my lord," said Odo carefully. "We're concerned she is...lost. The court wonders where their duchess has been for eight months. No one believes she'd visit relatives in Flanders this long."

"For their duchess, they can wait forever. She will recover." Her husband's voice roared with anger, and Odo waited before he spoke again.

"Is it fair to let her live in misery? Perhaps she should be removed to a convent."

A crash accompanied William's rebuttal, his tone heavy and menacing. "Listen to me, little brother. I believe you think what you're saying has everyone's best interests at heart. You spent years at Bec Abbey committing yourself to becoming smarter than me—and you did that—but today is the first time I can honestly say, with all sincerity, you're still an idiot." Odo stammered in the duke's powerful wake. "There will be no suggestion of any course of action regarding my wife's care unless anyone can think of a way to bring her back. Is that clear?" His men murmured around him, but William ignored their whispers. "What we should all be doing is focusing on the Breton raids in the west."

"Yes, Your Grace. FitzOsbern and Montgomery are in Coutances fighting them now."

Hearing footsteps in the hall, Maud crawled back to her bed, drowning herself in her diaphanous linens before Gundred appeared with a bowl of oatmeal.

The young lady-in-waiting smiled. "You're awake, Duchess! I brought you some breakfast. It's made with goat's milk, as you like it."

"I don't like it. But you all insist on feeding it to me to ensure I keep my strength up." The young lady-in-waiting stood over her duchess dutifully.

"You're looking healthier than before. Your cheeks are less hollow."

Sitting up in bed, Maud frowned. "Food sustains me, Gundred. But I'm still hollow."

"Bertrand says there's word from England." Her voice was enduringly cheerful. "The Countess of Northumbria is expecting again."

A hopefulness lit Gundred's eyes that Maud couldn't fathom. She was young and naive, as Maud had been once. "I'll pray for Judith," she said, fresh tears pouring over her cheeks.

"I'll pray for her too," agreed Gundred. Forcing a smile, Maud took the bowl of food and forced down a few bites. "The duke will be happy to know you're eating, Duchess."

The Virgin Mary stared at her while she ate, so she focused her attention on the plain-faced thirteen year old in her care. "I haven't been a very good mentor to you, Gundred. I haven't been good for anyone. I'm sorry."

"I understand, Duchess. My mother lost three children. Each one was hard on her, and on my father. No grief is greater."

Maud thought of William, and how she had neglected him too. "Leave me," she told Gundred, and her young maid nodded obediently. When she was alone, with only her guards standing outside her room, she glared at the omnipresent apparition. "Are there no other women who deserve you more?"

Nodding, Mother Mary looked toward the sky. Following her gaze, Maud let out a welcome smile, racing to the intricately carved stone window. The panes had no glass, and a pair of blue butterflies danced in the bouquet of lilies dressing Lady Emma's painted vase. Each morning, her maids cut fresh blooms to display them in the sunlight. Today, she laughed as the vase seemed to come to life before her eyes.

The butterflies danced in the air around Maud's outstretched hand, and one landed in her open palm. Tears flowed down her cheeks as it preened in the hot summer sun for a moment, before cocking its antenna and lifting itself back into the air with a flap of its wings.

Late summer bled into fall, with the apple orchards of Normandy harvested before the frost. Green leaves shifted to red, yellow, and sepia hues, lighting the skyline outside Maud's window like fire. Already her husband's men had boarded the opening for winter, but she could still peek through a few misshapen slats.

Some days she thought she heard her children playing in the yard, but they stayed in Beaumont for their safety. Her youngest, Matilda, was two now—almost a year older than when she first locked herself away. She wouldn't recognize Maud as her mother anymore. Though heartbroken, she still refused to see them, because Mother Mary watched her like a hawk.

A commotion outside the castle walls caught Maud's attention, but she couldn't see through the small holes in the wood. Trumpets blared from the courtyard, and Maud moved carefully toward the hallway.

"We haven't been expecting anyone," she told Mary. "I haven't heard of any visitors through the walls. Not this week. It's the Feast of All Saints."

The virgin nodded. Of course she knew. Maud peeked beyond the open doorway, spotting her soldiers standing guard outside the door, eyes forward, with hands on their sword hilts. She heard heavy footsteps echo at the end of the long, dark hall, until the figure of her steward emerged in the torchlight.

"You must dress, Duchess. Your mother has arrived."

"Who asked her to come here? I don't want to see her."

Bertrand eyed her fearfully. "You must! Your mother brings Tostig Godwinson and Lady Judith, and says she'll meet you in the throne room or she'll drag you from bed herself."

When Maud returned to her chambers to dress, the apparition of Mary had vanished.

Chapter Thirty-Four

November 1065 – Château de Caen in Caen, Normandy

Creeping anxiously down the stairwell, Maud could hear Tostig explaining their arrival. Frustration peppered his voice. "The king's old and growing weak, and the thegns in the north rebelled. They took York and I was outlawed. Harold agreed to depose me, and then he escorted us to the ship that sailed us to Flanders."

"Exile by your own brother seems excessive," said William. "Why would Harold agree to strip you of your earldom and remove a natural ally, unless he knew you weren't one?"

Turning into the throne room, with its vaulted stone arches and high wooden ceiling, Maud felt small. When he spotted her, William stood from his throne. With her auburn hair tucked under a pristine white veil for the first time in close to a year, she counted the eyes in the room silently judging her, feeling more exposed than ever. Countess Adela looked at her daughter with sad eyes, and Maud's gaze fell to the floor in quiet shame.

With her large, round stomach weighing her down, Judith carried herself to Maud's side, enveloping her in a hug so tight Maud realized she hadn't felt a touch like it since Adeliza's death. Terrified to allow it until now, she fell into Judith's comforting arms. Understanding a fraction of her persistent grief, what she knew had nearly been enough to break her. Glancing at Judith's expectant womb, Maud prayed this time would be different for her.

"She doesn't look half as bad as we'd heard," said Tostig.

"Your earldom, Godwinson." William eyed him distastefully.

"Harold thinks I'm a liability now he's aligned with Mercia. He killed King Gruffydd in Wales and married his widow, Aldgyth, the Earl of Mercia's daughter. He has his Christian marriage and his northern lords, and he's got the king's council convinced he's the choice for English unity after Edward's inevitable death over a twelve-year-old boy from the continent."

"If that's true, his vow to recognize me as Edward's heir in front of God and all our men at Bayeux Cathedral was quite a performance for a man who says he's a good Christian."

Tostig grinned under his long, faded scar, his wine-stained teeth a shade of sickly brown. "I'll fight him with your help."

"You're plotting an invasion against your own brother? To what end? Are you going to be king?" William tried not to laugh.

"Why shouldn't I be king? I..." The duke's intimidating glare shut him down.

"You've come to us knowing we have ambitions in England, hoping for our help to put a crown on your head, but the only support you bring are ladies to comfort my wife." He shifted, sitting forward in his throne. "Don't think I'm ungrateful for the gesture. As family, you know well my wife's comfort is of great value, but there's no chance in hell I'm giving you an entire army if I won't be your king."

Feeling all eyes on her again, she avoided her mother's gaze across the room. Content to hear what Tostig and her husband had to say, she listened quietly.

"King Harald Hardrada in Norway is prepared to add troops to the cause. He's spent half his life looking for a chance to avenge the Saint Swithun's Day massacre of English Danes."

With a shrug, William frowned. "He's well within his rights to want vengeance, but I don't want to share the spoils of a kingdom with another king, and I doubt he'll share them with you. If England won't pass to Edgar Aetheling and we're no longer allied with the English court, I'll lead the army that takes England myself. If you'd like to join my fight, you're welcome. I'll make sure you get an earldom in the south."

"Fuck your earldom." Tostig shook his head vigorously, his temper rising. "You have no familiarity with England. Harold tossed me out of the only home I've ever known with my wife in her delicate condition."

"You don't have any allies in England," William said. "You don't even have the support of men from the County of Flanders. How well do you think it's going to go?"

"And once the king's dead, what allies in England have you got? A twelve-year-old boy and his mother and sisters?"

"I know a fair few Normans who followed King Edward from his exile and settled in England's south already, but if I take England, I'll bring my own lords." He turned to Fitz, Beau, and Monty standing nearby. "They'll help ensure the support of the lords of Normandy if the rumors of King Edward's imminent demise prove true."

Tostig laughed ruefully. "That won't help you in the north. They're a different breed than the English in the south. Animals who'll eat their own young to survive a long winter."

"Those are just rumors, Tostig. It hasn't snowed in winter in England for ten years," argued Judith, as short with him as Maud had ever heard her.

"Just rumors like churches that kill a woman?" he shot back. Judith's gaze turned to stone. "It's a different world in the north," Tostig continued. "They have their own laws and observe their own customs—the Danelaw, they call it. The north of England is a dreary, miserable place full of savages more Norse than human."

"You're half Dane! And your wife descends from viking men," William said stiffly.

"And she's more human than Northman," he said. "You? You're half Dane, half man. The perfect Norman. That's why I want your help invading England when my brother steals the throne."

Maud thought of her youthful desire to win England without bloodshed, and of the bridge with heads on spikes she used to pass so often in Rouen. Her husband was capable of brutality then, but now, she was no different.

Glancing at her mother, who she judged so harshly once, the collar under Maud's veil felt hot and she frowned in discomfort. "Excuse me, I think I need to get some air."

Her mother perked up instantly. "Judith and I will join you."

Moving through the corridors of the castle to the courtyard, Maud could see more than a tiny portion of the sky for the first time in close to a year. She breathed in the scent of wet autumn leaves, walking slow on the uneven gravel beneath her linen soles. "You didn't have to come all the way here," she told them, but Judith shook her head vigorously.

"Tostig had to ask William for help in his plans to avenge his exile." She rolled her eyes. "We had to ensure he didn't make an ass of himself, but we needed to see you more."

"You're stronger than you think you are." Countess Adela wrapped her daughter in a long hug. "We all know how devastating the last year has been for you. Judith knows. Eleanor knows. You had a brother named Henry, when you were too young to remember, but he lived only a few weeks. Your father and I were beside ourselves, but when Robby came along our grief subsided. Still, we never talk about him. It hurts too much to think about all the years God took away from us."

Maud felt catharsis as she commiserated, sobbing as she mourned the brother she never knew she had. Her mother held herself together far better than she could. She pulled away and turned to her oldest friend. "Judith, you don't seem very happy with Tostig."

She stomped her foot, cradling her stomach. "I've had it with him in every way. He got himself exiled with his constant drunken outbursts, and he cares more about getting revenge on his brother than he does about this baby."

"How do you feel?" She placed a sympathetic hand on Judith's arm.

"I feel fine, except I think I hate my husband. William's right not to align with him. He's never led a successful fight on the king's behalf. Being by his side is like climbing a tree using only the weakest branches and hoping for the best. That's what it's been like since we married."

Tears glistened at the top of Maud's cheeks, but these weren't tears of grieving. Relieved to feel herself again, weight lifted from her shoulders into the open, overcast sky as she placed a comforting hand on Judith's shoulder. But adding her opinion of Tostig was unnecessary and she changed the subject. "How is Edie, by the way? If Harold's found his Christian wife, I can only imagine what's going through her mind."

"She'll be able to stay at Walsingham and Harold's promised never to bring his new wife or their infant son around once he's king," said Judith, her gaze darting sideways. "She offered to let me stay with her and the children until after the baby came, but I just wanted to get back to Flanders to be with our family."

"What's Papa's reason not to support Tostig's planned invasion?"

"While he's still King Philippe's co-regent, he won't spare his men for a cause of no benefit to Flanders or Francia." Adela shrugged her prim shoulders. "Certainly not for a misguided revenge plot by a drunk out to kill his own brother. Your father has regretted signing off on Judith's marriage from the day we returned home from the wedding and heard of the standoff at Dover."

"I'm so sorry for everything you've been through, Judith," Maud said. "I've prayed every day to Mother Mary herself for you to have a healthy child this time."

"These are your hallucinations?" interjected her mother.

"She may be gone." Maud averted her stern gaze. "When you got here, she left."

The countess looked upon her daughter with duress while Judith sighed. "It's not up to the Virgin Mary to protect me now," said Judith solemnly. "I regret not listening to you when we were younger, Maud, but a choice can't be unmade. I made mine."

The words hit Maud like a stone. "I didn't know anything when I was younger," she said. "I used to think the world was made up of good and bad people and we chose to be one or the other, then God treated us each accordingly."

"But sometimes He rewards the sinners and punishes the good," her mother said.

"The older I get, the more I think people aren't necessarily good or bad. I know I'm not."

Her mother looked softly upon her daughter's face. "You might be stubborn as an ox, but you're a good person, Maudie."

"I think most people who do bad things do them for what they think are good reasons."

She looked to the sky when she said this, and Judith and her mother eyed her quizzically.

"What is it you think God is punishing you for?" her mother pressed. "William says you've never told him, no matter how many ways he's tried to ask."

Meeting their concerned faces, she finally confessed. "Marguerite and Herbert of Maine got the poison from me." The faces of Judith and Adela turned ashen as Maud continued, events spilling out of her like a tapped barrel. "She begged me to help her. She said she loved her brother and would rather die than marry my son and be separated from him."

"Lady Berthe blamed your husband and sent her son's army to attack your own people in retaliation for their deaths." With anger in her eyes, Judith glared at Maud with a distrust she'd never known before.

"I wanted to save my children from them more than I wanted them to use the poison they asked for. I'd been trying to get William to call off the arrangement for years but all I could do was postpone it. Maine was too valuable to Normandy."

Noticing a guard pass by in the courtyard, Adela hushed them both quickly and stared sternly at her daughter. "If this information is too precious for your husband, why tell us now?"

The haughtiness in her mother's voice caught Maud by surprise, her nerves already on edge as tears flowed down her cheeks. "Years ago, I thought I hated you when I heard you might have poisoned your first husband, and now look at me."

"You protected your children, Maud," her mother said gently.

"You can't be serious, Countess." Judith scoffed, her voice barely above a whisper. "Marguerite and Herbert may have committed a deplorable sin, but they were still children."

"I need to know the truth," Maud begged, tears soaking the fabric of her veil. "Did you poison Duke Richard to marry my father? Am I like you? Or am I a monster?"

Standing over her daughter, Adela wrapped her tightly in her arms, and Maud drew in the scent of her rosewater oil perfume. "You protect those you love, first and forever, Maudie. I can't tell you what you want to hear, but you *are* like me."

Judith shook her head defiantly, placing her hands protectively around her bump. "If my child ever put yours in danger, would you at least think twice before murdering them too?" Maud tried to protest, but Judith turned on her heels in disdain. "I'd like to return to Flanders as soon as possible, Countess."

"I would never hurt your child."

"You'll never have a chance to." Judith stood her ground. "I don't want anything to do with anyone's fixation on the English Crown, now or ever." Waddling slowly down the corridor, she turned back when more to say found its way to her lips. "What makes you mad isn't what you did to Lady Berthe and her children. That makes you selfish." Her voice clipped and Maud cowered. She couldn't argue. "You're not mad because you feel guilty, or because monks crushed up mandrake root to make you think you saw the Virgin Mary. You're mad because you think you should be forgiven for something you know you didn't have to do."

At first, no one spoke. Maud looked at her hands, shaking nervously. "You made your choice," she hissed.

"Judith, please," Maud pleaded, but her lifelong "sister" looked upon her with disgust.

"I'm not your shadow anymore, Duchess."

Chapter Thirty-Five

December 1065 – Château de Caen in Caen, Normandy

A light dusting of snow painted the grounds surrounding the castle. Maud moved busily through the halls, straightening boughs of evergreen hung with ornaments of gold, draped across fireplace mantels in every room. Christmas would soon be upon them.

"How are you, Duchess?" William's brother, Robert, the Count of Mortain, gave several bushels of hunted goose to stewards to take to the kitchens. "We've all been happy to see you up and about the last few weeks."

She smiled politely. "I'm happy to be up and about again." Her brother-in-law bowed before returning to the courtyard, and Maud watched her servants dress the table with white linen cloth. "To the left slightly," she said, hoping they wouldn't notice her ragged breathing.

"Are you all right, Duchess?" Startled, Maud smiled when she recognized Gundred, her loyal lady-in-waiting. "I'm sorry, I didn't mean to surprise you."

"I'm just nervous about the children's return from Beaumont."

"Why? I thought you said the Virgin Mary hadn't come to you since your mother left with Judith and Tostig Godwinson."

Wrapping her hands together to keep from shaking, she frowned. "It's not that. I'm afraid they won't forgive me for pushing them away."

"You were sick, Duchess," Gundred pressed. "Beaumont was the best place for your children. You said so yourself."

She glanced wistfully toward the windows as her steward appeared in the doorway. "The duke's cortège isn't far now," said Bertrand. "A guardsman spotted them from the rampart wall."

With a long, careful breath, Maud steeled her nerves. "Please get my furs, Gundred. I'd like to greet my children in the courtyard as soon as they return."

Stepping outside, she pulled her cloak around her shoulders. Her ladies-in-waiting and their stewards lined up in less bountiful furs for the return of their duke and the children. They didn't shake as Maud did, so she knew the chill running down her spine was fear instead. As horses plodded toward the fortress walls, she stood strong in defiance of her desire to crumble.

Two tall carriages pulled into the yard, driven by four sturdy work-horses. William and two dozen of his men surrounded them on taller steeds. When he saw her waiting, he smiled.

"You look beautiful today, love." He pulled her in for a long embrace when he dismounted. His arms didn't enclose themselves around her with the energy they once did, but Maud couldn't dwell on it as their children began pouring out of the carriages. Lining up in the courtyard, they stood before her with cautious stares. Even Matilda, the baby, was perched upward on two legs now. Beau and his wife, Lina, stood with them.

"You've cared well for them," she said with a grateful smile.

"Beau and I forgot what a joy it is to have young children around," Lina replied. "We were more than happy to care for such well-behaved young guests while you convalesced."

"We'd be proud to welcome them again," said Beau gently, but Maud shook her head.

"I'm much better now, thank you." She smiled through gritted teeth. "We shouldn't need you to take them again for so long, but I'll never forget how you supported us this past year."

Her children's eyes brightened significantly as she spoke of her health, and Robert and Richard were the first to approach her. Richard, now thirteen, was over half a head taller than his older brother, but fourteen-year-old Robert was first to speak. "You don't look as though you've cried recently," he said. Her heart sank to know he remembered her that way.

"No." She willed herself not to tear up. "I'm too happy to see you again." Wrapping them in warm hugs, she turned to Lanfranc. "Were they good students while you were away?"

The old monk nodded. "The boys have applied themselves well this year," he said. "It shouldn't be long before they'll be able to say they've learned from every book worth reading."

"Maester Lanfranc promised us honey cakes for every book we

read between the full moons," explained Richard, and Maud chuckled softly.

"His bribery worked wonderfully," Lina said with a laugh. "I constantly found them up late trying to read by candlelight. Your daughters too. They would not be outdone."

"They're just like their mother," William said. "All she used to want to do was read."

"I still like to read," Maud protested softly, though she thought of Emma's vellum book, and how long it had been since she ran her hands across its pages.

Approaching next, Emma studied her mother with Cecilia close behind. Maud smiled upon the faces of her eldest daughters, now twelve and ten. Emma, especially, was growing into a woman, with her once round, rosy cheeks more refined beneath her long braids.

"Hello, my darlings. You're growing so big."

"We would in a year," Emma said stiffly as she pulled her mother toward her for a vacant hug. Cecilia's grasp felt more welcoming, but she watched Emma, who stood with her arms crossed in front of her chest protectively.

"Are you really better, Mama?" wondered Agatha, tugging her eight-year-old twin, Constance, by the hand. Nodding, Maud smiled down at them, laughing as they threw their arms around her heavy green robes.

"We missed you, Mama," said Constance, and Maud bent down to hold them in her arms and breathe them in. Finally, young William Rufus, now five, and Matilda joined the group hug. All but Emma wore smiles of joy and forgiveness.

"I missed you all too. So much. Mama got better for all of you, but I can't wait for you to tell me all about your adventures in Beaumont."

"We went out the other day for the Advent season and put coins in the shoes of all the peasants in the village," Agatha said excitedly. "We peeked at some of the children finding the coins, and they were dancing in the streets over the deniers."

"They were jumping for joy in the mud!" added Constance, eyes wide.

Small flakes of snow began to drift down from the clouds. Redheaded Rufus lifted his head, sticking his small pink tongue to the sky. "It melts, Mama!"

She laughed as the other children followed suit, catching crystal snowflakes on the ends of their tongues. Strengthened by their joyful embrace, Maud made sure to count her blessings as she caught a smile from her husband over her shoulder.

The family's return from church on Christmas Day was triumphant, despite Maud's desire to treat her return to public view with little importance. Many nobles were invited to a feast, as much for William to showcase his generosity as it was to parade his rejuvenated wife.

She played her part, mingling among the guests for their Christmas feast. The smile she wore was genuine; she was glad to feel better, but the crowds dragged her to exhaustion. It had been too long since she entertained like this. She felt as out of practice as ever when Ranulf de Warenne, one of William's distant cousins, droned on about his eminent livestock. Distracted, she fumbled her copper mug of ale, spilling the contents over Ranulf's leather turnshoes.

The mug clanged with an echo against the stone as the din of the party ceased. Maud felt the room watching. Moving quickly through the crowd, William put a comforting hand around his wife, while two stewards swarmed the puddle with rags. Almost as quickly as their eyes fell upon her, the guests returned to their conversations as though nothing had happened.

"Is everything all right, love?" he asked, his voice shaking.

"I'm fine. I'm sorry," she said, loosening her shoulders. "Maybe I should get some air."

He escorted her to the courtyard, where their breath formed clouds in front of their faces. Bundling against him to fight the chill, he waited before placing one arm around her weakly.

"Are you always going to treat me as if I might break, William?"

He sighed, shrugging slowly. "Won't you?"

"I hope not." She pulled out of his grasp as he buried his face in his hands.

"I've fought hundreds of battles, been on the run for my life, and I've never been more afraid of anything than I was of you."

"I'm scared too," she argued. "I lost myself, but I found my way back because of you and the children. I need you to believe I'm strong enough, like you used to."

He laughed ruefully. "I feel as though I haven't talked to the real you in a year."

"I'm right here."

She held her arms open as his chestnut eyes stared into her soul. "Why did Judith tell me to be careful around you before she left in such a hurry?"

Steeling herself, Maud took a deep breath. He had to know her shame if he wanted to know who his wife was now. "She's angry at me because I knew Marguerite and Herbert wanted to die, and I secured them the poison rather than tell you or Lady Berthe the reason why."

"Because they said they were in love and wanted to fuck the rest of their lives?"

Maud looked at her husband, eyes wide. "You knew?"

He nodded. "I didn't know you gave them the poison, but while you were in England, they were found in bed together. I told Lady Berthe I'd keep it quiet for her, but the marriage alliance would be called off as soon as you came home, which is why she thinks their deaths had something to do with me."

"But she launched a war against you with her son because they died."

He smiled, shaking his head. "Conan would have launched his war against me either way. She promised he would if I called off the marriage alliance and took Maine for myself."

"Why didn't you tell me you knew?"

"After they were dead, I didn't think you needed the details. I thought they'd mortify you, and I've still known her most of my life. I wanted to save Lady Berthe the embarrassment once she was grieving their deaths. I didn't realize you already knew."

Maud's muscles loosened in relief. "You're not angry at what I've done?"

"I've done worse. At the siege in Alençon shortly after Robert's birth and my mother's death, I had the lords cornered in the tavern. Rather than submit to a lost fight, they insulted my mother's heritage in front of hordes of villagers. To set an example, I cut off their thumbs."

"I remember, but the Gloved Lords of Alençon lived to see another day," Maud recalled. "I wasn't thinking about setting an example. All I thought about was our children. Then I didn't know how to tell you what I'd done, or if I should. I ignored it...until Adeliza."

William pulled her close, the strength of his touch returning in small measure as she leaned into him gratefully. "You were giving Herbert and Marguerite what they wished and saving them from their sins. Maine was always valuable to me, but I got it faster without them." He smiled devilishly. "Geoffrey of Anjou didn't know what hit him when the army at his gates wasn't led by a fifteen-year-old boy."

She sighed. "There's always a new battle. The next one might be England."

"You've given up hope of a diplomatic victory?" He cocked an eyebrow.

"I don't see how I can demand diplomacy with a straight face anymore, and I don't see how diplomacy will prevent Harold Godwinson stealing the Crown from Edgar Aetheling."

"We might have room for diplomacy if Edgar is crowned, but it doesn't sound like he will be. Tostig says the Aetheling has no allies since he's only been in England six years, and there's no way he'll amass an army that could take on Harold Godwinson. Tostig thinks he'll get numbers from the Norsemen, but King Harald Hardrada's backing the wrong man. Tostig's own wife thinks nothing of him now." He laughed snidely, enveloping Maud in his strong, warrior's arms. Steeling his gait in the moonlight, he spoke with conviction. "If Harold takes the throne, we'll have to invade."

PART EIGHT

Sacrifice

Chapter Thirty-Six

January 1066 – Château de Caen in Caen, Normandy

The twelve-day Christmas holiday ended in Normandy with a fresh coating of snow on the empty fields. Maud directed the household staff to put away the boughs and ornaments for another year as a lone messenger on a black horse rode into the courtyard, carrying the dispatch Tostig warned would come. King Edward of England was dead, and the council had named Harold the new monarch. William raged, kicking the frame of one of his carriages in frustration.

"War it is," he said darkly, turning to Fitz, Beau, and Monty behind him. "Gather every noble in the duchy. The time has come to build our offensive."

His stewards took their leave as Lanfranc returned from the site where their two churches neared completion. The beauty of their façades was evident even with some stones still out of place, obscured by tall scaffolds. "The builders say the churches should be ready for consecration by the summer," he reported.

"Just in time for us to ask God's blessing for our fight for England," said Maud. "King Edward is dead, and King Harold convinced the council to hand him the throne."

"You'll need more than God's blessing to rule over England," the priest reminded them.

"Rome," groused her husband, and Maud's heart sank. "Lanfranc, will you put together an embassy of bishops to present our cause to Pope Alexander on Normandy's behalf?"

"I would be honored, Your Grace." He leaned in close with a friendly smile and Duke William scratched his shaved face thoughtfully.

"When we've won England, I'll need an Archbishop of Canterbury I can trust, Lanfranc."

The monk's eyes grew wide, and he raised his hands in shock. "Your

Grace, I'm not even a bishop. I'm unworthy of such a high office, and England's Church is quite unlike Normandy. I met Stigand, the current Archbishop, when we were in London. Rome doesn't support him, but he refuses to leave his post. He just frightens the priests in England into supporting him."

With a laugh, William patted Lanfranc on the shoulder. "There's no one I know who understands the laws of God and Man better than you, my good friend. Get the Church on our side against Harold Godwinson, and no one on the continent would deserve it more."

With a humble smile, Lanfranc bowed to his duke and duchess before leaving them alone in the yard. Beyond the walls, the din of tools punctured the whir of crisp but mild winter winds. William scowled.

"When the cathedrals are finished, I'll finally stop hearing so much hammering."

"It's not that bad," she said with a laugh. "You should be used to it after so many years."

"You're a heavier sleeper than me, and they work into the night because I told them I'd pay them by the hour if they'd finish faster." He glowered, laughing ruefully to himself. "Construction picked up after we renegotiated, but I didn't think about the noise."

"Only a few more months until they're done," she reminded him, kissing him quickly on the lips. She still felt a distance between them, a wall that turned their kisses from passion to a matter of course. With sadness in her eyes, she forced a smile as Bertrand entered the yard.

"Pardon my interruption, but a tribute has arrived from England," said the steward. "From Edie Swanneck, the Lady Walsingham."

Maud thanked her steward as William followed her to the throne room. A gray wool blanket rested on a long table, held together with thick braids of twine. A note on parchment rested above the bow.

"*My friend Maud,*" she read aloud. "*I was clearing Walsingham Manor after Harold moved to London with his new wife and son, and I thought you might get better use of these items now. Sell them to help fund your army—show my husband his ambition will also be his downfall. I'm duty-bound to stand with him for the sake of my children, but all I ask in return is that your husband spare my sons on the inevitable battlefield.*"

"That depends on how much they want to fight their father's

battles," said William with a shrug. Unwrapping the twine, he pulled back the edges of the blanket to reveal Edie's elaborate gold necklace and several golden bracelets. Lifting the necklace by the clasp, he grunted.

"Edie told me it was a wedding present from Harold but felt like a noose."

"Her long neck might have been built for it," he mused. "But this is heavier than any sword."

"It's not really my style." She palmed the golden rings as William held the necklace with both hands. "But I have an idea what to do with it." William looked at her expectantly, but she shook her head. "It's a surprise, my love. After more than fifteen years of marriage, there are so few surprises. Expect this one."

Smiling down at his wife, he placed the necklace gently back on the table. "You've always managed to surprise me somehow."

She laughed, trying to ignore the niggling fear in the back of her mind that they'd never completely get back to who they were.

The wintry winds of January couldn't keep Maud from her weekly visits to Adeliza's grave. She often went alone, thinking about her year, convening with the memory of the Virgin Mary.

Before returning to Flanders with a dejected Tostig and Judith, her mother ordered the monks to stop grinding mandrake root into her food. "Monks don't know everything," she'd said stiffly. Maud thought back to her wedding night when Lady Eleanor revealed her mother's history with Flemish monks. The apparition of Mary hadn't returned—and Maud hoped she wouldn't—but she liked to think she was still there, guiding her through her grief.

This morning, wrapped in their fox furs, Emma, Cecilia, and the twins, Agatha and Constance, met her in the courtyard.

"Our tutor went to Rome with Maester Lanfranc and Uncle Odo, and the boys are practicing with their swords," protested Emma. "The skies are so dark this time of year, it's harder to focus on our reading."

"We want to visit Adeliza too." Agatha tugged at the fabric of her mother's red tunic, and Maud bent down to tighten the fur around her daughter's shoulders. From the looks on her daughters' faces, she'd have to be alone with her thoughts another time.

Making their way to Adeliza's stark gravestone, Constance and Agatha skipped together, ahead of their elder sisters. Emma and Cecilia stood back, walking on either side of their mother like a guard. "Robert says Papa will go to war for England," said Cecilia. "He says the whole of Normandy will fight."

"We don't know yet whether the Norman lords will join," she replied cautiously. "Robert gets easily excited. Fitz arranged a summit at Lillebonne, so in a few weeks we'll know for sure."

"I've been reading Lady Emma's book," said Emma. Maud smiled, but her eldest looked pleadingly at her mother. "When it talks about how King Cnut won England, it says they were foes on the land, and if they didn't conquer, they had no choice but to fight to their death."

"Your father is the greatest fighter on the continent and would never recklessly go into a war he can't win." She placed a comforting hand on Emma's shoulder. "No one wants a war, but Harold Godwinson stole the throne from the Wessex kings. We share their Wessex blood and it's a question of honor, but a fight doesn't have to be a war."

There was doubt in their eyes. As she spoke, Maud heard old Cecilia Drengot's croaky timbre in her ear: *"All of life is war."*

"Robert says he and Richard are going to fight with Papa," said Emma.

"That won't be happening. They're still too young."

"But Emma's book talks of the sacrifice of sons and daughters. Doesn't that mean children?"

"There are many ways for children to honor their families. Marching to war isn't one of them."

Agatha and Constance turned with interest as they overheard the conversation at Adeliza's black Tournai marble gravestone. "Why is sixteen honorable but fifteen too young?" Cecilia wondered thoughtfully.

The real reason Robert and Richard were too young to join their father in battle was because Maud said so, but this would be insufficient for her inquisitive daughters. "Boys become men at sixteen because they grow stronger and can better wield a sword and control a horse," she explained. "They're also a year older, so their minds are sharper from more experience."

"But Richard's taller and smarter than Robert already!" argued Constance. Maud raised a stern eyebrow, and her impish daughter silenced herself apologetically.

"Girls become women much younger than boys become men," Emma rued. "My ladies-in-waiting say I'm a woman already."

"You'll be married soon," teased Cecilia, and the twins giggled heartily.

"None of you will be married soon," Maud countered staunchly. "School is far more important."

"Our tutor says to know God is even more important than to know Latin," said Emma.

"I hope he's teaching you how important it is to know both."

"He says if God asked you to stop reading and you said, 'I can't stop. Reading is just as important as you,' it would be a sin."

"God wouldn't ask you to stop reading," Maud countered in frustration. "Women who read can spread His gospels. This is more valuable to God than simple devotion."

"I like reading," said Agatha.

"Books are dull," argued Constance, sticking out her tongue at her twin.

"Stop it, girls," admonished Emma. In the past year, she had taken to nurturing them in their mother's absence, and Maud looked upon her sadly, lamenting their time apart. Standing straighter, Emma made herself nearly as tall as her mother. "Maester Cluny says when the cathedrals are built, we'll learn to read there."

"It sounds like you don't want to." Maud creased her brow.

"I want to," Cecilia said quickly. "I want to read every book Emma has no time for."

"It's not that. I want to learn everything I can, but I'm happy here. Everything might be different if Papa invades England."

Placing a comforting arm around her two eldest daughters, Maud smiled at them warmly. "Different could be better," she said.

That night before bed, Maud was struck by an idea, inspired by her afternoon walk with her daughters. She brushed out her hair as

William entered her chambers slowly, his face lit by the din of torchlights hanging on the stone walls.

"You asked to see me?" He closed the newly carved door behind him.

She stood, her gown pulling tight across her chest. "I was thinking about the opening of the churches, and some of the tributes we'll offer on their consecration day."

"You have a vial with Jesus' blood from those Venetian merchants who toured the Holy Land, and I have those scrolls from Jerusalem that were returned from my father's belongings."

"And for you to part with those scrolls is a sacrifice, letting go of one of the last things remaining of your father," she agreed. "But a vial of Jesus' blood is more valuable to a church than it will ever be to me—yet without churches, or nuns, I may never have learned to read."

"The point is to give them something they would valuc, my love." He moved toward her, his eyes drawing lines along the shapes of her shoulders. He was beginning to recognize her again, and she felt relief in his wanton gaze.

"I remember something Lady Emma told me as a child, that power comes with great sacrifice. Even if Lanfranc returns from Rome with the blessing of the Pope, God will ultimately decide if we'll lead a kingdom in his name."

"Your sacrifices haven't been unworthy, Maud. You've raised eight of God's children and helped run a duchy so wealthy the Franks live in fear of their northern borders. Our daughters will make great men of worthy nobles some day, just like their mother."

Her lips curled into a smile. "That's just it. For me, there's no greater gift than our children. I could make no greater sacrifice to God than to commit one of our daughters to the Order on our cathedrals' consecration day, rather than benefit from her in a powerful marriage alliance."

William studied her face in the firelight. "How would you choose to send one away?"

"Maybe one will want to go, and we wouldn't send her away," she protested. "She'll be better educated than almost any woman in Normandy, and her sisters could go to school with her during the day when we're in Caen. I want them to have the very best possible education."

Pulling his wife in close, he sighed. "If none of them elects to go, we won't force them. But I have a feeling you already know one of them will volunteer."

"Let me talk to them," she said gently, picking at a loose thread on his tunic. "But for now, it's been so long since we were alone together." His breath danced on her skin as she lowered her robes, wrapping herself around his strong torso. "You still think I'm the fragile woman you're too afraid to touch. I want my husband to share my bed again."

With a long, ravenous kiss, he obliged her.

Chapter Thirty-Seven

February 1066 – the Nobles' Council at Lillebonne in Normandy

The Great Hall at Lillebonne teemed with nobles from all corners of Normandy, each escorted by an entourage denoting rank among their hierarchy. The wealthier nobles were accompanied by scores of relatives and friends, spectacularly dressed in decorative tunics and arms in the colors and traditions of their families. William stood, surrounded by both his brothers, and Fitz, Beau, and Monty by his side.

Looking on from a balcony, Maud watched the men below with careful interest. Maids moved about the wooden floors, serving mugs of ale to the gathered crowd. Her husband stood speaking to Ranulf de Warenne and his son, William, who had proven their might in dozens of battles at Duke William's side. She couldn't hear what they said over the din of conversation in the hall, but her husband's smile confirmed the Warennes were firm allies.

Spotting her brother-in-law, her neck stiffened, small hairs standing on edge beneath her veil. The entrance of Count Edo of Champagne meant his wife was somewhere in the same gallery where she stood. They hadn't shared a room for close to twelve years.

"William Warenne looks handsome today, don't you think?"

The soft, sweet voice of Gundred, now fourteen, cut through the tension building in Maud's mind. Young Warenne's gaze shifted skyward, meeting Gundred's adoringly. He was already in his mid-twenties, but the hair on his chin was still scant. Looking a shadow of his fellow warriors, his youthful face belied his skill with a sword. "When the time comes, I don't think he'll argue if we suggest a marriage contract with you."

The young girl's cheeks flushed with excitement at the thought, and Maud's gaze returned to the floor. Standing tall on an oak chair to get the barons' attention, Fitz held his silver mug above his head. He shouted over the babble echoing off the high wood ceilings.

"Gentlemen, I'd like to raise a toast to our most auspicious gathering," he said proudly, ale sloshing over the edges of his cup. "We've broken bread together time and again. Our wives are sisters and friends, but it's a rare occasion to see so many great Normans together in one place. Your duke is grateful to have you here, so please, enjoy the refreshments."

The men cheered gratefully, raising their cups aloft and drinking as William stepped to a raised platform. His face shaved and tunic lined with gold, his polished sword hung in an embossed leather sheath from his belt. The room fell silent in his magnificent presence.

"Great lords of Normandy, I've come before you today to tell you a story of treachery." The men murmured, and William hungrily devoured their interest.

"Who moves against you now?" asked Baldwin, the younger Brionne brother. The elder, Richard Brionne, stood next to him proudly. "We'll snuff them out too."

The room broke into raucous cheers among William's more fervent supporters and the younger men always primed for battle. But the older men, war-weary and protective of their hard-won assets, stood quieter amid the hollering.

"While I'm always grateful for the support of my brave nobles in defense of Norman lands, this is a story of treachery north of the sea, in England," William began. "The great King Edward died last month, leaving the Crown to his great-nephew, Edgar Aetheling, but the council selected Harold Godwinson. Long one of the king's most loyal men, but also his greatest adversary, Harold convinced them to break the Wessex line, claiming Edgar is too young to rule."

"It's not our business what goes on in England," said one of the elder nobles.

The duke gave his lords a charming smile. "My wife carries Wessex blood. I'm insulted in the name of my own sons. But over the years, Harold has been adversarial to me as well. Many times, he's recognized my claim to the English throne. King Edward was like a brother to me! But once Edgar Aetheling and his father were found in Hungary, Harold changed his allegiance, like a snake. Despite this, many of you witnessed him swear allegiance to me at Bayeux before he joined the battle against Brittany, which he did only in benefit to himself."

"If he doesn't cross the sea, it won't matter. Our lands will be protected," said another.

"He's crossed the sea before," said the duke. "What's to stop such a treacherous man from coming for your estates, your orchards, your livestock, or your families?"

"We're strong enough to defend our lands," the man argued. "We've proven it many times over."

The crowd murmured among themselves, and William stood taller. "Gentlemen, your ability to defend your own lands is not in question. I've brought you here to ask you to join me in defending our allies in England against the rule of a selfish man who wears a crooked crown."

One elder approached, studiously clearing his throat. "With respect, Your Grace, what do we gain from helping to install a boy on a foreign throne? Your rule prior to the victory at Val-ès-Dunes was unstable at best. We don't even know if Edgar would make a good king."

William grinned. "We've proven our might in battle time and again, in the name of our Norse ancestors and for love of the lands we tend so well. Some of you have fought against me, fiercely and with honor, only to realize we're stronger together. King Edward once said I would be a good king for England, and Harold himself concurred." The men drank as William continued proudly. "Edgar and his family are allies, and the boy would be easy to control, but my sons are both Norman and Wessex men. If you'll join me in battle for the future of England, together we can ensure the Crown for a new race of Anglo-Normans, from both sides of the sea." He stopped to let the men consider this with some interest, cocking his head with a cunning smirk. "If the matter of a boy king scares you, remember my reign as a boy duke survived and prospered along with Normandy, so let it fall to me." The men stirred, but he spoke over them confidently. "Though I might wear the crown, you would be doing it for much more than pride—in exchange for your assistance securing the throne, the great, green lands of England will be divided among all brave, noble men who join the cause. The size of your lands will be reflected in the size of the army you send forward."

"It's expensive enough to run my lands in Bellême," protested one.

"Think of it as a summer home," argued Monty jovially. "Or give the lands to your sons and let them worry about the investment."

More murmurs as Maud tried to read the faces in the crowd. Overhearing a familiar laugh behind her in the gallery, she turned to spy Adelaide chatting with the wives of Fitz, Beau, and Monty. Maud's stomach lurched as their eyes met. She forced a smile.

Standing over the uneasy crowd below, William raised his hand again to silence them. "Please, I implore you, talk amongst yourselves. I'm aware of the magnitude of my request. Enjoy the drink, but I say, in all sincerity, loyalty to me has never gone without reward. I am consistently a man of my word, and this could be our glory, gentlemen. Not just mine."

The men debated as Maud felt someone come to her side. "Sometimes I can't believe that's my idiot big brother."

Maud shook at the sound of her voice, not quite the same as when they last spoke. "He's a great man, Countess. I'm fortunate to have him."

Addie's blue eyes were shades darker after all these years. "Let's go for a walk."

Maud followed her out of the hall to the cobbled streets of Lillebonne. The weather was mild, but their long robes were enough with such little wind. "Congratulations on your wedding to Count Edo of Champagne. I was sorry to miss it. Has it been six years now?"

"It's just as well you weren't there," she said. "I didn't want to be there, but it was a sound business deal and I had two fatherless daughters and no other prospects. Champagne is nice, and the girls like their stepfather."

"I'm sorry I sent Count Lambert to war," she said. "I never meant for—"

Addie shook her head, silencing Maud with lips pursed. "Stop. You can't apologize for something that's done. I know you didn't mean to kill Lambert, but you meant to kill Herbert and Marguerite."

"Judith told you."

Nodding, Addie crossed her arms in front of her chest. "She wrote after her visit before winter. What you're capable of scares her to death and she wants nothing to do with you."

"I'm not the evil she thinks I am."

Adelaide laughed. "I know you're not. Believe it or not, I understand why you did it. Lady Berthe let it slip during one of her visits to Falaise. I said I'd keep her secret, but in truth I didn't say anything because I was mad at you. She knew about her children for years and hoped the marriage alliances would solve it, and she pushed too hard because she was desperate. You probably saved them from themselves, but you still played God. You were still wrong."

"I know I was wrong, but I would never harm Judith or her children."

"You used to say the same about me." She shrugged, unmoved by Maud's emotional appeal. "She had a baby boy in Flanders, by the way. She didn't want me to tell you, but she knows I love gossip. Healthy, happy, all his fingers and toes. His name's Skuli."

Maud's heart ached with joy and regret as tears flooded her cheeks. "If she'll accept, please send her my love."

Adelaide offered a piteous smile as a retinue of men on horses turned a corner. Pulling to a stop in front of the Great Hall, they carried flags adorned with the traditional black-and-white cross of Brittany. It didn't take long for Maud to spot Duke Conan and his mother, Lady Berthe, on a black steed near the front of the crowd. William's soldiers blocked the entrance.

"What are the Bretons doing here?"

Adelaide crossed her arms in frustration. "When my husband mentioned the council to his aunt, she vowed to show up uninvited. I begged against it, but Berthe hates my brother for what she thinks he did to her children. She's leading her only living son into a war he can't win."

"If you don't let me through, I'll lie in wait, and my men will attack every noble on their way out the door." Conan spoke gruffly, with menace in his stare. The Norman soldiers stood firm, greeting his threats with silent bravery. Sharing a quick, pensive glance with Lady Berthe, Maud and Adelaide slipped back inside.

Finding Beau standing near the entrance, the women informed him of the Bretons clamoring at the stone steps before returning to the upper gallery. They looked on as Beau spoke quietly to the duke. "Bring them in," said William loudly, swaying with his mug of ale as he waved his arm with an inviting smile.

Grasping the stone balustrade, Maud looked on from the gallery, and Adelaide stood at her side with shared interest. The nobles moved to the edges of the hall as Duke Conan of Brittany entered with his entourage. Lady Berthe stood behind her son. Her black lace veil showcased how her once thick, dark locks hung about her sallow cheeks in shades of silver.

"I don't suppose you've come to commit your men to the Norman cause?" William stared down his nose at his adversaries as Duke Conan stifled a pitiful laugh.

"You've struggled finding rebels strong enough to challenge border towns in Brittany!" Conan shot a snide glance to the men in the room. "No Breton lord would commit to a fool's errand with such a weak ruler. Any man in this room who will is just as foolish as their duke."

The Brionnes led a chorus of disgust at Duke Conan's accusation, threatening to raise their swords as the Bretons faced their anger with satisfaction. Several men emptied their mugs as William bellowed from the platform. "Enough!" he shouted with a menacing glare to Duke Conan. "If you want a fight, challenge me. Right here. Raise your sword against me like a man."

Conan scoffed. "You won't draw me into battle as easily as you might persuade these men. Go ahead and have your war with England. While your lords are occupied fighting rebellions from English lords who have no interest in being Norman, or killing one another over the spoils, Brittany will move in on Norman towns. We'll take your estates acre by acre, and you simply don't have enough men to be in two places at once. You won't stop me." Roaring to be heard over the objections of the crowd, he addressed William directly. "Your ambition for England will prove so disastrous, anyone who supports you will lose the faith of the Norman people. Rebellion will turn your friends to enemies and cost you both crowns."

Angrily staring him down, William allowed the nobles to object on his behalf. Surging forward, the crowd forced the Bretons back defensively. Steel swords sliding from their metal hilts echoed up to the gallery.

"Gentlemen!" William finally cried. "Withdraw your swords. Duke Conan has as much right to an incorrect opinion as any fool on the continent—don't waste your sword's polish." The crowd chuckled at the Bretons' expense. "Let the Duke of Brittany and his entourage leave this room with their lives, and if he should be so bold as to try to raid our towns while we march victorious into battle, let him know that I, as the mighty Duke of Normandy and King of England, will end him as ruthlessly as he deserves."

The nobles shouted with excitement as the Bretons were escorted outside surrounded by a ring of Normans brandishing spears. The maids moved about the floor with trays of fresh ale, which the men drank ravenously. The fighting spirits of even the most fiscal-minded elders had been awakened, and Fitz took the opportunity to return to his carved oak chair.

Standing tall over the men, he addressed his liege lord: "Duke Conan and his men may believe they could split Normandy apart but pay close attention to how he said he'd do it. He already believes we'll win England, presuming us spread too thin to mount a defense to his incursions. There's only one way to prove him wrong, which is to double our commitments of fighting men, ensuring ourselves the best English land to enrich our estates in Normandy!" A raucous debate rose from the chamber, but the mood of the majority had swayed toward war. "Any Norman lords who refuse to support the cause will be at risk of retaliation from more sides than Brittany." Fitz's words, delivered through a fog of bitter amber, sounded less like a threat than Duke Conan's vow, but still the holdouts quickly fell in line.

From the platform, William looked to the gallery, meeting his wife's smile with a satisfied grin.

Chapter Thirty-Eight

May 1066 – Caen, Normandy

"To think, these streets will be even more full of nobles and soldiers when Duke William is finally ready to sail for England." Gundred stared dreamily at the crowds of young, able-bodied men pouring into the castle courtyard to train for the coming invasion. "Even my brothers joined the mercenaries your father plans to send."

"My father plans to do nothing for the cause, officially. Any Flemish men who march alongside my husband will be there on my request." The duchess shared a sly smile with her young charge as they walked past the bailey walls to the village. Stepping inside a stone hut, Maud's eyes watered as the acidic stench of copper filled her nostrils. A goldsmith set down his iron hammer. "Maester d'Or," she said as he bowed before her. "I've come to see the design."

He fumbled with his leather cap. "Things have been busy in the shop, my lady, but nothing could keep me from designing the perfect figurehead for someone as generous as you." She followed him to his wooden desk as Gundred looked on silently in the corner of the small room. Through an open door to a courtyard, men with sweat-caked biceps pulled steel vats from stone ovens, grunting over the hiss of liquid metal through the open windows.

"The necklace and bracelets you provided will be more than enough to melt down and reshape." He nodded to the heavy pieces of Edie Swanneck's serpentine jewelry on his table. "So much English gold. The final piece will be quite symbolic."

She studied his design: a golden child, right hand pointing forward toward England, fashioned with precious metal from its own ground. With his left hand the child held a small horn of ivory, as if heralding a fortuitous victory.

Placing a hand over her small belly, she sighed with content. "It's wonderful, Maester. And it will be completed by the end of summer?"

"Yes, my lady. Once it's completed, I'll affixit to the ship in Barfleur myself."

"The figurehead must shine and be sturdy enough to hold a lantern for sailing into night."

"It will be more than worthy of the great longboat you're having built for your husband's crossing. I assure you it will be a fine symbol of everything you and your husband have built together, and it will point to the future of your rule over two proud domains."

Maud smiled at the charcoal sketches. "It does look so much like Rufus on the page." Her finger traced the dark lines of the design as the goldsmith chuckled soundly.

"The rambunctious youngster left an impression on me."

"I do hope the commission payment was more than enough to cover the costs to repair your oven," she said regretfully. The goldsmith waved her off politely.

"Your generosity is unmatched, my lady. Boys aren't known for their gracefulness, but young Rufus caused less damage than the explosion let on. We're just grateful no one was hurt."

She reached into a velvet pouch for two silver deniers, placing them in the goldsmith's unexpectant palm. "For your continued expertise in this top-secret project for my husband," she said. He beamed with gratitude, filling his shoe as she bid him good day.

Standing dutifully, Gundred followed from the goldsmith's workshop to the bustling streets of Caen. The fresh breeze of spring bounced off the cobbles, enveloping the ladies as they returned to their open-top carriage. Escorted by a retinue of Norman soldiers, horses pulled them through the well-kept streets. Many of the townspeople recognized their duchess as she passed, bowing or waving to get her attention as she looked upon them warmly.

"They'll be so happy when it's announced you're with child again," said Gundred, waving to the people from the carriage bench. Maud's heart skipped to hear it spoken aloud, and Gundred admonished herself with a gentle frown. "I'm sorry, Duchess."

"It's all right, Gundred. We're happy to be expecting again, with cau—"

"Cautious optimism. And I understand that, but I see your whole family think about it the same way, and a little unfettered optimism is good for balance. I'll take care of that."

"You constantly impress me," said Maud, and Gundred smiled proudly as the carriage pulled to a stop in front of a stone church. Though it paled in size to the two cathedrals nearing completion near the chateau, it stood taller than all structures in its vicinity.

Greeting her outside, the bishop kissed her hand. "Duchess, it's marvelous to see you again. We're perpetually honored by your patronage." Escorting them inside, he lit several lanterns affixed to stone columns, basking the small-windowed church in a firelit glow. She handed him a small blue sack and the deniers clinked as he grinned. "I'll leave you to your prayers in peace, as you like."

"Thank you. We'll close the doors behind us when we leave," she said. With a polite nod, he tucked the gift into his white robes before disappearing into his rectory.

"I'll pray for your child." Eagerly, Gundred crossed her chest and raised her hands. Maud left her to it, wondering instead if she might feel Mother Mary's presence. She knelt at the altar, communing silently with the spirit who no longer visited in ways Maud could see. Instead, she felt a connection transcending her known senses, but of late she felt her less than usual.

"Since I learned I was expecting, I haven't felt you," she said quietly, holding her stomach gently. "I'm scared to go through it again."

Her pleas met with silence as Maud overheard Gundred recite a long-winded prayer for the health of every person she'd ever met. She softened at the young teen's sweet nature, distracting herself from her fears, but as she faced the possibility of reliving grief unlike any she'd ever known, her heart ached for comfort. "Tell me all will be well with my husband and our child."

She waited a few more quiet minutes before crossing her chest and announcing their leave to young Gundred. Exiting the church with a heavy heart, a small boy distracted her in the town square. He chased a leather ball through a flock of pigeons, and Maud chuckled as the child waved his arms wildly, ducking the mess of feathered wings.

A wooden sign across the square advertised "great fortune." Struck by curiosity, she urged her soldiers to wait. Gundred followed as she turned into a small wooden hut, draped with pieces of green and blue silk fabric at the entrance instead of a door.

A woman with red locks under a red lace veil emerged from behind a wooden partition. "Welcome," she said grandly. "I am Mistress

Dzintra. What fortunes do you desire?"

Her bright-red satin robes hung low, revealing more of her freckled arms and chest than any woman in a noble court would dare.

"Duchess, what are we doing here?"

Gundred hung back nervously while Mistress Dzintra smiled. "Duchess Matilda, what worries you enough to visit me? Your bishops would be mortified."

"How do you operate so near a church?"

"When the church comes to do business with me, I'm just a humble pawnbroker."

With a satisfied nod, Maud lowered her voice as she continued. "What do you know of a prophecy for the English throne? By a fortune teller in the East."

"I've never encountered a prophecy for the English throne," she said apologetically. "Inceptions of the future are rarely so clear they'd be seen by more than one visionary."

"I'd like to know what my future holds," she said, careful not to tell Dzintra the details of the prophecy in case it should further influence her reading.

Smiling, the fortune teller led Maud to a round log sawed into a table. "Open your palms."

She studied the lines on Maud's hands closely, tracing them gently with her fingertips. Gasping, she dropped Maud's hand to the wood. She stared into the duchess' eyes with an unblinking, ice-blue stare, and Maud felt suddenly self-conscious. "What is it?"

The fortune teller stood. "I can't read your fortune, Duchess. You don't need it."

"What do you mean?"

Mistress Dzintra looked distressed. "I don't want your deniers. I haven't seen anything worth charging my usual fee."

Her eyes darted across the room as she spoke, and Maud knew she was lying. "I could make you tell me what you saw," she reminded her, but the fortune teller was unmoved.

"Please believe me when I say I saw nothing to suggest harm to your loved ones." She quivered, and Maud chose not to press her.

"I'll never understand why Agatha trusts all of you so much, or how you give her any comfort."

Stepping aside as Maud stood to leave, the fortune teller looked relieved.

"What do you think she saw?" Gundred struggled to keep up with her exasperated duchess as they crossed the square back to the carriage.

"Probably nothing. Rather than give me a false reading, she thought better than to take advantage of the Duchess of Normandy."

"Mother Mary is always with you, Duchess," called Mistress Dzintra from her hut. Maud stopped in her tracks. "She'll find a way to let you know soon. Keep an eye on the heavens."

The fortune teller disappeared into her hut and Maud regained her composure. Leaning toward Gundred, she scowled. "Tell no one I was so desperate to hear someone say my husband and child would survive the year, I sought it from a con artist."

Returning from town in time for a meal with her family, Maud listened with exhaustion while Robert begged to join his father's army.

"Some of the nobles' sons are joining the fight, and I'll almost be sixteen by the time you sail."

"You're not ready. Besides, if anything happens to me, I need you here to take care of your mother and manage the duchy."

"At least you're not being forced into a convent," Emma spat, her brow creased in an angry shadow as they dined. The golden light of early evening angled through long windows.

"I want to go to the convent," Cecilia protested quietly.

William roared. Slamming his fists on the wooden table, he stood to silence the children. Sending them to their chambers, they knew not to argue with him in this mood and went reasonably, kissing their mother's cheek as they retired.

To cool his temper, Maud suggested they take a walk in the courtyard, saying instead she wanted to take advantage of a seasonably warm eve. They walked close, his hand resting protectively on her stomach as she kept one eye on the sky.

"What are you looking for?" wondered William, but she didn't know until it was there. A bright, exquisite star sailed across the dusky sky, like an arrow pierced in fire, spilling stardust in its wake.

She smiled with relief, tears brimming her cheeks as they watched the star in awe. "I think all our prayers have been answered."

Chapter Thirty-Nine

July 1066 – The Abbey of Sainte Trinity in Caen, Normandy

The day before their first son was born, Maud and William made a deal with the Pope for two new cathedrals. Fifteen years, nine babies, and five pontiffs later, their towering stone houses of worship were finally complete.

To mark the occasion, a city-wide mass gathered at the steps of Saint Stephen's, built for the monks. The duke and his family would be guests of honor before Cecilia would enter the convent at Sainte Trinity's next door. Maud was determined the dedications would be the grand occasion the cathedrals deserved, having fretted over details with the bishops for months.

Emma sulked while Maud and her ladies-in-waiting dressed the girls for the ceremony. "I won't go," she protested, while Gundred pinned her veil. "I won't watch you give our sister away to the Catholic Church in exchange for the promise of war."

Maud exhaled in exasperation. "For the last time, Emma, we're not giving your sister away. We're devoting Ceci to God to honor Him."

"I don't even know why we need to do more for God now that Lanfranc secured the Pope's consent for the attack on England. He even convinced Rome to excommunicate the new King Harold for breaking his vow at Bayeux to support Papa."

"Some would be more grateful for His blessings than you," Maud shot back, staring down her challenging eldest daughter.

"What about the comet? Papa and everyone else in Normandy think it heralds his success. It even suits Agatha Wessex's prophecy. What God could need more?"

"I volunteered, Emma," insisted Cecilia from a wooden chair to quell the tension. Tossing her sister a sly grin, she added, "With the education I'll get at the convent, I'll definitely be smarter than you soon. Besides, I don't have to get dressed up like the rest of you, because fancy gowns won't be of any use with the nuns."

"Fancy dress or simple robes doesn't matter, Ceci, but you can still braid your hair."

She pouted softly. "Will you braid it, Mama?"

Taking strands of white ribbon and a horsehair brush from the vanity, Cecilia sat forward in her chair with a gleeful laugh. Maud untangled the mess of auburn hair in her hands, catching her breath to hold back a solemn tear. They'd clung to one another the past few months, their separation slowly dawning on them. Though Maud enjoyed every minute with her, today she had to stay strong for them both.

Finishing Cecilia's long braids, she tied them off and met her daughter's crooked smile. "I have a gift for you."

"I'm not allowed to take anything into the convent, Mama."

"We'll deliver it to the nun's library, but it will be yours. If you ever leave Sainte Trinity's, the book will go with you."

Reaching for Lady Emma's elaborate book near her bedside, she handed it to her wide-eyed daughter. "Won't you miss reading it, Mama?"

"I know it by heart now, and any good history should be shared."

Behind them, Emma scoffed in her coral veil and gown. "I'll be glad to see that book about my power-hungry namesake go."

"What are you talking about, Emma?" Maud eyed her daughter with frustration.

"I hate sharing her name," she whined. "Why did you have to name me after her?"

"You didn't know her. She was a great woman, and you should be proud to wear her name." Worried she might be driven to reaction by her daughter's moody insolence, Maud seethed, clasping her hands together in front of her long robes.

Emma stepped forward to embrace her sister in a tight hug, eyeing her mother bitterly. "You did this for us, Ceci. Your sisters—we won't forget this."

Maud's portly old steward appeared in the doorway. "You all look marvelous," said Bertrand. "Duke William and the boys are waiting downstairs."

"We're ready." Corralling her daughters, she scooped Matilda in her arms before they met William and their sons in the Great Hall.

"You look stunning," he said, placing one hand on his wife's stomach while the other cupped her chin. "How have you felt this morning?"

"The bounty of the apple orchards has done wonders keeping sickness at bay with this child," she said, and he smiled down at her small belly with relief. "It's a beautiful day, and we have much to be happy about. As we've all believed the comet heralds our victory in England, I've believed it confirms this one will be born healthy. When Lanfranc returned with news of Rome's support, we all knew: God is truly on our side."

Maud avoided Emma's disappointed gaze to embrace her husband. Piled into open-top carriages for the short journey from the castle to the cathedrals with her mother and siblings, Emma pouted as they rolled past cheering subjects. Maud tried in vain to ignore her sour mood, watching her sons with a satisfied smile as they rode on horseback beside their father. Even six-year-old Rufus rode a stocky brown pony, waving proudly at the rabble as he held the reins with one hand. She smiled at the crowds, reaching deeper into the thin streets around the square than Maud could see.

When the duke's cortège arrived at Saint Stephen's Cathedral, built in creamy yellow limestone quarried from hills northwest of Caen, the onlookers cheered louder. Standing atop stone steps, Lanfranc and a row of silent monks stood waiting, miniscule in comparison to the towering church.

William offered his hand to escort his wife from the carriage. Careful not to disturb the hem of her skirt, she absently cradled her stomach with her other hand. Ascending the cathedral steps slowly, arm-in-arm, they knelt before their old friend at the top, on two carefully placed velvet cushions. Serving as abbot to the new cathedral, Lanfranc delivered prayers, anointing their foreheads with holy water from a golden chalice. A hush fell as he spoke.

Dedicating the churches in their names, William gifted his father's scrolls to much fanfare from the crowds below. Then the family walked the short distance to Sainte Trinity's, where Benedictine nuns waited at the entrance to accept Cecilia into the Order. Tall, pointed spires with elaborate ironwork pierced the clear sky, and Cecilia looked upon the eminent structure with unease. She pulled back slowly, dragging her mother's hand.

"Mama, I'm scared. You promise you'll visit?"

"There's nothing to fear," she cooed gently. "We'll visit so often you'll get tired of us."

William knelt before his daughter to meet her nervous gaze. "A thousand promises, dear Ceci. One for every visit." Maud blinked a tear from her eye. Following her parents' example, Ceci knelt before the elder abbess at the entrance to the convent.

"Welcome." She rested weathered fingers on Ceci's small shoulders. "You may stand."

With one final glance to her family, Cecilia stood in the shadow of the tall doors of the convent. Beside her, William stood before his reverent subjects.

"Your duchess and I have been honored by your presence this afternoon." The crowd hung on his every word. "In celebration of the occasion, our chefs have been baking free loaves of fresh bread. Please, file orderly. There's enough for every citizen of Caen."

The people roared approval as court chefs wheeled out wagons of bread. Beaming, Maud wiped away tears as Cecilia marched inside, deep into the stone church with the nuns.

The harbor village of Barfleur smelled of salted fish, with pungent ocean zephyrs wafting southward from the windswept sea. Wooden ships dotted the breakwater, some small vessels fixed with fishing nets, and wider frames with taller masts bound for trade routes from London to Oslo. Maud felt the sun on her cheeks under clear skies and a warm September breeze, respite following a week of stormy weather.

Further out, hundreds of longships dotted the azure waters, already loaded with thousands of men, horses, and armor, with enough weaponry that the weight of the ships were precariously balanced to ensure safe crossing. All the nobles of Normandy had gathered in the harbor, each bringing as few as a dozen to as many as hundreds of men, depending on the size of their Norman lands.

"There's so many men, I can't count them all." Agatha gaped, wide-eyed, at the chaotic scene.

Her twin, Constance, stood in equal astonishment. "I can't even count the boats!"

Even Maud had never seen a flotilla so large. She led them to a long dock where an enormous drakkar longship floated in the harbor, a fire-breathing dragon carved into the stern. The sailing mast rocked in the gentle breeze, its carved wooden hull bobbing in the waves while men loaded crates from the shore. Gold accents glistened in the sunlight—none more brightly than the golden child perched atop the ship's bow, pointing north toward her husband's destiny.

"What a fine ship she is," mused William. "Which noble brought her?"

"You did, my love." Maud shot her husband an impish smile, and he watched his prized horse being loaded below deck. "Seven hundred ships in the harbor can't compete with the stature of this one. I had it made for you."

He was truly grateful for the elaborate surprise, staring upon his new ship and its multicolored sails with childlike joy. "She's stunning. What's her name?"

"I wanted a name befitting your destiny to lead a great royal house. Mora, for the Morinis who traded for the Romans and laid the foundations for the county of my birth, and because *Mora* and *amor* use the same letters, my love," she said cheekily. "It's also Latin for 'foolish woman,' which is unfortunate because it's a lovely word, but when I think of what people called me during my year of convalescence, it might be fitting too."

Emma scoffed from behind them. "What is it now, Emma?" William asked.

"Nothing, Papa," she said, but the scowl on her lips belied her answer.

"Speak now," he bellowed. "You might not get another chance to tell me."

Her sneer softened faster than her tongue. "I don't want you to die, Papa, but I don't understand why you want us to move back to Rouen. What about Ceci?"

"The castle at Rouen is tested against invading forces, and it's further from Brittany," he explained. "Ceci's safe with the nuns, but you'll be safer at my father's chateau."

"We promised her!"

"We'll be back to Caen soon," Maud insisted.

Emma shot her a deadly glare. "Not if we're in England."

"Please, Emma," said Richard gently. "We all know how you feel about it."

Anger silenced her frowning lips, allowing her siblings to say goodbye to their father without another sullen word. Certain she hadn't heard the last of her daughter's moody protestations, Maud felt relief for the momentary pause.

Meeting her husband's dark eyes, she smiled as he kissed the children—her warrior, decorated with scars and sins, and their stubborn but loving bear of a father. His two sides, both vital to the success of their family. If Maud let herself entertain the dangerous possibilities of his voyage, she knew victory was the only acceptable outcome.

He stood, enveloping his wife in his arms, and she fell into him for a long embrace. Fitz and Bishop Odo called to him from the stern of the *Mora*, while half a dozen men pulled ropes to raise the ship's multicolored flags. William's men loaded into the boat with Lanfranc, but Monty and Beau stayed behind. The duke turned to them and offered strong hugs.

"Watch over him. The duchy is his should anything happen, but he's still young."

Robert crossed his arms defensively, glaring at his father. "I'll do well as regent while you're gone. I'll take care of Mama and the baby and protect us all from the Duke of Brittany."

William chuckled, playfully punching his son's shoulder. Robert gritted his teeth. "Beau and Monty can handle the defenses if Duke Conan becomes a problem. You take care of your mother and help her run the duchy while I'm gone. The harvest will be soon, and you'll need to start taking collections. As duke, it will be one of the most important ways to raise money."

Robert nodded subserviently. "Yes, Papa."

William pulled him in for a hug, which at first surprised their eldest son, so unused to his father's affection. But Robert nimbly raised his arms and embraced him in return, accepting the burst of love he often longed for. Maud watched with tears in her eyes.

Pulling his wife away from the children, William leaned in for one last kiss, his hands caressing her stomach over billowing robes. "I hate to leave you with another one on the way."

"I know you're worried, William. I know your fear, but I choose to believe it will all go to plan, both in England and with this one's birth." She spoke with confidence, brushing his tunic. "Men can't help a woman in labor unless he can deliver a baby anyway."

"I'll send word while I'm away. I know I'm not always great with words, but I'll think of you every minute—even in battle." He grinned, pulling her close. "If I could ever turn off thoughts of you, my love, I wouldn't want to."

Holding back tears, Maud stood with her children embracing her as the fleet of ships sailed from the harbor. The *Mora*, largest of all, flew the white papal banner with its blue-and-gold cross atop the mast, announcing their legitimacy to all.

The boats far surpassed the number of vessels Maud remembered from the day she waved goodbye to Lady Emma in her youth, and hopeful anticipation filled her heart. Just as the old queen set sail to reclaim a place in her beloved England decades earlier, now she watched her husband sail to stake their claim on its future.

Captains blew horns in celebration. Families waved to their loved ones from the pier, watching as seven hundred boats, carrying thousands of men and beasts, slowly disappeared over the blue horizon.

Chapter Forty

The Book of William

October 1066 – Hastings, England

My dearest wife,

We left you and the children in Barfleur under sunny skies, getting caught in a shift in the weather soon after Normandy disappeared on the horizon at our backs. Taking no chances, we rerouted our fleet to harbor at Saint-Valery-sur-Somme to wait for good weather. I send this first dispatch from the Norman side of the narrow sea, with men anxious to cross and gain English lands for themselves.

Some questioned whether the sudden inclement weather was an omen, and to those men I said they were welcome to leave with their boots still on the continent if they lacked confidence in our victory, freeing them from the burden of the potential spoils. No surprise, they all chose to stay. They drink tonight, filling the streets with their merriment, but we'll prepare again for the journey in the morning.

I miss you already, my love, and count the days until I look upon your face again. God willing, it will be soon into the new year, and I'll bring you a crown as a late Christmas gift.

Your loving husband,
William

My dearest love,

We landed safely at a place called Pevensey, not far from where we landed at Borne all those years ago. Your ship is so fast, before we made landfall I had to stop for wine and bread to wait for the rest of the flotilla to catch us. The locals were in awe of all our ships when we arrived, but we blew the horn of war and gave them the chance to submit or flee. The majority fled, leaving us to raid their homes for supplies to build our camp.

Soon after our arrival we received the wonderful, if expected, news of Harold's victory over his brother and the Norwegian army in the north. Both Tostig and Harald Hardrada were killed at a crossing called Stamford Bridge, with the survivors sent back to Norway in disgrace. It's a mighty victory for Harold Godwinson and his men, but the Norwegians are tall and fierce and depleted much of the English army's resources.

Our late arrival due to the weather was perfectly timed—Harold's weakened army had no time to rest before they had to reform to the south on a hill in Hastings overlooking our battlements. We lay in wait now, as Harold has the high ground, plotting his next move.

Your love is the last thing I think of at night,
Your William

My beloved wife,

I dictate my latest letter from a bloody field. Harold Godwinson and many of his closest allies lie dead, their blood soiling the earth I declare in our name. I was victorious, my love. Harold and his men were fierce warriors, but no match for our fine companions.

Like most men defending such vast territory, Harold stubbornly refused to advance, so I waited him out until the soldiers began to feel restless. To prevent Harold's attack on an unmotivated gentry, I tried goading the former king to move downhill. We sent forward Ivo Taillefer, the court minstrel, singing "The Song of Roland" on his white horse. He sang better than ever, I swear it, distracting Harold's men into a daze. Their attack was uncoordinated as Taillefer charged forward alone, taking down five English soldiers before they gave him the honorable death he deserved. Once Harold's men had moved down the hill, I could send the cavalry charging in behind them.

The battle raged a day. Even Odo fought mightily with a club and not a sword, so as not to break his solemn vow to spill no blood as a man of the cloth. But despite our valor, it looked as though Harold and his men would defend their lands and send our weaker forces running for their ships, tearing our offensive apart. Fitz says I shouldn't tell you how close I came to being cut down, especially as my horse landed on me so hard when it was speared, I thought for a minute I had died. A mob swelled, but I ripped myself from the grasp of none other than Hakon Sweynson. He raised his sword to strike me, but the saber was mine before the poor fool finished his swing. I tore him from his horse and struck him down, then ordered my men to take his uncle, Wulf, into custody. He didn't even put up a fight.

I tore my helmet from my head in the confusion, to ensure my men knew I couldn't be beaten by a simple horse, nor any bands of fighting men. Swearing vengeance against any who would run from the field of battle, I vowed never to die until they'd all paid the price. Absurd, certainly, but this was enough to turn the tides, inspiring our men to fight as fiercely as me. I admit I delighted in making Wulf a prisoner again—this time entirely of his own accord. The land was won by late afternoon, and the orange sun set long shadows on the blood and mud-soaked field.

As I always do when the sun meets the horizon, I thought of you, and how we made this dream that day by the lake. I never would have achieved it without you, love. We must still make our way to London before I can claim the Kingdom of England, but if the autumn is mild, we should secure the southern towns and reach the city by December.

Edie Swanneck and Harold's mother, Gytha, came after the battle to identify his body and claim him for burial, battered though it was by arrows and swords. But most of the men thought releasing the former king to be buried with honor showed weakness. I don't favor dishonoring the bodies of those who die nobly in battle, but my men faced great blows to emerge victorious in our name, and the survivors thought this suitable vengeance against him for their troubles.

The women left with bitter understanding, as most of their sons had either died or fled before the battle was lost. The field littered with the bones of their allies, neither Edie nor Gytha shed a single tear for their army of dead men. I'll leave them be if they remain at least neutral in the coming months or years, but I'll never let my guard down with the Godwins.

I'll end this letter with one final declaration of my love for you, and gratitude for all we've built together. I long to bring you here to let the people fall as deeply in love with their new queen as I am forevermore. England will be ours, and tonight I'll rest dreaming of our future and all its possibilities.

I love you,
William

My dearest wife,

We're making our way north through a dreary rainy season, subduing any village revolts with superior force, and meeting any resistance with fire. The spoils help pay off our mercenaries to send them home, but we leave some Normans behind to manage rebuilding efforts and continue north toward London. We should reach the Thames in a few days, where I expect to meet their defenses with our proud fighting men, who've done much of what I've asked so far with bravery and dedication.

The days are always longer without you and the children to fill my time, but I keep busy meeting with town elders, negotiating to solidify our forts, and looking for potential allies among the English nobility. If most of them—especially those from the north—submit to my authority, we'll secure the throne with ease.

My next dispatch should come from the capital. Until then, all my love,

William

My dearest queen,

We arrived in London with the king's council about to crown Edgar Aetheling, but a short standoff with the Archbishop of Canterbury and his forces ended in the man's submission. We set fire to the wooden bridge under Southwark Cathedral and the buildings on the northern side of the river—they didn't even shoot a single arrow in response. It was too easy, and we quickly discovered none of the king's council truly had faith in the Boy King. They practically rolled out the welcome mat, but I hesitate to trust any of them, inwardly.

Outwardly, it's been all smiles and feasts for days, though I'm more disappointed than Lanfranc that I've had to leave the Anglo-Saxon Archbishop in charge at Canterbury for now. A smooth transition is important, and Archbishop Stigand, despite his excommunication, is well-connected to every clergyman in the kingdom. But no mind is more important to us than Lanfranc's, and he knows he must replace Stigand at the first legitimate opportunity. I haven't yet worn him down, but you know Lanfranc; I wonder if he's just playing coy to earn the trust of the English clergy.

The mood was tense with the local lords at first. Some of the northern earls escaped the Palace of Westminster with Harold's wife and son before we besieged it. I couldn't spare the men to go after them, but I stayed focused on the earls who stood before me. None of them wanted to face the same brutality as Harold's men. Even Edgar and his mother and sisters submitted to me.

Agatha tells me you wrote to her, to let her know we would be coming. She said she wants a peaceful life for her children and will align with our court if we can provide for them. I told her what I knew you expected me to say, which is that they're welcome to our support.

I protested again that I wanted to wait for a coronation until you and the baby are ready to join me, but everyone insists that a quick coronation is better for stability. We're rehearsing everything down to the minute, and will hold the ceremony with two bishops, in English and in French. On Christmas Day, I'll wear the crown of England, king in body and in name, and it's only a matter of time before you, too, will have your moment of crowning glory.

I love you. Today and every day.

Your loving husband,
William

Dearest Queen,

It's only days from my coronation and I received good news times two. First, I heard of your healthy childbirth with our sweet girl, Adela. I'm sure she'll embody the strength of your mother's spirit and the grace of her blessed sister. My heart burst with joy and satisfaction to know you're both well at home in Rouen.

Then I heard of the murder of Duke Conan of Brittany, gifted a poisoned glove before riding to his death. God smiles upon us, my love.

I'm told the prime suspect for the murder is me, which is to be expected, but the truth is I never gave the order. He hasn't mustered the devastating army he promised—not after I paid off enough Breton volunteers to make up one-third of my own invading force. Maybe all Lady Berthe's children are fools. I never would have come up with the idea if he didn't warn me he'd invade while I was gone.

While I'm not responsible for Conan's death, I have no kind words for Lady Berthe in her hour of loss this time around. I don't suppose you've heard anything about his poisoning back in Normandy.

Now, the Dukedom of Brittany falls to Duke Alain and Lady Berthe's last surviving child, a daughter with no sons. Even if she has one, we'll have decades before he's ready to avenge his uncle's death. If we play our cards right, he might not even want to.

Give the children kisses for me—with an extra one for Adela. Let her know we'll meet soon. All my love to you, my queen. I can't wait to hold you in my arms again.

Your loving husband,
William

PART NINE

Coronation

Chapter Forty-One

February 1067 – Château de Moulineaux in Rouen, Normandy

The new King William, Conqueror of England, marched into the Great Hall in Rouen, a golden crown perched atop his head. He carried an even greater confidence than his wife remembered when he was merely a duke. She presented their rosy-cheeked baby girl, sleeping peacefully against the diaphanous sleeves of her robes. With him were his stewards, Fitz, Beau, and Monty, their friend, Lanfranc, and dozens more—some she recognized, others were strangers yet—but she greeted all magnanimously for their roles in the great victory.

Her dress was new, in bright shades of pink and red, embroidered with gold thread in floral patterns. She had it made specifically for William's return from England, ostensibly to impress her husband, as well as the retinue of Anglo-Saxons who followed him across the sea to pay homage to their new monarch. Her gold-and-sapphire butterfly pin still shimmered, as it did when William gifted it to her before their engagement.

Beaming with joy, William cradled Adela in his arms while Maud greeted the Anglo-Saxon nobles gathered in a line behind their king. Introducing each of them with honor, he then turned to his elegantly dressed wife. "Gentlemen, your new queen," he said proudly. They bowed generously before her.

"It's a shame you couldn't be there for your husband's coronation, my lady," said Stigand, the Archbishop of Canterbury and most senior English official among William's entourage. "It was a most moving occasion, with a light snowfall right at the moment the Archbishop of York anointed his forehead with holy oil."

"I'm sorry to have missed it," she said warmly, with a nod to her peaceful baby girl. "But I was well occupied here."

"Yes, raising such a large household is busy work indeed."

"On top of helping maintain the duchy, I sometimes wonder how I manage." Laughing, she rolled her eyes to herself with discretion. "And I still managed daily visits to the chapel at Nôtre Dame du Pré to leave gifts and pray for the safety of a great many souls."

The archbishop nodded with a smug grin, and Maud shot a discreet look in Lanfranc's direction. He watched the room silently, his eyes fixed on the man still in the role William wanted him to fill. The way the English lords and bishops cowered in his presence made clear how Stigand held his position despite his excommunication.

"It was quite powerful," agreed Aldred, the Archbishop of York, with a meek but amiable expression. "I asked the gathered nobles if they accepted the Norman as their king, then the Bishop of Coutances asked the same of the Normans. It was quite unanimous indeed."

Young Edgar Aetheling shifted uncomfortably as his former allies spoke so well of another king. "Until the guards outside heard the hollering and thought the new king was under attack inside the church. Then the guards set fire to the houses."

"I set the guards to work immediately, rebuilding the homes they burned in the confusion," said William, eyeing the Aetheling with unease.

He stood with his mother, Agatha, and Margaret. Maud was taken aback when they bowed low before her, addressing her cordially as "Your Majesty."

Noticing, William chuckled. "You have time to get used to that, my love."

"Where is Cristina?" she wondered. "Keeping up her studies at Wilton Abbey?" Agatha nodded slowly. "And Margaret, you've chosen not to join King Malcolm in Scotland?"

"I met him again, my queen, and I thought he was very charming, but when it was thought Edgar would succeed King Edward, God rest his soul, the council believed a marriage alliance with the Scots would upset the north to rebellion."

"They pillage our farms and raid our villages, Your Majesties." One of the northern earls stepped forward, reintroducing himself to his new queen. "I'm Gospatric, Earl of Northumbria. I've driven off bands of Scottish raiders from my family's lands too many times to count."

"The Scottish people are no friends of the Anglo-Saxons, and the fact King Malcolm is allied with the Normans brings many in England no comfort," added Edwin, Earl of Mercia.

Maud flashed an understanding smile. "You're a brother of King Harold's second wife, aren't you, Lord Edwin? Isn't it strange that, though Harold wed your sister at the expense of his first wife, Edie Swanneck was the one who identified his body while your sister ran?"

"I wasn't a supporter of her marriage to Harold," he said assuredly. "My father agreed to it, but now he's dead and so is my brother-in-law. My fealty is to our new king, but Aldgyth has more devotion to her infant son than any other man. After my brothers and I sent them to Chester at the time of the conquest, we lost track of her."

She didn't believe him. A knowing glance between Maud and her husband said he held the same suspicion, but she was careful not to let it show in her smile to the English earl.

That careful presence faltered when Robert and Richard entered the room with Ulf Haroldson—no longer the meek young boy she remembered at Walsingham, but a gangly teenager with a ruddy-cheeked complexion. Since his appearance in Normandy before Christmas, Maud had been troubled and she couldn't hide it on her face.

"Father, this is Ulf Haroldson," said Robert proudly. William's face brightened.

"The killer of Conan of Brittany himself!" Gently, he passed baby Adela to Gundred van Oosterzele before rushing to shake the young man's hand. "When I heard it was you, I was honored, considering you'd just lost so many of your family at the hands of my men."

"Robert's offer of freedom was too good," Ulf admitted. "When he sent the boat, I said goodbye to my mother and our cursed home and left. When I pretended to submit to Duke Conan at Pouancé, I brought a leather riding glove in tribute, laced with arsenic." Smiling at his own murderous trick, he continued. "Once Conan knew I'd come from the English court, he believed without question I'd want to fight against you. I didn't even need to tell him who my father was."

William laughed heartily at the story. "You're cunning like your Godwin kin."

Ulf smiled with pride in his eyes. "But I'd achieve little trying to avenge my father's death. I have no interest in my father's lands or charging into battle. His territories will be divided among new barons anyway. I want only to move freely to pursue passions of my own."

William patted him on the back with a jovial laugh. "You'll have that and more. Stay as long as you wish at my court in Normandy. I know my sons are glad to have you here. Perhaps Edgar can join you young men when you head out to hunt tomorrow."

Nodding, Edgar barely raised a smile. He was no longer the outgoing little boy who pleaded with his mother to spend time with Maud's sons. As she looked sadly upon her eldest son, Robert, Maud understood how people could change.

When she discovered Duke Conan's assassination was plotted by her son, Maud was mortified. Yet she feared she had no right to be, suffering her regret in silence. Outwardly, she celebrated Robert's plan working in more ways than one, eliminating their adversary and impressing his father immensely.

"Robert, my boy," he said, his eyes twinkling as if the dismissive *Curthose* had never left his lips, "you may yet be the great leader our realms deserve."

Robert grinned with bursting pride, and William announced a great feast would be held in the hall that very evening. Maud presided over the chefs for most of the morning and knew the sumptuous feast of roasted eel—a delicacy prized for its rarity—would please even the most elegant appetites among the visiting nobles.

"You should mention the state visit from the King of Leon, Your Majesty." Lanfranc spoke carefully from his corner of the room, and William frowned.

Maud leaned into her husband. "A visit from a king? How soon?"

"The Dowager Queen of Leon and her son, King Alfonso, will arrive in a week. They wish to discuss a marriage alliance for one of our daughters."

Surrounded by men they couldn't trust, rage bubbled as she strained to keep her composure. "Surely you've said they're too young yet." Her blithe chuckle was unconvincing.

"If they wish to marry any of our girls, we'll request a few years before the actual marriage, once we're more settled on both sides of the narrow sea. But Emma's already thirteen. Defending a kingdom takes more than defending a duchy. We need powerful alliances with other kingdoms."

She bit her tongue, unwilling to express her true feelings in a crowded room, turning instead toward Ulf Haroldson to ease the building tension. "Have you heard anything from your mother since you left Norfolk?"

He shook his head. "No, my queen. The night I left she'd already let Gran Gytha take my sisters south to stay with Aunt Edith in retirement. My mother wanted them to continue their schooling, but she'd given away so many of her worldly goods in the months before the conquest, she could easily disappear into the night. She's not in Ireland with my brothers who escaped the battlefield, and I don't know if I'll hear from her again. I hope I do."

"Should you need resources to find her, you can always ask."

Maud frowned at the sound of her husband's voice. Anger filled her throat, but she held back. "I have great respect for your mother. Wherever she is now, I hope she's well." She spoke gently before excusing herself. Inviting Agatha and Margaret, they followed dutifully.

"Your little girl is quite beautiful, Your Majesty," Agatha said nervously as they walked a long, torchlit hallway. Maud looked at her with mild exasperation.

"You need not address me so formally. We're old friends."

Agatha shook her head firmly. "We are your subjects, not your friends. If we had any friends, the council would have crowned my son as King Edward intended."

"I said she refused to consider the throne being taken from Edgar after King Edward's death, even though she knew others had their eye on it," Margaret responded coyly. "We knew you eyed the throne, but Edgar was so close to more power than he's ever known. I don't think he'll let it go, and we're afraid to think what your husband may do to him someday."

Maud froze in step. "It seems everyone I trust with my life believes their lives aren't safe with me." She stared forlornly at the women. "Agatha, if you think your son will challenge my husband for the throne, I'll do everything I can to convince William to keep him alive. I promise you. King Malcolm is still unmarried, so there's still the option of exile in Scotland."

"But the northern earls!" Margaret betrayed her composure with a hopeful grin.

"Leave that to us. Say the word, and we'll send notice to Malcolm to deliver a ship."

Agatha bowed gratefully, promising to talk to her son. Maud could hear merriment echo through the dark stone walls as the chefs called the start of the feast. Loath to join them, she let the women return without her and listened as the men drunkenly compared tracts of English land now up for the taking. Still angry at her husband for agreeing to a marriage contract without her consent, she felt ill-prepared to present as his honorable queen this evening.

"You said we wouldn't have to marry for a long time." Emma's accusation cut through the raucous feast down the hall, startling Maud as her eldest daughter moved into the light.

"When I said it, it was true," she said, lifting her robes to march up the stairwell.

Emma tailed her. "I won't marry. I won't go with them. I'm not like you or Lady Emma."

"Act like this when Leon gets here, and I'm sure they'll avoid you," Maud sniped.

"I told you things would be different if Papa became king."

"I'm begging you, Emma, please leave me tonight. I've been invigorated enough to tolerate your constant disdain since Adela's birth, but I'm no happier about this than you are."

Emma's face softened. "I told my sisters you lied, and they're too upset to go to sleep."

"For someone who claims to hate war, you certainly don't mind sowing chaos."

Maud finished climbing the stairs, entering her daughters' large bedroom, with four beds facing a bearskin rug in the center of the room. Agatha, Constance, and Matilda clambered toward her, tearful at the prospect of marriage to a stranger.

She tried in vain to comfort them, because she couldn't be comforted herself, spotting something on Emma's bed which drove her to distraction. "Is that the translated scroll of *Beowulf* your father sent over before Christmas?"

Emma nodded. "I've been reading the Latin and studying the original English, but I can't make sense of most of the words and what they mean."

"Maybe we should find you a tutor who knows English," Maud suggested thoughtfully, picking up the scroll in her hands.

"What's the point?" Emma's shrug carried the weight of the world on her thin shoulders. "England's languages will be conquered just like their lands, and we'll be married off to men who'll decide how we spend our days."

"I know you're afraid because I've given you nothing but reasons to believe marriage this young is a terrible thing." She sighed at her daughters' rapt faces. "But it doesn't have to be, and your father and I will always defend you, even when you join another court."

Emma gave a spiteful curl of her lips. "I'd rather go back to Caen and go to school at the convent with Ceci, who we haven't visited in months."

"I want to visit Ceci!" parroted four-year-old Matilda, and Maud forced a smile.

"Soon we will," she said gently. "For now, what if we read Beowulf's story together?"

Excitement spread across their faces as they surrounded her in a carved wooden chair. With her daughters spread out at her feet, she fed their ravenous minds with the tale of a young Swedish warrior who defeated monsters to become a king on the English isle, staying with them until they finally tucked into their beds to sleep.

Chapter Forty-Two

February 1067 – Château de Moulineaux in Rouen, Normandy

Despite this quality time with her children—even Emma listened intently as she read—Maud returned angrily to her chambers that night. Passing an open door, she spotted William's desk and an unrolled parchment caught her eye. The scroll was so long it spilled onto the floor, and Maud curiously examined the penmanship.

Listed were the names and properties of dozens of Anglo-Saxon lords. Some, like Gospatric and Edwin, remained untouched. Other names, likely dead, were scratched out, the names of others, like Fitz, Monty, and Beau's two sons, replacing them next to the listed properties. Scanning the black ink, her eyes fell on one name, ever familiar. Brictric, son of Algar—his name uncrossed, with numerous properties still listed in his name.

William's letters never revealed the fate of Brictric, and she'd never wondered, but her heart sank to see he'd survived the conquest unscathed. So many other men had perished, but Brictric lived to chase young women another day. She frowned, reliving the embarrassment of her affections.

"It's so senseless," she muttered to herself. Reaching instinctively for William's feather quill, she dipped the shaft in a thick glass vial of black ink. Crossing out Brictric's name, she recorded her own in its place. With a blank sheet of parchment, she recorded an edict demanding his immediate arrest, and the confiscation of all his lands in the name of the new queen. Only his main property was to remain out of her control, as she left it to Goda, his long-faced wife.

Signing the edict in her husband's name, with the elaborate cross he used to distinguish his own signature, she warmed a small block of wax over a candle, gently dipping her husband's seal in the melted material.

"Where were you tonight? What are you doing?" She looked up

quickly, her face anxious as William approached. Seeing the letter in her hand he ripped it from her grasp. He didn't read well but read well enough to understand the note and his eyes darkened. "Is this a joke?"

She shook her head, staring him down with fire in her eyes.

"If it's no joke, then you hurt me. You make me look petty over the man I've spent a lifetime pretending means nothing to you."

"I saw his name and didn't know why he should keep his lands," she argued.

"He wasn't going to keep them, Maud." He threw the folded edict to her lap. "I hadn't decided what to do with them yet, but now I guess I don't need to." His eyes burned into her. "Seal it."

"I don't have to send it," she said. "We could call off the marriage alliance with the Kingdom of Leon and I'll burn the letter in that candle."

He balked, laughing spitefully. "After all these years he can still make you do impulsive, stupid things, but at least this isn't really about Brictric."

Cowed by his accurate assessment, she did as he asked, dipping his seal back into the wax on the table as he barked down the hall. Placing the edict in her husband's hand, her steward appeared eagerly in the doorway.

"Have this sent to my brother in England," William said stiffly. "Have the messenger tell him I expect it to be carried out within the week."

Bertrand nodded obediently, taking the sealed parchment. Leaving them alone in the room, he shut the door behind him on his way. Maud eyed her husband dubiously.

"You'd rather look petty than call off a marriage alliance none of our daughters want?"

"I can be petty," he cut back with a dismissive shrug. "I was going to give you the earldom of Kent and make you the wealthiest landowner in England. Lands even more vast than Brictric's, along with the title of countess. But I can't give you the County of Kent and all Brictric's land on top of that. Then you'd own more land than me."

"I don't need to be a countess. I'm already a duchess and a queen," she argued.

He sneered. "Now Odo will be a bishop and an earl."

"And one of our daughters will be a reluctant bride, but that doesn't matter because at least she'll be a queen." Sarcasm dripped from her lips.

"What the hell have you become?" he spat. "I rushed home from England to ensure your health following Adela's birth, dragging half of England's nobles back with me to keep them in line, and I found a woman who scorns my existence."

"You broke your word. You promised never to sign a marriage contract for any of our children without my consent, and you blind-sided me. You could have sent word before breaking the news of our daughters' future in front of the entire court."

"I'm sorry I agreed before consulting you," he said sincerely. "I never intended to hurt you, but you're acting as though I meant to hurt our daughters." She glared up at him, her angry eyes glistening in the candlelight. "A man knows his daughters will never be better cared for than if they marry a king. For our security and our children's future, we can't pass up this opportunity."

"A woman knows better," she shot back. "My grandmother, Constance, became the unfortunate Queen of Francia. She knew better. You can't just give them away."

Exasperated, William raised an accusatory finger in her face. "I didn't give our daughter to the Order out of guilt over Marguerite and Herbert's death."

His words punched her in the gut, and her cheeks burned red with anger. "Get out!" she hissed.

"You need to get on board with this plan before Dowager Queen Sancha arrives with King Alfonso. You have one week."

She seethed watching him storm from the room, slamming the door in his wake. She'd never felt such anger toward him, nor felt it from him in return.

For a week, Maud and William avoided each other. He busied himself with his nobles, tending to state affairs while out on gallant hunts in the woods north of Rouen. She preoccupied herself with the children while preparing for the arrival of a king to their court.

The castle was cleaned, the chalices polished, and beds made for the visitors and their entourage. Their finest tapestries were hung in the Great Hall, and on the morning of their arrival, an exhausted Maud looked around the room in satisfaction. But she couldn't raise a smile.

"The chateau looks immaculate, my queen," said Gundred, smiling sweetly. "The dowager queen and King of Leon will surely think so too."

William entered the Great Hall with Fitz at his side, slowing his step when he spotted his wife in the vicinity. "The chateau looks ready," he said cautiously. "Are you?"

"Gundred, please go see if the girls are ready to come downstairs." Her lady-in-waiting obliged, leaving them alone, and Maud sighed heavily. "For the strength of our alliance, most of our daughters are willing to agree to whatever happens today, but they're terrified. I hope you know what you're doing, William."

Before he could respond, they were interrupted by trumpeters atop the ramparts, heralding the arrival of their esteemed guests. The entourage from Leon was large, appearing drenched in golden jewelry in the courtyard. Befitting William and Maud's new status, the dowager queen and King of Leon bowed magnanimously.

"A prayer for your dearly departed husband, my lady," said William, taking note of Dowager Queen Sancha's long black veil and robes. The old woman nodded softly.

"The girls will meet us inside," said Maud, plastering on a fictitious smile as she led them to the Great Hall. King Alfonso, a long-haired, mustachioed man in his mid-twenties, interested himself in studying the tapestries until their daughters entered the room. Maud scooped Adela from Gundred's arms while Emma, Agatha, Constance, and Matilda stood in a row.

William introduced them with pride. In their best dresses, cut from fine Venetian fabrics, the girls paraded for the Iberian king. Alfonso looked down his long nose at all of them, his face unable to hide his disappointment. The dowager queen studied them closely, holding their faces in her slender fingers as if measuring the contours of their cheeks. She was a small, elderly woman with gray brows, arched as if performing a perpetual inquisition. Maud endured the interrogation, passing comforting glances to her daughters.

Dowager Queen Sancha stopped next to Emma with an admiring glance. "You're a pretty one."

"I'd very much like it if you wouldn't choose me," she responded curtly. William shifted uncomfortably as Sancha's jaw dropped, but King Alfonso laughed her off curiously.

"Honesty. How grand!" The young king studied her, but Emma looked past him with defiance. Unable to show it on her face, Maud finally found an appreciation for her attitude.

"You are too angry to be a queen, little girl," said Sancha, clucking her tongue in disapproval. Standing between the monarchs and their daughters, she pointed to Matilda and Adela, dangling long, translucent digits as she spoke. "These two are too young. My son is already twenty-six, and we can't wait for children this long."

William and Maud nodded with understanding. As Adela slept peacefully, Maud pulled her closer with a sigh of relief.

"These two are twins? They look nothing alike, and the pretty one is cursed." Maud sent discreet daggers toward Sancha behind her wide green eyes, but the old queen was defiant. She pointed at young Constance, who watched the faces of the adults as their attention fell upon her. "This one has fine features like her mother, but there's a black cloud behind her dark eyes. Blacker than the cloud around the rude one." She gestured at Emma, who curled her lip at the dowager queen like a hound.

William gently placed his hand over Maud's, silently pleading with her not to react. Conscious of the eyes on them in the room, she refrained from tearing her hand away as she spoke, her voice curt with clipped politeness. "Constance is only nine years old. How could she be cursed?"

Sancha shrugged. "Black clouds can be inherited from our parents."

Reading the tension in the room, King Alfonso stepped forward. "My mother is aging and doesn't know what she sees. Court doctors say the clouds are cataracts." The dowager queen shot her son a disparaging glance but let him speak. "The great Kingdom of Leon has watched your exploits from afar, Your Majesties, and we wish to ensure the combined strength of our territories. We could gain control of the gates to the open sea at the expense of the Aquitanians, Bretons, the Franks—we could contain them all, together."

William raised his brow, interested again following Sancha's insults for his daughters. "We're listening," he said, and Maud's stomach churned.

"Your daughters are quite young yet, but we men have much stronger virility."

"The other twin, with big blue eyes, will probably grow into her features." Sancha leaned toward her son with pleading eyes. "But I grow old. To see an heir before my death will help ensure the future of Leon."

"Agatha is not yet a woman and is still with her tutors," said William. "If you select her, we must request several years before the contract is fulfilled."

"She could finish her education in León," put forth Sancha. "She should become accustomed to the court before she rules as its queen."

"At the very least, she should be able to attend her mother's coronation in London. Following that, a boat can be arranged to bring her to Leon."

"I grow *old*," the dowager queen pressed, but the young king waved her off.

King Alfonso kneeled before Agatha with a gentle smile. "Would you say no to a proposal of marriage to become my queen?"

Agatha glanced cautiously at her parents before solemnly shaking her head.

"And would you like to be able to see your mother's coronation before journeying to Leon?"

Raising a smile, Agatha nodded. Sancha grumbled, but King Alfonso stood to shake King William's hand. "It is agreed. Following the coronation, we'll send for Agatha and bring her to be educated at our court. If it's grandchildren my mother wants, she'll have to live years yet."

King Alfonso sounded as eager to postpone the arrangement as Maud, which brought her immense comfort. The fear filling Agatha's wide blue-eyed gaze before the meeting had melted away, but now her twin, Constance, fidgeted with worry. "A black cloud?" she repeated quietly. Agatha shrugged.

"I don't see one," she whispered, gazing earnestly into her sister's dark eyes.

"Let's draw up the marriage contract," William said, glancing at his wife. "Your mother and my wife will sign as well, to ensure all abide by the terms."

Maud smiled dutifully to beat back her scowl.

Chapter Forty-Three

August 1067 – Château de Moulineaux in Rouen, Normandy

"Why have I been summoned to lunch in the Great Hall? I've been very clear. I prefer to dine without my husband when he's not in England."

Gundred eyed her queen nervously, stammering as their long robes brushed the stone tiles underfoot. "The king wishes to discuss your coronation. The nobles are all here."

"I've said there's no need to rush my coronation. Baby Adela is still too young for a sea voyage."

Startling them from behind, William cleared his throat. "No queen has ever had her own coronation in England," he said gruffly. "And you're the one with Wessex blood, not me. The ceremony will help legitimize our children in the line of English succession."

She scoffed. "It'll be a long time before we need to worry about English succession."

"I thought you wanted to be England's queen." She cocked her head in defiance of his anger.

"I'm sorry, I've been preoccupied convincing our nine year old that her future husband isn't a bad man, and her twin sister that she's not seriously cursed by a cloud."

He turned up his jaw and stalked past her into the Great Hall, where a long table was dressed with breads and pork meat. Their nobles took their seats, helping themselves to pitchers of ale and loading their trenchers with food. Maud sat next to Agatha and Margaret, while William sat between Stigand and Lanfranc across the table.

"Where is Edgar this morning?" wondered Maud with a welcoming smile.

Agatha froze. "G-Gone. He's gone, my queen."

"We think he wants to get to Scotland somehow," admitted Margaret. "He thinks Malcolm might support his claim, but he's never asked him before."

From across the banquet, William overheard, furiously slamming his mug on the table.

"So *who* is helping him?" he boomed, but Agatha and Margaret had no answers and pleaded for the king's mercy. "Send riders to all the harbors in Normandy, and men to every town in southern England," he barked, with an understanding nod from Fitz and Beau.

Maud's portly steward entered the hall with a parchment in his hand, dabbing sweat from his brow with a kerchief. "Are you all right, Bertrand?" Maud sat forward with concern.

"I'm sorry to interrupt, but there's a dispatch from the king's brother Odo in England. The earls have already rebelled. They're barring the Normans from passing the gates at the fort in Hereford."

"Edgar probably knew and left to join them," William roared.

"We'll find him," Fitz promised.

"Damn right we will, and I'll go back with you." Anger dripped from his voice. "I'll show the rebels I'll wield the sword that puts them down myself. Let them try to tear the crown from my head face-to-face!"

"I'll join you," volunteered Archbishop Stigand. "They trust me. I might get better information."

King William groused, giving in before he stalked angrily from the room. Plans for the coronation would have to wait.

Lips pursed, Maud stood to see off her husband and his men, but the departure was interrupted by a messenger in the familiar blue tunic and golden leg wraps of Flanders. As he dismounted, he pulled a rolled parchment from a leather satchel and bowed reverently to the monarchs in his midst. With a stoic expression, he passed the parchment to the queen. "A letter from the sister of Count Baudouin the Fifth, Your Majesty."

"Excuse me." Taking the parchment in her hands, she left the gathered nobles in the yard, pretending to be sad to go. William followed curiously.

When they were alone near a large window inside the keep, she stood in the angled rays of sunlight as she unfurled the roll of parchment. "*To Queen Matilda*," she read, surprised by the formality. "*I regret to inform you that your father has fallen very ill. Physicians say he is near death with a stomach ailment, and the only course of action left is to pray for my brother's soul. In sadness, Judith.*"

Maud's spine ran cold, her knees crumbling from the weight of fear as she imagined her strong, enigmatic father confined to his bed. Kneeling before her, William pulled her into a strong embrace. Sobbing, she rested her head against him for comfort.

"You still feel familiar, despite how far away you've been," she said quietly.

"I love you, Maud," he professed. "No matter what, that never changes."

"I love you," she said. "I must say goodbye to my father. Can we discuss the rest later?"

He nodded, holding her in both arms. "When we both return."

William crossed to England with Monty to put down the rebellion at Hereford while Beau managed the children and court affairs in Normandy. In a hurry to get to Flanders, Maud packed nothing, leaving on a tall stag with Fitz at her side. For her father, and the speed a horse could travel without a carriage on its back, she dealt with the discomforts without complaint.

After only two days they arrived in Lille, and Maud spotted the rebuilt stone towers of her family's keep on the horizon. She smiled as they pulled up to the old bridge over the River Deule. "The old wooden fortifications have been replaced by stone," she noted to Fitz as they sauntered past. "Lille looks larger, too, and the buildings are taller than I remember."

"Your father has been a good count," said Fitz with a smile. "Flanders prospers, thanks to him."

"He's been a good father too." She gazed forlornly at the chateau as they crossed the bridge. From the rampart wall—a new addition following the sacking of the old manor during Emperor Heinrich's war—a soldier spotted their horses and flags and called into the courtyard. "The Duchess Matild—*Her Majesty* the Queen of England approaches."

Crossing the wooden bridge connecting their estate to the rest of Lille, Maud entered the courtyard with a chill in her spine as Countess Adela met them outside, flanked by Lady Eleanor and Countess Richilde. Their veils hid their hair, but shades of gray in their brows marked the onset of age. Adela and Eleanor were both now in their late fifties, and Richilde neared fifty herself.

Dismounting with the grace of a turtle, Maud was unconcerned with her regrettable posture on a horse. Collapsing into her mother's comforting arms, Eleanor and Richilde lovingly joined the embrace. Richilde and Bodhi's preteen sons stood back, watching quietly. "I left as soon as I heard," said Maud, choking back tears. "Am I too late?"

"No, he's still with us," Countess Adela said with an assuring smile. "I think he was waiting for you."

Her brother, Robby, now a tall, handsome man in his early thirties, emerged from inside the castle with open arms. The weight of their father's death scarcely seemed to trouble his sly grin. "Sister! I thought they said a queen was here, but usually a queen needs a coronation."

"I see that charming smile of yours is just for show," Maud sniped. "How are your wife and children? Still looking for a title?"

"Trudi is well, and Ella and Robb are adorable," he replied. "But I've been traveling for the past year and haven't seen much of them, to tell you the truth." His lip curled with jealous rage. "As for the lack of title, we can't all marry someone who wins us so many crowns."

"That's quite enough!" Adela stared down her children with her hawkish glare. "Your father would be horrified to hear you right now, and you'll bring none of this into his chambers or I'll order you both away without a second thought. Baudouin deserves to spend his last few days in peace, surrounded by the love of his family. He's done enough as your father to earn something so simple in return."

Ashamed, Maud looked to the hard-packed dirt of the courtyard. "I'm sorry," she said quietly. Robby joined her almost in unison.

"Richilde, take Maud upstairs. I'd like to check with the kitchens about this evening's dinner. Robby and the boys can come with us. I bet there are fresh honey cakes still warm from the ovens." Despite the sadness in her eyes, Adela's voice sang for her grandsons.

Arnulf and Baldy—whose hair was long and dark—raced each other to the kitchens while Richilde led Maud to Count Baudouin's chambers. Maud ran her hand along the fortified stone walls. "It looks different from the outside after Papa rebuilt the chateau, but inside it feels like I never left, and it was never sacked by the Holy Roman Empire."

"Your father loves it here," said Richilde. "He sped up the rebuild in the last few years because he knew this was where he wanted to die. Wait until you see his new library."

Holding back tears, Maud stood straighter, carrying herself toward his bedchamber.

"I owe you an apology," Richilde said softly. "When I first arrived, that night on the ramparts in Bruges, I repeated a rumor and didn't know if it was true. I thought you deserved to know the rumor existed, but I didn't care what discord repeating it might bring. I miscalculated, and I'm sorry for the pain I caused you."

Maud sighed, shaking her head staunchly. "I don't blame you. I made my own choices."

"I do feel as though it was unfair of me," she admitted as they climbed the spiral stairs. "I've come to appreciate spending time with Countess Adela and Lady Eleanor over the years. They're riotous fun with good mead and something to bicker over." Laughing as they entered Count Baudouin's chambers, Bodhi and Judith eyed them questioningly. Maud looked sadly at her father, sleeping in his bed with Judith in a chair at his side. "We were just talking about how much Adela and Eleanor love good mead," Richilde said amiably, and her husband broke a friendly smile in her direction.

"So do you," he rebutted, chuckling.

Maud observed them with a smile. "It really is wonderful to see you two getting along."

"One important thing changed between us," Bodhi said proudly. "I grew up."

"Eighteen years ago, I never imagined I'd find a family with the court who stole my husband's throne, but Flanders and Hainault really are stronger together than apart—just like Count Baudouin said we'd be." She looked sadly upon her sickly father-in-law. Maud caught Judith roll her eyes, but Richilde didn't notice and continued. "My Gertrude is well on her way to becoming an abbess at Messines one day, and Roger will be a bishop at Chalons-sur-Marnes! Arnulf and Baldy are growing into fine young men. I really have nothing to want for."

"I promised you that the day we signed our marriage contract," said Bodhi with a grin.

"You did." She laughed. "But back then, even you weren't sure you meant it."

Maud returned her attention to Judith, who watched her father closely. "How is he?" she asked, but Judith wouldn't look at her. Bodhi stepped forward.

"He takes valerian to rest. He's often nauseous when awake, so sleep is easier for him."

"He's so thin," she observed, frowning at the sight of his shallow cheekbones.

"He barely eats. Even liquids he struggles to hold down."

Taking the empty chair on the other side of her father's wide bed, his linens soaked with sweat, she held his bony hand. He barely stirred, his chest bobbing with labored breaths, and a tear dropped down her cheek. "I'm here, Papa," she said quietly.

With her gaze bouncing from Maud to Judith, Richilde turned to Bodhi. "We should make sure the boys aren't ruining their dinner with honey cakes," she suggested wryly.

When the door closed behind them and their laughter followed, a hollow, vacant silence seeped into the walls, punctured by Count Baudouin's uneven breathing. Maud eyed Judith anxiously, but her aunt kept her eyes on the bed. The dead air in the room livened with a knock. They both looked toward the door.

A maid entered holding a smiling baby boy in white robes. The blond-haired, blue-eyed child sat upright in her arms, but when he spotted Judith he babbled, reaching for her excitedly.

"Skuli woke from his nap and wanted to see his mama." Judith stood, beaming as she took her giggling son in her arms. With a quiet nod, the maid left them alone again.

Maud wiped a tear from her eye but couldn't hide a smile. "I know what you think of me. I won't beg to change your opinion, but please allow me to say, with no agenda, I'm truly overcome with joy to see you as a mother. I'm grateful to God for your happiness."

Judith kept her focus on her son. "Skuli has no father and I have no permanent home. He's the only thing I have that brings me any happiness."

As Judith bounced Skuli on her hip, the boy hiccupped, spitting his lunch on his mother's purple robes. Cringing, Maud reached for him instinctively as Judith heaved. Letting Maud pull her son from her arms, she wiped Skuli's vomit onto a pile of soiled linens.

"I can stay with him if you want to change," offered Maud. Judith wavered. Skuli giggled away so she ultimately relented, trying not to gag as she left the room. Alone again, with Skuli babbling gently over Count Baudouin's labored breathing, Maud sat back at her father's side. "It's Maudie," she said. "I don't really know what to say, but I love you. I..." She bowed her head, and his hand jerked gently within her grasp. She looked up, and he stared back at her with pale eyes. "Words fail me," she said tearfully. "What is living without those who give life to you?"

"Maudie, you'll figure it out," he whispered, his voice dry and cracking as he forced himself up against his pillow. Tears rolled down her face. "You always figure it out."

"Thank you for the life I live. I owe so much to you and Mama."

He shook his head, reaching over to take her hand with an earnest smile. Gathering his energy with a long, careful breath, he looked upon her with pride in his eyes. "You're among the strongest women I know, Maudie. We gave you life, but you've seized your own destiny. I'll deny this to your brothers as long as I live, but our great legacy is you."

Chapter Forty-Four

September 1067 – Lille, Flanders

Count Baudouin lived just a few more days, passing in the evening with his family surrounding his bed. He took his final breaths to a chorus of quiet sobs, his hand falling limp in Countess Adela's slender grasp as his eyes closed one last time. While monks worked to prepare his body for the funeral, his family gathered by candlelight to mourn his passing. A bishop read prayers until Adela's ducts ran dry and she asked to be taken to bed.

Before retiring, Adela knelt before her eldest son, placing a gold ring studded with rubies around his finger. "Your father never liked to wear this much, but his father's father received it from his own father, and so now it goes to you." Her voice broke with disbelief to speak of her husband in the past tense. "Long live the new Count Baudouin the Sixth of Flanders."

Richilde knelt to kiss her husband's ring, followed by Maud, Eleanor, Judith, and finally Robby, who didn't wish long life to the new count as the women had done. Maud eyed him suspiciously, but he retired soon after their mother, bidding the family good night.

Spending the first night in her father's library among his books, Maud sat by the window. Her favorite spot in his library in Bruges, the place in Lille still felt familiar, comforting her grief. Reading by candlelight until her eyes were sore, she finally carried herself to sleep as roosters crowed in the fields beyond the castle walls.

A week later, Count Baudouin's funeral attracted every noble and bishop in the county of Flanders. Countess Adela and Lady Eleanor hosted an elegant dinner the night before the funeral procession, where Robby weaved between tables and Maud watched from her seat at the head banquet. "He's up to something," she said to Bodhi and Richilde at her sides.

"Robby's always up to something." Bodhi glared across the room at his brother.

"You're sure you can trust Papa's allies to support you." This wasn't a question and Maud pressed further when he gave a slight nod. "You need to make sure they'll support you, Bodhi. Robby married into money with Trudi, and money buys otherwise loyal men."

He nodded. Adela, who could still hear better than anyone they'd ever met, glared down the long table to silence them.

The next morning, the men and women emerged from the castle dressed head to toe in black. A long coffin raised on wooden boards was foisted by a dozen soldiers. Marching in blue tunics and yellow leg wraps, they proudly displayed the colors of the Flemish flag.

Maud and her relatives followed on foot for the long march to the cathedral—the first time she'd made the grievous walk since her grandfather's death as a child. The procession was long, their faces heavy with tears, as it was more than thirty years earlier for her grandfather. But this time her father wasn't there to carry her the rest of the way. She soldiered forward, stepping inside the Cathedral Church of Saint Pierre with its long nave and tall sunburst window over the entrance, where her father's earthly body would rest for eternity.

Her father's crypt was opened and his body removed from the coffin, displayed to hundreds of gathered mourners. Two golden coins stamped with his insignia covered his eyes. As the bishop led the cathedral in prayer, Maud distracted herself with memories of her father as her eyes brimmed full with tears.

The prayers and hymns finished, punctured by solemn wails from the gathered mourners. Her father's body was lowered into his crypt before a slab of marble from a quarry in Tournai was dragged across the top to seal his body inside. Locals watched curiously as mourners poured into the street with the bishop, some offering prayers for the departed count. Maud and her siblings accepted flowers from peasant women in the market square, while their mother accepted condolences from her nobles.

King Philippe of Francia, still only fifteen, stood among the funeral guests. "Dear Auntie," he said warmly, "I'm sorry we meet again under such circumstances. Count Baudouin was a good regent, but don't tell my mother I said that."

Adela managed a smile through her grief. "She may try to re-exert her influence now that my husband is gone," she warned, but Philippe cocked a sideways grin.

"Don't worry, Auntie. Count Baudouin made me strong allies. I'm grateful, and I'll continue to show loyalty to the next Count Baudouin." He nodded politely in Bodhi's direction, then offered Maud a cartoonish bow. "And Your Majesty," he said with wild eyes, his entire demeanor shifting. "What a pleasure to be among one nearly so regal as me. Of course, to be a queen of English savages can't compare to the refined kingdom of Francia."

"Thank you for coming, Your Majesty," said Maud, offering a diplomatic bow as she ignored his sneering condescension, embracing the strength that made her father proud. "I've been to England twice before and met wonderful people. It's with gratitude that I look forward to reigning as their queen."

His snide display undone by her lack of intimidation, Philippe turned up his nose. His stewards helped him remount his white horse in the cathedral square, and he sped off before another word was spoken. Bodhi chuckled at her side.

"He might hate England now, but he'll want it just because you've got it, I'll bet."

"She hasn't got it," Robby cut in. "The duke still has rebellions to subdue."

She rolled her eyes as the women piled into a carriage for the return to the castle, with Bodhi and Robby riding alongside them on horseback. Judith sat silently, staring at the crowds, careful not to look at Maud directly.

"I'll head back in a day or two," Maud said to her mother, sensing how little Judith was tolerating her presence. "I should get back to the children, and William says putting down the rebellion is going well."

"Your coronation should be soon then," said Countess Adela.

"The sooner the better, for William."

"For you and the children too," remarked her mother.

"You sound just like him."

From the opposite end of the carriage, Judith shushed them haughtily. "We should be more respectful, and silent, in Count Baudouin's memory."

To keep Judith happy, they stayed quiet the rest of the ride to the castle. Maud straightened her robes as her linen shoes touched down upon the dirt with her brother's help. He turned back to lend a hand to Lady Eleanor, but a rolling, thunderous shudder made him pause.

"Look out!" shouted a stablehand. "Get out of the way!"

Maud's feet turned toward the sound. Her stomach lurched. A dozen hooves pounded in their direction. Fitz rode at the back of the procession and could only watch in horror as the duchess stood in the path of three wild horses, their torn leather reins flapping against the wind.

She froze. The horses grew before her eyes as though she was the same small eight year old in the market. Bodhi leapt for her, throwing them both to the ground. He yowled. His leg crunched as one brown steed's iron-leaden hoof trampled overfoot. The women screamed in terror from the carriage, but Maud went to the ground in dead silence.

Racing after the horses, the stablehands reined them in as the women scrambled from the benches. "The bones need to be set quickly. Call for the monks!" ordered Lady Eleanor. Stewards raced to help the new Count Baudouin stand on his good leg, dragging him inside.

Robby approached the women with concern etched on his face, but Maud knew guilt and saw through his façade. "That could have been disastrous," he said. "Gratefully, it looks like the horse just clipped him."

She seethed, accepting Eleanor's hand to help her stand. "One of those horses is yours." Winded, she dusted off her black robes. "Did you mean to kill us both?"

"I don't know what you're talking about." He offered a charming smile for their mother. Adela wore fatigue and heartbreak on her face, her hands clenched under long sleeves.

"Robby, you must swear fealty to your brother," pressed Maud. "You're playing with fire if you think attacking him or his sons is the answer."

"The horses were excited by a cat in the yard," he insisted coolly.

"King Philippe needs a wife, and you could recommend your stepdaughter," Maud suggested, hoping to bargain with him. "I know you love your titles, and she might not be a princess, but she's also scarcely royal. Normandy will throw its support behind the union. The Church won't be able to bar it on grounds of consanguinity, and you'll probably get a castle in Francia."

Robby was quiet as his mother glowered. "Your sister's right, Robby. You could be more than just another man who kills his brother for a crown."

"I'm insulted, Mother." He barely masked snide laughter.

Stepping protectively between him and Maud, Fitz sneered back at Robby. "That day I saved you from drowning wasn't a mistake, was it?"

"I don't know, FitzOsbern, how often is it a mistake to save a six year old from dying?" Robby stiffened his stance as Maud neared.

"Fitz, I'd like you to join my husband in Hereford." She eyed her younger brother cautiously. "Let him know I must stay in Flanders the next few months to ensure the support of the nobles for Bodhi, Richilde, and their sons *after* Robby returns home to Trudi and the children."

Robby grinned. "I don't believe you have the power to ask me to leave."

Richilde, the new Countess of Flanders, said stiffly, "I do. After swearing Count Baudouin an oath of fealty, you're free to go."

"Is that a threat?"

Richilde stood her ground as he closed in on her menacingly. "You'll soon find out."

The impact of Bodhi and Richilde's alliance with William and Maud could scarcely be overstated. Flemish nobles rushed to honor their homegrown queen, and she left Flanders confident they could hold the county against Robby's reckless ambitions.

When Maud returned to Normandy, the verdant fields had faded to brown and gold before the snowfall. Stepping from the carriage driven by her Flemish escorts, her children surrounded her with eager smiles. Even Emma seemed pleased to see her again, and she basked in their affection under the setting Norman sun.

"When will Papa come home, Mama?"

"He is home, Rufus," said Constance. "England is our home now too."

"He sent a letter to say he expects to be back to Normandy in the new year." Maud smiled for her children but shared worried glances with Beau and William's brother, Robert, the Count of Mortain.

"Children, leave your mother and get ready for supper," ordered Beau. They obeyed him like the second father he'd become, filing into the castle where their attendants waited.

When the children were out of sight, her smile faded. "Have you heard anything from England? I had no news on the road from Flanders."

"Hereford's quieted now, but the larger rebellion at Exeter rages on, my queen," said Beau. "The city's loyalty to Lady Gytha makes them fierce fighters, but our king will prevail."

Maud eyed him dubiously. "Are you convinced, or are you trying to convince me?" He didn't answer right away, but his silence told Maud the truth. Frowning, she straightened her neck to stand taller. "Where are Agatha and Margaret?"

The Count of Mortain sighed. "Agatha says while her son is a prisoner in England, she and her daughter are no better than prisoners here in Rouen."

"Why? They had nothing to do with Edgar's involvement in the Hereford rebellion."

"Are you sure?" questioned Beau. "They benefit more than most if Edgar has the Crown."

"What Margaret wants, the north will never allow if her brother is the king," Maud countered, and the men's faces fell.

"We thought Edgar's desires more pressing, my queen," said Count Robert, glancing anxiously at his leather turnshoes.

"Do Agatha and Margaret feel like prisoners in Normandy because they've been treated like prisoners since Edgar was apprehended?"

"We've done only what we think best for Normandy and the Crown," Beau stammered.

A wave of guilt washed over her. "A mother will always support her child, no matter how evil he may be," she said darkly. "Even after Robby trampled Bodhi with his horse, my mother still accepts his letters. Bodhi's leg barely healed, and he walks now with a terrible limp."

Beau and Count Robert listened quietly to their queen. "Though I don't share my mother's affection for Robby, I understand a mother's love for her children. But Agatha is not responsible for Edgar's lust for the English throne. She doesn't even wish him to be king."

"You trust her too easily," said Beau carefully, but she stared them down with defiance.

"I've been so preoccupied helping my brother, I let them down. Please tell me their imprisonment wasn't my husband's idea."

They shook their heads. "No, my queen," said Beau. "We took the precaution ourselves."

"Edgar admitted he only received help from Archbishop Stigand, and both have been arrested in England. *They* may be our enemies, not Agatha and her daughter. Release them."

Chapter Forty-Five

May 1068 – London, England

Maud hadn't been inside the Palace of Westminster since her visit to England with Robert and Richard six years earlier, but the tapestries adorning the walls were still leftover from the end of King Edward's reign. Having seen them all before, she gazed at them now like foreign curiosities.

William could read this expression on her face and smiled. "We're building a new fortress along the Thames with Caen stone," he said. "Our men have been building castles since we made land a year and a half ago, and soon everything will feel more Norman and familiar."

"It's not that the tapestries and carvings are more Anglo-Saxon than Norman, and everything looks wonderful for the coronation. So many people are here, but I can't help thinking of those who won't be."

"The children will all be there, and all the nobles of Normandy have brought their wives and families to celebrate and take ownership of their new lands." Maud couldn't match his excitement. She sighed, placing a hand on her small stomach, growing once again with new life.

"Your mother and Lady Eleanor are too old to travel now, and Bodhi can't leave Flanders in case Robby pounces on his throne while he's gone," he said. "Judith is safe in Denmark with Skuli, just as you wanted for her."

"I know." She heaved her shoulders with a defeated frown. "When Gytha fled to her homeland after you put down her rebellion, it gave Judith somewhere to go. She needed that. I still regret she's so scared of me but not the woman who called for dozens of your men to be flayed in the center of Exeter, but so be it." She steeled herself, straightening her spine. "Addie says Gytha will introduce Judith to men at the Danish court who could make a suitable second husband. For her sake, I hope she'll be successful."

"Addie will be at the coronation," William said with hopefulness in his voice. "You two have been more than civil to each other lately."

"We're still not friends," Maud insisted. "You're also being crowned again, don't forget. She missed your first coronation too. But unlike Judith, Addie and I want the same things. Her daughters are getting closer to marrying age, so she'll be at court often in the coming years." Her husband frowned, but she smiled. "We'll be on our best behavior, William. For the Crown."

"I am grateful you've changed your tune on several things for the good of the Crown, my love. When Dowager Queen Sancha died, I thought you'd try to call off the marriage contract."

"For the Crown," she repeated. "King Alfonso gave us permission to keep Agatha in our care longer than his mother would have. Even though she'll still be too young, as far as I'm concerned, when she does sail for Leon, he seems like a fair man. Agatha hopes he'll be kind."

"He will, or I'll declare war on him myself."

She leaned into him expectantly. "Let's hope there will be no more wars for some time now, and this is the last time I think I'd like to be with child. It never used to exhaust me this much when I was younger, but it might be nice, for once, if you're not off in battle and we're in the same city when this one greets the world."

"For my last child, I hope I won't need to miss it," he said earnestly, holding her close with his hand protectively on her growing bump. Their steward rushed into the castle's Great Hall carrying golden chalices with an anxious bluster.

"Which should it be for the first sip of wine at the feast?" One was forged with colored glass in red and green adorning the outside of the cup, the other stamped with intricate half-moon shapes. William chuckled at his expense.

"Every detail will be perfect, Bertrand. Because of the importance of the day, the colors of the chalices will be perfect no matter which is selected," he said calmly.

"You've been at ease lately," noted Maud. "Do you no longer fear rebellion by the English lords?"

"I never *fear* rebellion. But it is perhaps a blessing Exeter was so difficult to put down." William grinned at the cloudless sky. "Deciding to wait for the snows of another winter to melt before staging your coronation leaves us with fine weather. The people will be more inclined to join us in the celebration, which will only solidify our legitimacy."

"Won't people be excited for the Feast of the Pentecost anyway?"

"Another reason to have the coronation now, to mark the end of the winter chill," he said. "Everyone will want to be on the streets at a time like this."

Agatha and Margaret Wessex entered the Great Hall side-by-side, their faces long as they eyed the familiar tapestries. "It looks the same, but completely foreign at the same time," observed Agatha politely.

"I know what you mean," said Maud, but only Margaret managed to raise a smile.

"We visited Edgar in his room this morning, and his spirits are so low he brought Mother down with him." Margaret was apologetic, her eyes pleading. "He says he'll give up his claim if you'll let us bring him north to Scotland. King Malcolm says he'll shelter us in exile."

"I don't believe him," said William haughtily.

"Edgar understands I'd like to wed King Malcolm to ensure the security of our family, and he knows if I do he can't hope to be king. He knows the northern lords won't accept an English king in a marriage alliance with the Scots." William glared at her with doubt in his eyes. "He promises, my king."

Margaret and Agatha bowed before them reverently, their pained faces begging mercy for their kin. Maud empathized with the drawn circles hanging low under Agatha's eyes, sleepless with worry for the fate of her rebellious young son. Maud felt their distance, wearing their significant unhappiness on her heavy heart in the months since her return from Flanders.

"Leave my husband and me for a moment. I wish to discuss something with him."

Agatha and Margaret left the room with quiet nods as their long robes brushed against the wood flooring at their feet. William eyed his wife cautiously. "Is something wrong, love?"

She sighed. "Not exactly wrong. I've felt such guilt for failing to keep Agatha and her children safe. We made a vow."

"You had more than enough to worry about, with your father and the tension between your brothers. Edgar is probably a lost cause. Even if he never challenges the throne, he'll never fight with us. Our vow didn't include his treachery, but I still don't know what to do about him and Archbishop Stigand. The people won't stand for an executed Wessex prince, and the Church won't stand for an executed bishop—even an excommunicated one."

"Keep Stigand working under guard until you and Lanfranc can come up with a reason to depose him," she agreed. "But what if, to celebrate our joint coronation, you show mercy to Edgar Wessex as a sign of good faith to our lords?"

"Because it sounds like a show of weakness."

"You won't lead everybody with fear, William. Some people are just reckless. If we show Edgar good faith and he betrays us again, we'll have that to show the nobles, most of whom will be Norman once you've handed out the land. But if it bothers you, we could say he escaped in the crowds and chaos before the coronation."

William grinned. "It really is a sight watching all the boats glide up the Thames. Thousands of Normans want to follow us here to—what was it you said when we visited for Judith's wedding? The mythical garden of your childhood."

"It really is so much more than I could have imagined," she admitted, beaming as she looked out a window to the sprawling metropolis of wood and stone huts beyond their castle walls. Dozens of longships glided along the sun-soaked river to the south.

William joined her at the window, staring proudly out at his domain. "To be its king and queen... The Norman lords will love it here in England as much as we do. I'm sure of it."

"Not everyone loves it here at court as we do," she pressed.

"I have no problem providing safe passage to Agatha and Margaret. Even Cristina—"

"They won't go without Edgar."

He let out an exasperated growl, finally relenting to his wife's idea. "Fine," he hissed. "But if he breaks his word, I won't kill him. He'll just wish he was dead."

"Agatha and Margaret want him to stop," she said. "I believe this wholeheartedly. They'll do everything in their power to keep him distracted in Scotland."

Resigning himself to obliging his wife's wishes, he grumbled. Still, he wouldn't leave without a quick kiss before stalking from the Great Hall. Agatha and Margaret returned, their eyes devoid of hope, and Maud met them with a warm smile.

"We've worked it out," she announced. "Your passage to Scotland will be under our protection."

Before dawn the next morning, Maud bid Agatha and Margaret goodbye at the gates of the Palace of Westminster. Edgar sat in the back of a simple carriage, ropes binding his hands and feet. Their small entourage, provided by William's men, dressed plainly to avoid drawing attention for the ride north, in hopes they'd avoid detection so William could insist he never let them go. "I'm sorry we'll miss your coronation, my queen." Agatha's warmth returned to her voice for the first time since the invasion. "But it's better if Edgar isn't in London for it."

"You'll both be missed," Maud told them, pulling them in for one final embrace. "Our men can take you safely as far as Norfolk, where a ship will deliver you north to Scotland. Please write as soon as you're safely in Dunfermline."

They nodded, bowing their heads in reverence before climbing into the wooden carriage. "Thank you," Margaret called, waving as horses hauled their carriage through the gates.

Turning back toward the castle, she found her husband waiting in the courtyard. She laughed. "You had to make sure they left quietly?"

"It's a risk, love," he said honestly. "The northern lords know much more about Scotland than we do, and they say the Scottish kings would support anyone who might help them grab English lands for themselves."

"Then they'd support anyone—it wouldn't have to be Edgar," she reasoned. "We have a blood claim to the Wessex throne, too, and our joint coronation is this afternoon. In a matter of hours, Edgar's claim will be even weaker than it is right now."

With a smile, he pulled his wife toward him, lifting her excitedly from the ground. "It's finally happening. We'll finally be king and queen, just like we've always planned." His gushing joy warmed her heart, and she laughed as he swayed with her aloft in his arms. "Today, my love, you'll be a queen."

Westminster Abbey was **King Edward's** great cathedral, and he witnessed its completion in time to be buried in a crypt behind the altar. Now, just over two years later, it belonged to William and Maud, and the new king and queen were to be crowned in an elaborate ritual.

Following the short procession to the cathedral, the new monarchs walked the long nave together, past the choir where monks sang Latin hymns to mark the occasion. Their baritone voices echoed off the high-arched ceilings. Barons, both Norman and Anglo-Saxon, filled the aisles, kneeling before their king and queen.

Their heavy crowns shone in the candlelight, and Maud thought the weight appropriate considering what power had cost. She knelt before the altar, the embroidered butterflies on her skirt pooling over the tiles and her gold-and-sapphire brooch glistening as she moved.

It was too late for regret. The Archbishop of York anointed their chests and foreheads with holy oil, leading the nobles in prayer. As he crowned them both, they vowed to protect England in the name of God.

The bishops bowed reverently to the stone floors. As the ritual ended William and Maud stood, drenched in gold, entrusted with England's throne.

Their children filled the carriage directly behind their own, while extended relatives and allies piled into a dozen more for the procession back to the palace for the coronation feast. With a gentle prod, the carter ordered the horses forward in a slow, respectable march.

Maud keenly felt the absence of those who weren't there. For the sake of her husband and herself, she forced herself to stay in the moment, engaged and smiling throughout the day. At the coronation feast, William and Maud sipped ceremonial toasts from a golden chalice encrusted with shimmering glass—ultimately decided upon by Bertrand because it looked "more impressive" than the one embossed with half-moons.

Corralling the attention of their allies in the dining hall by ringing his knife off the base of his golden goblet, William took the opportunity to announce his plans for the Church in England. He grinned at his stewards, who watched Archbishop's Stigand's every move. "As you know, the excommunicated Stigand remains in his post at Canterbury, but my respected prior, Lanfranc, is well connected in Rome and will take up his own office at Canterbury to ensure a smooth transition." The humble monk nodded dutifully, raising his chalice to the king. "With the help of the Archbishop of York who anointed me, the English and Norman Churches will soon be united, just like their people."

The crowd cheered, and King William glanced at his wife with a crooked smile. "Esteemed gentlemen and ladies of the court, dear friends, we're full of gratitude. Your support led to this day—this important day honoring the feast of the Holy Spirit, and this crowning glory for myself and my most profoundly incredible beloved: Queen Matilda of the English."

They raised their goblets and cheered, in great spirits as the wine flowed like a river to accompany the enormous feast. New tapestries adorned with blue butterflies hung over their heads, commissioned to match Maud's specially embroidered gown. They drank in celebration with their hall full of raucous nobles.

Gazing upon the festivities, Maud made sure her smile stayed pinned across her face to mask her conflictions, giving their subjects the grandeur expected of a queen.

PART TEN

Conquest

Chapter Forty-Six

July 1068 – Winchester, England

The summer sun beat down on the open-top carriage pulling Queen Maud through the streets of Winchester. She waved at the curious people lining the cobblestones, beckoning back to their king and queen with enthusiasm.

"The people always love a queen," William mused. Sitting atop his speckled gray horse marching alongside the carriage, he grinned at the people. Gundred sat dutifully at Maud's side, though her gaze was mostly fixed to the opposite side of the carriage. Handpicked by the king and queen to join their escort, next to them sat William Warenne on a brown steed.

"I wish this one loved the heat as much as people here seem to enjoy breaks in the rainy weather." Maud chuckled softly, caressing her stomach as her husband looked down to her with concern.

"We're nearly at the cathedrals to meet with the bishops. I know the journey is arduous in your condition, but the people respond to you so well."

She sighed wearily. "It's good for them to see us face-to-face, to know better who leads them now. I've always liked touring Normandy to meet the people, and I'm equally invigorated to meet with our people in England. Our child knows we have a duty as their king and queen."

"We should be at the old Royal Lodge before nightfall. You can rest there before we head north."

Though she looked forward to the end of their day, she threw herself into charming the bishops on their arrival in Winchester, giving deniers generously. The two limestone cathedrals—Old and New Minster—loomed over the city as they did when Maud visited Lady Emma years earlier. On this day, she entered to pay respects at Emma's marble grave, carved with the same design as her beloved desk.

The cacophonic, competing song of the monks inside each choir still dominated the sprawling town, though the arrival of the king and queen meant it hummed with more activity than usual.

At a busy market erected in the square below the cathedral towers, William instructed his stewards to buy goods from every stand. "We must support the locals," he insisted, sacks of deniers jingling in the stewards' hands. "If there's anything of value besides embroideries and woven baskets, like jewels or marbleworks, purchase it for the treasury."

"And food will go to the children in the streets," Maud said from behind him. The stewards nodded dutifully before fanning out across the marketplace. The king and queen marched regally through the square, stopping at various stalls to chat with the artisans, growers, and merchants about their wares. Women approached Maud to place their hands on her growing stomach, predicting the sex of the child as they studied how she carried. None of the peasants spoke French, but Maud was glad to practice her English.

"Your chest and belly hang low like church bells, Your Majesty," said one woman with a pitiful produce stall. Her teeth had rotted from her blackened gums, but she smiled as though she'd never miss them. "Only a man would drag you down that much!"

Laughing heartily at her own joke, the haggard old woman barely noticed Maud's awkward, polite grin. "Boy or girl, we're looking forward to welcoming one who'll be born on English soil, just like you wonderful people." The gathered crowds in Winchester met the couple's charm offensive with broad smiles, as they had throughout the southern settlements they'd visited since the coronation. They planned to head north during the harvest to meet the English known to Tostig Godwinson as monsters, returning before the winter frost and their last child's birth. "They won't have as much goodwill for us the further north we go, so I'll put up with a rude joke or two."

William laughed, his brown eyes twinkling as he shot his wife a teasing grin. "It's almost genius how she insulted men and women equally with that one."

Returning to their cortège, William supported his wife as she climbed into the carriage. Adoring crowds waved merrily as they pulled out of the square, their horses directed northward toward the Royal Lodge. But instead of continuing to Kings Worthy, the horses turned west at a fork in the long gravel road. "Are we going somewhere?"

William kept his eyes forward. "Winchester Gaol."

"A jail?" He shot her the pained look she remembered each time she spoke of Brictric, and suddenly she knew. The horses pulled to a stop outside a small stone fortress with crossed iron bars in every window. Her stomach ached as fear washed over her. "I don't want to see him."

"We have to," he said staunchly. "We stole his life away without even asking if he'd switch sides. He deserves to hear your reason why."

With a heavy sigh she dragged herself forward, entering the fortress through a steel door hinged into the stone. William followed and her eyes adjusted to the poorly lit room with tiny windows too tall for most men. A black-robed gatekeeper stood watch inside, eyeing a single cell marked by thick bars.

"Leave us," William said. The gatekeeper nodded obligingly, closing the door behind him with a thud.

Sitting on the earth-packed floor beyond the bars, Brictric frowned when he recognized his visitors. His clothes ragged and dirty, with unkempt hair fading to white, he grumbled with a distant stare. "My humiliation must never cease." He nodded in the direction of her pert belly beneath her green robes. "You're looking well, Queen Matilda. How many is that now?"

"All ten of my children are blessed with a great father," she said coolly.

He laughed ruefully, letting go of a cavernous cough that sounded as though it was tearing him apart from inside. "Sorry, I inhale so much dust in here." He spit onto his soiled tunic.

"You must know the edict was my idea," Maud said to him, eyeing his bare feet with chains locked around his blood-caked ankles.

"When you left Goda our main property but put the rest in your name, she knew." He grimaced with self-loathing. "She didn't want to risk upsetting the new king and queen by continuing to pretend she supported me, and with the house in her name, she didn't need me anymore. You did that for her, Your Majesties. Congratulations, she left me."

"I never forgave you for using me before Bodhi's wedding," she admitted. "And I thought I'd made peace with it until I found out you were doing the same to Margaret Wessex."

"It was her choice. Just as you made a choice, so did she."

"You're careless," she shot back. "I behaved no worse than you that night, but in this world, even women who appear to have everything at their fingertips are a scandal away from ruin. You could live a life of sin in the open and still rise to become one of the greatest thegns of King Edward's reign, but your lack of care for the women in your life says more about you than it does any of the women you've bedded across the continent."

With darkness in his eyes, he glared from his spot on the floor. "You *wanted* to break your vows to God for me."

"Watch yourself, Brictric." William unsheathed his sword with a satisfying clink, raising it protectively between Maud and the iron bars. He angrily bared his teeth. "I could run you through with my sword and never think of you again."

"Do it." Brictric shrugged with a distant, defeated gaze.

"It's a death too quick for you." William lowered his blade.

The thegn gave a rueful laugh, choking as it scratched his dry throat. "Do you know the only reason I rose through the ranks as I did? I wasn't even a first son, paying down my father's debt to Earl Godwin. He chose me specifically to escort the old Queen Emma from Flanders. I had no idea why he asked me, but he knew as soon as Emma learned my father's name, she'd obsess over me. My father was Queen Emma's first friend in England."

"Algar, the carpenter."

"He was the son of a builder at King Aethelred's court. The young queen was lonely, desperate for friends when she first sailed from Normandy. Rumors of their friendship spread, and King Aethelred and the Bishop of Winchester made her perform a public penance. She survived the ordeal, and they couldn't pin the rumors on her, but my father was removed from court. For his silence, he was given his estates and even the woman who became my mother, but he was still made to work in debt to Earl Godwin." He spoke of the late earl with disgust. "Godwin hoped it would reveal her secrets and discredit her when she convinced King Edward to make me an ambassador, but Lady Emma was too discreet. I proved myself to Earl Godwin and the king enough that they never saw fit to use the connection against me."

Maud considered what she'd learned, reminiscing about her youth and her beloved Lady Emma. "Are you lying?" Her cheeks burned hot.

He shook his head, wearing satisfaction on his face and relishing her agony. The setting sun peeked through the tiny windows, casting shadows on his face.

"What does it matter if your father and Lady Emma loved each other once?" William cut the tension with his brusqueness. "They're both gone now, God rest their souls. And one of us should be joining them sooner than later." He glared at Brictric, who refused to meet his gaze. "You might wish to declare a hunger strike to save face with any Anglo-Saxons you may keep in contact with outside these walls. No one will question why food deliveries to Winchester Gaol have ceased indefinitely, but anyone who thinks your death suspicious will die for it, like you. Better to die with some honor than starved like a dog who's enjoyed his last bone, don't you think?"

Maud looked pitifully on Brictric's dirt-smeared cheeks. He spoke bitterly. "You're cursed with good fortune, Your Majesties, and you wield it like a weapon. The dragon of Wessex lives and breathes fire in you."

Returning to the open air beyond the steel door of the fortress, the gatekeeper bowed to the king and queen before returning dutifully to his post. Maud caught William's wounded gaze.

"How do you feel?" he asked.

"It doesn't matter if Lady Emma was fond of him," she said. "She didn't know him like I did."

"That's not what I meant."

Placing her hand on her chest to confirm a slow, steady rhythm, she frowned. "I don't feel anything. At eighteen I might have mortified myself, but maybe it's all really gotten to me."

William pulled her close, letting her rest her head against his powerful chest. "I used to say I wondered about my heart, and whether I was a good person. But even after everything we've been through, I still never worry about you, Maud."

Chapter Forty-Seven

August 1068 – Durham Castle in Northumbria, England

"For an earldom I've heard so many complaints about, it comes with quite the stunning castle. Judith's descriptions in her letters never quite did it justice."

Visiting English towns and nobles along the way, another six weeks on the road brought them to Durham, where their cortège pulled up to the gates of the castle Judith once called home with Tostig Godwinson. Maud gazed at the moss-covered stone fortress where Gospatric, the Earl of Northumbria, stood in the yard to greet the king and queen with his household.

"As beautiful as she is, she is much to maintain, Your Majesty." Gospatric bowed low to the king and queen. "And it's a labor of love to maintain her."

"She seems to flourish with your love, Earl Gospatric."

"It really is wonderful you've decided to tour this great land since the coronation, even in your delicate condition."

"The pleasure is ours," said Queen Maud. "The people have been wonderful, and the weather this summer has been splendid. Our child is learning to appreciate the size and splendor of this fine kingdom from the womb."

"Education can never begin too early," agreed Gospatric.

"We're pleased to be here," said William. "The north isn't half as wild as we've heard."

"Sometimes it's even wilder, but the roads have calmed of late. The Scots have paused their raids in celebration of King Malcolm's betrothal to Margaret Wessex."

Maud nodded approvingly. "We trust the northern barons understand the marriage alliance will only strengthen relations between England and Scotland."

Gospatric sighed. "That's not the issue, Your Majesties. The problem in the north is we don't care if relations strengthen between Scotland and the south. We know the Scots aren't coming for Pevensey, or even London. They're coming for northern homes. Northern people."

William placed his hand proudly on his chest. "I'm not king of the south of England, Earl Gospatric. As king of *all* England, it's my sworn duty to protect the people under my domain. Normandy has prospered under my leadership and England will prosper much the same, but it will require trust from the northern lords to follow our plan."

"I don't mean to imply I don't trust you, Your Majesty. But it is a lot to ask. Reports from the Midlands say you've charmed the English everywhere, but you've never ventured this far north. We barely know you." Maud understood his wary smile, but still she found it off-putting.

"What we know of northern people is impressive," she said.

Accepting her compliment with a smile, he turned to his steward. "Bring the desk we found in the attic." Turning to William and Maud, he explained himself. "When we moved in, we found a desk among the belongings your kin left behind. I remember Judith once told me the desk was her most prized possession, and they left in such a hurry."

The steward and another servant slowly carried the desk into the courtyard. Maud smiled at the familiar Celtic carvings running down the legs, the smooth finish still pristine.

"We'll gladly have it sent to her in Denmark," said William, noting the burst of nostalgia creeping into the fine lines on his wife's face. Maud circled the old oak desk in the courtyard, running her fingers along the surface. On the back, tucked against the left leg, she noticed letters carved into the sanded timber. *Algar*.

Her beloved Lady Emma's dear friend, a lowly carpenter, sired the man whose betrayal proved too much for Maud to bear. Her breath caught, but she tightened her expression with William and the Gospatrics eyeing her with interest. "It was so good of you to think to save this for Judith," she said, forcing a magnanimous smile. "Our gratitude is enduring."

"We are distant cousins, you and I. My great-grandfather was King Aethelred, and Queen Emma was kind to my family after Aethelred's murder by King Cnut. None of those rulers were much for peace, but perhaps a new dawn is calling."

Detecting snide tones in his voice as he spoke, Maud relayed her concerns to William in their guest quarters that night. "He's playing a game, but Earl Gospatric isn't with us."

"He's been more generous than any of the English lords who've kept their holdings."

"Robby gave generously to Bodhi before he tried to kill him too."

"I've told you, I don't fear rebellions, and not because I doubt they'll happen. I don't fear anyone on the continent enough to lose what we've gained." Relenting, she rested against his chest in the bed. He stared at the curve of her bulging stomach under the wool and linen blankets, letting his gaze travel slowly toward her face. "You're the most beautiful woman in the world, my love."

"Lately I feel like the world's most beautiful whale."

They laughed, and he offered a long, meandering kiss. His breath playing on her skin, she smiled dreamily, sinking into the soft, cottony eiderdown stuffing of the mattress.

Maud and William's cortège was headed south again by early September, continuing their tour of settlements throughout the fields and forests of Yorkshire.

In York, a wood-and-stone cathedral with thirty altars rose tall and imposing above the huts and taverns of the city. They accompanied the bishops to a local hospital, St. Peter's, where high ceilings and large, ornate windows impressed the king and queen. The smell of vinegar, so common in hospitals, faded somewhat on the breeze through an open section of window as several monks shuffled from bed to bed.

"We've built hospitals in several cities in Normandy," Maud said to the abbot. "But none as impressive as this. The ceilings are awe-inspiring."

"The high ceilings and large windows are better for removing bad air and helping the healing process," said the abbot. "And the ornate windows help the spirits of the sick. Beauty is one of life's most favorable distractions."

They were introduced to patients nearing recovery, who spoke gratefully of the work of the monks at St. Peter's. "I lost my leg in the River Tyne last year, trying to defend English lands against Scottish raiders," said one man, leaning on a carved wooden stick propped under his shoulder to hold his balance. "Our boat was hit and ran aground, pinning me against the riverbank. By the time I'd been brought home to York the leg was dead, but the monks saved my life and have been teaching me to walk again. I owe them everything."

"We're quite in awe of this place, Abbot. You've done wonderful work, and the Crown will be eager to support your endeavors," William promised.

"We should hope other priories will follow your lead," added Maud. "All people deserve such care as you provide here."

Everywhere they stopped they charmed their subjects, drenched in tributes in return. In addition to Lady Emma's desk, they collected an entire carriage full of elaborate trinkets to take back to London, from tapestries to golden vases and more precious metals. As their cortège continued south from the city, a leather strap holding the overflowing carriage snapped, sending wooden crates tumbling to the ground.

"We're going to need a cart for our travel carriage." King William laughed as Warenne helped him tighten new straps around the crates to hold them in place. Stretching her spine, Maud forced a smile in the heat.

The sound of lulling lutes wafted over them on the wind, and through the trees Maud spotted colorful tents surrounded by people. Curiously, she stepped forward, Gundred following close behind. "It looks like there may be a faire," she announced to her husband.

"Go with them," he told William Warenne. "We'll let the horses feed while we wait."

Warenne marched ahead, cutting the brush with his sword to prevent the women's robes from tangling as they passed through the wood. "It's quite beautiful music," said Gundred dreamily, the melodic rancor growing louder as they came through the trees.

When the oaks cleared to a meadow, Maud smiled at the joyful scene. Children ran after one another with sticks, laughing and jumping in the grass. Women in plain brown robes stood chattering in the late-summer heat, standing over tables serving food. At one end of the field, men gambled over tunic-clad brawlers amid a cheering rabble. At the other, barefoot children sat watching performers with powdered white faces and red-painted noses.

She scanned the crowd of happy faces, spotting a woman with navy robes and a long hood pulled low over her eyes. Meeting her gaze for only a moment, in that instant Maud was certain she knew her. "Edie," she said breathlessly as the woman sped toward the trees. Maud shouted, "Edie Swanneck!"

"I'll retrieve her." Warenne took off beyond the tree line, and Maud noticed the curious onlookers they'd attracted. Without an introduction alongside her husband, they didn't know her from any other noblewoman, so she nodded stiflyin the face of their gawking glances before carrying her large stomach toward the woods. "I've got her, Your Majesty." Maud and Gundred heard Warenne's call before meeting in the mossy brush. Edie's hood had fallen, revealing silvery blonde locks pulled back behind her swan-like neck. Warenne pinned her hands behind her, forcing her to her knees.

Brandishing their swords, King William and three of his soldiers raced up behind them. When he recognized their capture, he halted. "I thought you were in danger when I heard you shout." The king relaxed his shoulders to see his wife unharmed.

"Unhand her, Warenne," Maud demanded calmly. "She's a noblewoman who supported the Norman cause with donations of gold."

As Warenne let go, he recognized her. "She's the one who found Harold Godwinson's body at Hastings field."

"I was Lady of Walsingham," she said. "King Harold was my husband before he was Aldgyth of Mercia's. His sons and brothers who died on the field with him were my family. His mother took my youngest to Denmark in hopes it will save her life, and all that protects my other daughter are the nuns at Wilton Abbey."

"Not all your sons died on the battlefield," William reminded her. "Some take shelter in Dublin, and Ulf walks free in our court in Normandy."

Edie frowned. "He told me his plans for Conan of Brittany before he left. He used to be so sweet, but now he's a menace like his father was." Anguish pulled at the lines on her face. "The destruction of my family is by your hands."

"You donated to the cause," Warenne said gruffly, but she refused to cower.

"I didn't say I don't wear their deaths on my heart. Revenge was my ruin. I came north but all my mother's relatives are gone now. I live, day by day, with nothing to want and nothing to run to. I live like a ghost."

"We can provide you with a home, Lady Wals—"

"No! I'm not Lady Walsingham anymore, and I'm not Edie Swan-neck. I'm of no consequence. Just let me be."

"Your mother-in-law staged a violent rebellion in Exeter," reasoned William. "If Normans know you live free in England after our men were flayed in the sun in the name of the Godwins, you'll be in danger without our protection."

"Then kill me."

"Edie," Maud pressed, but the woman glared at her captors.

"Kill me!" she repeated, resignation dripping fearlessly from her lips. "I have nothing to die for except my sins."

With a curt nod from William, Warenne unsheathed his dagger from inside his leather shoe. "Look away," he said. Gundred obliged him, shaking, but Maud wouldn't turn around. "I've never killed a woman before."

Warenne nervously adjusted the dagger in his hands. Edie guided the blade to the point between her ribs. When Warenne hesitated, she clasped his gloved hand. Driving the golden dagger through her heart, she fell limply to the forest bed with one final gasp.

Chapter Forty-Eight

September 1068 – Selby, Yorkshire

"She deserves a more honorable burial than this."

Maud spoke with regret while Warenne and her husband shoveled earth over Edie Swanneck's bloodied corpse. Two gold coins were placed over her eyes before the men lowered her into the pit, only half as deep as a typical grave. She said a quiet prayer to the Virgin Mary as dirt was piled atop her body. Just as she had, Edie Swanneck had seen visions of Mother Mary, though Maud was unsure whether she'd seen her since their conversation by candlelight years earlier. Perhaps she'd left her, too, content to let her face the rest of her life out from under her watch; if so, the state of her implied she'd left too soon, and Maud tried to push this fear from her mind.

"The vicar here in Selby let us use the chapel grounds," said William, dabbing his sweat-caked brow with his tunic. "We didn't mention how she died because the Church would condemn her for it, but we're carrying too much as it is and have nowhere to take her. This is the best we can do for her under the circumstances."

"She wasn't always a Christian. We don't even know if she would have preferred the funeral pyre," she lamented. "Do you think when your father died in Nicaea, the men he was with had a conversation like this?"

"For his honor, I hope they did." Loose dirt fell from his shovel over the corpse.

"It's quiet here," noted Gundred, listening to the whistle of birds in the wind, and the lutes from the faire barely audible through the woods. Mud-and-straw homes dotted gravel paths leading to a chapel, which stood up the road from an inn and tavern. South of bustling York, the village was more forest than fortification.

"The townspeople must still be at the faire," said Warenne with a welcoming smile. Gundred stared back at him dreamily.

Maud held back a lump in her throat. "Her children will be devastated. We can't do anything for the exiled sons in Dublin, and Gytha has her youngest in Denmark, but we owe it to Edie to protect the other two," she insisted. "Ulf is already safe in our court, but we have a responsibility to Gunhilda while she's studying at Wilton Abbey, for Lady Walsingham's sake."

William tossed another pile of earth into the grave, letting the shovel fall to his side while Warenne kept working. "You're upset, love."

She sighed. "Edie had things to live for."

"She didn't think so." He gave a slight shrug. "She decided what she could live with, and she turned down what we offered her."

"I know I never knew truly what life was like for Edie Swanneck, but it just feels so tragic."

"The vicar's coming back," whispered Gundred. "We should stop talking about Lady Walsingham's real manner of death."

Turning to the vicar, Maud gave a gracious nod. "Thank you for allowing us a plot of ground to bury a dear friend," she said, and the vicar bowed to them both with a charming smile.

"Anything you wish, Your Majesties."

"You will perform a short service for the lady?"

"I would be honored." The vicar smiled, showcasing his brown and crooked teeth.

Warenne finished covering Edie's corpse with dirt, using his shovel to pack the earth flat. Ushering Edie into the Kingdom of Heaven with the Lord's Prayer, the vicar blessed the loose earth over her body.

"We will remember your sacrifice and protect your youngest children," Maud promised, crossing her hands over her chest as the vicar's prayer came to an end.

Gundred placed round stones over the grave. "I'm marking her place in case her children can visit someday."

"When we return to London, we can arrange for a real tombstone to replace it," William said. As they left the churchyard, he placed his wife's hand through his arm to escort her to the carriages. She picked up her heavy heart and smiled, but as she stepped forward, she crumbled in sudden pain. After so many children, she recognized the beginnings of childbirth.

"It's early, my queen," said Gundred urgently. "Before she died,

Celeste tried to teach me everything she could. She said you might feel contractions before the baby is ready to be born."

Maud grimaced against the pain rolling across her abdomen. "It might be false labor, but I don't think I can bear a long carriage ride like this."

"You won't have to," said William, marching up to the inn. He knocked on the wooden door, but no one answered. Warenne peered inside the front windows.

"They must be at the faire," he said.

Trying the door and finding it locked, William kicked the wooden threshold off its hinges. "We'll explain everything when they return."

"What if the innkeepers turn out to be rebels?"

"Then we won't apologize for the door, Warenne. But the Queen of England won't give birth in the woods." He flinched, Adeliza's still-birth clearly weighing on his mind. As another contraction brought her to her knees, Maud squeezed her husband's arm for comfort.

William bent down to pick her up, but Gundred stopped him before they entered the abandoned inn. "If the baby's head is down, the queen should move herself," she explained. Fighting the pain from her contractions, Maud followed the men up the dark stairwell. A room at the top of the stairs lay empty, with a wooden bed in the center of the room. A ceramic bowl sat on a table. "We need that filled with water."

"I saw a well around the corner," volunteered Warenne.

"We need towels, and we need some light in here," Gundred pressed.

"You know how to deliver a baby?" Warenne eyed her with awe. "Midwives are all peasants."

"Midwives are vitally important," she corrected him. "Babies come into the world so often. Whether a peasant or a noblewoman has the skills doesn't matter. Hopefully it just means more healthy mothers and babies."

Warenne flashed an impressed grin before racing off to fetch the water. William stood helpless, watching his wife remove her under-garments, clinging to the bedpost for support.

"You're sure you can deliver a child on your own?" He looked to Gundred with fear in his eyes. "I'm sorry. I don't mean... I've never been faced with this myself. It wasn't my intention to miss all my children's births."

"She assisted with Adela's birth and trained with midwives when I went to Flanders last year," Maud sputtered through long, steady breaths. "She even impressed Roger de Montgomery's cruel wife, Mabel, at the birth of her grandson."

"The queen has been healthy while expecting this one, and before she died Celeste said she thought I was a great student," said Gundred. Even her pride sounded humble.

"We trust Gundred, William," Maud remarked.

His shoulders dropped as his tension waned. "I'll make a fire to bring light in here," he said, relieved to make himself useful.

When he returned with lit torches, he set them up on opposite sides of the room, pressed into the wooden slats of the floorboards to keep them upright. Warenne returned with white towels and the ceramic basin full of water, and Gundred smiled graciously before setting to work. She wet a towel, handing it to William. "Keep her forehead cool with this."

"Men shouldn't be here," said Warenne nervously.

"If we were back in London, I'd have at least one other midwife with me. I don't need you both but having one to focus on the queen while I focus on the baby will be safer."

"You go outside, Warenne." William's resolute voice masked his nerves. "I'll stay. Keep watch for the innkeepers."

Maud labored late into the evening with her husband at her side, dutifully dabbing her forehead and offering his fist for her to squeeze while she pushed. At first terrified to look, curiosity finally led William to watch how his wife's body shifted as their baby crowned. Maud groaned in agony, and William understood why. Moving back to her side, he held her as she made her final pushes, delivering a healthy boy who squealed with great strength in his lungs.

With one of the towels, Gundred cleaned off their son. Wrapped in fresh blankets, she placed him on the breast of Maud's underdress with a smile. "He's perfect."

"Thank you, Gundred." William eyed his newborn son with amazement. His parents cooed, exhaustion worn across their faces as the babe lay sleepily in his mother's arms. The king placed his hand over the swaddling to note the child's leg was scarcely larger than his thumb. "I've never seen one this small."

"He's not that small," said Maud. "Constance was smaller, but she didn't come this early."

"Boys eat like savages, even in the womb." He looked lovingly upon his wife cradling their newborn. "I never understood just what women go through to have children. I'd heard stories, but to see it... I'm in awe of you, love." She blushed as he spoke, like she did when their love was new. "To know you've put your body through hell to give us ten healthy children..." His voice paled, practically speechless. "We owe our entire legacy to you, my love."

With a tired smile, she pulled her husband's cheek toward her for a kiss. "Everything we have is impossible without you, William."

"You're a great team," said Gundred, quietly wringing bloody towels in a poorly lit corner of the room. "I've seen for years how you make each other stronger, even when you're challenging each other."

They smiled at one another, then back at Gundred before the lady-in-waiting dumped the dirty water from the basin out the window. "I'll leave you to bond with your son for a while. If you need anything, I'll be downstairs."

The door shut, and Maud passed the infant to his father. Cradling him in his wide, strong arms, the king gazed upon his youngest son with pride. "Two crowns, four sons," he mused.

"I'd be content if our conquering days are over. The younger sons will find their purpose, but I'll be happy if they go through life not coveting their brothers' crowns."

"Our sons won't be like Robby." He scoffed. "Our sons scarcely know Robby. They'll learn loyalty by example."

She sighed. "I hope you're right."

"I'm certainly right that Robby won't be around to corrupt them. After he tried to kill you, he should hope I never catch him on my lands." At the sound of his father's voice, their son's eyes opened curiously. "Hello, little one," he said as his tone softened, placing his finger in the child's tiny hand. "Have you thought of what we should call him?"

Maud shook her head. "I thought about naming him for my father, but Baldy wears his grandfather's name so well already. What names do you like?"

He shrugged. "I'm so stunned by what I witnessed of your strength, I lack inspiration."

With a contented smile, she thought for a moment. "What about Henry?"

"For your uncle, the Frankish king who attacked our borders and tried to knock me down?"

"Not exactly," she protested. "Perhaps nothing I have in life would be possible without sacrifice, but I think it's more than that. I don't think often enough of the sacrifice of the man I told you about, who pushed me and Judith from a horse's path on the same day you and I first met as children—but Draco is quite a name."

"Explaining Agatha's name has been hard enough," he replied with a lighthearted smile.

"When she visited after Adeliza, my mother told me of her own experience losing a child. His name was Henry in honor of her brother, the king, but I like the name because it reminds me of my mother's strength, and the sacrifices she made for me."

William grinned. "Who am I to argue with honoring the woman who pushed so hard for you to fall in love with me? We could have named all our daughters Adela." She laughed as her husband repeated the name several times, their son watching him groggily. Finally, William beamed. "He looks like a Henry." Shouting rose to the second-story windows from the gravel road below. "They must be coming home from the faire," said William as Maud burrowed into the pillows with a yawn. "Rest, my love. I'll watch over young Henry."

As she drifted into restful slumber, the shouts rose again from the road below. "What are they saying?" Maud spoke groggily. William moved toward the window, jumping backward as a fiery rock of hot coal pierced the thin glass windows. She screamed as Henry wailed. William kicked the simmering rock toward the stone wall with his boot.

"Your Majesty, the rebels!" Warenne's panicked voice came from inside the doorless inn, and seconds later he was up the stairs. Gundred followed, furiously gathering the queen's robes. Stirring with exhaustion, Maud hoped to wrest away the distractions, but Warenne insisted, "I think it's just a drunken rabble, but they've got torches and pitchforks, and they're declaring this land for the north. If we send some men forward it'll buy time to escape, but we must go. Now."

The urgency in his voice pushed William to action. Gundred took Henry in the billowing folds of Maud's robes, racing outside the inn with Warenne at her side. Scooping up his wife with both arms, William held her close as he hurried behind.

Ducking behind the inn, the foursome and their soldiers disappeared beyond the tree line. Weary and exhausted, they hid among the brush, watching helplessly while the inn, and their overflowing carriage of tributes, was set alight by rebel torches. Rioters marched through the dark night calling for their heads, murdering the soldiers who defended the line.

"In the name of Edgar Aetheling, England's true king!"

Chapter Forty-Nine

September 1068 – Selby, Yorkshire

Long after the mob had returned to their beds, the king's soldiers found an abandoned hunting lodge they could reach before morning. William employed more than a dozen soldiers to stand guard outside, ensuring his wife and son were as comfortable as they could be, given the circumstances. "The guards collected a few of the horses that ran off before the start of the blaze. We'll ride to York and find a new carriage to bring you back to London."

Maud looked at her husband with exhaustion as the midday sun peered through the tiny windows of the hunter's simple den. A stone-rimmed firepit lay in the center of the room under an angled thatch roof with a hole at the top for escaping smoke. A straw-stuffed linen mattress lay on the earthen floor of the mud-walled hut.

"You're not just going to York for a carriage, are you?"

He shook his head. Wearing his chainmail armor, he was ready for a fight. "We need reinforcements in case last night's mob is a sign of wider rebellion in the north. I'll need to stay behind with Warenne to shore up our alliances." He scowled. "Edgar Wessex is behind this. I'm sure Stigand's involved somehow, with King Malcolm, and the northern barons too."

"They haven't all turned on us yet," she reminded him gently. With a kiss for the road, William reluctantly left his wife and son with his men in the Yorkshire woods.

"We'll be back before nightfall," he assured her, and she waved him off with an anxious smile. When she returned to the earthen lodge, Gundred offered Maud a broth of weeds and herbs. Henry stirred in her arms, fussing as his tiny face contorted into a whimper.

"He's hungry, Your Majesty. You'll have to keep yourself full to feed him from your breast."

She stammered in response. "I don't—I've never."

"I hoped when the innkeepers returned, they'd know someone in town who could feed him at least until we got to London, but we may not be back to London for weeks."

She swallowed hard, feeling the weight of the milk in her engorged breasts. "Does it hurt?"

"Some say it does." Gundred cradled restless Henry in her arms. "I could give him more water."

"My son must eat. I want to try." Steadfast, she took a long, nervous breath. "Even at thirty-seven, I can still learn new things."

Slipping out of her loose robes, she cupped one breast, guiding it toward Henry's small, agape lips. The sensation as he suckled sent strange tingles to the ends of her skin. She smiled down at her son, who gazed up at her with wide blue eyes while he feasted.

"You're both naturals," Gundred said, caressing the soft hairs on Henry's nearly bald head before leaving them to continue in peace.

Alone with her thoughts, Maud tried not to worry as she considered what might befall her husband in York. The woods were quiet beyond the hut, with only the voices of her husband's men audible above the light wind. With no one to hear her, she vented to her infant son. He stared back with clueless eyes, transfixed on the sound of her voice. "I was bringing a desk back to London to send to Judith in Denmark. It belonged to a great woman I loved very dearly, meant for another I loved just as much. But she wants nothing to do with me."

Henry finished suckling, spitting up the last of the milk on a towel Gundred placed over Maud's shoulder. While feeding from her breast may have been a new experience, she knew what to do here, and gently rubbed her son's small back, propped upright to aid in his digestion. She'd seen it done by wetnurses many times before, even taking it on herself from time to time—when the urge to cradle her own children strengthened her willful impatience.

"The desk was burned to ash last night, like the embers of our lifelong friendship. Sadly fitting." She glanced out the window to the sky beyond. "I was so tired from giving birth to you, I watched fire light the sky with blurred vision, including the inn where you—" Her mind raced as she recalled the fortune teller's prophecy. "But our crowns have been won!" she protested. Henry cooed sleepily in her arms and Gundred hurried back inside.

"Did you need something, my queen?"

Staring gravely at her loyal lady-in-waiting, Maud shuddered. "I have a terrible feeling my husband's trip to York will be more than he bargained for."

Placing a hand on her queen's shoulder, Gundred tried to comfort her. "The king left for the city with vigilance. He's seen the rebellious rumblings for himself and always handles himself well. Besides, he has Warenne at his side."

Maud smiled despite her anguish as Gundred's heart revealed itself again, but she couldn't distract her mind from troubled thoughts. "What if the prophecy didn't foretell the comet as a sign of victory, but a war to unite the north and south?" Maud's voice shook nervously as she spoke.

"I would say don't put too much stake in prophecies," said Gundred. "If Mistress Dzintra was a con artist, Agatha Wessex's old fortune teller may have been too."

"The prophecy doesn't matter," she said unconvincingly. "It never really mattered. We never let the prophecy alter the course of our plans for England. But war matters, Gundred. If war is coming to England, my husband, and the lives of thousands more, will be in danger."

Nodding quietly, Gundred objected no further.

By morning, Maud paced nervously inside the hunter's lodge, treading a dip in the earth under her feet. The faint smell of smoke wafted in the air. "He promised to return before dark."

"Perhaps they're delayed by the hospitality of the nobles and bishops." Hopeful as always, even Gundred knew her optimism was useless to Maud. Cradling Henry as he slept, she pleaded with her queen. "You must rest, or you'll be less able to feed Henry before we can leave this place."

"I can't rest. Something's wrong." The voices of their soldiers stirred outside the windows, and Maud heard William FitzOsbern's familiar call from beyond the lodge's short wooden door. "Help me dress, Gundred."

Laying Henry on the straw-packed mattress, Gundred helped her queen step into the blue robes she'd escaped with from the inn.

Tightening a sash under her breast, Maud's stomach still poked out beneath her robes so soon after delivery. "Some women say that goes down faster with breastfeeding," said Gundred, but Maud shrugged.

"It says I've had another healthy son, and I'm proud of it."

When she'd returned her veil to her head, Maud stepped out to greet Fitz amid the commotion.

"My queen," he said, falling to one knee in a regal bow. She looked up in surprise to see her second son, Richard, atop a horse at Fitz' side. "Robert and Lanfranc knew your itinerary, so we rode for two straight days."

She could hear the fear in his voice as he stumbled over his words. "Please don't waste the silence, FitzOsbern. My husband left yesterday for York and hasn't returned as expected. I have no time for trepidation."

Richard spewed the words Fitz was terrified to say. "Emma's missing. She ran away after Robert said she'd probably have to marry one of the English barons for the sake of the Crown and eat spit-roasted squirrel at the wedding like a savage."

Reeling from the news, Maud composed herself. "She's fourteen years old. She couldn't have gotten very far."

Fitz wavered. "A maid at Westminster thought she heard of a young girl buying her way aboard a merchant ship bound for the continent."

"When did she go?"

Fitz' voice cracked. "Three days ago."

"She could have landed on the continent by now. Oh, Emma, what have you done?" Maud was horrified, imagining her aboard a merchant ship of adventurous, hungry-eyed men. "No one helped her?"

Her second son shook his head. "Emma's determined, Mama."

"We've sent word to Beau and Odo in Normandy. They'll put the entire duchy on guard until they find her," vowed Fitz. "They'll put your brother in Flanders on alert too."

"I must get back to Normandy as soon as possible to join the search, but I can't leave the north without knowing if my husband is alive."

"Richard can take you back to London now. I'll head to York."

"I'm coming with you."

Gundred joined Fitz in protest. "Your Majesty, you're in no condition to—"

"I know you're right," she said, her legs throbbing from a dull muscle ache. "But I don't care."

Finally, Fitz relented, but just as Maud was preparing to drag herself up to perch side-saddle on Fitz' stocky steed, a mess of hooves clattered through the trees. William and Warenne led a charge of a handful of soldiers.

"They left with at least a dozen more." Maud waited with a rueful gaze, though they returned toting a nondescript wooden cart led by two strong horses.

"They sacked it!" William cried. "The rebels sacked the city and drove the people to seek shelter in the forests. They attacked St. Peter's hospital!" His tunic singed and covered in another man's blood, he leapt from his horse, stocky and strong as ever. "Earl Gospatric arrived with Edwin of Mercia and three hundred men. They announced to the people of York the hour of their death had arrived, for their support of the king who stole the Wessex throne. This rebellion goes beyond the north. They all lied right to my face, in my own castle in Normandy."

His voice raged as Warenne continued, his tunic equally asunder and his face stained with soot and mud. "Thatched roofs caught like wildfire, and those who didn't join them in laying waste to everything their torches could destroy were targeted."

William wore a look of stunned disgust, and Maud had never seen him so surprised by the violence of his adversaries. "We lost most of our men trying to evacuate women and children. This blood on my hands is the blood of children too small to withstand the wall of fire the northern rebels built around the city."

"Thank God you're all right." Maud pulled her husband close, his soiled tunic caked with soot staining the linen of her robes. "Was Edgar involved?"

"We didn't see him, but Earl Gospatric reminded the citizens he was a true Wessex heir." His eyes fell upon their sixteen-year-old son. "Richard. What are you doing here? And Fitz?"

"Emma's run away, William." Maud clenched her jaw as she spoke. "Apparently she got to the docks in London three days ago and boarded a ship for the continent before anyone realized she was gone."

"Anyone?" His jaw dropped, and he glanced accusingly at Fitz. "How could she slip from a castle full to the brim with Normans, Anglo-Saxons, and even Danes?"

Fitz stammered, "Lanfranc is concerned with the bishops and helping *Curthos*—helping Robert manage in your absence. The rest of us have our hands full with the barons and our new lands. Without the queen in London, there's no one to manage the household staff."

William frowned. "I should have asked Addie to stay after the coronation."

"She wanted to get back to Champagne. Away from me, just like Emma." Maud shook her head reluctantly before an idea struck her. "Put the nuns in Caen on alert. If Emma's determined to get somewhere, it must be to Ceci at Sainte Trinity's."

"Beau and Odo will never let her get that far," said Fitz. "It's too rare for young girls to travel alone. Someone will find her before Caen."

"However resourceful our daughter may be, I'm not worried how far she'll get, but who might find her alone out there." She turned to her husband with conviction. "I must get back, and not just to London. I must reach Normandy before the winter to help look for Emma."

He nodded easily. "I want you and all the children to return in case rebellion spreads."

"What about Henry? He's too young for a sea voyage."

Turning to her lady-in-waiting, Maud was determined. "We'll protect him."

Warenne stood before Gundred with a comforting smile. "I'm sure Emma will be found quickly, but the queen is still a duchess, and right now her place is in Normandy, not England."

"You're staying in the north with the king, aren't you?" Gundred's tone was accusing, as though they'd had an entire silent conversation in plain view.

Warenne spoke apologetically. "We must defend and secure the north."

William's eyes darkened as he nodded in agreement. "With what we witnessed in York last night? Those who'd see Edgar Wessex on the throne tried to burn my wife and son alive the night before. There's no hell on earth the rebels won't suffer."

"What will you do to bring them in?" Maud feared the answer. "If the north is loyal to their lords, they won't give the rebels up so easily."

"If they'd burn a town, I'll burn their castles. I'll burn down the half of York they left standing for themselves," he warned. "And if I find Edgar Wessex, his life will be a living hell."

"You might provoke a war."

His nostrils flared as he paced the clearing, his son stirring in Gundred's arms. "I'm already provoked! The north might think itself independent of the south, but that's only because the Wessexes were weak enough to let them believe it."

Chapter Fifty

September 1068 – the road south from Yorkshire to London, England

As horses dragged the carriage from the muddy woods of Yorkshire, Maud looked back to wave at her husband through the window. He'd remounted alongside Warenne and Fitz, and as soon as Maud's cortège disappeared beyond the tree line, his remaining men hitched their steeds to head north again. "They'll be all right, Your Majesty," said Gundred, endlessly optimistic. "They're strong, and King William has never lost a battle." Her voice faded as the horses pulled the carriage over a ridge.

"At what cost?" Beyond the thick row of oaks at the end of the gravel road, black smoke rose over the northern horizon into the cloudy skies above. Maud's heart sank. "York is still burning."

"King William will set things right in the north."

Maud worried despite Gundred's assertion. "We won't celebrate what that means."

Richard's horse whinnied, bucking in distress. "Whoa, girl," he said calmly as their caravan pulled to a stop. Maud poked her head outside the window. "Mama, don't look." His voice was low and ominous but couldn't prevent his mother from following his gaze. Lining the side of the road, brown-robed women and children lay face-down in the brush, blindfolded with rags, and torn through with arrows.

Stepping from the carriage despite her son's protest, drawn to the corpses in the road, Maud's breathing grew ragged. Beyond the bodies, fields of wheat smoldered under heavy ash as embers wafted in the air. "This was an execution," she said. "The northern rebels are slaughtering their own, razing their crops to frighten them into fighting against us."

"Father will make the rebels pay," Richard said. Quietly, her heart raced. The whole north risked its head mounted on a spike.

From inside the carriage, Henry started to wail. The soldiers gazed beyond the ridge, hands on their swords and ready for movement. "He's hungry, Your Majesty," called Gundred.

"We should continue south. The rebels who did this may not be far away," Richard urged, trying to get his mother back to the carriage.

"We can't travel while Henry feeds," argued Gundred. "The uneven road will make it too difficult. The baby could choke."

Richard needed to hear no more, raising his hands in surrender before helping his mother up the carriage steps. "If you might hurry," he said with gentle pleading. "I don't mean to sound uncaring, but again, these lands could be teeming with rebels."

"Henry's screams are a sign he gains strength despite his premature birth," Maud said proudly, straightening her robes to sit on the bench. "I'm all too happy to quiet him in such hostile territory, but I never rushed you or your brothers and sisters when you fed from the wetnurses. I want to get back to find Emma more than anything, but even she'll have to wait."

Unlike his emotional brother, Robert, Richard protested no further. With his hand on his sword hilt, he stood watch, his back to the carriage while his mother's robes were open and exposing her. Though she refused to rush his suckling, Maud was grateful when Henry finished, handing him to Gundred to tighten her robes over her shoulders. "He'll be asleep again shortly."

With a smile, Richard called his soldiers to order. "Ready, men! We move south again!"

As he spoke, a figure in a black-hooded cloak peeled around the back of the carriage. He lunged through the window, grabbing violently for the women. Queen Maud fought as the hooded figure tried to rip her son from Gundred's grasp. She curled her body sideways to protect him.

A band of half a dozen men poured down from the ridge at their backs. With a hail of arrows raining over them from beyond the ridge, the other soldiers engaged the rebels in close combat. Richard finally managed to wrest the man from the window ledge with a violent roar, tearing him down with the blade of his sword. He sounded so much like his father. The steel dripped with the blood of their assailant, and she met her son's remorseless gaze.

Her lungs heavy, she craned her neck out the window after Richard joined the fray, dodging arrows as the rebels fought the Norman swords with their axes. Maud watched the brutal violence, impotent, even with the power of a queen. Soldiers on horseback tore the heads from men in brown tunics, but one sliced Richard's arm beneath his chainmail vest. Maud screamed, but ever the skilled swordsman, Richard threw his blade to his right hand, stabbing his assailant in the chest. Blood bubbled to his lips as he fell to the gravel.

"Get over the ridge now!" Richard ordered his men as an arrow pierced the roof of the carriage. Gundred gasped, trying in vain to calm Henry while she shook in fear herself. "Halt their fire in the name of the king!"

Three of the men raced over the ridge while the last rebel combatant dropped his axe, raising his hands in surrender before his arms were yanked roughly behind his back. Twelve broken bodies lay bloody in the road, downwind from the billowing smoke of York and the stench of rotting corpses. The hail of arrows ceased.

Richard stood with authority next to the carriage, waiting for the prisoner to be dropped at his feet. The last rebel wore a black hood tied tight around his face with rope. All they could see clearly was his nose, until Richard yanked the hood from his head. Their eyes fell upon a boy no older than fifteen. "You attack the caravan belonging to the Queen of England. Who do you fight for?" Richard bellowed.

At first, the young boy refused to speak. He held his tongue despite Richard's tall, imposing gait, until another soldier grabbed his wrist. "What if we cut off his thumb? Let's see his skill with an axe then."

The soldiers laughed, but Richard shook his head. "Gentlemen, we're not savages." Charm dripped from his voice. The boy cowered.

"The Earl of Mercia paid us to attack anyone passing this road," he stammered, looking fearfully toward the carriage. "When we saw you, we thought you'd be wealthy enough to rob. We wanted the ladies' gold jewelry, but we didn't know she was the queen."

"And why does the Earl of Mercia want you robbing gold?"

The boy said nothing, but Richard twisted his ear with his gloved hand. Crying out in pain as Richard dropped his head to the dirt, he sputtered with as much conviction as he could through his squeals, "We fight in the name of King Edgar, the true king of England!"

Richard grinned, letting go of the boy's cartilage. "Do you have a name?"

The boy was defiant again in the face of Richard's confidence, returning to his knees with forced stoicism. "It doesn't matter."

"It will matter to your mother. We'd like to inform her when you're dead."

Eyeing the sword in Richard's blood-covered fist, the fearful boy relented. "Alwi—"

Before he could give enough of his name to find his parents, the sword plunged into his heart by Richard's hand, quick and efficient. As the boy lay dead, Richard pulled a cloth from his bag, casually wiping the blood from the tip of his blade before sliding it back into its sheath. He nodded confidently in the direction of his men. "We'll reach Norfolk by morning if we move quickly."

Maud's heart ached for the boy, despite his treachery, and she gazed with sad eyes as blood pooled under his stiff frame. "If this is what our men are up against in the north, they'll need reinforcements," she said.

"They'll come," said Richard assuredly. "The Normans are loyal. They've multiplied their wealth by more deniers than any of them can count since the battle at Hastings, and if they think there's more land up for grabs in the north, they'll come get it with swords up."

Maud failed to enjoy the English scenery as the small cortège continued toward London. The air felt thick with fire and blood, and she couldn't push the rebel confrontation from her mind.

She returned to the castle in Caen, welcomed by her brothers-in-law, but disheartened when Bishop Odo and Count Robert reported they'd yet to find any trace of her daughter. Returning upstairs to her old bedroom with a heavy heart, she found her father's weathered blue-and-yellow shield on the floor. Apart from a small scuff in the wood at the base where it fell, it looked as she'd left it. The iron hook holding it to the wall had slipped in the years the fortress hadn't been lived in, but with the help of her stewards, her shield was remounted even stronger.

Lady Emma's blue butterfly-painted vase followed her to Rouen and then to London, but it returned to its familiar place on her windowsill. She let out a comfortable sigh. "Home again," she said to herself, sniffing the fresh, pink peonies in the vase. Before her crates of embellished robes were unpacked, Maud was out the door again, and Gundred followed. "I'll be at Sainte Trinity's with Ceci," she informed Bishop Odo, before stepping into her ornate black carriage with a golden-winged leopard painted on the side. The two enormous churches rose on the horizon as her carter led them from the courtyard, and she turned to her loyal maid with sadness in her eyes. "I don't think I deserve to set foot in that abbey," she said ruefully.

Gundred laughed. "It's your church. You can go wherever you like."

"Both my sons are killers, just like their parents."

"And men of the church attacked your mother, and collude with kings to murder their enemies," Gundred reminded her. She'd grown into a confident, assured young woman since their harrowing trip to the north, shedding her meek outer layer like a butterfly emerging from its cocoon.

"That's not even what makes me feel most guilty. I promised to visit Ceci so much more than I have. I won't be surprised if she won't even see me."

Twelve-year-old Cecilia welcomed her as any nun would greet a queen, with deference and distance. "I bear no ill will to you for not visiting as promised the past few years," she said, dressed in the gray habit of young nuns on their way to taking their vows and joining the Order. Her tone of voice was curt, sharper than her gentle words. "I pray Emma's reasons for running away bring her safety, and if she returns, I won't keep it from you." Ceci listened as her mother spoke of her siblings and their relatives but had little to share of her own. "I spend days praying and reading with my tutor, but when I go outside, it's never beyond these walls. The abbess says I could be her one day, when she's gone, so I think of my life, and how it will always be here, and how I'm grateful the builders made such beautiful big windows."

She left her daughter with a long embrace. "While I'm still in Caen, I'll visit weekly."

"You don't have to," said Ceci, but the corners of her lips pulled into a slight smile.

Flowers bloomed in shades of pink, blue, red, and gold when spring returned to the castle grounds. The bright colors contrasted with Maud's mood, but she raised a smile for her aging steward as he approached her in the castle hall. "Is there any word of Emma?"

Shaking his head apologetically, Bertrand handed her a letter on rolled parchment. "It's from Margaret Wessex." With a grateful nod, she pulled at the unbroken wax seal.

To Your Majesty, Queen Maud,

I know I may be the last person you wish to hear from, but I write with news of my mother.

After Edgar fled Scotland for Northumbria to join the rebels, our mother was so distraught she fell into sickness, and the violence of the harrying drew her further into misery. Such persecution for one belief over another was something she avoided before coming west, isolated and sheltered as she was. She never got used to it.

King Malcolm's court physicians did all they could, but she passed after the Feast of the Pentecost. My only solace is she didn't suffer long, but I'm in the right place here in Dunfermline, and betrothed to the right man. I knew for sure as soon as a storm hit on our way into the harbor. Our ship ran aground on some rocks, but Malcolm and his men ferried us safely to shore to a cheering welcome.

I feel safe here. Malcolm is comforting and kind, and I never would have opened myself up to it without your advice. We'll be married next year and would be honored by your presence, but we all know the state of the rebellions means we likely won't celebrate together.

I've found a cave not far from the castle. I pray there every morning, recommitting myself to God just as you suggested. I owe my future to you as much as my own mother, dear queen. I hope I can one day help guide Malcolm in diplomacy toward more peaceful relations with England's north, guided by your strong example.

Yours in hope of forgiveness,
Margaret Wessex

Clutching the parchment in her hand, Maud squeezed anxiously, crumpling it into a jagged ball. "Are you all right, Your Majesty?"

Regaining her composure, she smiled at her portly old steward.

"Margaret Wessex sounds like me when I was her age," she said sadly. "Agatha Wessex has died, and I can't help but think of how my husband hunts down her son day and night across his lands."

"Edgar Wessex is unlike his mother, my queen."

She gave Bertrand a spiteful laugh. "No, he's like us. My husband ordered the deaths of almost one thousand people inside Durham Castle," she reminded him. "They all burned alive for Earl Gospatric, who fled to safety in Scotland and left them to die. The new Earl of Northumbria may be loyal to us, but he's hunted day and night by the rebels."

"Things are calmer now. Your husband was just here for a feast at Easter," he said, but she waved him off, her voice wavering.

"William still fights them. He had to sail straight back. Farms and livestock have been turned to ash, and northern lands are unlivable. Now, the south is filled with northerners who need homes, and I don't know when I'll see my husband or my daughter again. Most days, I think none of it was worth all this."

Bertrand faltered before placing a comforting hand on her shoulder and offering a gentle smile. "You and King William are capable administrators, my queen. You'll find your way, but not if you doubt yourself like this." Straightening her spine, Maud stood tall under his proud, fatherly gaze. "Forward, Your Majesty."

With his advice in her ear, she headed to the Abbey of Sainte Trinity to visit Ceci, confirming once again that Emma's whereabouts remained unknown. In desperation, she instructed her carter to take her to the town square, where she ordered him to stop in front of a small hut with hanging scarves in place of the door.

But a puppet show first drew her attention in front of the nearby church. Gundred stayed close to her queen while gallant knights on a wooden stage battled a long, green dragon with a painted scowl, made from a stuffed sock. The marionettes fought valiantly with wooden swords, felling the dragon in a fiery blaze of glory, and when the fighting was over their ladies raced out to congratulate them. The puppets drank and danced, until the lady in blue raced to the window of the castle tower, calling for another dragon.

Looking down at her own blue robes, Maud frowned. The story wasn't exactly the same, but she remembered this show from her childhood.

A bigger, fiercer dragon flew in front of the painted backdrop—a long, black sock with a menacing grin. Maud remembered well what happened next, feeling the same punch to her gut when the blue-dressed lady and her knight betrayed their friends. She thought sadly of Addie, Judith, Lady Berthe, and even Agatha. Now she was a queen, but none of them stood with her. "You have no one to blame but yourself," she muttered quietly. When the show ended, Gundred clapped gleefully, but Maud returned to her original intention. "Wait for me," she told her. "But if anyone asks, we were never here."

Stepping through the silk curtains, which brushed against her fingers, she waited only a moment for Mistress Dzintra to emerge from the courtyard behind her tiny shack. Her blue eyes widened in surprise, and she curtsied awkwardly as her freckled cheeks flushed. "Your Majesty, I—"

"What did you see that day that scared you so?"

"I don't remember." Her gaze shifted to the floor.

"Are you cowering from the weight of your obvious lie, or because you're afraid of me?"

Mistress Dzintra stumbled, straightening her lace veil over her fiery locks. "Both."

The queen sighed. "I'm not here to punish you, though I do wonder why you didn't tell me how horrific the harrying in the north would be."

"You couldn't change the visions even if you knew, and if you thought me insulting, it could've been my head on a spike."

She sat at Mistress Dzintra's sawed log table, emotional exhaustion dragging at her bones. "I wouldn't have believed you," she admitted. "Not until I saw it for myself. We won our conquest, but I feel as though I sacrificed my soul."

Mistress Dzintra sat across from her. "Would you like another fortune, Your Majesty?"

Laughing miserably, Maud shook her head. "I'm done with prophecies and visions of the future."

The fortune teller smiled warmly. "That's perfectly understandable."

With little left to say, Maud stood to excuse herself from the small hut. "Thank you, Mistress Dzintra, for your discretion."

"Always." She bowed dutifully, locking eyes with her queen. "For your own discretion, I'll remind you of something I said when you paid me a visit years ago: I've seen nothing to indicate harm to any of your loved ones."

The queen whimpered. "Emma?"

"Let her come to you, Your Majesty. If you don't give her time, she won't stay."

Stepping back into the warm spring air, Maud spotted a blue-winged butterfly floating overhead. Beaming with renewed hope as it sailed on the wind, lightness returned to her heart.

Waiting behind her, Mother Mary watched Queen Maud with a forlorn stare.

Acknowledgements and Notes

If you've made it to this point, first and foremost, thank you for spending your time with these characters. I hope you've grown to love, or love to hate them, as much as I do. Though many of them were living, breathing people and not characters, the versions of them you've just experienced are, of course, deeply fictional.

If you're anything like me, you read historical fiction with an eye on real history, and some of the creative choices here may not be to your liking. I know I've experienced this myself more than once, so when I set out to write *The Dragon and the Butterfly*, I tried to stay as close to historical record as possible, embellishing elements that were not immediately disproven by historical fact. Some of the character names are anachronistic (Bodhi, anyone?) but so many historical figures had similar names that it was a choice to differentiate characters from their fathers or daughters. Others are invented—no daughter of William and Matilda was named Emma according to historical record, but two were named Adeliza and Adela, and the novel already features another Adela, Adeliza, and two Adelaides. In this vein I chose to call the protagonist by the diminutive Maud, instead of the more formal name she's known by historically, as a nod to the character's Flemish origins. The Flemish version of Matilda is *Mahaut*, which is phonetically more like Maud than Matilda.

The story of William's "rough wooing" of his queen is one of the enduring tales of the warrior king's vicious legacy, but turned somewhat on its head in this tale. Some would argue this fundamentally alters William as a person, but as I read about this pair, I knew my love story wouldn't tell a tale of rape or beating leading to a lifetime of mutual devotion as the chroniclers posit. I considered what, in the context of the era, would be a truth deemed far worse, and settled on Brictric.

The truth of Queen Matilda's past with the English thegn and ambassador, Brictric, is widely unknown. One story says she wrote him a letter requesting he marry her, but he turned her down, running from Flanders in the middle of the night rather than face her. Their story picks up almost two decades later, after her husband has conquered England and Brictric is arrested and thrown in jail, with all his lands transferred to Queen Matilda. Absolutely, this is a story of revenge, but the exact details are hazy.

Queen Matilda may well have been an embittered woman forced into a marriage with a duke she didn't want in an era where women had few choices and no agency, having been forsaken by the man she really loved. She may have been so disturbed by the circumstances of her own marriage that most of her daughters became nuns. That tale exists and may very well be her biographical story, but it isn't this story.

The greatest invention in *The Dragon and the Butterfly*, and the two real people I would owe the greatest apology for creative license if seated with them in a room, is that of the fate of Marguerite and Herbert of Maine. Herbert is recorded to have died in March 1062, while Marguerite's death is given as circa 1063. As such, the manner of their deaths in this novel, and events leading to it, are invented. However, chronicles note their deaths as suspicious, and it appears their deaths ended marriage alliances brokered with the House of Normandy, after which William is known to have seized control of the County of Maine for himself.

Similarly, the death of Duke Conan of Brittany is believed to have been on William's orders, but this is unproven. No evidence suggests it was Ulf Haroldson who did the deed, and he spent several years imprisoned by King William, but the exact details and timing of his imprisonment are only assumed, and he's also said to have been a friend of Robert Curthose. I took creative license by leaning on the notion that many of the surviving chronicles from the Middle Ages were written for self-interested patrons, and often by members of the Church. The chance remains their chronicles are fictional, like mine, though they were nonetheless fantastic resources for me while I wrote and researched this novel.

So thank you, Orderic Vitalis, William of Jumieges, and contemporary historians of the Middle Ages like Tracy Borman, Dr. Eleanor

Janega, and Dan Jones for inspiring me with their incredible work (they had nothing to do with this novel specifically, but I owe them gratitude for their work just the same). Thank you to Sean Perry, Kenzie Millar, and Liz Ward for being unreal betas. You read so many words when they were in the first draft, I can't thank any of you enough for putting yourselves through all that! Thank you to Dzintra Sullivan for inspiring me as an indie author and a character. Thank you to Sabrina Shaw and Kimmy Mills for the very early encouragement when this story was just an unhatched egg. Thank you to Keith Feltz for your beautiful poetry and allowing me to use your voice as Tostig Godwinson during his proposal. But thank you to Ashley Hutchison, Dewi Hargreaves, and the entire team at Lost Boys Press most of all. You saw my vision and gave me the tools to polish it, all before you went and made my dreams of becoming a published novelist come true. You truly are the greatest of small presses in my wholly unbiased opinion, and working with you is objectively spectacular.

Once again, thank you, and if you've read this and still have concerns about the story, I hope you'll follow me into book two, which just may give you answers and everything you ever wanted to know about William and Maud's *Cursed Daughter*.

Family Trees

House Normandy

pre 1050 AD

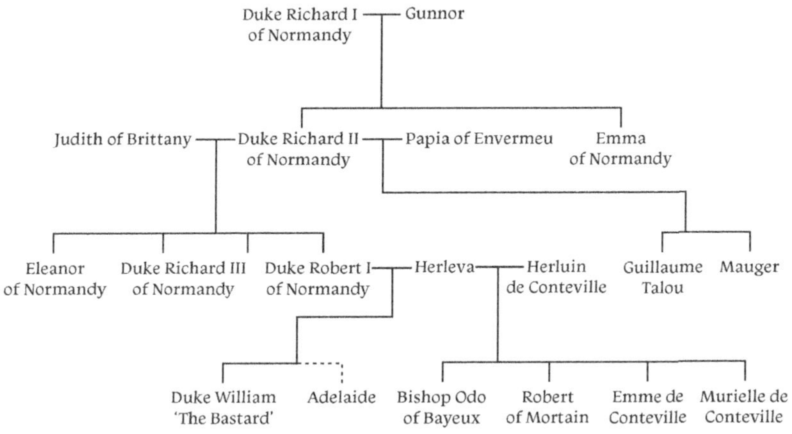

post 1050 AD

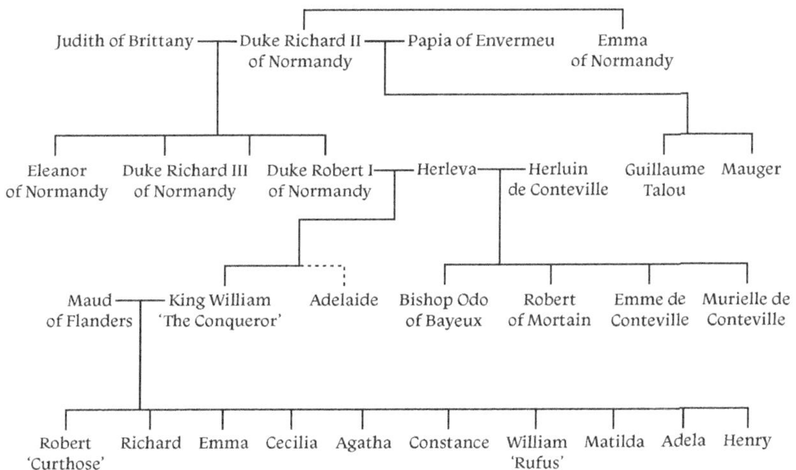

House Flanders

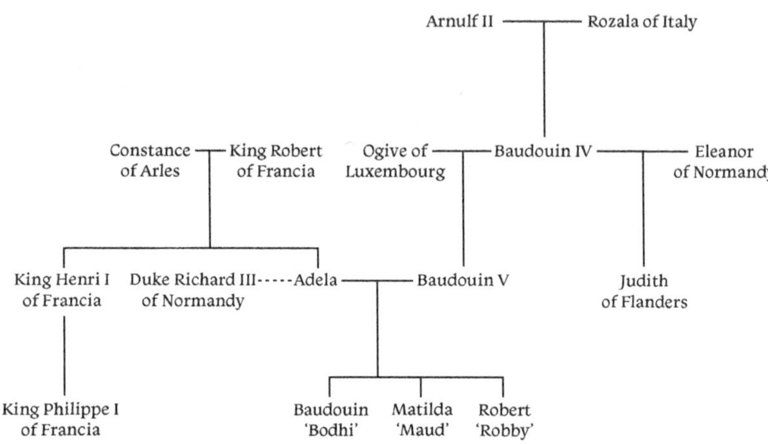

House Godwin

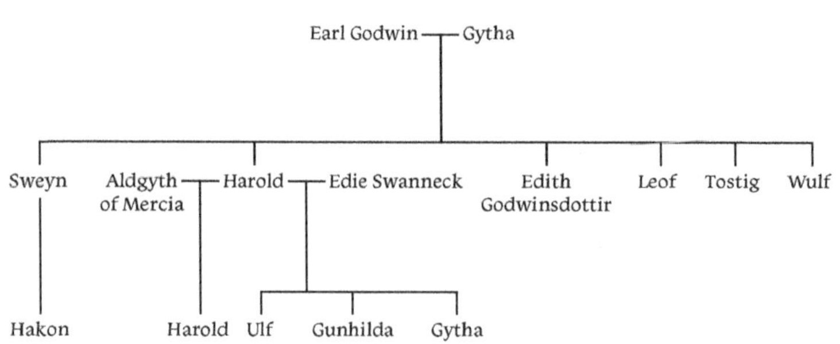

House Wessex

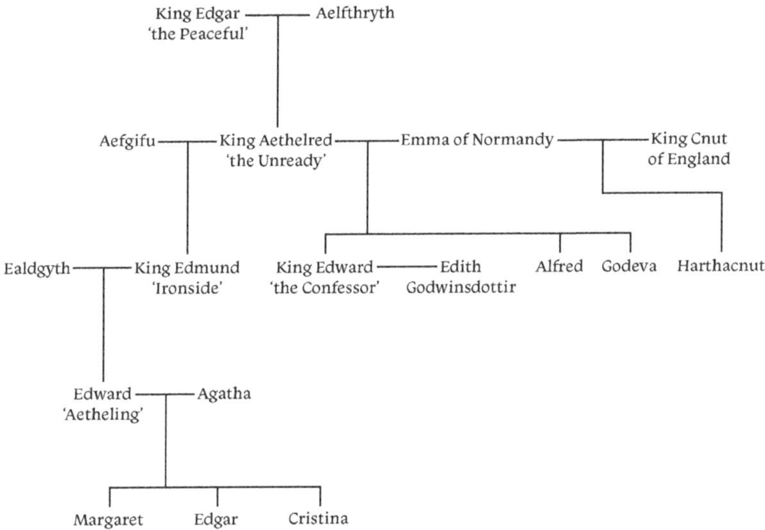

Abby Simpson is a Vancouver-based author and freelancer releasing her debut novel with Lost Boys Press. She holds a degree in political science from Simon Fraser University, but her love of storytelling and passion for history and politics brought The Dragon and the Butterfly to life. Her short fiction and non-fiction commentary has appeared in Vamp Cat Magazine, Gestalt Media, DeanBlundell.com, and more.

Lost Boys Press

Like an intrepid ship's captain, Lost Boys Press is exploring new horizons, riding the high seas and interstellar winds of cutting edge science fiction and fantasy. We're committed to the powerful storytelling, the expression of self, and the breaking of conventions readers expect from the indie scene, nurturing bright new voices as we go.

Our mission is to bring the vibrancy and color of indie speculative fiction to as wide an audience as possible. In our books, you'll find tried-and-tested elements of science fiction and fantasy alongside genre-mashing, boundary-pushing, and occasional forays into history and creative non-fiction, especially where new stories can be told or expectations subverted.

We seek out imaginative speculative fiction with heart, hoping to show you things you haven't seen before and to leave you enriched when you turn the final page.

Find Out More

Head to our website to find our **indie bookstore**, where you can buy books and Lost Boys merch, and sign up to our **newsletter** to receive news, exclusive offers, and advance information on our upcoming releases!

WWW.LOSTBOYSPRESS.COM

SUPPORT INDIE

Find us on social media at 'lostboyspress.'

Printed in Great Britain
by Amazon